ILLUSTRATIONS BY RICK LIEDER

BRUCE STERLING

ARKHAM HOUSE PUBLISHERS, INC.

ACKNOWLEDGMENTS

"The Beautiful and the Sublime," copyright © 1986 by Davis Publications, Inc., for *Isaac Asimov's Science Fiction Magazine*, June 1986.

"Cicada Queen," copyright © 1983 by Terry Carr for *Universe 13*, edited by Terry Carr.

"Dinner in Audoghast," copyright © 1985 by Davis Publications, Inc., for *Isaac Asimov's Science Fiction Magazine*, May 1985.

"Flowers of Edo," copyright © 1987 by Davis Publications, Inc., for *Isaac Asimov's Science Fiction Magazine*, May 1987; first published in *Hayakawa's Science Fiction Magazine*.

"Green Days in Brunei," copyright © 1985 by Davis Publications, Inc., for *Isaac Asimov's Science Fiction Magazine*, October 1985.

"The Little Magic Shop," copyright © 1987 by Davis Publications, Inc., for *Isaac Asimov's Science Fiction Magazine*, October 1987.

"Spider Rose," copyright © 1982 by Mercury Press, Inc., for *The Magazine of Fantasy and Science Fiction*, August 1982.

"Spook," copyright © 1983 by Mercury Press, Inc., for *The Magazine of Fantasy and Science Fiction*, April 1983.

"Sunken Gardens," copyright © 1984 by Omni Publications International, Ltd., for *Omni*, June 1984.

"Swarm," copyright © 1982 by Mercury Press, Inc., for *The Magazine of Fantasy and Science Fiction*, April 1982.

"Telliamed," copyright © 1984 by Mercury Press, Inc., for *The Magazine of Fantasy and Science Fiction*, September 1984.

"Twenty Evocations," copyright © 1984 by Bruce Sterling for *Interzone*, Spring 1984; first published as "Life in the Mechanist/Shaper Era: Twenty Evocations."

Library of Congress Cataloging-in-Publication Data

Sterling, Bruce.
 Crystal express.

 1. Fantastic fiction, American. I. Title.
PS3569.T3876C79 1989 813'.0876 89-31079
ISBN 0-87054-158-7 (alk. paper)

Typographic modifications by Dan X
Printed in the United States of Ame
First Edition

We cannot separate the historic accidents of the society in which we were born from the axiomatic bases of the universe.

— J. D. BERNAL, 1925

The deadliest bullshit is odorless and transparent.

— WM. GIBSON, 1988

CONTENTS

FANTASY STORIES

SWARM

"I WILL MISS your conversation during the rest of the voyage," the alien said.

Captain-Doctor Simon Afriel folded his jeweled hands over his gold-embroidered waistcoat. "I regret it also, ensign," he said in the alien's own hissing language. "Our talks together have been very useful to me. I would have paid to learn so much, but you gave it freely."

"But that was only information," the alien said. He shrouded his bead-bright eyes behind thick nictitating membranes. "We Investors deal in energy, and precious metals. To prize and pursue mere knowledge is an immature racial trait." The alien lifted the long ribbed frill behind his pinhole-sized ears.

"No doubt you are right," Afriel said, despising him. "We humans are as children to other races, however; so a certain immaturity seems natural to us." Afriel pulled off his sunglasses to rub the bridge of his nose. The starship cabin was drenched in searing blue light, heavily ultraviolet. It was the light the Investors preferred, and they were not about to change it for one human passenger.

"You have not done badly," the alien said magnanimously. "You are the kind of race we like to do business with: young, eager, plastic, ready for a wide variety of goods and experiences. We would have contacted you much earlier, but your technology was still too feeble to afford us a profit."

"Things are different now," Afriel said. "We'll make you rich."

"Indeed," the Investor said. The frill behind his scaly head flickered rapidly, a sign of amusement. "Within two hundred years you will be wealthy enough to buy from us the secret of our starflight. Or perhaps your Mechanist faction will discover the secret through research."

Afriel was annoyed. As a member of the Reshaped faction, he did not appreciate the reference to the rival Mechanists. "Don't put too much stock in mere technical expertise," he said. "Consider the aptitude for languages we Shapers have. It makes our faction a much better trading partner. To a Mechanist, all Investors look alike."

The alien hesitated. Afriel smiled. He had appealed to the alien's personal ambition with his last statement, and the hint had been taken. That was where the Mechanists always erred. They tried to treat all Investors consistently, using the same programmed routines each time. They lacked imagination.

Something would have to be done about the Mechanists, Afriel thought. Something more permanent than the small but deadly confrontations between isolated ships in the Asteroid Belt and the ice-rich Rings of Saturn. Both factions maneuvered constantly, looking for a decisive stroke, bribing away each other's best talent, practicing ambush, assassination, and industrial espionage.

Captain-Doctor Simon Afriel was a past master of these pursuits. That was why the Reshaped faction had paid the millions of kilowatts necessary to buy his passage. Afriel held doctorates in biochemistry and alien linguistics, and a master's degree in magnetic weapons engineering. He was thirty-eight years old and had been Reshaped according to the state of the art at the time of his conception. His hormonal balance had been altered slightly to compensate for long periods spent in free-fall. He had no appendix. The structure of his heart had been redesigned for greater efficiency, and his large intestine had been altered to produce the vitamins normally made by intestinal bacteria. Genetic engineering and rigorous training in childhood had given him an intelligence quotient of one hundred and eighty. He was not the brightest of the agents of the Ring Council, but he was one of the most mentally stable and the best trusted.

"It seems a shame," the alien said, "that a human of your accomplishments should have to rot for two years in this miserable, profitless outpost."

"The years won't be wasted," Afriel said.

"But why have you chosen to study the Swarm? They can teach you nothing, since they cannot speak. They have no wish to trade, having no tools or technology. They are the only spacefaring race that is essentially without intelligence."

"That alone should make them worthy of study."

"Do you seek to imitate them, then? You would make monsters of yourselves." Again the ensign hesitated. "Perhaps you could do it. It would be bad for business, however."

There came a fluting burst of alien music over the ship's speakers, then a screeching fragment of Investor language. Most of it was too high-pitched for Afriel's ears to follow.

The alien stood, his jeweled skirt brushing the tips of his clawed birdlike feet. "The Swarm's symbiote has arrived," he said.

"Thank you," Afriel said. When the ensign opened the cabin door, Afriel could smell the Swarm's representative; the creature's warm yeasty scent had spread rapidly through the starship's recycled air.

Afriel quickly checked his appearance in a pocket mirror. He touched powder to his face and straightened the round velvet hat on his shoulder-length reddish-blond hair. His earlobes glittered with red impact-rubies, thick as his thumbs' ends, mined from the Asteroid Belt. His knee-length coat and waistcoat were of gold brocade; the shirt beneath was of dazzling fineness, woven with red-gold thread. He had dressed to impress the Investors, who expected and appreciated a prosperous look from their customers. How could he impress this new alien? Smell, perhaps. He freshened his perfume.

Beside the starship's secondary airlock, the Swarm's symbiote was chittering rapidly at the ship's commander. The commander was an old and sleepy Investor, twice the size of most of her crewmen. Her massive head was encrusted in a jeweled helmet. From within the helmet her clouded eyes glittered like cameras.

The symbiote lifted on its six posterior legs and gestured feebly with its four clawed forelimbs. The ship's artificial gravity, a third again as strong as Earth's, seemed to bother it. Its rudimentary eyes, dangling on stalks, were shut tight against the glare. It must be used to darkness, Afriel thought.

The commander answered the creature in its own language. Afriel grimaced, for he had hoped that the creature spoke Investor. Now he would have to learn another language, a language designed for a being without a tongue.

After another brief interchange the commander turned to Afriel. "The symbiote is not pleased with your arrival," she told Afriel in the Investor language. "There has apparently been some disturbance here involving humans, in the recent past. However, I have prevailed upon it to admit you to the Nest. The episode has been recorded. Payment for my diplomatic services will be arranged with your faction when I return to your native star system."

"I thank Your Authority," Afriel said. "Please convey to the symbiote my best personal wishes, and the harmlessness and humility of my intentions. . . . " He broke off short as the symbiote lunged toward him, biting him savagely in the calf of his left leg. Afriel jerked free and leapt backward in the heavy artificial gravity, going into a defensive position. The symbiote had ripped away a long shred of his pants leg; it now crouched quietly, eating it.

"It will convey your scent and composition to its nestmates," said the commander. "This is necessary. Otherwise you would be classed as an invader, and the Swarm's warrior caste would kill you at once."

Afriel relaxed quickly and pressed his hand against the puncture wound to stop the bleeding. He hoped that none of the Investors had noticed his reflexive action. It would not mesh well with his story of being a harmless researcher.

"We will reopen the airlock soon," the commander said phlegmatically, leaning back on her thick reptilian tail. The symbiote continued to munch the shred of cloth. Afriel studied the creature's neckless segmented head. It had a mouth and nostrils; it had bulbous atrophied eyes on stalks; there were hinged slats that might be radio receivers, and two parallel ridges of clumped wriggling antennae, sprouting among three chitinous plates. Their function was unknown to him.

The airlock door opened. A rush of dense, smoky aroma entered the departure cabin. It seemed to bother the half-dozen Investors, who left rapidly. "We will return in six hundred and twelve of your days, as by our agreement," the commander said.

"I thank Your Authority," Afriel said.

"Good luck," the commander said in English. Afriel smiled.

The symbiote, with a sinuous wriggle of its segmented body, crept into the airlock. Afriel followed it. The airlock door shut behind them. The creature said nothing to him but continued munching loudly. The second door opened, and the symbiote sprang through it, into a wide, round stone tunnel. It disappeared at once into the gloom.

Afriel put his sunglasses into a pocket of his jacket and pulled out a pair of infrared goggles. He strapped them to his head and stepped out of the airlock. The artificial gravity vanished, replaced by the almost imperceptible gravity of the Swarm's asteroid nest. Afriel smiled, comfortable for the first time in weeks. Most of his adult life had been spent in free-fall, in the Shapers' colonies in the Rings of Saturn.

Squatting in a dark cavity in the side of the tunnel was a disk-headed furred animal the size of an elephant. It was clearly visible in the infrared of its own body heat. Afriel could hear it breathing. It waited patiently until Afriel had launched himself past it, deeper into the tunnel. Then it took its place in the end of the tunnel, puffing itself up with air until its swollen head securely plugged the exit into space. Its multiple legs sank firmly into sockets in the walls.

The Investors' ship had left. Afriel remained here, inside one of the millions of planetoids that circled the giant star Betelgeuse in a girdling ring with almost five times the mass of Jupiter. As a source of potential wealth it dwarfed the entire solar system, and it belonged, more or less, to the Swarm. At least, no other race had challenged them for it within the memory of the Investors.

Afriel peered up the corridor. It seemed deserted, and without other bodies to cast infrared heat, he could not see very far. Kicking against the wall, he floated hesitantly down the corridor.

He heard a human voice. "Dr. Afriel!"

"Dr. Mirny!" he called out. "This way!"

He first saw a pair of young symbiotes scuttling toward him, the tips of their clawed feet barely touching the walls. Behind them came a woman wearing goggles like his own. She was young, and attractive in the trim, anonymous way of the genetically reshaped.

She screeched something at the symbiotes in their own language, and they halted, waiting. She coasted forward, and Afriel caught her arm, expertly stopping their momentum.

"You didn't bring any luggage?" she said anxiously.

He shook his head. "We got your warning before I was sent out. I have only the clothes I'm wearing and a few items in my pockets."

She looked at him critically. "Is that what people are wearing in the Rings these days? Things have changed more than I thought."

Afriel glanced at his brocaded coat and laughed. "It's a matter of policy. The Investors are always readier to talk to a human who looks ready to do business on a large scale. All the Shapers' representatives dress like this these days. We've stolen a jump on the Mechanists; they still dress in those coveralls."

He hesitated, not wanting to offend her. Galina Mirny's intelligence was rated at almost two hundred. Men and women that bright were sometimes flighty and unstable, likely to retreat into private fantasy worlds or become enmeshed in strange and impenetrable webs of plotting and rationalization. High intelligence was the strategy the Shapers had chosen in the struggle for cultural dominance, and they were obliged to stick to it, despite its occasional disadvantages. They had tried breeding the Superbright—those with quotients over two hundred—but so many had defected from the Shapers' colonies that the faction had stopped producing them.

"You wonder about my own clothing," Mirny said.

"It certainly has the appeal of novelty," Afriel said with a smile.

"It was woven from the fibers of a pupa's cocoon," she said. "My original wardrobe was eaten by a scavenger symbiote during the troubles last year. I usually go nude, but I didn't want to offend you by too great a show of intimacy."

Afriel shrugged. "I often go nude myself, I never had much use for clothes except for pockets. I have a few tools on my person, but most are of little importance. We're Shapers, our tools are here." He tapped his head. "If you can show me a safe place to put my clothes. . . ."

She shook her head. It was impossible to see her eyes for the goggles, which made her expression hard to read. "You've made your first mistake, Doctor. There are no places of our own here. It was the same mistake the Mechanist agents made, the same one that almost killed me as well. There is no concept of privacy or property here. This is the Nest. If you seize any part of it for yourself—to store equipment, to sleep in, whatever—then you become an intruder, an enemy. The two Mechanists—a man and a woman—tried to secure an empty chamber for their computer lab. Warriors broke down their door and devoured them. Scavengers ate their equipment, glass, metal, and all."

Afriel smiled coldly. "It must have cost them a fortune to ship all that material here."

Mirny shrugged. "They're wealthier than we are. Their machines, their mining. They meant to kill me, I think. Surreptitiously, so the warriors wouldn't be upset by a show of violence. They had a computer that was learning the language of the springtails faster than I could."

"But you survived," Afriel pointed out. "And your tapes and reports—especially the early ones, when you still had most of your equipment—were of tremendous interest. The Council is behind you all the way. You've become quite a celebrity in the Rings, during your absence."

"Yes, I expected as much," she said.

Afriel was nonplused. "If I found any deficiency in them," he said carefully, "it was in my own field, alien linguistics." He waved vaguely at the two symbiotes who accompanied her. "I assume you've made great progress in communicating with the symbiotes, since they seem to do all the talking for the Nest."

She looked at him with an unreadable expression and shrugged. "There are at least fifteen different kinds of symbiotes here. Those that accompany me are called the springtails, and they speak only for themselves. They are savages, Doctor, who received attention from the Investors only because they can still talk. They were a spacefaring race once, but they've forgotten it. They discovered the Nest and they were absorbed, they became parasites." She tapped one of them on the head. "I tamed these two because I learned to steal and beg food better than they can. They stay with me now and protect me from the larger ones. They are jealous, you know. They have only been with the Nest for perhaps ten thousand years and are still uncertain of their position. They still think, and wonder sometimes. After ten thousand years there is still a little of that left to them."

"Savages," Afriel said. "I can well believe that. One of them bit me while I was still aboard the starship. He left a lot to be desired as an ambassador."

"Yes, I warned him you were coming," said Mirny. "He didn't much like the idea, but I was able to bribe him with food. . . . I hope he didn't hurt you badly."

"A scratch," Afriel said. "I assume there's no chance of infection."

"I doubt it very much. Unless you brought your own bacteria with you."

"Hardly likely," Afriel said, offended. "I have no bacteria. And I wouldn't have brought microorganisms to an alien culture anyway."

Mirny looked away. "I thought you might have some of the special genetically altered ones. . . . I think we can go now. The springtail will have spread your scent by mouth-touching in the subsidiary chamber, ahead of us. It will be spread throughout the Nest in a few hours. Once it reaches the Queen, it will spread very quickly."

She jammed her feet against the hard shell of one of the young springtails and launched herself down the hall. Afriel followed her. The air was warm and he was beginning to sweat under his elaborate clothing, but his antiseptic sweat was odorless.

They exited into a vast chamber dug from the living rock. It was arched and oblong, eighty meters long and about twenty in diameter. It swarmed with members of the Nest. There were hundreds of them. Most of them were workers, eight-legged and furred, the size of Great Danes. Here and there were members of the warrior caste, horse-sized furry monsters with heavy fanged heads the size and shape of overstuffed chairs.

A few meters away, two workers were carrying a member of the sensor caste, a being whose immense flattened head was attached to an atrophied body that was mostly lungs. The sensor had great platelike eyes, and its furred chitin sprouted long coiled antennae that twitched feebly as the workers bore it along. The workers clung to the hollowed rock of the chamber walls with hooked and suckered feet.

A paddle-limbed monster with a hairless, faceless head came sculling past them, through the warm reeking air. The front of its head was a nightmare of sharp grinding jaws and blunt armored acid spouts. "A tunneler," Mirny said. "It can take us deeper into the Nest —come with me." She launched herself toward it and took a handhold on its furry, segmented back. Afriel followed her, joined by the two immature springtails, who clung to the thing's hide with their forelimbs. Afriel shuddered at the warm, greasy feel of its rank, damp fur. It continued to scull through the air, its eight fringed paddle feet catching the air like wings.

"There must be thousands of them," Afriel said.

"I said a hundred thousand in my last report, but that was before I had fully explored the Nest. Even now there are long stretches I haven't seen. They must number close to a quarter of a million. This asteroid is about the size of the Mechanists' biggest base—Ceres. It still has rich veins of carbonaceous material. It's far from mined out."

Afriel closed his eyes. If he was to lose his goggles, he would have to feel his way, blind, through these teeming, twitching, wriggling thousands. "The population's still expanding, then?"

"Definitely," she said. "In fact, the colony will launch a mating swarm soon. There are three dozen male and female alates in the chambers near the Queen. Once they're launched, they'll mate and start new Nests. I'll take you to see them presently." She hesitated. "We're entering one of the fungal gardens now."

One of the young springtails quietly shifted position. Grabbing the tunneler's fur with its forelimbs, it began to gnaw on the cuff of Afriel's pants. Afriel kicked it soundly, and it jerked back, retracting its eyestalks.

When he looked up again, he saw that they had entered a second chamber, much larger than the first. The walls around, overhead, and below were buried under an explosive profusion of fungus. The most common types were swollen barrellike domes, multibranched massed thickets, and spaghettilike tangled extrusions that moved very slightly in the faint and odorous breeze. Some of the barrels were surrounded by dim mists of exhaled spores.

"You see those caked-up piles beneath the fungus, its growth medium?" Mirny said.

"Yes."

"I'm not sure whether it is a plant form or just some kind of complex biochemical sludge," she said. "The point is that it grows in sunlight, on the outside of the asteroid. A food source that grows in naked space! Imagine what that would be worth, back in the Rings."

"There aren't words for its value," Afriel said.

"It's inedible by itself," she said. "I tried to eat a very small piece of it once. It was like trying to eat plastic."

"Have you eaten well, generally speaking?"

"Yes. Our biochemistry is quite similar to the Swarm's. The fungus itself is perfectly edible. The regurgitate is more nourishing, though. Internal fermentation in the worker hindgut adds to its nutritional value."

Afriel stared. "You grow used to it," Mirny said. "Later I'll teach you how to solicit food from the workers. It's a simple matter of reflex tapping—it's not controlled by pheromones, like most of their behavior." She brushed a long lock of clumped and dirty hair from the side of her face. "I hope the pheromonal samples I sent back were worth the cost of transportation."

"Oh, yes," said Afriel. "The chemistry of them was fascinating. We managed to synthesize most of the compounds. I was part of the research team myself." He hesitated. How far did he dare trust her? She had not been told about the experiment he and his superiors had planned. As far as Mirny knew, he was a simple, peaceful researcher, like herself. The Shapers' scientific community was suspicious of the minority involved in military work and espionage.

As an investment in the future, the Shapers had sent researchers to each of the nineteen alien races described to them by the Investors. This had cost the Shaper economy many gigawatts of precious energy and tons of rare metals and isotopes. In most cases, only two or three researchers could be sent; in seven cases, only one. For the Swarm, Galina Mirny had been chosen. She had gone peacefully, trusting in her intelligence and her good intentions to keep her alive and sane. Those who had sent her had not known whether her find-ings would be of any use or importance. They had only known that it was imperative that she be sent, even alone, even ill-equipped, before some other faction sent their own people and possibly dis-covered some technique or fact of overwhelming importance. And Dr. Mirny had indeed discovered such a situation. It had made her mission into a matter of Ring security. That was why Afriel had come.

"You synthesized the compounds?" she said. "Why?"

Afriel smiled disarmingly. "Just to prove to ourselves that we could do it, perhaps."

She shook her head. "No mind-games, Dr. Afriel, please. I came this far partly to escape from such things. Tell me the truth."

Afriel stared at her, regretting that the goggles meant he could not meet her eyes. "Very well," he said. "You should know, then, that I have been ordered by the Ring Council to carry out an experi-ment that may endanger both our lives."

Mirny was silent for a moment. "You're from Security, then?"

"My rank is captain."

"I knew it. . . . I knew it when those two Mechanists arrived. They were so polite, and so suspicious—I think they would have killed me at once if they hadn't hoped to bribe or torture some secret out of me. They scared the life out of me, Captain Afriel. . . . You scare me, too."

"We live in a frightening world, Doctor. It's a matter of faction security."

"Everything's a matter of faction security with your lot," she said. "I shouldn't take you any farther, or show you anything more. This Nest, these creatures—they're not *intelligent,* Captain. They can't think, they can't learn. They're innocent, primordially innocent. They have no knowledge of good and evil. They have no knowledge of *anything.* The last thing they need is to become pawns in a power struggle within some other race, light-years away."

The tunneler had turned into an exit from the fungal chambers and was paddling slowly along in the warm darkness. A group of creatures like gray, flattened basketballs floated by from the oppo-site direction. One of them settled on Afriel's sleeve, clinging with frail whiplike tentacles. Afriel brushed it gently away, and it broke loose, emitting a stream of foul reddish droplets.

"Naturally I agree with you in principle, Doctor," Afriel said smoothly. "But consider these Mechanists. Some of their extreme factions are already more than half machine. Do you expect humanitarian motives from them? They're cold, Doctor—cold and soulless creatures who can cut a living man or woman to bits and never feel their pain. Most of the other factions hate us. They call us racist supermen. Would you rather that one of these cults do what we must do, and use the results against us?"

"This is double-talk." She looked away. All around them workers laden down with fungus, their jaws full and guts stuffed with it, were spreading out into the Nest, scuttling alongside them or disappearing into branch tunnels departing in every direction, including straight up and straight down. Afriel saw a creature much like a worker, but with only six legs, scuttle past in the opposite direction, overhead. It was a parasite mimic. How long, he wondered, did it take a creature to evolve to look like that?

"It's no wonder that we've had so many defectors, back in the Rings," she said sadly. "If humanity is so stupid as to work itself into a corner like you describe, then it's better to have nothing to do with them. Better to live alone. Better not to help the madness spread."

"That kind of talk will only get us killed," Afriel said. "We owe an allegiance to the faction that produced us."

"Tell me truly, Captain," she said. "Haven't you ever felt the urge to leave everything—everyone—all your duties and constraints, and just go somewhere to think it all out? Your whole world, and your part in it? We're trained so hard, from childhood, and so much is demanded from us. Don't you think it's made us lose sight of our goals, somehow?"

"We live in space," Afriel said flatly. "Space is an unnatural environment, and it takes an unnatural effort from unnatural people to prosper there. Our minds are our tools, and philosophy has to come second. Naturally I've felt those urges you mention. They're just another threat to guard against. I believe in an ordered society. Technology has unleashed tremendous forces that are ripping society apart. Some one faction must arise from the struggle and integrate things. We Shapers have the wisdom and restraint to do it humanely. That's why I do the work I do." He hesitated. "I don't expect to see our day of triumph. I expect to die in some brush-fire conflict, or through assassination. It's enough that I can foresee that day."

"But the arrogance of it, Captain!" she said suddenly. "The arrogance of your little life and its little sacrifice! Consider the Swarm, if you really want your humane and perfect order. Here it is! Where it's always warm and dark, and it smells good, and food is easy to get, and everything is endlessly and perfectly recycled. The only resources that are ever lost are the bodies of the mating swarms, and a little air. A Nest like this one could last unchanged for hundreds of thousands of years. Hundreds . . . of thousands . . . of years. Who, or what, will remember us and our stupid faction in even a thousand years?"

Afriel shook his head. "That's not a valid comparison. There is no such long view for us. In another thousand years we'll be machines, or gods." He felt the top of his head; his velvet cap was gone. No doubt something was eating it by now.

The tunneler took them deeper into the asteroid's honeycombed free-fall maze. They saw the pupal chambers, where pallid larvae twitched in swaddled silk; the main fungal gardens; the graveyard pits, where winged workers beat ceaselessly at the soupy air, feverishly hot from the heat of decomposition. Corrosive black fungus ate the bodies of the dead into coarse black powder, carried off by blackened workers themselves three-quarters dead.

Later they left the tunneler and floated on by themselves. The woman moved with the ease of long habit; Afriel followed her, colliding bruisingly with squeaking workers. There were thousands of them, clinging to ceiling, walls, and floor, clustering and scurrying at every conceivable angle.

Later still they visited the chamber of the winged princes and princesses, an echoing round vault where creatures forty meters long hung crooked-legged in midair. Their bodies were segmented and metallic, with organic rocket nozzles on their thoraxes, where wings might have been. Folded along their sleek backs were radar antennae on long sweeping booms. They looked more like interplanetary probes under construction than anything biological. Workers fed them ceaselessly. Their bulging spiracled abdomens were full of compressed oxygen.

Mirny begged a large chunk cf fungus from a passing worker, deftly tapping its antennae and provoking a reflex action. She handed most of the fungus to the two springtails, which devoured it greedily and looked expectantly for more.

Afriel tucked his legs into a free-fall lotus position and began chewing with determination on the leathery fungus. It was tough, but tasted good, like smoked meat—a delicacy he had tasted only once. The smell of smoke meant disaster in a Shaper's colony.

Mirny maintained a stony silence. "Food's no problem," Afriel said. "Where do we sleep?"

She shrugged. "Anywhere . . . there are unused niches and tunnels here and there. I suppose you'll want to see the Queen's chamber next."

"By all means."

"I'll have to get more fungus. The warriors are on guard there and have to be bribed with food."

She gathered an armful of fungus from another worker in the endless stream, and they moved on. Afriel, already totally lost, was further confused in the maze of chambers and tunnels. At last they exited into an immense lightless cavern, bright with infrared heat from the Queen's monstrous body. It was the colony's central factory. The fact that it was made of warm and pulpy flesh did not conceal its essentially industrial nature. Tons of predigested fungal pap went into the slick blind jaws at one end. The rounded billows of soft flesh digested and processed it, squirming, sucking, and undulating, with loud machinelike churnings and gurglings. Out of the other end came an endless conveyorlike blobbed stream of eggs, each one packed in a thick hormonal paste of lubrication. The workers avidly licked the eggs clean and bore them off to nurseries. Each egg was the size of a man's torso.

The process went on and on. There was no day or night here in the lightless center of the asteroid. There was no remnant of a diurnal rhythm in the genes of these creatures. The flow of production was as constant and even as the working of an automated mine.

"This is why I'm here," Afriel murmured in awe. "Just look at this, Doctor. The Mechanists have cybernetic mining machinery that is generations ahead of ours. But here—in the bowels of this nameless little world, is a genetic technology that feeds itself, maintains itself, runs itself, efficiently, endlessly, mindlessly. It's the perfect organic tool. The faction that could use these tireless workers could make itself an industrial titan. And our knowledge of biochemistry is unsurpassed. We Shapers are just the ones to do it."

"How do you propose to do that?" Mirny asked with open skepticism. "You would have to ship a fertilized queen all the way to the solar system. We could scarcely afford that, even if the Investors would let us, which they wouldn't."

"I don't need an entire Nest," Afriel said patiently. "I only need the genetic information from one egg. Our laboratories back in the Rings could clone endless numbers of workers."

"But the workers are useless without the Nest's pheromones. They need chemical cues to trigger their behavior modes."

"Exactly," Afriel said. "As it so happens, I possess those

pheromones, synthesized and concentrated. What I must do now is test them. I must prove that I can use them to make the workers do what I choose. Once I've proven it's possible, I'm authorized to smuggle the genetic information necessary back to the Rings. The Investors won't approve. There are, of course, moral questions involved, and the Investors are not genetically advanced. But we can win their approval back with the profits we make. Best of all, we can beat the Mechanists at their own game."

"You've carried the pheromones here?" Mirny said. "Didn't the Investors suspect something when they found them?"

"Now it's you who has made an error," Afriel said calmly. "You assume that the Investors are infallible. You are wrong. A race without curiosity will never explore every possibility, the way we Shapers did." Afriel pulled up his pants cuff and extended his right leg. "Consider this varicose vein along my shin. Circulatory problems of this sort are common among those who spend a lot of time in free-fall. This vein, however, has been blocked artificially and treated to reduce osmosis. Within the vein are ten separate colonies of genetically altered bacteria, each one specially bred to produce a different Swarm pheromone."

He smiled. "The Investors searched me very thoroughly, including X-rays. But the vein appears normal to X-rays, and the bacteria are trapped within compartments in the vein. They are indetectable. I have a small medical kit on my person. It includes a syringe. We can use it to extract the pheromones and test them. When the tests are finished—and I feel sure they will be successful, in fact I've staked my career on it—we can empty the vein and all its compartments. The bacteria will die on contact with air. We can refill the vein with the yolk from a developing embryo. The cells may survive during the trip back, but even if they die, they can't rot inside my body. They'll never come in contact with any agent of decay. Back in the Rings, we can learn to activate and suppress different genes to produce the different castes, just as is done in nature. We'll have millions of workers, armies of warriors if need be, perhaps even organic rocketships, grown from altered alates. If this works, who do you think will remember me then, eh? Me and my arrogant little life and little sacrifice?"

She stared at him; even the bulky goggles could not hide her new respect and even fear. "You really mean to do it, then."

"I made the sacrifice of my time and energy. I expect results, Doctor."

"But it's kidnapping. You're talking about breeding a slave race." Afriel shrugged, with contempt. "You're juggling words, Doctor. I'll cause this colony no harm. I may steal some of its workers' labor while they obey my own chemical orders, but that tiny theft won't be missed. I admit to the murder of one egg, but that is no more a crime than a human abortion. Can the theft of one strand of genetic material be called 'kidnapping'? I think not. As for the scandalous idea of a slave race—I reject it out of hand. These creatures are genetic robots. They will no more be slaves than are laser drills or cargo tankers. At the very worst, they will be our domestic animals."

Mirny considered the issue. It did not take her long. "It's true. It's not as if a common worker will be staring at the stars, pining for its freedom. They're just brainless neuters."

"Exactly, Doctor."

"They simply work. Whether they work for us or the Swarm makes no difference to them."

"I see that you've seized on the beauty of the idea."

"And if it worked," Mirny said, "if it worked, our faction would profit astronomically."

Afriel smiled genuinely, unaware of the chilling sarcasm of his expression. "And the personal profit, Doctor . . . the valuable expertise of the first to exploit the technique." He spoke gently, quietly. "Ever see a nitrogen snowfall on Titan? I think a habitat of one's own there —larger, much larger than anything possible before. . . . A genuine city, Galina, a place where a man can scrap the rules and discipline that madden him. . . ."

"Now it's you who are talking defection, Captain-Doctor."

Afriel was silent for a moment, then smiled with an effort. "Now you've ruined my perfect reverie," he said. "Besides, what I was describing was the well-earned retirement of a wealthy man, not some self-indulgent hermitage . . . there's a clear difference." He hesitated. "In any case, may I conclude that you're with me in this project?"

She laughed and touched his arm. There was something uncanny about the small sound of her laugh, drowned by a great organic rumble from the Queen's monstrous intestines. . . . "Do you expect me to resist your arguments for two long years? Better that I give in now and save us friction."

"Yes."

"After all, you won't do any harm to the Nest. They'll never know anything has happened. And if their genetic line is successfully reproduced back home, there'll never be any reason for humanity to bother them again."

"True enough," said Afriel, though in the back of his mind he instantly thought of the fabulous wealth of Betelgeuse's asteroid system. A day would come, inevitably, when humanity would move to the stars en masse, in earnest. It would be well to know the ins and outs of every race that might become a rival.

"I'll help you as best I can," she said. There was a moment's silence. "Have you seen enough of this area?"

"Yes." They left the Queen's chamber.

"I didn't think I'd like you at first," she said candidly. "I think I like you better now. You seem to have a sense of humor that most Security people lack."

"It's not a sense of humor," Afriel said sadly. "It's a sense of irony disguised as one."

There were no days in the unending stream of hours that followed. There were only ragged periods of sleep, apart at first, later together, as they held each other in free-fall. The sexual feel of skin and body became an anchor to their common humanity, a divided, frayed humanity so many light-years away that the concept no longer had any meaning. Life in the warm and swarming tunnels was the here and now; the two of them were like germs in a bloodstream, moving ceaselessly with the pulsing ebb and flow. Hours stretched into months, and time itself grew meaningless.

The pheromonal tests were complex, but not impossibly difficult. The first of the ten pheromones was a simple grouping stimulus, causing large numbers of workers to gather as the chemical was spread from palp to palp. The workers then waited for further instructions; if none were forthcoming, they dispersed. To work effectively, the pheromones had to be given in a mix, or series, like computer commands; number one, grouping, for instance, together with the third pheromone, a transferral order, which caused the workers to empty any given chamber and move its effects to another. The ninth pheromone had the best industrial possibilities; it was a building order, causing the workers to gather tunnelers and dredgers and set them to work. Others were annoying; the tenth pheromone provoked grooming behavior, and the workers' furry palps stripped off the remaining rags of Afriel's clothing. The eighth pheromone sent the workers off to harvest material on the asteroid's surface, and in their eagerness to observe its effects the two explorers were almost trapped and swept off into space.

The two of them no longer feared the warrior caste. They knew that a dose of the sixth pheromone would send them scurrying off to defend the eggs, just as it sent the workers to tend them. Mirny and Afriel took advantage of this and secured their own chambers, dug by chemically hijacked workers and defended by a hijacked air-lock guardian. They had their own fungal gardens to refresh the air, stocked with the fungus they liked best, and digested by a worker they kept drugged for their own food use. From constant stuffing and lack of exercise the worker had swollen up into its replete form and hung from one wall like a monstrous grape.

Afriel was tired. He had been without sleep recently for a long time; how long, he didn't know. His body rhythms had not adjusted as well as Mirny's, and he was prone to fits of depression and irritability that he had to repress with an effort. "The Investors will be back sometime," he said. "Sometime soon."

Mirny was indifferent. "The Investors," she said, and followed the remark with something in the language of the springtails, which he didn't catch. Despite his linguistic training, Afriel had never caught up with her in her use of the springtails' grating jargon. His training was almost a liability; the springtail language had decayed so much that it was a pidgin tongue, without rules or regularity. He knew enough to give them simple orders, and with his partial control of the warriors he had the power to back it up. The springtails were afraid of him, and the two juveniles that Mirny had tamed had developed into fat, overgrown tyrants that freely terrorized their elders. Afriel had been too busy to seriously study the springtails or the other symbiotes. There were too many practical matters at hand.

"If they come too soon, I won't be able to finish my latest study," she said in English.

Afriel pulled off his infrared goggles and knotted them tightly around his neck. "There's a limit, Galina," he said, yawning. "You can only memorize so much data without equipment. We'll just have to wait quietly until we can get back. I hope the Investors aren't shocked when they see me. I lost a fortune with those clothes."

"It's been so dull since the mating swarm was launched. If it weren't for the new growth in the alates' chamber, I'd be bored to death." She pushed greasy hair from her face with both hands. "Are you going to sleep?"

"Yes, if I can."

"You won't come with me? I keep telling you that this new growth is important. I think it's a new caste. It's definitely not an alate. It has eyes like an alate, but it's clinging to the wall."

"It's probably not a Swarm member at all, then," he said tiredly, humoring her. "It's probably a parasite, an alate mimic. Go on and see it, if you want to. I'll be here waiting for you."

He heard her leave. Without his infrareds on, the darkness was still not quite total; there was a very faint luminosity from the steaming, growing fungus in the chamber beyond. The stuffed worker replete moved slightly on the wall, rustling and gurgling. He fell asleep.

When he awoke, Mirny had not yet returned. He was not alarmed. First, he visited the original airlock tunnel, where the Investors had first left him. It was irrational—the Investors always fulfilled their contracts—but he feared that they would arrive someday, become impatient, and leave without him. The Investors would have to wait, of course. Mirny could keep them occupied in the short time it would take him to hurry to the nursery and rob a developing egg of its living cells. It was best that the egg be as fresh as possible.

Later he ate. He was munching fungus in one of the anterior chambers when Mirny's two tamed springtails found him. "What do you want?" he asked in their language.

"Food-giver no good," the larger one screeched, waving its forelegs in brainless agitation. "Not work, not sleep."

"Not move," the second one said. It added hopefully, "Eat it now?"

Afriel gave them some of his food. They ate it, seemingly more out of habit than real appetite, which alarmed him. "Take me to her," he told them.

The two springtails scurried off; he followed them easily, adroitly dodging and weaving through the crowds of workers. They led him several miles through the network, to the alates' chamber. There they stopped, confused. "Gone," the large one said.

The chamber was empty. Afriel had never seen it empty before, and it was very unusual for the Swarm to waste so much space. He felt dread. "Follow the food-giver," he said. "Follow the smell."

The springtails snuffled without much enthusiasm along one wall; they knew he had no food and were reluctant to do anything without an immediate reward. At last one of them picked up the scent, or pretended to, and followed it up across the ceiling and into the mouth of a tunnel.

It was hard for Afriel to see much in the abandoned chamber; there was not enough infrared heat. He leapt upward after the springtail.

He heard the roar of a warrior and the springtail's choked-off screech. It came flying from the tunnel's mouth, a spray of clotted fluid bursting from its ruptured head. It tumbled end over end until it hit the far wall with a flaccid crunch. It was already dead.

The second springtail fled at once, screeching with grief and terror. Afriel landed on the lip of the tunnel, sinking into a crouch as his legs soaked up momentum. He could smell the acrid stench of the warrior's anger, a pheromone so thick that even a human could scent it. Dozens of other warriors would group here within minutes, or seconds. Behind the enraged warrior he could hear workers and tunnelers shifting and cementing rock.

He might be able to control one enraged warrior, but never two, or twenty. He launched himself from the chamber wall and out an exit.

He searched for the other springtail—he felt sure he could recognize it, since it was so much bigger than the others—but he could not find it. With its keen sense of smell, it could easily avoid him if it wanted to.

Mirny did not return. Uncountable hours passed. He slept again. He returned to the alates' chamber; there were warriors on guard there, warriors that were not interested in food and brandished their immense serrated fangs when he approached. They looked ready to rip him apart; the faint reek of aggressive pheromones hung about the place like a fog. He did not see any symbiotes of any kind on the warriors' bodies. There was one species, a thing like a huge tick, that clung only to warriors, but even the ticks were gone.

He returned to his chambers to wait and think. Mirny's body was not in the garbage pits. Of course, it was possible that something else might have eaten her. Should he extract the remaining pheromone from the spaces in his vein and try to break into the alates' chamber? He suspected that Mirny, or whatever was left of her, was somewhere in the tunnel where the springtail had been killed. He had never explored that tunnel himself. There were thousands of tunnels he had never explored.

He felt paralyzed by indecision and fear. If he was quiet, if he did nothing, the Investors might arrive at any moment. He could tell the Ring Council anything he wanted about Mirny's death; if he had the genetics with him, no one would quibble. He did not love her; he respected her, but not enough to give up his life, or his faction's investment. He had not thought of the Ring Council in a long time, and the thought sobered him. He would have to explain his decision. . . .

He was still in a brown study when he heard a whoosh of air as his living airlock deflated itself. Three warriors had come for him. There was no reek of anger about them. They moved slowly and carefully. He knew better than to try to resist. One of them seized him gently in its massive jaws and carried him off.

It took him to the alates' chamber and into the guarded tunnel. A new, large chamber had been excavated at the end of the tunnel. It was filled almost to bursting by a black-splattered white mass of flesh. In the center of the soft speckled mass were a mouth and two damp, shining eyes, on stalks. Long tendrils like conduits dangled, writhing, from a clumped ridge above the eyes. The tendrils ended in pink, fleshy pluglike clumps.

One of the tendrils had been thrust through Mirny's skull. Her body hung in midair, limp as wax. Her eyes were open, but blind.

Another tendril was plugged into the braincase of a mutated worker. The worker still had the pallid tinge of a larva; it was shrunken and deformed, and its mouth had the wrinkled look of a human mouth. There was a blob like a tongue in the mouth, and white ridges like human teeth. It had no eyes.

It spoke with Mirny's voice. "Captain-Doctor Afriel . . ."

"Galina . . ."

"I have no such name. You may address me as Swarm."

Afriel vomited. The central mass was an immense head. Its brain almost filled the room.

It waited politely until Afriel had finished.

"I find myself awakened again," Swarm said dreamily. "I am pleased to see that there is no major emergency to concern me. Instead it is a threat that has become almost routine." It hesitated delicately. Mirny's body moved slightly in midair; her breathing was inhumanly regular. The eyes opened and closed. "Another young race."

"What are you?"

"I am the Swarm. That is, I am one of its castes. I am a tool, an adaptation; my specialty is intelligence. I am not often needed. It is good to be needed again."

"Have you been here all along? Why didn't you greet us? We'd have dealt with you. We meant no harm."

The wet mouth on the end of the plug made laughing sounds. "Like yourself, I enjoy irony," it said. "It is a pretty trap you have found yourself in, Captain-Doctor. You meant to make the Swarm work for you and your race. You meant to breed us and study us and use us. It is an excellent plan, but one we hit upon long before your race evolved."

Stung by panic, Afriel's mind raced frantically. "You're an intelligent being," he said. "There's no reason to do us any harm. Let us talk together. We can help you."

"Yes," Swarm agreed. "You will be helpful. Your companion's memories tell me that this is one of those uncomfortable periods when galactic intelligence is rife. Intelligence is a great bother. It makes all kinds of trouble for us."

"What do you mean?"

"You are a young race and lay great stock by your own cleverness," Swarm said. "As usual, you fail to see that intelligence is not a survival trait."

Afriel wiped sweat from his face. "We've done well," he said. "We came to you, and peacefully. You didn't come to us."

"I refer to exactly that," Swarm said urbanely. "This urge to expand, to explore, to develop, is just what will make you extinct. You naively suppose that you can continue to feed your curiosity indefinitely. It is an old story, pursued by countless races before you. Within a thousand years—perhaps a little longer—your species will vanish."

"You intend to destroy us, then? I warn you it will not be an easy task—"

"Again you miss the point. Knowledge is power! Do you suppose that fragile little form of yours—your primitive legs, your ludicrous arms and hands, your tiny, scarcely wrinkled brain—can *contain* all that power? Certainly not! Already your race is flying to pieces under the impact of your own expertise. The original human form is becoming obsolete. Your own genes have been altered, and you, Captain-Doctor, are a crude experiment. In a hundred years you will be a relic. In a thousand years you will not even be a memory. Your race will go the same way as a thousand others."

"And what way is that?"

"I do not know." The thing on the end of the Swarm's arm made a chuckling sound. "They have passed beyond my ken. They have all discovered something, learned something, that has caused them to transcend my understanding. It may be that they even transcend *being*. At any rate, I cannot sense their presence anywhere. They seem to do nothing, they seem to interfere in nothing; for all intents and purposes, they seem to be dead. Vanished. They may have become gods, or ghosts. In either case, I have no wish to join them."

"So then—so then you have—"

"Intelligence is very much a two-edged sword, Captain-Doctor. It is useful only up to a point. It interferes with the business of living. Life, and intelligence, do not mix very well. They are not at all closely related, as you childishly assume."

"But you, then—you are a rational being—"

"I am a tool, as I said." The mutated device on the end of its arm made a sighing noise. "When you began your pheromonal experiments, the chemical imbalance became apparent to the Queen. It triggered certain genetic patterns within her body, and I was reborn. Chemical sabotage is a problem that can best be dealt with by intelligence. I am a brain replete, you see, specially designed to be far more intelligent than any young race. Within three days I was fully self-conscious. Within five days I had deciphered these markings on my body. They are the genetically encoded history of my race . . . within five days and two hours I recognized the problem at hand and knew what to do. I am now doing it. I am six days old."

"What is it you intend to do?"

"Your race is a very vigorous one. I expect it to be here, competing with us, within five hundred years. Perhaps much sooner. It will be necessary to make a thorough study of such a rival. I invite you to join our community on a permanent basis."

"What do you mean?"

"I invite you to become a symbiote. I have here a male and a female, whose genes are altered and therefore without defects. You make a perfect breeding pair. It will save me a great deal of trouble with cloning."

"You think I'll betray my race and deliver a slave species into your hands?"

"Your choice is simple, Captain-Doctor. Remain an intelligent, living being, or become a mindless puppet, like your partner. I have taken over all the functions of her nervous system; I can do the same to you."

"I can kill myself."

"That might be troublesome, because it would make me resort to developing a cloning technology. Technology, though I am capable of it, is painful to me. I am a genetic artifact; there are fail-safes within me that prevent me from taking over the Nest for my own uses. That would mean falling into the same trap of progress as other intelligent races. For similar reasons, my life span is limited. I will live for only a thousand years, until your race's brief flurry of energy is over and peace resumes once more."

"Only a thousand years?" Afriel laughed bitterly. "What then? You kill off my descendants, I assume, having no further use for them."

"No. We have not killed any of the fifteen other races we have taken for defensive study. It has not been necessary. Consider that small scavenger floating by your head, Captain-Doctor, that is feeding on your vomit. Five hundred million years ago its ancestors made the galaxy tremble. When they attacked us, we unleashed their own kind upon them. Of course, we altered our side, so that they were smarter, tougher, and, naturally, totally loyal to us. Our Nests were the only world they knew, and they fought with a valor and inventiveness we never could have matched. . . . Should your race arrive to exploit us, we will naturally do the same."

"We humans are different."

"Of course."

"A thousand years here won't change us. You will die and our descendants will take over this Nest. We'll be running things, despite you, in a few generations. The darkness won't make any difference."

"Certainly not. You don't need eyes here. You don't need anything."

"You'll allow me to stay alive? To teach them anything I want?"

"Certainly, Captain-Doctor. We are doing you a favor, in all truth. In a thousand years your descendants here will be the only remnants of the human race. We are generous with our immortality; we will take it upon ourselves to preserve you."

"You're wrong, Swarm. You're wrong about intelligence, and you're wrong about everything else. Maybe other races would crumble into parasitism, but we humans are different."

"Certainly. You'll do it, then?"

"Yes. I accept your challenge. And I will defeat you."

"Splendid. When the Investors return here, the springtails will say that they have killed you, and will tell them to never return. They will not return. The humans should be the next to arrive."

"If I don't defeat you, they will."

"Perhaps." Again it sighed. "I'm glad I don't have to absorb you. I would have missed your conversation."

SPIDER ROSE

NOTHING WAS what Spider Rose felt, or almost nothing. There had been some feelings there, a nexus of clotted two-hundred-year-old emotions, and she had mashed it with a cranial injection. Now what was left of her feelings was like what is left of a roach when a hammer strikes it.

Spider Rose knew about roaches; they were the only native animal life in the orbiting Mechanist colonies. They had plagued spacecraft from the beginning, too tough, prolific, and adaptable to kill. Of necessity, the Mechanists had used genetic techniques stolen from their rivals the Shapers to turn the roaches into colorful pets. One of Spider Rose's special favorites was a roach a foot long and covered with red and yellow pigment squiggles against shiny black chitin. It was clinging to her head. It drank sweat from her perfect brow, and she knew nothing, for she was elsewhere, watching for visitors.

She watched through eight telescopes, their images collated and fed into her brain through a nerve-crystal junction at the base of her skull. She had eight eyes now, like her symbol, the spider. Her ears were the weak steady pulse of radar, listening, listening for the weird distortion that would signal the presence of an Investor ship.

Rose was clever. She might have been insane, but her monitoring techniques established the chemical basis of sanity and maintained it artificially. Spider Rose accepted this as normal.

And it was normal; not for human beings, but for a two-hundred-year-old Mechanist, living in a spinning web of a habitat orbiting Uranus, her body seething with youth hormones, her wise old-young face like something pulled fresh from a plaster mold, her long white hair a rippling display of implanted fiber-optic threads with tiny beads of light oozing like microscopic gems from their slant-cut tips. . . . She was old, but she didn't think about that. And she was lonely, but she had crushed those feelings with drugs. And she had something that the Investors wanted, something that those reptilian alien traders would give their eye-fangs to possess.

Trapped in her polycarbon spiderweb, the wide-stretched cargo net that had given her her name, she had a jewel the size of a bus.

And so she watched, brain-linked to her instruments, tireless, not particularly interested but certainly not bored. Boredom was dangerous. It led to unrest, and unrest could be fatal in a space habitat, where malice or even plain carelessness could kill. The proper survival behavior was this: to crouch in the center of the mental web, clean euclidean web-lines of rationality radiating out in all directions, hooked legs alert for the slightest tremble of troubling emotion. And when she sensed that feeling tangling the lines, she rushed there, gauged it, shrouded it neatly, and pierced it cleanly and lingeringly with a spiderfang hypodermic. . . .

There it was. Her octuple eyes gazed a quarter of a million miles into space and spotted the star-rippling warp of an Investor ship. The Investor ships had no conventional engines, and radiated no detectable energies; the secret of their star drive was closely guarded. All that any of the factions (still loosely called "humanity" for lack of a better term) knew for sure about the Investor drive was that it sent long parabolic streamers of distortion from the sterns of ships, causing a rippling effect against the background of stars.

Spider Rose came partially out of her static observation mode and felt herself in her body once more. The computer signals were muted now, overlaid behind her normal vision like a reflection of her own face on a glass window as she gazed through it. Touching a keyboard, she pinpointed the Investor ship with a communications laser and sent it a pulse of data: a business offer. (Radio was too chancy; it might attract Shaper pirates, and she had had to kill three of them already.)

She knew she had been heard and understood when she saw the

Investor ship perform a dead stop and an angled acceleration that broke every known law of orbital dynamics. While she waited, Spider Rose loaded an Investor translator program. It was fifty years old, but the Investors were a persistent lot, not so much conservative as just uninterested in change.

When it came too close to her station for star-drive maneuvers, the Investor ship unfurled a decorated solar sail with a puff of gas. The sail was big enough to gift-wrap a small moon and thinner than a two-hundred-year-old memory. Despite its fantastic thinness, there were molecule-thin murals worked onto it: titanic scenes of Investor argosies where wily Investors had defrauded pebbly bipeds and gullible heavy-planet gasbags swollen with wealth and hydrogen. The great jewel-laden queens of the Investor race, surrounded by adoring male harems, flaunted their gaudy sophistication above miles-high narratives of Investor hieroglyphs, placed on a musical grid to indicate the proper pitch and intonation of their half-sung language.

There was a burst of static on the screen before her and an Investor face appeared. Spider Rose pulled the plug from her neck. She studied the face: its great glassy eyes half-shrouded behind nictitating membranes, rainbow frill behind pinhole-sized ears, bumpy skin, reptile grin with peg-sized teeth. It made noises: "Ship's ensign here," her computer translated. "Lydia Martinez?"

"Yes," Spider Rose said, not bothering to explain that her name had changed. She had had many names.

"We had profitable dealings with your husband in the past," the Investor said with interest. "How does he fare these days?"

"He died thirty years ago," Spider Rose said. She had mashed the grief. "Shaper assassins killed him."

The Investor officer flickered his frill. He was not embarrassed. Embarrassment was not an emotion native to Investors. "Bad for business," he opined. "Where is this jewel you mentioned?"

"Prepare for incoming data," said Spider Rose, touching her keyboard. She watched the screen as her carefully prepared sales spiel unrolled itself, its communication beam shielded to avoid enemy ears.

It had been the find of a lifetime. It had started existence as part of a glacierlike ice moon of the protoplanet Uranus, shattering, melting, and recrystallizing in the primeval eons of relentless bombardment. It had cracked at least four different times, and each time mineral flows had been forced within its fracture zones under tremendous pressure: carbon, manganese silicate, beryllium, aluminum oxide. When the moon was finally broken up into the famous Ring complex, the massive ice chunk had floated for eons, awash in shock waves of hard radiation, accumulating and losing charge in the bizarre electromagnetic flickerings typical of all Ring formations.

And then one crucial moment some millions of years ago it had been ground-zero for a titanic lightning flash, one of those soundless invisible gouts of electric energy, dissipating charges built up over whole decades. Most of the ice-chunk's outer envelope had flashed off at once as a plasma. The rest was . . . changed. Mineral occlusions were now strings and veins of beryl, shading here and there into lumps of raw emerald big as Investors' heads, crisscrossed with nets of red corundum and purple garnet. There were lumps of fused diamond, weirdly colored blazing diamond that came only from the strange quantum states of metallic carbon. Even the ice itself had changed into something rich and unique and therefore by definition precious.

"You intrigue us," the Investor said. For them, this was profound enthusiasm. Spider Rose smiled. The ensign continued: "This is an unusual commodity and its value is hard to establish. We offer you a quarter of a million gigawatts."

Spider Rose said, "I have the energy I need to run my station and defend myself. It's generous, but I could never store that much."

"We will also give you a stabilized plasma lattice for storage." This unexpected and fabulous generosity was meant to overwhelm her. The construction of plasma lattices was far beyond human technology, and to own one would be a ten years' wonder. It was the last thing she wanted. "Not interested," she said.

The Investor lifted his frill. "Not interested in the basic currency of galactic trade?"

"Not when I can spend it only with you."

"Trade with young races is a thankless lot," the Investor observed. "I suppose you want information, then. You young races always want to trade in technology. We have some Shaper techniques for trade within their faction—are you interested in those?"

"Industrial espionage?" Spider Rose said. "You should have tried me eighty years ago. No, I know you Investors too well. You would only sell Mechanist techniques to them to maintain the balance of power."

"We like a competitive market," the Investor admitted. "It helps us avoid painful monopoly situations like the one we face now, dealing with you."

"I don't want power of any kind. Status means nothing to me. Show me something new."

"No status? What will your fellows think?"

"I live alone."

The Investor hid his eyes behind nictitating membranes. "Crushed your gregarious instincts? An ominous development. Well, I will take a new tack. Will you consider weaponry? If you will agree to various conditions regarding their use, we can give you unique and powerful armaments."

"I manage already."

"You could use our political skills. We can strongly influence the major Shaper groups and protect you from them by treaty. It would take ten or twenty years, but it could be done."

"It's up to them to be afraid of me," Spider Rose said, "not vice versa."

"A new habitat, then." The Investor was patient. "You can live within solid gold."

"I like what I have."

"We have some artifacts that might amuse you," the Investor said. "Prepare for incoming data."

Spider Rose spent eight hours examining the various wares. There was no hurry. She was too old for impatience, and the Investors lived to bargain.

She was offered colorful algae cultures that produced oxygen and alien perfumes. There were metafoil structures of collapsed atoms for radiation shielding and defense. Rare techniques that transmuted nerve fibers to crystal. A smooth black wand that made iron so malleable that you could mold it with your hands and set it in shape. A small luxury submarine for the exploration of ammonia and methane seas, made of transparent metallic glass. Self-replicating globes of patterned silica that, as they grew, played out a game simulating the birth, growth, and decline of an alien culture. A land-sea-and-aircraft so tiny that you buttoned it on like a suit. "I don't care for planets," Spider Rose said. "I don't like gravity wells."

"Under certain circumstances we could make a gravity generator available," the Investor said. "It would have to be tamper-proof, like the wand and the weapons, and loaned rather than sold outright. We must avoid the escape of such a technology."

She shrugged. "Our own technologies have shattered us. We can't assimilate what we already have. I see no reason to burden myself with more."

"This is all we can offer you that's not on the interdicted list," he said. "This ship in particular has a great many items suitable only for races that live at very low temperature and very high pressure. And we have items that you would probably enjoy a great deal, but they would kill you. Or your whole species. The literature of the [untranslatable], for instance."

"I can read the literature of Earth if I want an alien viewpoint," she said.

"[Untranslatable] is not really a literature," the Investor said benignly. "It's really a kind of virus."

A roach flew onto her shoulder. "Pets!" he said. "Pets! You enjoy them?"

"They are my solace," she said, letting it nibble the cuticle of her thumb.

"I should have thought," he said. "Give me twelve hours."

She went to sleep. After she woke, she studied the alien craft through her telescope while she waited. All Investor ships were covered with fantastic designs in hammered metal: animal heads, metal mosaics, scenes and inscriptions in deep relief, as well as cargo bays and instruments. But experts had pointed out that the basic shape beneath the ornamentation was always the same: a simple octahedron with six long rectangular sides. The Investors had gone to some pains to disguise this fact; and the current theory held that the ships had been bought, found, or stolen from a more advanced race. Certainly the Investors, with their whimsical attitude toward science and technology, seemed incapable of building them themselves.

The ensign reopened contact. His nictitating membranes looked whiter than usual. He held up a small winged reptilian being with a long spiny crest the color of an Investor's frill. "This is our Commander's mascot, called 'Little Nose for Profits.' Beloved by us all! It costs us a pang to part from him. We had to choose between losing face in this business deal or losing his company." He toyed with it. It grasped his thick digits with little scaly hands.

"He's . . . cute," she said, finding a half-forgotten word from her childhood and pronouncing it with a grimace of distaste. "But I'm not going to trade my find for some carnivorous lizardkin."

"And think of us!" the Investor lamented. "Condemning our little Nose to an alien lair swarming with bacteria and giant vermin. . . . However, this can't be helped. Here's our proposal. You take our mascot for seven hundred plus or minus five of your days. We will return here on our way out of your system. You can choose then between owning him or keeping your prize. In the meantime you must promise not to sell the jewel or inform anyone else of its existence."

"You mean that you will leave me your pet as a kind of earnest money on the transaction."

The Investor covered his eyes with the nictitating membranes and squeezed his pebbly lids half-shut. It was a sign of acute distress. "He is a hostage to your cruel indecision, Lydia Martinez. Frankly we doubt that we can find anything in this system that can satisfy you better than our mascot can. Except perhaps some novel mode of suicide."

Spider Rose was surprised. She had never seen an Investor become so emotionally involved. Generally they seemed to take a detached view of life, even showing on occasion behavior patterns that resembled a sense of humor.

She was enjoying herself. She was past the point when any of the Investor's normal commodities could have tempted her. In essence, she was trading her jewel for an interior mind-state: not an emotion, because she mashed those, but for a paler and cleaner feeling: interestedness. She wanted to be interested, to find something to occupy herself besides dead stones and space. And this looked intriguing.

"All right," she said. "I agree. Seven hundred plus or minus five days. And I keep silence." She smiled. She hadn't spoken to another human in five years and was not about to start.

"Take good care of our Little Nose for Profits," the Investor said, half pleading, half warning, accenting those nuances so that her computer would be sure to pick them up. "We will still want him, even if, through some utter corrosion of the spirit, you do not. He is valuable and rare. We will send you instructions on his care and feeding. Prepare for incoming data."

They fired the creature's cargo capsule into the tight-stretched polycarbon web of her spider habitat. The web was built on a framework of eight spokes, and these spokes were pulled taut by centrifugal force from the wheeling rotation of eight teardrop-shaped capsules. At the impact of the cargo shot, the web bowed gracefully and the eight massive metal teardrops were pulled closer to the web's center in short, graceful free-fall arcs. Wan sunlight glittered along the web as it expanded in recoil, its rotation slowed a little by the energy it had spent in absorbing the inertia. It was a cheap and effective docking technique, for a rate of spin was much easier to manage than complex maneuvering.

Hook-legged industrial robots ran quickly along the polycarbon fibers and seized the mascot's capsule with clamps and magnetic palps. Spider Rose ran the lead robot herself, feeling and seeing through its grips and cameras. The robots hustled the cargo craft to an airlock, dislodged its contents, and attached a small parasitic rocket to boost it back to the Investor mother ship. After the small rocket had returned and the Investor ship had left, the robots trooped back to their teardrop garages and shut themselves off, waiting for the next tremor of the web.

Spider Rose disconnected herself and opened the airlock. The mascot flew into the room. It had seemed tiny compared to the Investor ensign, but the Investors were huge. The mascot was as tall as her knee and looked like it weighed close to twenty pounds. Wheezing musically on the unfamiliar air, it flew around the room, ducking and darting unevenly.

A roach launched itself from the wall and flew with a great clatter of wings. The mascot hit the deck with a squawk of terror and lay there, comically feeling its spindly arms and legs for damage. It half-closed its rough eyelids. Like the eyes of an Investor baby, Spider Rose thought suddenly, though she had never seen a young Investor and doubted if anyone human ever had. She had a dim memory of something she had heard a long time before—something about pets and babies, their large heads, their large eyes, their softness, their dependence. She remembered scoffing at the idea that the sloppy dependence of, say, a "dog" or "cat" could rival the clean economy and efficiency of a roach.

The Investor mascot had recovered its composure and was crouching bent-kneed on the algae carpet, warbling to itself. There was a sort of sly grin on its miniature dragon face. Its half-slitted eyes were alert and its matchstick ribs moved up and down with each breath. Its pupils were huge. Spider Rose imagined that it must find the light very dim. The lights in Investor ships were like searing blue arc-lamps, drenched in ultraviolet.

"We have to find a new name for you," Spider Rose said. "I don't speak Investor, so I can't use the name they gave you."

The mascot fixed her with a friendly stare, and it arched little half-transparent flaps over its pinhole ears. Real Investors had no such flaps, and she was charmed at this further deviation from the norm. Actually, except for the wings, it looked altogether too much like a tiny Investor. The effect was creepy.

"I'll call you Fuzzy," she said. It had no hair. It was a private joke, but all her jokes were private.

The mascot bounced across the floor. The false centrifugal gravity was lighter here, too, than the 1.3 g's that the massive Investors used. It embraced her bare leg and licked her kneecap with a rough sandpaper tongue. She laughed, more than a little alarmed, but she knew the Investors were strictly nonaggressive. A pet of theirs would not be dangerous.

It made eager chirping sounds and climbed onto her head, clutching handfuls of glittering optic fibers. She sat at her data console and called up the care and feeding instructions.

Clearly the Investors had not expected to trade their pet, because the instructions were almost indecipherable. They had the air of a second- or third-hand translation from some even more profoundly alien language. However, true to Investor tradition, the blandly pragmatic aspects had been emphasized.

Spider Rose relaxed. Apparently the mascots would eat almost anything, though they preferred dextrorotatory proteins and required certain easily acquirable trace minerals. They were extremely resistant to toxins and had no native intestinal bacteria. (Neither did the Investors themselves, and they regarded races who did as savages.)

She looked for its respiratory requirements as the mascot leapt from her head and capered across the control board, almost aborting the program. She shooed it off, hunting for something she could comprehend amid dense clusters of alien graphs and garbled technical material. Suddenly she recognized something from her old days in technical espionage: a genetics chart.

She frowned. It seemed she had run past the relevant sections and on to another treatise entirely. She advanced the data slightly and discovered a three-dimensional illustration of some kind of fantastically complex genetic construct, with long helical chains of alien genes marked out in improbable colors. The gene chains were wrapped around long spires or spicules that emerged radially from a dense central knot. Further chains of tightly wound helices connected spire to spire. Apparently these chains activated different sections of genetic material from their junctions on the spires, for she could see ghost chains of slave proteins peeling off from some of the activated genes.

Spider Rose smiled. No doubt a skilled Shaper geneticist could profit spectacularly from these plans. It amused her to think that they never would. Obviously this was some kind of alien industrial genetic complex, for there was more genetic hardware there than any actual living animal could ever possibly need.

She knew that the Investors themselves never tampered with

genetics. She wondered which of the nineteen known intelligent races had originated this thing. It might even have come from outside the Investors' economic realm, or it might be a relic from one of the extinct races.

She wondered if she ought to erase the data. If she died, it might fall into the wrong hands. As she thought of her death, the first creeping shades of a profound depression disturbed her. She allowed the sensation to build for a moment while she thought. The Investors had been careless to leave her with this information; or perhaps they underestimated the genetic abilities of the smooth and charismatic Shapers with their spectacularly boosted IQs.

There was a wobbling feeling inside her head. For a dizzying moment the chemically repressed emotions gushed forth with all their pent-up force. She felt an agonized envy for the Investors, for the dumb arrogance and confidence that allowed them to cruise the stars screwing their purported inferiors. She wanted to be with them. She wanted to get aboard a magic ship and feel alien sunlight burn her skin in some place light-years from human weakness. She wanted to scream and feel like a little girl had screamed and felt one hundred and ninety-three years ago on a roller coaster in Los Angeles, screaming in total pure intensity of feeling, in swept-away sensation like she had felt in the arms of her husband, her man dead now thirty years. Dead . . . Thirty years . . .

Her hands trembling, she opened a drawer beneath the control board. She smelled the faint medicinal reek of ozone from the sterilizer. Blindly she pushed her glittering hair from the plastic duct into her skull, pressed the injector against it, inhaled once, closed her eyes, inhaled twice, pulled the hypo away. Her eyes glazed over as she refilled the hypo and slipped it back into its velcro holster in the drawer.

She held the bottle and looked at it blankly. There was still plenty left. She would not have to synthesize more for months. Her brain felt like someone had stepped on it. It was always like this right after a mash. She shut off the Investor data and filed it absently in an obscure corner of computer memory. From its stand on the laser-com interface the mascot sang briefly and groomed its wing.

Soon she was herself again. She smiled. These sudden attacks were something she took for granted. She took an oral tranquilizer to stop the trembling of her hands and antacid for the stress on her stomach.

Then she played with the mascot until it grew tired and went to sleep. For four days she fed it carefully, being especially careful not to overfeed it, for like its models the Investors, it was a greedy little creature and she was afraid it would hurt itself. Even despite its rough skin and cold-bloodedness she was growing fond of it. When it grew tired of begging for food, it would play with string for hours or sit on her head watching the screen as she monitored the mining robots she had out in the Rings.

On the fifth day she found on awakening that it had killed and eaten her four largest and fattest roaches. Filled with a righteous anger she did nothing to blunt, she hunted for it throughout the capsule.

She did not find it. Instead, after hours of search, she found a mascot-sized cocoon wedged under the toilet.

It had gone into some sort of hibernation. She forgave it for eating the roaches. They were easy to replace, anyway, and rivals for her affections. In a way it was flattering. But the sharp pang of worry she felt overrode that. She examined the cocoon closely. It was made of overlapping sheets of some brittle translucent substance—dried mucus?—that she could chip easily with her fingernail. The cocoon was not perfectly rounded; there were small vague lumps that might have been its knees and elbows. She took another injection.

The week it spent in hibernation was a period of acute anxiety for her. She pored over the Investor tapes, but they were far too cryptic for her limited expertise. At least she knew it was not dead, for the cocoon was warm to the touch and the lumps within it sometimes stirred.

She was asleep when it began to break free of the cocoon. She had set up monitors to warn her, however, and she rushed to it at the first alarm.

The cocoon was splitting. A rent appeared in the brittle overlapping sheets, and a warm animal reek seeped out into the recycled air.

Then a paw emerged: a tiny five-fingered paw covered in glittering fur. A second paw poked through, and the two paws gripped the edges of the rent and ripped the cocoon away. It stepped out into the light, kicking the husk aside with a little human shuffle, and it grinned.

It looked like a little ape, small and soft and glittering. There were tiny human teeth behind the human lips of its grin. It had small soft baby's feet on the ends of its round springy legs, and it had lost its wings. Its eyes were the color of her eyes. The smooth mammalian skin of its round little face had the faint rosy flush of perfect health. It jumped into the air, and she saw the pink of its tongue as it babbled aloud in human syllables.

It skipped over and embraced her leg. She was frightened, amazed, and profoundly relieved. She petted the soft perfect glittering fur on its hard little nugget of a head.

"Fuzzy," she said. "I'm glad. I'm very glad."

"Wa wa wa," it said, mimicking her intonation in its piping child's voice. Then it skipped back to its cocoon and began to eat it by the double handful, grinning.

She understood now why the Investors had been so reluctant to offer their mascot. It was a trade item of fantastic value. It was a genetic artifact, able to judge the emotional wants and needs of an alien species and adapt itself to them in a matter of days.

She began to wonder why the Investors had given it away at all; if they fully understood the capabilities of their pet. Certainly she doubted that they had understood the complex data that had come with it. Very likely, they had acquired the mascot from other Investors, in its reptilian form. It was even possible (the thought chilled her) that it might be older than the entire Investor race.

She stared at it: at its clear, guileless, trusting eyes. It gripped her fingers with small warm sinewy hands. Unable to resist, she hugged it to her, and it babbled with pleasure. Yes, it could easily have lived for hundreds or thousands of years, spreading its love (or equivalent emotions) among dozens of differing species.

And who would harm it? Even the most depraved and hardened of her own species had secret weaknesses. She remembered stories of guards in concentration camps who butchered men and women without a qualm, but meticulously fed hungry birds in the winter. Fear bred fear and hatred, but how could anyone feel fear or hatred toward this creature, or resist its brilliant powers?

It was not intelligent; it didn't need intelligence. It was sexless as well. An ability to breed would have ruined its value as a trade item. Besides, she doubted that anything so complex could have grown in a womb. Its genes would have to be built, spicule by spicule, in some unimaginable lab.

Days and weeks reeled by. Its ability to sense her moods was little short of miraculous. When she needed it, it was always there, and when she didn't it vanished. Sometimes she would hear it chattering to itself as it capered in strange acrobatics or chased and ate roaches. It was never mischievous, and on the odd occasions where it spilled

food or upset something, it would unobtrusively clean up after itself. It dropped its small inoffensive fecal pellets into the same recycler she used.

These were the only signs it showed of patterns of thought that were more than animal. Once, and only once, it had mimicked her, repeating a sentence letter-perfect. She had been shocked, and it had sensed her reaction immediately. It never tried to parrot her again.

They slept in the same bed. Sometimes while she slept she would feel its warm nose snuffling lightly along the surface of her skin, as if it could smell her suppressed moods and feelings through the pores. Sometimes it would rub or press with its small firm hands against her neck or spine, and there was always a tightened muscle there that relaxed in gratitude. She never allowed this in the day, but at night, when her discipline was half-dissolved in sleep, there was a conspiracy between them.

The Investors had been gone over six hundred days. She laughed when she thought of the bargain she was getting.

The sound of her own laughter no longer startled her. She had even cut back on her dosages of suppressants and inhibitors. Her pet seemed so much happier when she was happy, and when it was at hand her ancient sadnesses seemed easier to bear. One by one she began to face old pains and traumas, holding her pet close and shedding healing tears into its glittering fur. One by one it licked her tears, tasting the emotional chemicals they contained, smelling her breath and skin, holding her as she was racked with sobbing. There were so many memories. She felt old, horribly old, but at the same time she felt a new sense of wholeness that allowed her to bear it. She had done things in the past—cruel things—and she had never put up with the inconvenience of guilt. She had mashed it instead.

Now for the first time in decades she felt the vague reawakening of a sense of purpose. She wanted to see people again—dozens of people, hundreds of people, all of whom would admire her, protect her, find her precious, whom she could care for, who would keep her safer than she was with only one companion. . . .

Her web station entered the most dangerous part of its orbit, where it crossed the plane of the Rings. Here she was busiest, accepting the drifting chunks of raw materials—ice, carbonaceous chondrites, metal ores—that her telepuppet mining robots had discovered and sent her way. There were killers in these Rings: rapacious pirates, paranoid settlers anxious to lash out.

In her normal orbit, far off the plane of the ecliptic, she was safe. But here there were orders to be broadcasted, energies to be spent, the telltale traces of powerful mass drivers hooked to the captive asteroids she claimed and mined. It was an unavoidable risk. Even the best-designed habitat was not a completely closed system, and hers was big, and old.

They found her.

Three ships. She tried bluffing them off at first, sending them a standard interdiction warning routed through a telepuppet beacon. They found the beacon and destroyed it, but that gave her their location and some blurry data through the beacon's limited sensors.

Three sleek ships, iridescent capsules half-metal, half-organic, with long ribbed insect-tinted sun-wings thinner than the scum of oil on water. Shaper spacecraft, knobbed with the geodesics of sensors, the spines of magnetic and optical weapons systems, long cargo manipulators folded like the arms of mantises.

She sat hooked into her own sensors, studying them, taking in a steady trickle of data: range estimation, target probabilities, weapons status. Radar was too risky; she sighted them optically. This was fine for lasers, but her lasers were not her best weapons. She might get one, but the others would be on her. It was better that she stay quiet while they prowled the Rings and she slid silently off the ecliptic.

But they had found her. She saw them fold their sails and activate their ion engines.

They were sending radio. She entered it on screen, not wanting the distraction filling her head. A Shaper's face appeared, one of the Oriental-based gene lines, smooth raven hair held back with jeweled pins, slim black eyebrows arched over dark eyes with the epicanthic fold, pale lips slightly curved in a charismatic smile. A smooth, clean actor's face with the glittering ageless eyes of a fanatic. "Jade Prime," she said.

"*Colonel-Doctor* Jade Prime," the Shaper said, fingering a golden insignia of rank in the collar of his black military tunic. "Still calling yourself 'Spider Rose' these days, Lydia? Or have you wiped that out of your brain?"

"Why are you a soldier instead of a corpse?"

"Times change, Spider. The bright young lights get snuffed out, by your old friends, and those of us with long-range plans are left to settle old debts. You remember old debts, Spider?"

"You think you're going to survive this meeting, don't you, Prime?" She felt the muscles of her face knotting with a ferocious hatred she had no time to kill. "Three ships manned with your own clones. How long have you holed up in that rock of yours, like a maggot in an apple? Cloning and cloning. When was the last time a woman let you touch her?"

His eternal smile twisted into a leer with bright teeth behind it. "It's no use, Spider. You've already killed *thirty-seven* of me, and I just keep coming back, don't I? You pathetic old bitch, what the hell is a maggot, anyway? Something like that mutant on your shoulder?"

She hadn't even known the pet was there, and her heart was stabbed with fear for it. "You've come too close!"

"Fire, then! Shoot me, you germy old cretin! Fire!"

"You're not him!" she said suddenly. "You're not First Jade! Hah! He's dead, isn't he?"

The clone's face twisted with rage. Lasers flared, and three of her habitats melted into slag and clouds of metallic plasma. A last searing pulse of intolerable brightness flashed in her brain from three melting telescopes.

She cut loose with a chugging volley of magnetically accelerated iron slugs. At four hundred miles per second they riddled the first ship and left it gushing air and brittle clouds of freezing water.

Two ships fired. They used weapons she had never seen before, and they crushed two habitats like a pair of giant fists. The web lurched with the impact, its equilibrium gone. She knew instantly which weapons systems were left, and she returned fire with metal-jacketed pellets of ammonia ice. They punched through the semiorganic sides of a second Shaper craft. The tiny holes sealed instantly, but the crew was finished; the ammonia vaporized inside, releasing instantly lethal nerve toxins.

The last ship had one chance in three to get her command center. Two hundred years of luck ran out for Spider Rose. Static stung her hands from the controls. Every light in the habitat went out, and her computer underwent a total crash. She screamed and waited for death.

Death did not come.

Her mouth gushed with the bile of nausea. She opened the drawer in the darkness and filled her brain with liquid tranquillity. Breathing hard, she sat back in her console chair, her panic mashed. "Electromagnetic pulse," she said. "Stripped everything I had."

The pet warbled a few syllables. "He would have finished us by now if he could," she told her pet. "The defenses must have come through from the other habitats when the mainframe crashed."

She felt a thump as the pet jumped into her lap, shivering with terror. She hugged it absently, rubbing its slender neck. "Let's see," she said into the darkness. "The ice toxins are down, I had them over-ridden from here." She pulled the useless plug from her neck and plucked her robe away from her damp ribs. "It was the spray, then. A nice, thick cloud of hot ionized metallic copper. Blew every sensor he had. He's riding blind in a metallic coffin. Just like us."

She laughed. "Except old Rose has a trick left, baby. The In-vestors. They'll be looking for me. There's nobody left to look for him. And I still have my rock."

She sat silently, and her artificial calmness allowed her to think the unthinkable. The pet stirred uneasily, sniffing at her skin. It had calmed a little under her caresses, and she didn't want it to suffer.

She put her free hand over its mouth and twisted its neck till it broke. The centrifugal gravity had kept her strong, and it had no time to struggle. A final tremor shook its limbs as she held it up in the darkness, feeling for a heartbeat. Her fingertips felt the last pulse behind its frail ribs.

"Not enough oxygen," she said. Mashed emotions tried to stir, and failed. She had plenty of suppressor left. "The carpet algae will keep the air clean a few weeks, but it dies without light. And I can't eat it. Not enough food, baby. The gardens are gone, and even if they hadn't been blasted, I couldn't get food in here. Can't run the robots. Can't even open the airlocks. If I live long enough, they'll come and pry me out. I have to improve my chances. It's the sensible thing. When I'm like this I can only do the sensible thing."

When the roaches—or at least all those she could trap in the darkness—were gone, she fasted for a long dark time. Then she ate her pet's undecayed flesh, half hoping even in her numbness that it would poison her.

When she first saw the searing blue light of the Investors glaring through the shattered airlock, she crawled back on bony hands and knees, shielding her eyes.

The Investor crewman wore a spacesuit to protect himself from bacteria. She was glad he couldn't smell the reek of her pitch-black crypt. He spoke to her in the fluting language of the Investors, but her translator was dead.

She thought then for a moment that they would abandon her, leave her there starved and blinded and half-bald in her webs of shed fiber-hair. But they took her aboard, drenching her with stinging an-tiseptics, scorching her skin with bactericidal ultraviolet rays.

They had the jewel, but that much she already knew. What they wanted—(this was difficult)—what they wanted to know was what had happened to their mascot. It was hard to understand their gestures and their pidgin scraps of human language. She had done something bad to herself, she knew that. Overdoses in the dark. Struggling in the darkness with a great black beetle of fear that broke the frail meshes of her spider's web. She felt very bad. There was something wrong inside of her. Her malnourished belly was as tight as a drum, and her lungs felt crushed. Her bones felt wrong. Tears wouldn't come.

They kept at her. She wanted to die. She wanted their love and understanding. She wanted—

Her throat was full. She couldn't talk. Her head tilted back, and her eyes shrank in the searing blaze of the overhead lights. She heard painless cracking noises as her jaws unhinged.

Her breathing stopped. It came as a relief. Antiperistalsis throbbed in her gullet, and her mouth filled with fluid.

A living whiteness oozed from her lips and nostrils. Her skin tingled at its touch, and it flowed over her eyeballs, sealing and soothing them. A great coolness and lassitude soaked into her as wave after wave of translucent liquid swaddled her, gushing over her skin, coating her body. She relaxed, filled with a sensual, sleepy gratitude. She was not hungry. She had plenty of excess mass.

In eight days she broke from the brittle sheets of her cocoon and fluttered out on scaly wings, eager for the leash.

CICADA QUEEN

T BEGAN THE NIGHT the Queen called off her dogs. I'd been under the dogs for two years, ever since my defection. My initiation, and my freedom from the dogs, were celebrated at the home of Arvin Kulagin. Kulagin, a wealthy Mechanist, had a large domestic-industrial complex on the outer perimeter of a midsized cylindrical suburb.

Kulagin met me at his door and handed me a gold inhaler. The party was already roaring. The Polycarbon Clique always turned out in force for an initiation.

As usual, my entrance was marked by a subtle freezing up. It was the dogs' fault. Voices were raised to a certain histrionic pitch, people handled their inhalers and drinks with a slightly more studied elegance, and every smile turned my way was bright enough for a team of security experts.

Kulagin smiled glassily. "Landau, it's a pleasure. Welcome. I see you've brought the Queen's Percentage." He looked pointedly at the box on my hip.

"Yes," I said. A man under the dogs had no secrets. I had been working off and on for two years on the Queen's gift, and the dogs had taped everything. They were still taping everything. Czarina-Kluster Security had designed them for that. For two years they'd taped every moment of my life and everything and everyone around me.

"Perhaps the Clique can have a look," Kulagin said. "Once we've whipped these dogs." He winked into the armored camera face of the watchdog, then looked at his timepiece. "Just an hour till you're out from under. Then we'll have some fun." He waved me on into the room. "If you need anything, use the servos."

Kulagin's place was spacious and elegant, decorated classically and scented by gigantic suspended marigolds. His suburb was called the Froth and was the Clique's favorite neighborhood. Kulagin, living at the suburb's perimeter, profited by the Froth's lazy spin and had a simulated tenth of a gravity. His walls were striped to provide a vertical referent, and he had enough space to affect such luxuries as "couches," "tables," "chairs," and other forms of gravity-oriented furniture. The ceiling was studded with hooks, from which were suspended a dozen of his favorite marigolds, huge round explosions of reeking greenery with blossoms the size of my head.

I walked into the room and stood behind a couch, which partially hid the two offensive dogs. I signaled one of Kulagin's spidery servos and took a squeezebulb of liquor to cut the speedy intensity of the inhaler's phenethylamine.

I watched the party, which had split into loose subcliques. Kulagin was near the door with his closest sympathizers, Mechanist officers from Czarina-Kluster banks and quiet Security types. Nearby, faculty from the Kosmosity-Metasystem campus talked shop with a pair of orbital engineers. On the ceiling, Shaper designers talked fashion, clinging to hooks in the feeble gravity. Below them a manic group of C-K folk, "Cicadas," spun like clockwork through gravity dance steps.

At the back of the room, Wellspring was holding forth amid a herd of spindly-legged chairs. I leapt gently over the couch and glided toward him. The dogs sprang after me with a whir of propulsive fans.

Wellspring was my closest friend in C-K. He had encouraged my defection when he was in the Ring Council, buying ice for the Martian terraforming project. The dogs never bothered Wellspring. His ancient friendship with the Queen was well known. In C-K, Wellspring was a legend.

Tonight he was dressed for an audience with the Queen. A coronet of gold and platinum circled his dark, matted hair. He wore a loose blouse of metallic brocade with slashed sleeves that showed a black underblouse shot through with flickering pinpoints of light. This was complemented by an Investor-style jeweled skirt and knee-high scaled boots. The jeweled cables of the skirt showed Wellspring's massive legs, trained to the heavy gravity favored by the reptilian Queen. He was a powerful man, and his weaknesses, if he had any, were hidden within his past.

Wellspring was talking philosophy. His audience, mathematicians and biologists from the faculty of C-K K-M, made room for me with strained smiles. "You asked me to define my terms," he said urbanely. "By the term we, I don't mean merely you Cicadas. Nor do I mean the mass of so-called humanity. After all, you Shapers are constructed of genes patented by Reshaped genetics firms. You might be properly defined as industrial artifacts."

His audience groaned. Wellspring smiled. "And conversely, the Mechanists are slowly abandoning human flesh in favor of cybernetic modes of existence. So. It follows that my term, we, can be attributed to any cognitive metasystem on the Fourth Prigoginic Level of Complexity."

A Shaper professor touched his inhaler to the painted line of his nostril and said, "I have to take issue with that, Wellspring. This occult nonsense about levels of complexity is ruining C-K's ability to do decent science."

"That's a linear causative statement," Wellspring riposted. "You conservatives are always looking for certainties outside the level of the cognitive metasystem. Clearly every intelligent being is separated from every lower level by a Prigoginic event horizon. It's time we learned to stop looking for solid ground to stand on. Let's place ourselves at the center of things. If we need something to stand on, we'll have it orbit us."

He was applauded. He said, "Admit it, Yevgeny. C-K is blooming in a new moral and intellectual climate. It's unquantifiable and unpredictable, and, as a scientist, that frightens you. Posthumanism offers fluidity and freedom, and a metaphysic daring enough to think a whole world into life. It enables us to take up economically absurd projects such as the terraforming of Mars, which your pseudopragmatic attitude could never dare to attempt. And yet think of the gain involved."

"Semantic tricks," sniffed the professor. I had never seen him before. I suspected that Wellspring had brought him along for the express purpose of baiting him.

I myself had once doubted some aspects of C-K's Posthumanism.

But its open abandonment of the search for moral certainties had liberated us. When I looked at the eager, painted faces of Wellspring's audience, and compared them to the bleak strain and veiled craftiness that had once surrounded me, I felt as if I would burst. After twenty-four years of paranoid discipline under the Ring Council, and then two more years under the dogs, tonight I would be explosively released from pressure.

I sniffed at the phenethylamine, the body's own "natural" amphetamine. I felt suddenly dizzy, as if the space inside my head were full of the red-hot Ur-space of the primordial de Sitter cosmos, ready at any moment to make the Prigoginic leap into the "normal" space-time continuum, the Second Prigoginic Level of Complexity. . . . Posthumanism schooled us to think in terms of fits and starts, of structures accreting along unspoken patterns, following the lines first suggested by the ancient Terran philosopher Ilya Prigogine. I directly understood this, since my own mild attraction to the dazzling Valery Korstad had coalesced into a knotted desire that suppressants could numb but not destroy.

She was dancing across the room, the jeweled strings of her Investor skirt twisting like snakes. She had the anonymous beauty of the Reshaped, overlaid with the ingenious, enticing paint of C-K. I had never seen anything I wanted more, and from our brief and strained flirtations I knew that only the dogs stood between us.

Wellspring took me by the arm. His audience had dissolved as I stood rapt, lusting after Valery. "How much longer, son?"

Startled, I looked at the watch display on my forearm. "Only twenty minutes, Wellspring."

"That's fine, son." Wellspring was famous for his use of archaic terms like *son*. "Once the dogs are gone, it'll be your party, Hans. I won't stay here to eclipse you. Besides, the Queen awaits me. You have the Queen's Percentage?"

"Yes, just as you said." I unpeeled the box from the stick-tight patch on my hip and handed it over.

Wellspring lifted its lid with his powerful fingers and looked inside. Then he laughed aloud. "Jesus! It's beautiful!"

Suddenly he pulled the open box away and the Queen's gift hung in midair, glittering above our heads. It was an artificial gem the size of a child's fist, its chiseled planes glittering with the green and gold of endolithic lichen. As it spun it threw tiny glints of fractured light across our faces.

As it fell, Kulagin appeared and caught it on the points of four extended fingertips. His left eye, an artificial implant, glistened darkly as he examined it.

"Eisho Zaibatsu?" he asked.

"Yes," I said. "They handled the synthesizing work; the lichen is a special variety of my own." I saw that a curious circle was gathering and said aloud, "Our host is a connoisseur."

"Only of finance," Kulagin said quietly, but with equal emphasis. "I understand now why you patented the process in your own name. It's a dazzling accomplishment. How could any Investor resist the lure of a living jewel, friends? Someday soon our initiate will be a wealthy man."

I looked quickly at Wellspring, but he unobtrusively touched one finger to his lips. "And he'll need that wealth to bring Mars to fruition," Wellspring said loudly. "We can't depend forever on the Kosmosity for funding. Friends, rejoice that you too will reap the profits of Landau's ingenious genetics." He caught the jewel and boxed it. "And tonight I have the honor of presenting his gift to the Queen. A double honor, since I recruited its creator myself." Suddenly he leapt toward the exit, his powerful legs carrying him quickly above our heads. As he flew he shouted, "Goodbye, son! May another dog never darken your doorstep!"

With Wellspring's exit, the non-Polycarbon guests began leaving, forming a jostling knot of hat-fetching servos and gossiping well-wishers. When the last was gone, the Clique grew suddenly quiet.

Kulagin had me stand at a far corner of his studio while the Clique formed a long gauntlet for the dogs, arming themselves with ribbons and paint. A certain dark edge of smoldering vengeance only added a tang to their enjoyment. I took a pair of paint balloons from one of Kulagin's scurrying servos.

The time was almost on me. For two long years I'd schemed to join the Polycarbon Clique. I needed them. I felt they needed me. I was tired of suspicion, of strained politeness, of the glass walls of the dogs' surveillance. The keen edges of my long discipline suddenly, painfully, crumbled. I began shaking uncontrollably, unable to hold it back.

The dogs were still, taping steadily to the last appointed instant. The crowd began to count down. Exactly at the count of zero the two dogs turned to go.

They were barraged with paint and tangled streamers. A moment earlier they would have turned savagely on their tormentors, but now they had reached the limits of their programming, and at long last they were helpless. The Clique's aim was deadly, and with every splattering hit they split the air with screams of laughter. They knew no mercy, and it took a full minute before the humiliated dogs could hop and stagger, blinded, to the door.

I was overcome with mob hysteria. Screams escaped my clenched teeth. I had to be grappled back from pursuing the dogs down the hall. As firm hands pulled me back within the room I turned to face my friends, and I was chilled at the raw emotion on their faces. It was as if they had been stripped of skin and watched me with live eyes in slabs of meat.

I was picked up bodily and passed from hand to hand around the room. Even those that I knew well seemed alien to me now. Hands tore at my clothing until I was stripped; they even took my computer gauntlet, then stood me in the middle of the room.

As I stood shivering within the circle, Kulagin approached me, his arms rigid, his face stiff and hieratic. His hands were full of loose black cloth. He held the cloth over my head, and I saw that it was a black hood. He put his lips close to my ear and said softly, "Friend, go the distance." Then he pulled the hood over my head and knotted it.

The hood had been soaked in something; I could smell that it reeked. My hands and feet began to tingle, then go numb. Slowly, warmth crept like bracelets up my arms and legs. I could hear nothing, and my feet could no longer feel the floor. I lost all sense of balance, and suddenly I fell backward, into the infinite.

My eyes opened, or my eyes closed, I couldn't tell. But at the limits of vision, from behind some unspoken fog, emerged pinpoints of cold and piercing brightness. It was the Great Galactic Night, the vast and pitiless emptiness that lurks just beyond the warm rim of every human habitat, emptier even than death.

I was naked in space, and it was so bitterly cold that I could taste it like poison in every cell I had. I could feel the pale heat of my own life streaming out of me like plasma, ebbing away in aurora sheets from my fingertips. I continued to fall, and as the last rags of warmth pulsed off into the devouring chasm of space, and my body grew stiff and white and furred with frost from every pore, I faced the ultimate horror: that I would not die, that I would fall forever backward into the unknown, my mind shriveling into a single frozen spore of isolation and terror.

Time dilated. Eons of silent fear telescoped into a few heartbeats and I saw before me a single white blob of light, like a rent from this cosmos into some neighboring realm full of alien radiance. This time

I faced it as I fell toward it, and through it, and then, finally, jarringly, I was back behind my own eyes, within my own head, on the soft floor of Kulagin's studio.

The hood was gone. I wore a loose black robe, closed with an embroidered belt. Kulagin and Valery Korstad helped me to my feet. I wobbled, brushing away tears, but I managed to stand, and the Clique cheered.

Kulagin's shoulder was under my arm. He embraced me and whispered, "Brother, remember the cold. When we your friends need warmth, be warm, remembering the cold. When friendship pains you, forgive us, remembering the cold. When selfishness tempts you, renounce it, remembering the cold. For you have gone the distance, and returned to us renewed. Remember, remember the cold." And then he gave me my secret name, and pressed his painted lips to mine.

I clung to him, choked with sobs. Valery embraced me and Kulagin pulled away gently, smiling.

One by one the Clique took my hands and pressed their lips quickly to my face, murmuring congratulations. Still unable to speak, I could only nod. Meanwhile Valery Korstad, clinging to my arm, whispered hotly in my ear, "Hans, Hans, Hans Landau, there still remains a certain ritual, which I have reserved to myself. Tonight the finest chamber in the Froth belongs to us, a sacred place where no glassy-eyed dog has ever trespassed. Hans Landau, tonight that place belongs to you, and so do I."

I looked into her face, my eyes watering. Her eyes were dilated, and a pink flush had spread itself under her ears and along her jawline. She had dosed herself with hormonal aphrodisiacs. I smelled the antiseptic sweetness of her perfumed sweat and I closed my eyes, shuddering.

Valery led me into the hall. Behind us, Kulagin's door sealed shut, cutting the hilarity to a murmur. Valery helped me slip on my air fins, whispering soothingly.

The dogs were gone. Two chunks of my reality had been edited like tape. I still felt dazed. Valery took my hand, and we threaded a corridor upward toward the center of the habitat, kicking along with our air fins. I smiled mechanically at the Cicadas we passed in the halls, members of another day crowd. They were soberly going about their day shift's work while the Polycarbon Clique indulged in bacchanalia.

It was easy to lose yourself within the Froth. It had been built in rebellion against the regimented architecture of other habitats, in C-K's typical defiance of the norm. The original empty cylinder had been packed with pressurized plastic, which had been blasted to foam and allowed to set. It left angular bubbles whose tilted walls were defined by the clean topologies of close packing and surface tension. Halls had been snaked through the complex later, and the doors and airlocks cut by hand. The Froth was famous for its delirious and welcome spontaneity.

And its discreets were notorious. C-K showed its civic spirit in the lavish appointments of these citadels against surveillance. I had never been in one before. People under the dogs were not allowed across the boundaries. But I had heard rumors, the dark and prurient scandal of bars and corridors, those scraps of licentious speculation that always hushed at the approach of dogs. Anything, anything at all, could happen in a discreet, and no one would know of it but the lovers or survivors who returned, hours later, to public life. . . .

As the centrifugal gravity faded we began floating, Valery half-towing me. The bubbles of the Froth had swollen near the axis of rotation, and we entered a neighborhood of the quiet industrial domiciles of the rich. Soon we had floated to the very doorstep of the infamous Topaz Discreet, the hushed locale of unnumbered elite frolics. It was the finest in the Froth.

Valery looked at her timepiece, caressing away a fine film of sweat that had formed on the flushed and perfect lines of her face and neck. We hadn't long to wait. We heard the mellow repeated bonging of the discreet's time alarm, warning the present occupant that his time was up. The door's locks unsealed. I wondered just what member of C-K's inner circle would emerge. Now that I was free of the dogs, I longed to boldly meet his eyes.

Still we waited. Now the discreet was ours by right and every moment lost pained us. To overstay in a discreet was the height of rudeness. Valery grew angry, and pushed open the door.

The air was full of blood. In free-fall, it floated in a thousand clotting red blobs.

Near the center of the room floated the suicide, his flaccid body still wheeling slowly from the gush of his severed throat. A scalpel glittered in the mechanically clenched fingers of the cadaver's outstretched hand. He wore the sober black overalls of a conservative Mechanist.

The body spun, and I saw the insignia of the Queen's Advisers stitched on his breast. His partially metallic skull was sticky with his own blood; the face was obscured. Long streamers of thickened blood hung from his throat like red veils.

We had cometaried into something very much beyond us. "I'll call Security," I said.

She said two words. "Not yet." I looked into her face. Her eyes were dark with fascinated lust. The lure of the forbidden had slid its hooks into her in a single moment. She kicked languidly across one tessellated wall, and a long streak of blood splattered and broke along her hip.

In discreets one met the ultimates. In a room with so many hidden meanings, the lines had blurred. Through constant proximity pleasure had wedded with death. For the woman I adored, the private rites transpiring there had become of one unspoken piece.

"Hurry," she said. Her lips were bitter with a thin grease of aphrodisiacs. We interlaced our legs to couple in free-fall while we watched his body twist.

That was the night the Queen called off her dogs.

It had thrilled me in a way that made me sick. We Cicadas lived in the moral equivalent of de Sitter space, where no ethos had validity unless it was generated by noncausative free will. Every level of Prigoginic Complexity was based on a self-dependent generative catalyst: space existed because space existed, life was because it had come to be, intelligence was because it is. So it was possible for an entire moral system to accrete around a single moment of profound disgust. . . . Or so Posthumanism taught. After my blighted consummation with Valery I withdrew to work and think.

I lived in the Froth, in a domestic-industrial studio that reeked of lichen and was much less chic than Kulagin's.

On the second day-shift of my meditation I was visited by Arkadya Sorienti, a Polycarbon friend and one of Valery's intimates. Even without the dogs there were elements of a profound strain between us. It seemed to me that Arkadya was everything that Valery was not: blonde where Valery was dark, covered with Mechanist gimmickry where Valery had the cool elegance of the genetically Reshaped, full of false and brittle gaiety where Valery was prey to soft and melancholy gloom. I offered her a squeezebulb of liqueur; my apartment was too close to the axis to use cups.

"I haven't seen your apartment before," she said. "I love your air-frames, Hans. What kind of algae is it?"

"It's lichen," I said.

"They're beautiful. One of your special kinds?"

"They're all special," I said. "Those have the Mark III and IV varieties for the terraforming project. The others have some delicate strains I was working on for contamination monitors. Lichen are very sensitive to pollution of any sort." I turned up the air ionizer. The intestines of Mechanists seethed with bacteria, and their effects could be disastrous.

"Which one is the lichen of the Queen's jewel?"

"It's locked away," I said. "Outside the environs of a jewel its growth becomes very distorted. And it smells." I smiled uneasily. It was common talk among Shapers that Mechanists stank. It seemed to me that I could already smell the reek of her armpits.

Arkadya smiled and nervously rubbed the skin-metal interface of a silvery blob of machinery grafted along her forearm. "Valery's in one of her states," she said. "I thought I'd come see how you were."

In my mind's eye flickered the nightmare image of our naked skins slicked with blood. I said, "It was . . . unfortunate."

"C-K's full of talk about the Comptroller's death."

"It was the Comptroller?" I said. "I haven't seen any news."

Slyness crept into her eyes. "You saw him there," she said.

I was shocked that she should expect me to discuss my stay in a discreet. "I have work," I said. I kicked my fins so that I drifted off our mutual vertical. Facing each other sideways increased the social distance between us.

She laughed quietly. "Don't be a prig, Hans. You act as if you were still under the dogs. You have to tell me about it if you want me to help the two of you."

I stopped my drift. She said, "And I want to help. I'm Valery's friend. I like the way you look together. It appeals to my sense of aesthetics."

"Thanks for your concern."

"I am concerned. I'm tired of seeing her on the arm of an old lecher like Wellspring."

"You're telling me they're lovers?" I said.

She fluttered her metal-clad fingers in the air. "You're asking me what the two of them do in his favorite discreet? Maybe they play chess." She rolled her eyes under lids heavy with powdered gold. "Don't look so shocked, Hans. You should know his power as well as anyone. He's old and rich; we Polycarbon women are young and not too terribly principled." She looked quickly up and away from beneath long lashes. "I've never heard that he took anything from us that we weren't willing to give." She floated closer. "Tell me what you saw, Hans. C-K's crazy with the news, and Valery does nothing but mope."

I opened the refrigerator and dug among Petri dishes for more liqueur. "It strikes me that you should be doing the talking, Arkadya."

She hesitated, then shrugged and smiled. "Now you're showing some sense, my friend. Open eyes and ears can take you a long way in C-Kluster." She took a stylish inhaler from a holster on her enameled garter. "And speaking of eyes and ears, have you had your place swept for bugs yet?"

"Who'd bug me?"

"Who wouldn't?" She looked bored. "I'll stick to what's common knowledge, then. Hire us a discreet sometime, and I'll give you all the rest." She fired a stream of amber liqueur from arm's length and sucked it in as it splashed against her teeth. "Something big is stirring in C-K. It hasn't reached the rank and file yet, but the Comptroller's death is a sign of it. The other Advisers are treating it like a personal matter, but it's clear that he wasn't simply tired of life. He left his affairs in disorder. No, this is something that runs back to the Queen herself. I'm sure of it."

"You think the Queen ordered him to take his own life?"

"Maybe. She's getting erratic with age. Wouldn't you, though, if you had to spend your life surrounded by aliens? I feel for the Queen, I really do. If she needs to kill a few stuffy rich old bastards for her own peace of mind, it's perfectly fine by me. In fact, if that's all there was to it, I'd sleep easier."

I thought about this, my face impassive. The entire structure of Czarina-Kluster was predicated on the Queen's exile. For seventy years, defectors, malcontents, pirates, and pacifists had accreted around the refuge of our alien Queen. The powerful prestige of her fellow Investors protected us from the predatory machinations of Shaper fascists and dehumanized Mechanist sects. C-K was an oasis of sanity amid the vicious amorality of humanity's warring factions. Our suburbs spun in webs around the dark hulk of the Queen's blazing, jeweled environment.

She was all we had. There was a giddy insecurity under all our success. C-K's famous banks were backed by the Cicada Queen's tremendous wealth. The academic freedom of C-K's teaching centers flourished only under her shadow.

And we did not even know why she was disgraced. Rumors abounded, but only the Investors themselves knew the truth. Were she ever to leave us, Czarina-Kluster would disintegrate overnight.

I said offhandedly, "I've heard talk that she's not happy. It seems these rumors spread, and they raise her Percentage for a while and panel a new room with jewels, and then the rumors fade."

"That's true. . . . She and our sweet Valery are two of a kind where these dark moods are concerned. It's clear, though, that the Comptroller was left no choice but suicide. And that means disaster is stirring at the heart of C-K."

"It's only rumors," I said. "The Queen is the heart of C-K, and who knows what's going on in that huge head of hers?"

"Wellspring would know," Arkadya said intently.

"But he's not an Adviser," I said. "As far as the Queen's inner circle is concerned, he's little better than a pirate."

"Tell me what you saw in Topaz Discreet."

"You'll have to allow me some time," I said. "It's rather painful." I wondered what I should tell her, and what she was willing to believe. The silence began to stretch.

I put on a tape of Terran sea sounds. The room began to surge ominously with the roar of alien surf.

"I wasn't ready for it," I said. "In my crèche we were taught to guard our feelings from childhood. I know how the Clique feels about distance. But that kind of raw intimacy, from a woman I really scarcely know—especially under that night's circumstances—it wounded me." I looked searchingly into Arkadya's face, longing to reach through her to Valery. "Once it was over, we were further apart than ever."

Arkadya tilted her head to the side and winced. "Who composed this?"

"What? You mean the music? It's a background tape—sea sounds from Earth. It's a couple of centuries old."

She looked at me oddly. "You're really absorbed by the whole planetary thing, aren't you? 'Sea sounds.'"

"Mars will have seas someday. That's what our whole Project is about, isn't it?"

She looked disturbed. "Sure . . . We're working at it, Hans, but that doesn't mean we have to live there. I mean, that's centuries from now, isn't it? Even if we're still alive, we'll be different people by then. Just think of being trapped down a gravity well. I'd choke to death."

I said quietly, "I don't think of it as being for the purposes of settlement. It's a clearer, more ideal activity. The instigation by Fourth-Level cognitive agents of a Third-Level Prigoginic Leap. Bringing life itself into being on the naked bedrock of space-time. . . . "

But she was shaking her head and backpedaling toward the door. "I'm sorry, Hans, but those sounds, they're just . . . getting into my blood somehow. . . . She shook herself, shuddering, and the filigree beads woven into her blonde hair clattered loudly. "I can't bear it."

"I'll turn it off."

But she was already leaving. "Goodbye, goodbye . . . We'll meet again soon."

She was gone. I was left to steep in my own isolation, while the roaring surf gnawed and mumbled at its shore.

One of Kulagin's servos met me at his door and took my hat. Kulagin was seated at a workplace in a screened-off corner of his marigold-reeking domicile, watching stock quotations scroll down a display screen. He was dictating orders into a microphone on his forearm gauntlet. When the servo announced me he unplugged the jack from his gauntlet and stood, shaking my hand with both of his. "Welcome, friend, welcome."

"I hope I haven't come at a bad time."

"No, not at all. Do you play the Market?"

"Not seriously," I said. "Later, maybe, when the royalties from Eisho Zaibatsu pile up."

"You must allow me to guide your eyes, then. A good Posthumanist should have a wide range of interests. Take that chair, if you would."

I sat beside Kulagin as he sat before the console and plugged in. Kulagin was a Mechanist, but he kept himself rigorously antiseptic. I liked him.

He said, "Odd how these financial institutions tend to drift from their original purpose. In a way, the Market itself has made a sort of Prigoginic Leap. On its face, it's a commercial tool, but it's become a game of conventions and confidences. We Cicadas eat, breathe, and sleep rumors, so the Market is the perfect expression of our zeitgeist."

"Yes," I said. "Frail, mannered, and based on practically nothing tangible."

Kulagin lifted his plucked brows. "Yes, my young friend, exactly like the bedrock of the cosmos itself. Every level of complexity floats freely on the last, supported only by abstractions. Even natural laws are only our attempts to strain our vision through the Prigoginic event horizon. . . . If you prefer a more primal metaphor, we can compare the Market to the sea. A sea of information, with a few blue-chip islands here and there for the exhausted swimmer. Look at this."

He touched buttons, and a three-dimensional grid display sprang

into being. "This is Market activity in the past forty-eight hours. It
looks rather like the waves and billows of a sea, doesn't it? Note
these surges of transaction." He touched the screen with the light
pen implanted in his forefinger, and gridded areas flushed from cool
green to red. "That was when the first rumors of the iceteroid came
in—"

"What?"

"The asteroid, the ice-mass from the Ring Council. Someone has
bought it and is mass-driving it out of Saturn's gravity well right now,
bound for Martian impact. Someone very clever, for it will pass
within a few thousands of klicks from C-K. Close enough for naked-
eyed view."

"You mean they've really done it?" I said, caught between shock
and joy.

"I heard it third-, fourth-, maybe tenth-hand, but it fits in well with
the parameters the Polycarbon engineers have set up. A mass of ice
and volatiles, well over three klicks across, targeted for the Hellas
Depression south of the equator at sixty-five klicks a second, impact
expected at UT 20:14:53, 14-4-'54. . . . That's dawn, local time. Local
Martian time, I mean."

"But that's months from now," I said.

Kulagin smirked. "Look, Hans, you don't push a three-klick ice
lump with your thumbs. Besides, this is just the first of dozens. It's
more of a symbolic gesture."

"But it means we'll be moving out! To Martian orbit!"

Kulagin looked skeptical. "That's a job for drones and monitors,
Hans. Or maybe a few rough and tough pioneer types. Actually,
there's no reason why you and I should have to leave the comforts of
C-K."

I stood up, knotting my hands. "You want to *stay*? And miss the
Prigoginic catalyst?"

Kulagin looked up with a slight frown. "Cool off, Hans, sit down,
they'll be looking for volunteers soon enough, and if you really mean
to go I'm sure you can manage somehow. . . . The point is that the effect on the Market has been spectacular. . . . It's been fairly giddy
ever since the Comptroller's death, and now some very big fish indeed is rising for the kill. I've been following his movements for three
day-shifts straight, hoping to feast on his scraps, so to speak. . . . Care
for an inhale?"

"No, thanks."

Kulagin helped himself to a long pull of stimulant. He looked ragged. I'd never seen him without his face paint before. He said, "I don't have the feeling for mob psychology that you Shapers have, so I have to make do with a very, very good memory. . . . The last time I saw something like this was thirteen years ago. Someone spread the rumor that the Queen had tried to leave C-K, and the Advisers had restrained her by force. The upshot of that was the Crash of 'Forty-one, but the real killing came in the Rally that followed. I've been reviewing the tapes of the Crash, and I recognize the fins and flippers and big sharp teeth of an old friend. I can read his style in his maneuvering. It's not the slick guile of a Shaper. It's not the cold persistence of a Mechanist, either."

I considered. "Then you must mean Wellspring."

Wellspring's age was unknown. He was well over two centuries old. He claimed to have been born on Earth in the dawn of the Space Age, and to have lived in the first generation of independent space colonies, the so-called Concatenation. He had been among the founders of Czarina-Kluster, building the Queen's habitat when she fled in disgrace from her fellow Investors.

Kulagin smiled. "Very good, Hans. You may live in moss, but there's none on you. I think Wellspring engineered the Crash of 'Forty-one for his own profit."

"But he lives very modestly."

"As the Queen's oldest friend, he was certainly in a perfect position to start rumors. He even engineered the parameters of the Market itself, seventy years ago. And it was after the Rally that the Kosmosity-Metasystems Department of Terraformation was set up. Through anonymous donations, of course."

"But contributions came in from all over the system," I objected. "Almost all the sects and factions think that terraforming is humanity's sublimest effort."

"To be sure. Though I wonder just how that idea became so widely spread. And to whose benefit. Listen, Hans. I love Wellspring. He's a *friend,* and I remember the cold. But you have to realize just what an anomaly he is. He's not one of us. He wasn't even born in space." He looked at me narrowly, but I took no offense at his use of the term *born.* It was a deadly insult against Shapers, but I considered myself a Polycarbon first and Cicada second, with Shaperism a distant third.

He smiled briefly. "To be sure, Wellspring has a few Mechanist knickknacks implanted, to extend his life span, but he lacks the whole Mech style. In fact he actually *predates* it. I'd be the last to deny the genius of you Shapers, but in a way it's an artificial genius. It works out well enough on IQ tests, but it somehow lacks that, well, primeval quality that Wellspring has, just as we Mechanists can use cybernetic modes of thinking but we can never be actual machines. . . . Wellspring simply is one of those people at the farthest reaches of the bell curve, one of those titans that spring up only once a generation. I mean, think what's become of his normal human contemporaries."

I nodded. "Most of them have become Mechs."

Kulagin shook his head fractionally, staring at the screen. "I was born here in C-K. I don't know that much about the old-style Mechs, but I do know that most of the first ones are dead. Outdated, crowded out. Driven over the edge by future shock. A lot of the first life-extension efforts failed, too, in very ugly ways. . . . Wellspring survived that, too, from some innate knack he has. Think of it, Hans. Here we sit, products of technologies so advanced that they've smashed society to bits. We trade with aliens. We can even hitchhike to the stars, if we pay the Investors' fare. And Wellspring not only holds his own, he rules us. We don't even know his real name."

I considered what Kulagin had said while he switched to a Market update. I felt bad. I could hide my feelings, but I couldn't shake them off. "You're right," I said. "But I trust him."

"I trust him too, but I know we're cradled in his hands. In fact, he's protecting us right now. This terraforming project has cost megawatt after megawatt. All those contributions were anonymous, supposedly to prevent the factions from using them for propaganda. But I think it was to hide the fact that most of them were from Wellspring. Any day now there's going to be an extended Market crash. Wellspring will make his move, and that will start the rally. And every kilowatt of his profits will go to us."

I leaned forward in my chair, interlacing my fingers. Kulagin dictated a series of selling orders into his microphone. Suddenly I laughed.

Kulagin looked up. "That's the first time I've ever heard you laugh like you meant it, Hans."

"I was just thinking. . . . You've told me all this, but I came here to talk about Valery."

Kulagin looked sad. "Listen, Hans. What I know about women you could hide under a microchip, but, as I said, my memory is excellent. The Shapers blundered when they pushed things to the limits. The Ring Council tried to break the so-called Two-Hundred

Barrier last century. Most of the so-called Superbrights went mad, defected, turned against their fellows, or all three. They've been hunted down by pirates and mercenaries for decades now.

"One group found out somehow that there was an Investor Queen living in exile, and they managed to make it to her shadow, for protection. And someone—you can imagine who—talked the Queen into letting them stay, if they paid a certain tax. That tax became the Queen's Percentage, and the settlement became Czarina-Kluster. Valery's parents—yes, *parents;* it was a natural birth—were among those Superbrights. She didn't have the schooling Shapers use, so she ranks in at only one forty-five or so.

"The problem is those mood cycles of hers. Her parents had them, she's had them since she was a child. She's a dangerous woman, Hans. Dangerous to herself, to all of us. She should be under the dogs, really. I've suggested that to my friends in Security, but someone stands in my way. I have my ideas who."

"I'm in love with her. She won't speak to me."

"I see. Well, I understand she's been full of mood suppressants lately; that probably accounts for her reticence. . . . I'll speak frankly. There's an old saying, Hans, that you should never enter a discreet with someone crazier than you are. And it's good advice. You can't trust Valery."

He held up his hand. "Hear me out. You're young. You've just come out from under the dogs. This woman has enchanted you, and admittedly she has the famous Shaper charm in full measure. But a liaison with Valery is like an affair with five women, three of whom are crazy. C-K is full to bursting with the most beautiful women in human history. Admittedly you're a bit stiff, a bit of an obsessive perhaps, but you have a certain idealistic charm. And you have that Shaper intensity, fanaticism even, if you don't mind my saying so. Loosen up a little, Hans. Find some woman who'll rub the rough edges off of you. Play the field. It's a good way to recruit new friends to the Clique."

"I'll keep what you said in mind," I said.

"Right. I knew it was wasted effort." He smiled ironically. "Why should I blight the purity of your emotions? A tragic first love may become an asset to you, fifty or a hundred years from now." He turned his attention back to the screen. "I'm glad we had this talk, Hans. I hope you'll get in touch again when the Eisho Zaibatsu money comes through. We'll have some fun with it."

"I'd like that," I said, though I knew already that every kilowatt

not spent on my own research would go—anonymously—to the terraforming fund. "And I don't resent your advice. It's just that it's of no
use to me."

"Ah, youth," Kulagin said. I left.

Back to the simple beauty of the lichens. I had been trained for years
to specialize in them, but they had taken on beauty and meaning for
me only after my Posthumanist enlightenment. Viewed through C-K's
philosophies, they stood near the catalysis point of the Prigoginic
Leap that brought life itself into being.

Alternately, a lichen could be viewed as an extended metaphor
for the Polycarbon Clique: a fungus and an alga, potential rivals,
united in symbiosis to accomplish what neither could do alone, just
as the Clique united Mechanist and Shaper to bring life to Mars.

I knew that many viewed my dedication as strange, even unhealthy. I was not offended by their blindness. Just the names of my
genetic stocks had a rolling majesty: *Alectoria nigricans, Mastodia
tessellata, Ochrolechia frigida, Stereocaulon alpinum.* They were
humble but powerful: creatures of the cold desert whose roots and
acids could crumble naked, freezing rock.

My gel frames seethed with primal vitality. Lichens would drench
Mars in one green-gold tidal wave of life. They would creep irresistibly from the moist craters of the iceteroid impacts, proliferating re-
lentlessly amid the storms and earthquakes of terraformation, surviv-
ing the floods as permafrost melted. Gushing oxygen, fixing nitrogen.

They were the best. Not because of pride or show. Not because
they trumpeted their motives, or threatened the cold before they
broke it. But because they were silent, and the first.

My years under the dogs had taught me the value of silence.
Now I was sick of surveillance. When the first royalty payment came
in from Eisho Zaibatsu, I contacted one of C-K's private security firms
and had my apartments swept for bugs. They found four.

I hired a second firm to remove the bugs left by the first.

I strapped myself in at a floating workbench, turning the spy eyes
over and over in my hands. They were flat videoplates, painted with
one-way colorshifting polymer camouflage. They would fetch a nice
price on the unofficial market.

I called a post office and hired a courier servo to take the bugs to
Kulagin. While I awaited the servo's arrival, I turned off the bugs and
sealed them into a biohazard box. I dictated a note, asking Kulagin to
sell them and invest the money for me in C-K's faltering Market. The
Market looked as if it could use a few buyers.

When I heard the courier's staccato knock, I opened my door with a gauntlet remote. But it was no courier that whirred in. It was a guard dog.

"I'll take that box, if you please," said the dog.

I stared at it as if I had never seen a dog before. This dog was heavily armored in silver. Thin powerful limbs jutted from its silver-seamed black-plastic torso, and its swollen head bristled with spring-loaded taser darts and the blunt nozzles of restraint webs. Its swiveling antenna tail showed that it was under remote control.

I spun my workbench so that it stood between me and the dog. "I see you have my comm lines tapped as well," I said. "Will you tell me where the taps are, or do I have to take my computer apart?"

"You sniveling little Shaper upstart," commented the dog, "do you think your royalties can buy you out from under everyone? I could sell you on the open market before you could blink."

I considered this. On a number of occasions, particularly trouble-some meddlers in C-K had been arrested and offered for sale on the open market by the Queen's Advisers. There were always factions outside C-K willing to pay good prices for enemy agents. I knew that the Ring Council would be overjoyed to make an example of me. "You're claiming to be one of the Queen's Advisers, then?"

"*Of course* I'm an Adviser! Your treacheries haven't lured us all to sleep. Your friendship with Wellspring is notorious!" The dog whirred closer, its clumped camera eyes clicking faintly. "What's inside that freezer?"

"Lichen racks," I said impassively. "You should know that well enough."

"Open it."

I didn't move. "You're going beyond the bounds of normal operations," I said, knowing that this would trouble any Mechanist. "My Clique has friends among the Advisers. I've done nothing wrong."

"Open it, or I'll web you and open it myself, with this dog."

"Lies," I said. "You're no Adviser. You're an industrial spy, trying to steal my gemstone lichen. Why would an Adviser want to look into my freezer?"

"Open it! Don't involve yourself more deeply in things you don't understand."

"You've entered my domicile under false pretenses and threatened me," I said. "I'm calling Security."

The dog's chromed jaws opened. I twisted myself free of the workbench, but a thready spray of white silk from one of the dog's facial nozzles caught me as I dodged. The filaments clung and hardened instantly, locking my arms in place where I had instinctively raised them to block the spray. A second blast caught my legs as I struggled uselessly, bouncing off a tilted Froth-wall.

"Troublemaker," muttered the dog. "Everything would have gone down smooth without you Shapers quibbling. We had the soundest banks, we had the Queen, the Market, everything. . . . You parasites gave C-K nothing but your fantasies. Now the system's crumbling. Everything will crash. Everything. I ought to kill you."

I gasped for breath as the spray rigidified across my chest. "Life isn't banks," I wheezed.

Motors whined as the dog flexed its jointed limbs. "If I find what I expect in that freezer, you're as good as dead."

Suddenly the dog stopped in midair. Its fans whirred as it wheeled to face the door. The door clicked convulsively and began to slide open. A massive taloned forelimb slammed through the opening.

The watchdog webbed the door shut. Suddenly the door shrieked and buckled, its metal peeling back like foil. The goggling head and spiked legs of a tiger crunched and thrashed through the wreckage. "Treason!" the tiger roared.

The dog whirred backward, cringing, as the tiger pulled its armored hindquarters into the room. The jagged wreckage of the door didn't even scratch it. Armored in black and gold, it was twice the size of the watchdog. "Wait," the dog said.

"The Council warned you against vigilante action," the tiger said heavily. "I warned you myself."

"I had to make a choice, Coordinator. It's *his* doing. He turned us against one another, you have to see that."

"You have only one choice left," the tiger said. "Choose your discreet, Councilman."

The dog flexed its limbs indecisively. "So I'm to be the second," he said. "First the Comptroller, now myself. Very well, then. Very well. He has me. I can't retaliate." The dog seemed to gather itself up for a rush. "But I can destroy his favorite!"

The dog's legs shot open like telescopes, and it sprang off a wall for my throat. There was a terrific flash with the stench of ozone, and the dog slammed bruisingly into my chest. It was dead, its circuits stripped. The lights flickered and went out as my home computer faltered and crashed, its programming scrambled by incidental radiation from the tiger's electromagnetic pulse.

Flanges popped open on the tiger's bulbous head, and two spotlights emerged. "Do you have any implants?" it said.

"No," I said. "No cybernetic parts. I'm all right. You saved my life."

"Close your eyes," the tiger commanded. It washed me with a fine mist of solvent from its nostrils. The web peeled off in its talons, taking my clothing with it.

My forearm gauntlet was ruined. I said, "I've committed no crime against the state, Coordinator. I love C-K."

"These are strange days," the tiger rumbled. "Our routines are in decay. No one is above suspicion. You picked a bad time to make your home mimic a discreet, young man."

"I did it openly," I said.

"There are no rights here, Cicada. Only the Queen's graces. Dress yourself and ride the tiger. We need to talk. I'm taking you to the Palace."

The Palace was like one gigantic discreet. I wondered if I would ever leave its mysteries alive.

I had no choice.

I dressed carefully under the tiger's goggling eyes, and mounted it. It smelled of aging lubrication. It must have been in storage for decades. Tigers had not been seen at large in C-K for years.

The halls were crowded with Cicadas going on and off their day shifts. At the tiger's approach they scattered in terror and awe.

We exited the Froth at its cylinder end, into the gimbaling cluster of interurban tube roads.

The roads were transparent polycarbon conduits, linking C-K's cylindrical suburbs in an untidy web. The sight of these shining habitats against the icy background of the stars gave me a sharp moment of vertigo. I remembered the cold.

We passed through a thickened knot along the web, a swollen intersection of tube roads where one of C-K's famous highway bistros had accreted itself into being. The lively gossip of its glittering habitués froze into a stricken silence as I rode by, and swelled into a chorus of alarm as I left. The news would permeate C-K in minutes.

The Palace imitated an Investor starship: an octahedron with six long rectangular sides. Genuine Investor ships were crusted with fantastic designs in hammered metal, but the Queen's was an uneven dull black, reflecting her unknown shame. With the passage of time it had grown by fits and starts, and now it was lumped and flanged with government offices and the Queen's covert hideaways. The ponderous hulk spun with dizzying speed.

We entered along one axis into a searing bath of blue-white light. My eyes shrank painfully and began oozing tears.

The Queen's Advisers were Mechanists, and the halls swarmed with servos. They passively followed their routines, ignoring the tiger, whose chromed and plated surfaces gleamed viciously in the merciless light.

A short distance from the axis the centrifugal force seized us and the tiger sank creaking onto its massive legs. The walls grew baroque with mosaics and spun designs in filamented precious metals. The tiger stalked down a flight of stairs. My spine popped audibly in the increasing gravity, and I sat erect with an effort.

Most of the halls were empty. We passed occasional clumps of jewels in the walls that blazed like lightning. I leaned against the tiger's back and locked my elbows, my heart pounding. More stairs. Tears ran down my face and into my mouth, a sensation that was novel and disgusting. My arms trembled with fatigue.

The Coordinator's office was on the perimeter. It kept him in shape for audiences with the Queen. The tiger stalked creaking through a pair of massive doors, built to Investor scale.

Everything in the office was in Investor scale. The ceilings were more than twice the height of a man. A chandelier overhead gushed a blistering radiance over two immense chairs with tall backs split by tail holes. A fountain surged and splattered feebly, exhausted by strain.

The Coordinator sat behind a keyboarded business desk. The top of the desk rose almost to his armpits, and his scaled boots dangled far above the floor. Beside him a monitor scrolled down the latest Market reports.

I heaved myself, grunting, off the tiger's back and up into the scratchy plush of an Investor chair seat. Built for an Investor's scaled rump, it pierced my trousers like wire.

"Have some sun shades," the Coordinator said. He opened a cavernous desk drawer, fished elbow-deep for a pair of goggles, and hurled them at me. I reached high, and they hit me in the chest.

I wiped my eyes and put on the goggles, groaning with relief. The tiger crouched at the foot of my chair, whirring to itself.

"Your first time in the Palace?" the Coordinator said.

I nodded with an effort.

"It's horrible, I know. And yet, it's all we have. You have to understand that, Landau. This is C-K's Prigoginic catalyst."

"You know the philosophy?" I said.

"Surely. Not all of us are fossilized. The Advisers have their factions. That's common knowledge." The Coordinator pushed his chair back. Then he stood up in its seat, climbed up onto his desk top, and sat on its forward edge facing me, his scaled boots dangling.

He was a blunt, stocky, powerfully muscled man, moving easily in the force that flattened me. His face was deeply and ferociously creased with two centuries of seams and wrinkles. His black skin gleamed dully in the searing light. His eyeballs had the brittle look of plastic. He said, "I've seen the tapes the dogs made, and I feel I understand you, Landau. Your sin is distance."

He sighed. "And yet you are less corrupt than others. . . . There is a certain threshold, an intensity of sin and cynicism, beyond which no society can survive. . . . Listen. I know about Shapers. The Ring Council. Stitched together by black fear and red greed, drawing power from the momentum of its own collapse. But C-K's had hope. You've lived here, you must have at least seen it, if you can't feel it directly. You must know how precious this place is. Under the Cicada Queen, we've drawn survival from a state of mind. Belief counts, confidence is central." The Comptroller looked at me, his dark face sagging. "I'll tell you the truth. And depend on your good-will. For the proper response."

"Thank you."

"C-K is in crisis. Rumors of the Queen's disaffection have brought the Market to the point of collapse. This time they're more than rumors, Landau. The Queen is on the point of defection from C-K."

Stunned, I slumped suddenly into my chair. My jaw dropped. I closed it with a snap.

"Once the Market collapses," the Coordinator said, "it means the end of all we had. The news is already spreading. Soon there will be a run against the Czarina-Kluster banking system. The system will crash, C-K will die."

"But . . . ," I said. "If it's the Queen's own doing. . . . " I was having trouble breathing.

"It's *always* the doing of the Investors, Landau; it's been that way ever since they first swept in and made our wars into an institution. . . . We Mechanists had you Shapers at bay. We ruled the entire system while you hid in terror in the Rings. It was your trade with the Investors that got you on your feet again. In fact, they deliberately built you up, so that they could maintain a competitive trade market, pit the human race against itself, to their own profit. . . . Look at C-K. We live in harmony here. That could be the case everywhere. It's their doing."

"Are you saying," I said, "that the history of C-K is an Investor scheme? That the Queen was never really in disgrace?"

"They're not infallible," the Coordinator said. "I can save the Market, and C-K, if I can exploit their own greed. It's your jewels, Landau. Your jewels. I saw the Queen's reaction when her . . . damned lackey Wellspring presented your gift. You learn to know their moods, these Investors. She was livid with greed. Your patent could catalyze a major industry."

"You're wrong about Wellspring," I said. "The jewel was his idea. I was working with endolithic lichens. 'If they can live within stones they can live within jewels,' he said. I only did the busywork."

"But the patent's in your name." The Coordinator looked at the toes of his scaled boots. "With one catalyst, I could save the Market. I want you to transfer your patent from Eisho Zaibatsu to me. To the Czarina-Kluster People's Corporate Republic."

I tried to be tactful. "The situation does seem desperate," I said, "but no one within the Market really wants it destroyed. There are other powerful forces preparing for a rebound. Please understand— it's not for any personal gain that I must keep my patent. The revenue is already pledged. To terraforming."

A sour grimace deepened the crevasses in the Coordinator's face. He leaned forward, and his shoulders tightened with a muffled creaking of plastic. "Terraforming! Oh, yes, I'm familiar with the so-called moral arguments. The cold abstractions of bloodless ideologues. What about respect? Obligation? Loyalty? Are these foreign terms to you?"

I said, "It's not that simple. Wellspring says—"

"Wellspring!" he shouted. "He's no Terran, you fool, he's only a renegade, a traitor scarcely a hundred years old, who sold himself utterly to the aliens. They fear us, you see. They fear our energy. Our potential to invade their markets, once the star drive is in our hands. It should be obvious, Landau! They want to divert human energies into this enormous Martian boondoggle. We could be competing with them, spreading to the stars in one fantastic wave!" He held his arms out rigid before him, his wrists bent upward, and stared at the tips of his outstretched fingers.

His arms began to tremble. Then he broke, and cradled his head in his corded hands. "C-K could have been great. A core of unity, an island of safety in the chaos. The Investors mean to destroy it. When the Market crashes, when the Queen defects, it means the end."

"Will she really leave?"

"Who knows what she means to do." The Coordinator looked exhausted. "I've suffered seventy years from her little whims and humiliations. I don't know what it is to care anymore. Why should I break my heart trying to glue things together with your stupid knick-knacks? After all, there's still the discreet!"

He looked up ferociously. "That's where your meddling sent the

Councilman. Once we've lost everything, they'll be thick enough with blood to swim in!"

He leapt from his desk top, bounced across the carpet, and dragged me bodily from the chair. I grabbed feebly at his wrists. My arms and legs flopped as he shook me. The tiger scuttled closer, clicking. "I hate you," he roared, "I hate everything you stand for! I'm sick of your Clique and their philosophies and their pudding smiles. You've killed a good friend with your meddling.

"Get out! Get out of C-K. You have forty-eight hours. After that I'll have you arrested and sold to the highest bidder." He threw me contemptuously backward. I collapsed at once in the heavy gravity, my head thudding against the carpet.

The tiger pulled me to my feet as the Coordinator clambered back into his oversized chair. He looked into his Market screen as I climbed trembling onto the tiger's back.

"Oh, no," he said softly. "Treason." The tiger took me away.

I found Wellspring, at last, in Dogtown. Dogtown was a chaotic subcluster, pinwheeling slowly to itself above the rotational axis of C-K. It was a port and customhouse, a tangle of shipyards, storage drogues, quarantines, and social houses, catering to the vices of the footloose, the isolated, and the estranged.

Dogtown was the place to come when no one else would have you. It swarmed with transients: prospectors, privateers, criminals, derelicts from sects whose innovations had collapsed, bankrupts, defectors, purveyors of hazardous pleasures. Accordingly the entire area swarmed with dogs, and with subtler monitors. Dogtown was a genuinely dangerous place, thrumming with a deranged and predatory vitality. Constant surveillance had destroyed all sense of shame.

I found Wellspring in the swollen bubble of a tubeway bar, discussing a convoluted business deal with a man he introduced as "the Modem." The Modem was a member of a small but vigorous Mechanist sect known in C-K slang as Lobsters. These Lobsters lived exclusively within skin-tight life-support systems, flanged here and there with engines and input-output jacks. The suits were faceless and dull black. The Lobsters looked like chunks of shadow.

I shook the Modem's rough room-temperature gauntlet and strapped myself to the table.

I peeled a squeezebulb from the table's adhesive surface and had a drink. "I'm in trouble," I said. "Can we speak before this man?"

Wellspring laughed. "Are you joking? This is Dogtown! Everything we say goes onto more tapes than you have teeth, young Landau.

Besides, the Modem is an old friend. His skewed vision should be of some use."

"Very well." I began explaining. Wellspring pressed for details. I omitted nothing.

"Oh, dear," Wellspring said when I had finished. "Well, hold on to your monitors, Modem, for you are about to see rumor break the speed of light. Odd that this obscure little bistro should launch the news that is certain to destroy C-K." He said this quite loudly, and I looked quickly around the bar. The jaws of the clientele hung open with shock. Little blobs of saliva oscillated in their mouths.

"The Queen is gone, then," Wellspring said. "She's probably been gone for weeks. Well, I suppose it couldn't be helped. Even an Investor's greed has limits. The Advisers couldn't lead her by the nose forever. Perhaps she'll show up somewhere else, some habitat more suited to her emotional needs. I suppose I had best get to my monitors and cut my losses while the Market still has some meaning."

Wellspring parted the ribbons of his slashed sleeve and looked casually at his forearm computer. The bar emptied itself, suddenly and catastrophically, the customers trailed by their personal dogs. Near the exit, a vicious hand-to-hand fight broke out between two Shaper renegades. They spun with piercing cries through the crunching grip-and-tumble of free-fall jujitsu. Their dogs watched impassively.

Soon the three of us were alone with the bar servos and half a dozen fascinated dogs. "I could tell from my last audience that the Queen would leave," Wellspring said calmly. "C-K had outlived its usefulness, anyway. It was important only as the motivational catalyst for the elevation of Mars to the Third Prigoginic Level of Complexity. It was fossilizing under the weight of the Advisers' programs. Typical Mech shortsightedness. Pseudopragmatic materialism. They had it coming."

Wellspring showed an inch of embroidered undercuff as he signaled a servo for another round. "The Councilman you mentioned has retired to a discreet. He won't be the last one they haul out by the heels."

"What will I do?" I said. "I'm losing everything. What will become of the Clique?"

Wellspring frowned. "Come on, Landau! Show some Posthuman fluidity. The first thing to do, of course, is to get you into exile before you're arrested and sold. I imagine our friend the Modem here can help with that."

"To be sure," the Modem enunciated. He had a vocoder unit

strapped to his throat, and it projected an inhumanly beautiful synthesized voice. "Our ship, the Crowned Pawn, is hauling a cargo of iceteroid mass drivers to the Ring Council. It's for the Terraforming Project. Any friend of Wellspring's is welcome to join us."

I laughed incredulously. "For me, that's suicide. Go back to the Council? I might as well open my throat."

"Be at ease," the Modem soothed. "I'll have the medimechs work you over and graft on one of our shells. One Lobster is very much like another. You'll be perfectly safe, under the skin."

I was shocked. "Become a Mech?"

"You don't have to stay one," Wellspring said. "It's a simple procedure. A few nerve grafts, some anal surgery, a tracheotomy . . . You lose on taste and touch, but the other senses are vastly expanded."

"Yes," said the Modem. "And you can step alone into naked space, and laugh."

"Right!" said Wellspring. "More Shapers should wear Mech technics. It's like your lichens, Hans. Become a symbiosis for a while. It'll broaden your horizons."

I said, "You don't do . . . anything cranial, do you?"

"No," said the Modem offhandedly. "Or, at least, we don't have to. Your brain's your own."

I thought. "Can you do it in"—I looked at Wellspring's forearm—"thirty-eight hours?"

"If we hurry," the Modem said. He detached himself from the table.

I followed him.

The Crowned Pawn was under way. My skin clung magnetically to a ship's girder as we accelerated. I had my vision set for normal wavelengths as I watched Czarina-Kluster receding.

Tears stung the fresh tracks of hair-thin wires along my deadened eyeballs. C-K wheeled slowly, like a galaxy in a jeweled web. Here and there along the network, flares pulsed as suburbs began the tedious and tragic work of cutting themselves loose. C-K was in the grip of terror.

I longed for the warm vitality of my Clique. I was no Lobster. They were alien. They were solipsistic pinpoints in the galactic night, their humanity a forgotten pulp behind black armor.

The Crowned Pawn was like a ship turned inside out. It centered around a core of massive magnetic engines, fed by drones from a chunk of reaction mass. Outside these engines was a skeletal metal framework where Lobsters clung like cysts or skimmed along on induced magnetic fields. There were cupolas here and there on the skeleton where the Lobsters hooked into fluidic computers or sheltered themselves from solar storms and ring-system electrofluxes.

They never ate. They never drank. Sex involved a clever cyberstimulation through cranial plugs. Every five years or so they "molted" and had their skins scraped clean of the stinking accumulation of mutated bacteria that scummed them over in the stagnant warmth.

They knew no fear. Agoraphobia was a condition easily crushed with drugs. They were self-contained and anarchical. Their greatest pleasure was to sit along a girder and open their amplified senses to the depths of space, watching stars past the limits of ultraviolet and infrared, or staring into the flocculate crawling plaque of the surface of the sun, or just sitting and soaking in watts of solar energy through their skins while they listened with wired ears to the warbling of Van Allen belts and the musical tick of pulsars.

There was nothing evil about them, but they were not human. As distant and icy as comets, they were creatures of the vacuum, bored with the outmoded paradigms of blood and bone. I saw within them the first stirrings of the Fifth Prigoginic Leap—that postulated Fifth Level of Complexity as far beyond intelligence as intelligence is from amoebic life, or life from inert matter.

They frightened me. Their bland indifference to human limitations gave them the sinister charisma of saints.

The Modem came skimming along a girder and latched himself soundlessly beside me. I turned my ears on and heard his voice above the radio hiss of the engines. "You have a call, Landau. From C-K. Follow me."

I flexed my feet and skimmed along the rail behind him. We entered the radiation lock of an iron cupola, leaving it open, since the Lobsters disliked closed spaces.

Before me, on a screen, was the tear-streaked face of Valery Korstad. "Valery!" I said.

"Is that you, Hans?"

"Yes. Yes, darling. It's good to see you."

"Can't you take that mask off, Hans? I want to see your face."

"It's not a mask, darling. And my face is, well, not a pretty sight. All those wires . . . "

"You sound different, Hans. Your voice sounds different."

"That's because this voice is a radio analogue. It's synthesized."

"How do I know it's really you, then? God, Hans . . . I'm so afraid. Everything . . . it's just evaporating. The Froth is . . . there's a bio-hazard scare, something smashed the gel frames in your domicile, I guess it was the dogs, and now the lichen, the damned lichen is sprouting everywhere. It grows so fast!"

"I designed it to grow fast, Valery, that was the whole point. Tell them to use a metal aerosol or sulfide particulates; either one will kill it in a few hours. There's no need for panic."

"No need! Hans, the discreets are suicide factories. C-K is through! We've lost the Queen!"

"There's still the Project," I said. "The Queen was just an excuse, a catalyst. The Project can draw as much respect as the damned Queen. The groundwork's been laid for years. This is the moment. Tell the Clique to liquidate all they have. The Froth must move to Martian orbit."

Valery began to drift sideways. "That's all you cared about all along, wasn't it? The Project! I degraded myself, and you, with your cold, that Shaper distance, you left me in despair!"

"Valery!" I shouted, stricken. "I called you a dozen times, it was you who closed yourself off, it was me who needed warmth after those years under the dogs—"

"You could have done it!" she screamed, her face white with passion. "If you cared you would have broken in to prove it! You expected me to come crawling in humiliation? Black armor or dog's eyeglass, Hans, what's the difference? You're still not with me!"

I felt the heat of raw fury touching my numbed skin. "Blame me, then! How was I to know your rituals, your sick little secrets? I thought you'd thrown me over while you sneered and whored with Wellspring! Did you think I'd compete with the man who showed me my salvation? I would have slashed my wrists to see you smile, and you gave me nothing, nothing but disaster!"

A look of cold shock spread across her painted face. Her mouth opened, but no words came forth. Finally, with a small smile of total despair, she broke the connection. The screen went black.

I turned to the Modem. "I want to go back," I said.

"Sorry," he said. "First, you'd be killed. And second, we don't have the wattage to turn back. We're carrying a massive cargo." He shrugged. "Besides, C-K is in dissolution. We've known it was coming for a long time. In fact, some colleagues of ours are arriving there within the week with a second cargo of mass drivers. They'll fetch top prices as the Kluster dissolves."

"You knew?"

"We have our sources."

"Wellspring?"

"Who, him? He's leaving, too. He wants to be in Martian orbit when *that* hits." The Modem glided outside the cupola and pointed along the plane of the ecliptic. I followed his gaze, shifting clumsily along the visual wavelengths.

I saw the etched and ghostly flare of the Martian asteroid's mighty engines. "The iceteroid," I said.

"Yes, of course. The comet of your disaster, so to speak. A useful symbol for C-K's decay."

"Yes," I said. I thought I recognized the hand of Wellspring in this. As the ice payload skimmed past C-K the panicked eyes of its inhabitants would follow it. Suddenly I felt a soaring sense of hope.

"How about *that?*" I said. "Could you land me there?"

"On the asteroid?"

"Yes! They're going to detach the engines, aren't they? In orbit! I can join my fellows there, and I won't miss the Prigoginic catalyst!"

"I'll check." The Modem fed a series of parameters into one of the fluidics. "Yes . . . I could sell you a parasite engine that you could strap on. With enough wattage and a cybersystem to guide you, you could match trajectory within, say, seventy-two hours."

"Good! Good! Let's do that, then."

"Very well," he said."There remains only the question of price."

I had time to think about the price as I burned along through the piercing emptiness. I thought I had done well. With C-K's Market in collapse I would need new commercial agents for the Eisho jewels. Despite their eeriness, I felt I could trust the Lobsters.

The cybersystem led me to a gentle groundfall on the sunside of the asteroid. It was ablating slowly in the heat of the distant sun, and infrared wisps of volatiles puffed here and there from cracks in the bluish ice.

The iceteroid was a broken spar calved from the breakup of one of Saturn's ancient glacial moons. It was a mountainous splintered crag with the fossilized scars of primordial violence showing themselves in wrenched and jagged cliffs and buttresses. It was roughly egg-shaped, five kilometers by three. Its surface had the bluish pitted look of ice exposed for thousands of years to powerful electric fields.

I roughened the gripping surfaces of my gauntlets and pulled myself and the parasite engine hand over hand into shadow. The en-

gine's wattage was exhausted, but I didn't want it drifting off in the
ablation.

I unfolded the radio dish the Modem had sold me and anchored
it to a crag, aligning it with C-K. Then I plugged in.

The scope of the disaster was total. C-K had always prided itself
on its open broadcasts, part of the whole atmosphere of freedom
that had vitalized it. Now open panic was dwindling into veiled
threats, and then, worst of all, into treacherous bursts of code. From
all over the system, pressures long held back poured in.

The offers and threats mounted steadily, until the wretched
cliques of C-K were pressed to the brink of civil war. Hijacked dogs
prowled the tubes and corridors, tools of power elites made cruel by
fear. Vicious kangaroo courts stripped dissidents of their status and
property. Many chose the discreets.

Crèche cooperatives broke up. Stone-faced children wandered
aimlessly through suburban halls, dazed on mood suppressants.
Precious few dared to care any longer. Sweating Marketeers collapsed across their keyboards, sinuses bleeding from inhalants.
Women stepped naked out of commandeered airlocks and died in
sparkling gushes of frozen air. Cicadas struggled to weep through altered eyes, or floated in darkened bistros, numbed with disaster and
drugs.

Centuries of commercial struggle had only sharpened the teeth
of the cartels. They slammed in with the cybernetic precision of the
Mechanists, with the slick unsettling brilliance of the Reshaped. With
the collapse of the Market, C-K's industries were up for grabs. Commercial agents and arrogant diplomats annexed whole complexes.
Groups of their new employees stumbled through the Queen's
deserted Palace, vandalizing anything they couldn't steal outright.

The frightened subfactions of C-K were caught in the classic double bind that had alternately shaped and splintered the destinies of
humanity in Space. On the one hand their technically altered modes
of life and states of mind drove them irresistibly to distrust and
fragmentation; on the other, isolation made them the prey of united
cartels. They might even be savaged by the pirates and privateers
that the cartels openly condemned and covertly supported.

And instead of helping my Clique, I was a black dot clinging like a
spore to the icy flank of a frozen mountain.

It was during those sad days that I began to appreciate my skin. If
Wellspring's plans had worked, then there would come a flowering. I
would survive this ice in my sporangial casing, as a windblown speck

of lichen will last out decades to spread at last into devouring life. Wellspring had been wise to put me here. I trusted him. I would not fail him.

As boredom gnawed at me I sank gently into a contemplative stupor. I opened my eyes and ears past the point of overload. Consciousness swallowed itself and vanished into the roaring half existence of an event horizon. Space-time, the Second Level of Complexity, proclaimed its noumenon in the whine of stars, the rumble of planets, the transcendent crackle and gush of the uncoiling sun.

There came a time when I was roused at last by the sad and empty symphonies of Mars.

I shut down the suit's amplifiers. I no longer needed them. The catalyst, after all, is always buried by the process.

I moved south along the asteroid's axis, where I was sure to be discovered by the team sent to recover the mass driver. The driver's cybersystem had reoriented the asteroid for partial deceleration, and the south end had the best view of the planet.

Only moments after the final burn, the ice mass was matched by a pirate. It was a slim and beautiful Shaper craft, with long ribbed sun wings of iridescent fabric as thin as oil on water. Its shining organo-metallic hull hid eighth-generation magnetic engines with marvelous speed and power. The blunt nodes of weapons systems knobbed its sleekness.

I went into hiding, burrowing deep into a crevasse to avoid radar. I waited until curiosity and fear got the better of me. Then I crawled out and crept to a lookout point along a fractured ice ridge.

The ship had docked and sat poised on its cocked manipulator arms, their mantislike tips anchored into the ice. A crew of Mechanist mining drones had decamped and were boring into the ice of a clean-sheared plateau.

No Shaper pirate would have mining drones on board. The ship itself had undergone systems deactivation and sat inert and beautiful as an insect in amber, its vast sun wings folded. There was no sign of any crew.

I was not afraid of drones. I pulled myself boldly along the ice to observe their operations. No one challenged me.

I watched as the ungainly drones rasped and chipped the ice. Ten meters down they uncovered the glint of metal.

It was an airlock.

There they waited. Time passed. They received no further orders. They shut themselves down and crouched inert on the ice, as dead as the boulders around us.

For safety's sake I decided to enter the ship first.

As its airlock opened, the ship began switching itself back on. I entered the cabin. The pilot's couch was empty.

There was no one on board.

It took me almost two hours to work my way into the ship's cybersystem. Then I learned for certain what I had already suspected. It was Wellspring's ship.

I left the ship and crawled across the ice to the airlock. It opened easily. Wellspring had never been one to complicate things unnecessarily.

Beyond the airlock's second door a chamber blazed with blue-white light. I adjusted my eye systems and crawled inside.

At the far end, in the iceteroid's faint gravity, there was a bed of jewels. It was not a conventional bed. It was simply a huge, loose-packed heap of precious gems.

The Queen was asleep on top of it.

I used my eyes again. There was no infrared heat radiating from her. She lay quite still, her ancient arms clutching something to her chest, her three-toed legs drawn up along her body, her massive tail curled up beneath her rump and between her legs. Her huge head, the size of a man's torso, was encased in a gigantic crowned helmet encrusted with blazing diamonds. She was not breathing. Her eyes were closed. Her thick, scaled lips were drawn back slightly, showing two blunt rows of peg-shaped yellowing teeth.

She was ice-cold, sunk in some kind of alien cryosleep. Wellspring's coup was revealed. The Queen had joined willingly in her own abduction. Wellspring had stolen her in an act of heroic daring, robbing his rivals in C-K to begin again in Martian orbit. It was an astounding fait accompli that would have put him and his disciples into unquestioned power.

I was overcome with admiration for his plan. I wondered, though, why he had not accompanied his ship. Doubtless there were medicines aboard to wake the Queen and spirit her off to the nascent Kluster.

I moved nearer. I had never seen an Investor face to face. Still, I could tell after a moment that there was something wrong with her skin. I'd thought it was a trick of the light at first. But then I saw what she had in her hands.

It was the lichen jewel. The rapacity of her clawed grip had split it along one of the fracture planes, already weakened by the lichens' acids. Released from its crystalline prison, and spurred to frenzy by the powerful light, the lichens had crept onto her scaly fingers, and then up her wrist, and then, in an explosive paroxysm of life, over her entire body. She glittered green and gold with devouring fur. Even her eyes, her gums.

I went back to the ship. It was always said of us Shapers that we were brilliant under pressure. I reactivated the drones and had them refill their borehole. They tamped ice chips into it and melted them solid with the parasite rocket.

I worked on intuition, but all my training told me to trust it. That was why I had stripped the dead Queen and loaded every jewel aboard the ship. I felt a certainty beyond any chain of logic. The future lay before me like a drowsing woman awaiting the grip of her lover.

Wellspring's tapes were mine. The ship was his final sanctum, programmed in advance. I understood then the suffering and the ambition that had driven him, and that now were mine.

His dead hand had drawn representatives of every faction to witness the Prigoginic impact. The protoKluster already in orbit was made up exclusively of drones and monitors. It was natural that the observers would turn to me. My ship controlled the drones.

The first panic-stricken refugees told me of Wellspring's fate. He had been dragged heels first from a discreet, followed closely by the bloodless corpse of sad Valery Korstad. Never again would she create delight. Never again would his charisma enthrall the Clique. It might have been a double suicide. Or, perhaps more likely, she murdered him and then herself. Wellspring could never believe that there was anything beyond his abilities to cure. A madwoman and a barren world were part and parcel of the same challenge. Eventually he met his limit, and it killed him. The details scarcely matter. A discreet had swallowed them in any case.

When I heard the news, the ice around my heart sealed shut, seamless and pure.

I had Wellspring's will broadcast as the iceteroid began its final plunge into the atmosphere. Tapes sucked the broadcast in as volatiles peeled smoking into the thin, starved air of Mars.

I lied about the will. I invented it. I had Wellspring's taped memories to hand; it was a simple thing to change my artificial voice to counterfeit his, to set the stage for my own crucial ascendancy. It was necessary for the future of T-K, Terraform-Kluster, that I proclaim myself Wellspring's heir.

Power accreted around me like rumors. It was said that beneath my armor I *was* Wellspring, that the real Landau had been the one to die with Valery in C-K. I encouraged the rumors. Misconceptions would unite the Kluster. I knew T-K would be a city without rival. Here, abstractions would take on flesh, phantoms would feed us. Once our ideals had slammed it into being, T-K would gather strength, unstoppably. My jewels alone gave it a power base that few cartels could match.

With understanding came forgiveness. I forgave Wellspring. His lies, his deceptions, had moved me better than the chimeric "truth." What did it matter? If we needed solid bedrock, we would have it orbit us.

And the fearsome beauty of that impact! The searing linearity of its descent! It was only one of many, but the one most dear to me. When I saw the milk-drop splatter of its collision into Mars, the concussive orgasmic gush of steam from the Queen's covert and frozen tomb, I knew at once what my mentor had known. A man driven by something greater than himself dares everything and fears nothing. Nothing at all.

From behind my black armor, I rule the Polycarbon Clique. Their elite are my Advisers. I remember the cold, but I no longer fear it. I have buried it forever, as the cold of Mars is buried beneath its seething carpet of greenery. The two of us, now one, have stolen a whole planet from the realm of Death. And I do not fear the cold. No, not at all.

SUNKEN GARDENS

IRASOL'S CRAWLER loped across the badlands of the Mare Hadriacum, under a tormented Martian sky. At the limits of the troposphere, jet streams twisted, dirty streaks across pale lilac. Mirasol watched the winds through the fretted glass of the control bay. Her altered brain suggested one pattern after another: nests of snakes, nets of dark eels, maps of black arteries.

Since morning the crawler had been descending steadily into the Hellas Basin, and the air pressure was rising. Mars lay like a feverish patient under this thick blanket of air, sweating buried ice.

On the horizon thunderheads rose with explosive speed below the constant scrawl of the jet streams.

The basin was strange to Mirasol. Her faction, the Patternists, had been assigned to a redemption camp in northern Syrtis Major. There, two-hundred-mile-an-hour surface winds were common, and their pressurized camp had been buried three times by advancing dunes.

It had taken her eight days of constant travel to reach the equator.

From high overhead, the Regal faction had helped her navigate. Their orbiting city-state, Terraform-Kluster, was a nexus of monitor satellites. The Regals showed by their helpfulness that they had her under close surveillance.

The crawler lurched as its six picklike feet scrabbled down the slopes of a deflation pit. Mirasol suddenly saw her own face reflected in the glass, pale and taut, her dark eyes dreamily self-absorbed. It was a bare face, with the anonymous beauty of the genetically Reshaped. She rubbed her eyes with nail-bitten fingers.

To the west, far overhead, a gout of airborne topsoil surged aside and revealed the Ladder, the mighty anchor cable of the Terraform-Kluster.

Above the winds the cable faded from sight, vanishing below the metallic glitter of the Kluster, swinging aloofly in orbit.

Mirasol stared at the orbiting city with an uneasy mix of envy, fear, and reverence. She had never been so close to the Kluster before, or to the all-important Ladder that linked it to the Martian surface. Like most of her faction's younger generation, she had never been into space. The Regals had carefully kept her faction quarantined in the Syrtis redemption camp.

Life had not come easily to Mars. For one hundred years the Regals of Terraform-Kluster had bombarded the Martian surface with giant chunks of ice. This act of planetary engineering was the most ambitious, arrogant, and successful of all the works of man in space.

The shattering impacts had torn huge craters in the Martian crust, blasting tons of dust and steam into Mars's threadbare sheet of air. As the temperature rose, buried oceans of Martian permafrost roared forth, leaving networks of twisted badlands and vast expanses of damp mud, smooth and sterile as a television. On these great playas and on the frost-caked walls of channels, cliffs, and calderas, transplanted lichen had clung and leapt into devouring life. In the plains of Eridania, in the twisted megacanyons of the Coprates Basin, in the damp and icy regions of the dwindling poles, vast clawing thickets of its sinister growth lay upon the land—massive disaster areas for the inorganic.

As the terraforming project had grown, so had the power of Terraform-Kluster.

As a neutral point in humanity's factional wars, T-K was crucial to financiers and bankers of every sect. Even the alien Investors, those star-traveling reptiles of enormous wealth, found T-K useful, and favored it with their patronage.

And as T-K's citizens, the Regals, increased their power, smaller factions faltered and fell under their sway. Mars was dotted with bankrupt factions, financially captured and transported to the Martian surface by the T-K plutocrats.

Having failed in space, the refugees took Regal charity as ecologists of the sunken gardens. Dozens of factions were quarantined in cheerless redemption camps, isolated from one another, their lives pared to a grim frugality.

And the visionary Regals made good use of their power. The factions found themselves trapped in the arcane bioaesthetics of Posthumanist philosophy, subverted constantly by Regal broadcasts, Regal teaching, Regal culture. With time even the stubbornest faction would be broken down and digested into the cultural bloodstream of T-K. Faction members would be allowed to leave their redemption camp and travel up the Ladder.

But first they would have to prove themselves. The Patternists had awaited their chance for years. It had come at last in the Ibis Crater competition, an ecological struggle of the factions that would prove the victors' right to Regal status. Six factions had sent their champions to the ancient Ibis Crater, each one armed with its group's strongest biotechnologies. It would be a war of the sunken gardens, with the Ladder as the prize.

Mirasol's crawler followed a gully through a chaotic terrain of rocky permafrost that had collapsed in karsts and sinkholes. After two hours, the gully ended abruptly. Before Mirasol rose a mountain range of massive slabs and boulders, some with the glassy sheen of impact melt, others scabbed over with lichen.

As the crawler started up the slope, the sun came out, and Mirasol saw the crater's outer rim jigsawed in the green of lichen and the glaring white of snow.

The oxygen readings were rising steadily. Warm, moist air was drooling from within the crater's lip, leaving a spittle of ice. A half-million-ton asteroid from the Rings of Saturn had fallen here at fifteen kilometers a second. But for two centuries rain, creeping glaciers, and lichen had gnawed at the crater's rim, and the wound's raw edges had slumped and scarred.

The crawler worked its way up the striated channel of an empty glacier bed. A cold alpine wind keened down the channel, where flourishing patches of lichen clung to exposed veins of ice.

Some rocks were striped with sediment from the ancient Martian seas, and the impact had peeled them up and thrown them on their backs.

It was winter, the season for pruning the sunken gardens. The treacherous rubble of the crater's rim was cemented with frozen mud. The crawler found the glacier's root and clawed its way up the ice face. The raw slope was striped with winter snow and storm-blown summer dust, stacked in hundreds of red-and-white layers. With the years the stripes had warped and rippled in the glacier's flow.

Mirasol reached the crest. The crawler ran spiderlike along the crater's snowy rim. Below, in a bowl-shaped crater eight kilometers deep, lay a seething ocean of air.

Mirasol stared. Within this gigantic airsump, twenty kilometers across, a broken ring of majestic rain clouds trailed their dark skirts, like duchesses in quadrille, about the ballroom floor of a lens-shaped sea.

Thick forests of green-and-yellow mangroves rimmed the shallow water and had overrun the shattered islands at its center. Pinpoints of brilliant scarlet ibis spattered the trees. A flock of them suddenly spread kitelike wings and took to the air, spreading across the crater in uncounted millions. Mirasol was appalled by the crudity and daring of this ecological concept, its crass and primal vitality.

This was what she had come to destroy. The thought filled her with sadness.

Then she remembered the years she had spent flattering her Regal teachers, collaborating with them in the destruction of her own culture. When the chance at the Ladder came, she had been chosen. She put her sadness away, remembering her ambitions and her rivals.

The history of mankind in space had been a long epic of ambitions and rivalries. From the very first, space colonies had struggled for self-sufficiency and had soon broken their ties with the exhausted Earth. The independent life-support systems had given them the mentality of city-states. Strange ideologies had bloomed in the hothouse atmosphere of the o'neills, and breakaway groups were common.

Space was too vast to police. Pioneer elites burst forth, defying anyone to stop their pursuit of aberrant technologies. Quite suddenly the march of science had become an insane, headlong scramble. New sciences and technologies had shattered whole societies in waves of future shock.

The shattered cultures coalesced into factions, so thoroughly alienated from one another that they were called humanity only for lack of a better term. The Shapers, for instance, had seized control of their own genetics, abandoning mankind in a burst of artificial evolution. Their rivals, the Mechanists, had replaced flesh with advanced prosthetics.

Mirasol's own group, the Patternists, was a breakaway Shaper faction.

The Patternists specialized in cerebral asymmetry. With grossly expanded right-brain hemispheres, they were highly intuitive, given to metaphors, parallels, and sudden cognitive leaps. Their inventive minds and quick, unpredictable genius had given them a competitive edge at first. But with these advantages had come grave weaknesses: autism, fugue states, and paranoia. Patterns grew out of control and became grotesque webs of fantasy.

With these handicaps their colony had faltered. Patternist industries went into decline, outpaced by industrial rivals. Competition had grown much fiercer. The Shaper and Mechanist cartels had turned commercial action into a kind of endemic warfare. The Patternist gamble had failed, and the day came when their entire habitat was bought out from around them by Regal plutocrats. In a way it was a kindness. The Regals were suave and proud of their ability to assimilate refugees and failures.

The Regals themselves had started as dissidents and defectors. Their Posthumanist philosophy had given them the moral power and the bland assurance to dominate and absorb factions from the fringes of humanity. And they had the support of the Investors, who had vast wealth and the secret techniques of star travel.

The crawler's radar alerted Mirasol to the presence of a landcraft from a rival faction. Leaning forward in her pilot's couch, she put the craft's image on screen. It was a lumpy sphere, balanced uneasily on four long, spindly legs. Silhouetted against the horizon, it moved with a strange wobbling speed along the opposite lip of the crater, then disappeared down the outward slope.

Mirasol wondered if it had been cheating. She was tempted to try some cheating herself—to dump a few frozen packets of aerobic bacteria or a few dozen capsules of insect eggs down the slope—but she feared the orbiting monitors of the T-K supervisors. Too much was at stake—not only her own career but that of her entire faction, huddled bankrupt and despairing in their cold redemption camp. It was said that T-K's ruler, the posthuman being they called the Lobster King, would himself watch the contest. To fail before his black abstracted gaze would be a horror.

On the crater's outside slope, below her, a second rival craft appeared, lurching and slithering with insane, aggressive grace. The craft's long supple body moved with a sidewinder's looping and coiling, holding aloft a massive shining head, like a faceted mirror ball.

Both rivals were converging on the rendezvous camp, where the six contestants would receive their final briefing from the Regal Adviser. Mirasol hurried forward.

When the camp first flashed into sight on her screen, Mirasol was shocked. The place was huge and absurdly elaborate: a drug dream of paneled geodesics and colored minarets, sprawling in the lichenous desert like an abandoned chandelier. This was a camp for Regals.

Here the arbiters and sophists of the BioArts would stay and judge the crater as the newly planted ecosystems struggled among themselves for supremacy.

The camp's airlocks were surrounded with shining green thickets of lichen, where the growth feasted on escaped humidity. Mirasol drove her crawler through the yawning airlock and into a garage. Inside the garage, robot mechanics were scrubbing and polishing the coiled hundred-meter length of the snake craft and the gleaming black abdomen of an eight-legged crawler. The black crawler was crouched with its periscoped head sunk downward, as if ready to pounce. Its swollen belly was marked with a red hourglass and the corporate logos of its faction.

The garage smelled of dust and grease overlaid with floral perfumes. Mirasol left the mechanics to their work and walked stiffly down a long corridor, stretching the kinks out of her back and shoulders. A latticework door sprang apart into filaments and resealed itself behind her.

She was in a dining room that clinked and rattled with the high-pitched repetitive sound of Regal music. Its walls were paneled with tall display screens showing startlingly beautiful garden panoramas. A pulpy-looking servo, whose organometallic casing and squat, smiling head had a swollen and almost diseased appearance, showed her to a chair.

Mirasol sat, denting the heavy white tablecloth with her knees. There were seven places at the table. The Regal Adviser's tall chair was at the table's head. Mirasol's assigned position gave her a sharp idea of her own status. She sat at the far end of the table, on the Adviser's left.

Two of her rivals had already taken their places. One was a tall, red-haired Shaper with long, thin arms, whose sharp face and bright, worried eyes gave him a querulous birdlike look. The other was a sullen, feral Mechanist with prosthetic hands and a paramilitary tunic marked at the shoulders with a red hourglass.

Mirasol studied her two rivals with silent, sidelong glances. Like her, they were both young. The Regals favored the young, and they encouraged captive factions to expand their populations widely.

This strategy cleverly subverted the old guard of each faction in a tidal wave of their own children, indoctrinated from birth by Regals.

The birdlike man, obviously uncomfortable with his place directly at the Adviser's right, looked as if he wanted to speak but dared not. The piratical Mech sat staring at his artificial hands, his ears stoppered with headphones.

Each place setting had a squeezebulb of liqueur. Regals, who were used to weightlessness in orbit, used these bulbs by habit, and their presence here was both a privilege and a humiliation.

The door fluttered open again, and two more rivals burst in, almost as if they had raced. The first was a flabby Mech, still not used to gravity, whose sagging limbs were supported by an extraskeletal framework. The second was a severely mutated Shaper whose elbowed legs terminated in grasping hands. The pedal hands were gemmed with heavy rings that clicked against each other as she waddled across the parquet floor.

The woman with the strange legs took her place across from the birdlike man. They began to converse haltingly in a language that none of the others could follow. The man in the framework, gasping audibly, lay in obvious pain in the chair across from Mirasol. His plastic eyeballs looked as blank as chips of glass. His sufferings in the pull of gravity showed that he was new to Mars, and his place in the competition meant that his faction was powerful. Mirasol despised him.

Mirasol felt a nightmarish sense of entrapment. Everything about her competitors seemed to proclaim their sickly unfitness for survival. They had a haunted, hungry look, like starving men in a lifeboat who wait with secret eagerness for the first to die.

She caught a glimpse of herself reflected in the bowl of a spoon and saw with a flash of insight how she must appear to the others. Her intuitive right brain was swollen beyond human bounds, distorting her skull. Her face had the blank prettiness of her genetic heritage, but she could feel the bleak strain of her expression. Her body looked shapeless under her quilted pilot's vest and dun-drab, general-issue blouse and trousers. Her fingertips were raw from biting. She saw in herself the fey, defeated aura of her faction's older generation, those who had tried and failed in the great world of space, and she hated herself for it.

They were still waiting for the sixth competitor when the plonk-ing music reached a sudden crescendo and the Regal Adviser ar-rived. Her name was Arkadya Sorienti, Incorporated. She was a mem-ber of T-K's ruling oligarchy, and she swayed through the bursting door with the careful steps of a woman not used to gravity.

She wore the Investor-style clothing of a high-ranking diplomat. The Regals were proud of their diplomatic ties with the alien Inves-tors, since Investor patronage proved their own vast wealth. The Sorienti's knee-high boots had false birdlike toes, scaled like Investor hide. She wore a heavy skirt of gold cords braided with jewels, and a stiff wrist-length formal jacket with embroidered cuffs. A heavy collar formed an arching multicolored frill behind her head. Her blonde hair was set in an interlaced style as complex as computer wiring. The skin of her bare legs had a shiny, glossy look, as if freshly enam-eled. Her eyelids gleamed with soft reptilian pastels.

One of her corporate ladyship's two body-servos helped her to her seat. The Sorienti leaned forward brightly, interlacing small, pretty hands so crusted with rings and bracelets that they resembled gleaming gauntlets.

"I hope the five of you have enjoyed this chance for an informal talk," she said sweetly, just as if such a thing were possible. "I'm sorry I was delayed. Our sixth participant will not be joining us."

There was no explanation. The Regals never publicized any ac-tion of theirs that might be construed as a punishment. The looks of the competitors, alternately stricken and calculating, showed that they were imagining the worst.

The two squat servos circulated around the table, dishing out courses of food from trays balanced on their flabby heads. The com-petitors picked uneasily at their plates.

The display screen behind the Adviser flicked into a schematic diagram of the Ibis Crater. "Please notice the revised boundary lines," the Sorienti said. "I hope that each of you will avoid trespassing—not merely physically but biologically as well." She looked at them seriously. "Some of you may plan to use herbicides. This is permissi-ble, but the spreading of spray beyond your sector's boundaries is considered crass. Bacteriological establishment is a subtle art. The spreading of tailored disease organisms is an aesthetic distortion. Please remember that your activities here are a disruption of what should ideally be natural processes. Therefore the period of biotic seeding will last only twelve hours. Thereafter, the new complexity level will be allowed to stabilize itself without any other interference at all. Avoid self-aggrandizement, and confine yourselves to a primal role, as catalysts."

The Sorienti's speech was formal and ceremonial. Mirasol studied the display screen, noting with much satisfaction that her territory had been expanded.

Seen from overhead, the crater's roundness was deeply marred. Mirasol's sector, the southern one, showed the long flattened scar of a major landslide, where the crater wall had slumped and flowed into the pit. The simple ecosystem had recovered quickly, and mangroves festooned the rubble's lowest slopes. Its upper slopes were gnawed by lichens and glaciers.

The sixth sector had been erased, and Mirasol's share was almost twenty square kilometers of new land.

It would give her faction's ecosystem more room to take root before the deadly struggle began in earnest.

This was not the first such competition. The Regals had held them for decades as an objective test of the skills of rival factions. It helped the Regals' divide-and-conquer policy, to set the factions against one another.

And in the centuries to come, as Mars grew more hospitable to life, the gardens would surge from their craters and spread across the surface. Mars would become a warring jungle of separate creations. For the Regals the competitions were closely studied simulations of the future.

And the competitions gave the factions motives for their work. With the garden wars to spur them, the ecological sciences had advanced enormously. Already, with the progress of science and taste, many of the oldest craters had become ecoaesthetic embarrassments.

The Ibis Crater had been an early, crude experiment. The faction that had created it was long gone, and its primitive creation was now considered tasteless.

Each gardening faction camped beside its own crater, struggling to bring it to life. But the competitions were a shortcut up the Ladder. The competitors' philosophies and talents, made into flesh, would carry out a proxy struggle for supremacy. The sine-wave curves of growth, the rallies and declines of expansion and extinction, would scroll across the monitors of the Regal judges like stock-market reports. This complex struggle would be weighed in each of its aspects: technological, philosophical, biological, and aesthetic. The winners would abandon their camps to take on Regal wealth and power. They would roam T-K's jeweled corridors and revel in its perquisites: extended life spans, corporate titles, cosmopolitan tolerance, and the interstellar patronage of the Investors.

When red dawn broke over the landscape, the five were poised around the Ibis Crater, awaiting the signal. The day was calm, with only a distant nexus of jet streams marring the sky. Mirasol watched pink-stained sunlight creep down the inside slope of the crater's western wall. In the mangrove thickets birds were beginning to stir.

Mirasol waited tensely. She had taken a position on the upper slopes of the landslide's raw debris. Radar showed her rivals spaced along the interior slopes: to her left, the hourglass crawler and the jewel-headed snake; to her right, a mantislike crawler and the globe on stilts.

The signal came, sudden as lightning: a meteor of ice shot from orbit and left a shock-wave cloud plume of ablated steam. Mirasol charged forward.

The Patternists' strategy was to concentrate on the upper slopes and the landslide's rubble, a marginal niche where they hoped to excel. Their cold crater in Syrtis Major had given them some expertise in alpine species, and they hoped to exploit this strength. The landslide's long slope, far above sea level, was to be their power base. The crawler lurched downslope, blasting out a fine spray of lichenophagous bacteria.

Suddenly the air was full of birds. Across the crater, the globe on stilts had rushed down to the waterline and was laying waste the mangroves. Fine wisps of smoke showed the slicing beam of a heavy laser.

Burst after burst of birds took wing, peeling from their nests to wheel and dip in terror. At first, their frenzied cries came as a high-pitched whisper. Then, as the fear spread, the screeching echoed and reechoed, building to a mindless surf of pain. In the crater's dawn-warmed air, the scarlet motes hung in their millions, swirling and coalescing like drops of blood in free-fall.

Mirasol scattered the seeds of alpine rock crops. The crawler picked its way down the talus, spraying fertilizer into cracks and crevices. She pried up boulders and released a scattering of invertebrates: nematodes, mites, sowbugs, altered millipedes. She splattered the rocks with gelatin to feed them until the mosses and ferns took hold.

The cries of the birds were appalling. Downslope the other factions were thrashing in the muck at sea level, wreaking havoc, destroying the mangroves so that their own creations could take hold. The great snake looped and ducked through the canopy, knotting itself, ripping up swathes of mangroves by the roots. As Mirasol watched, the top of its faceted head burst open and released a cloud of bats.

The mantis crawler was methodically marching along the borders of its sector, its saw-edged arms reducing everything before it into kindling. The hourglass crawler had slashed through its territory, leaving a muddy network of fire zones. Behind it rose a wall of smoke.

It was a daring ploy. Sterilizing the sector by fire might give the new biome a slight advantage. Even a small boost could be crucial as exponential rates of growth took hold. But the Ibis Crater was a closed system. The use of fire required great care. There was only so much air within the bowl.

Mirasol worked grimly. Insects were next. They were often neglected in favor of massive sea beasts or flashy predators, but in terms of biomass, gram by gram, insects could overwhelm. She blasted a carton downslope to the shore, where it melted, releasing aquatic termites. She shoved aside flat shelves of rock, planting egg cases below their sun-warmed surfaces. She released a cloud of leaf-eating midges, their tiny bodies packed with bacteria. Within the crawler's belly, rack after automatic rack was thawed and fired through nozzles, dropped through spiracles or planted in the holes jabbed by picklike feet.

Each faction was releasing a potential world. Near the water's edge, the mantis had released a pair of things like giant black sail planes. They were swooping through the clouds of ibis, opening great sieved mouths. On the islands in the center of the crater's lake, scaled walruses clambered on the rocks, blowing steam. The stilt ball was laying out an orchard in the mangroves' wreckage. The snake had taken to the water, its faceted head leaving a wake of V-waves.

In the hourglass sector, smoke continued to rise. The fires were spreading, and the spider ran frantically along its network of zones. Mirasol watched the movement of the smoke as she released a horde of marmots and rock squirrels.

A mistake had been made. As the smoky air gushed upward in the feeble Martian gravity, a fierce valley wind of cold air from the heights flowed downward to fill the vacuum. The mangroves burned fiercely. Shattered networks of flaming branches were flying into the air.

The spider charged into the flames, smashing and trampling. Mirasol laughed, imagining demerits piling up in the judges' data banks. Her talus slopes were safe from fire. There was nothing to burn.

The ibis flock had formed a great wheeling ring above the shore. Within their scattered ranks flitted the dark shapes of airborne predators. The long plume of steam from the meteor had begun to twist and break. A sullen wind was building up.

Fire had broken out in the snake's sector. The snake was swimming in the sea's muddy waters, surrounded by bales of bright-green kelp. Before its pilot noticed, fire was already roaring through a great piled heap of the wreckage it had left on shore. There were no windbreaks left. Air poured down the denuded slope. The smoke column guttered and twisted, its black clouds alive with sparks.

A flock of ibis plunged into the cloud. Only a handful emerged; some of them were flaming visibly. Mirasol began to know fear. As smoke rose to the crater's rim, it cooled and started to fall outward and downward. A vertical whirlwind was forming, a torus of hot smoke and cold wind.

The crawler scattered seed-packed hay for pygmy mountain goats. Just before her an ibis fell from the sky with a dark squirming shape, all claws and teeth, clinging to its neck. She rushed forward and crushed the predator, then stopped and stared distractedly across the crater.

Fires were spreading with unnatural speed. Small puffs of smoke rose from a dozen places, striking large heaps of wood with uncanny precision. Her altered brain searched for a pattern. The fires springing up in the mantis sector were well beyond the reach of any falling debris.

In the spider's zone, flames had leapt the firebreaks without leaving a mark. The pattern felt wrong to her, eerily wrong, as if the destruction had a force all its own, a raging synergy that fed upon itself.

The pattern spread into a devouring crescent. Mirasol felt the dread of lost control—the sweating fear an orbiter feels at the hiss of escaping air or the way a suicide feels at the first bright gush of blood.

Within an hour the garden sprawled beneath a hurricane of hot decay. The dense columns of smoke had flattened like thunderheads at the limits of the garden's sunken troposphere. Slowly a spark-shot gray haze, dripping ash like rain, began to ring the crater. Screaming birds circled beneath the foul torus, falling by tens and scores and hundreds. Their bodies littered the garden's sea, their bright plumage blurred with ash in a steel-gray sump.

The landcraft of the others continued to fight the flames, smashing unharmed through the fire's charred borderlands. Their efforts were useless, a pathetic ritual before the disaster.

Even the fire's malicious purity had grown tired and tainted. The oxygen was failing. The flames were dimmer and spread more slowly, releasing a dark nastiness of half-combusted smoke.

Where it spread, nothing that breathed could live. Even the flames were killed as the smoke billowed along the crater's crushed and smoldering slopes.

Mirasol watched a group of striped gazelles struggle up the barren slopes of the talus in search of air. Their dark eyes, fresh from the laboratory, rolled in timeless animal fear. Their coats were scorched, their flanks heaved, their mouths dripped foam. One by one they collapsed in convulsions, kicking at the lifeless Martian rock as they slid and fell. It was a vile sight, the image of a blighted spring.

An oblique flash of red downslope to her left attracted her attention. A large red animal was skulking among the rocks. She turned the crawler and picked her way toward it, wincing as a dark surf of poisoned smoke broke across the fretted glass.

She spotted the animal as it broke from cover. It was a scorched and gasping creature like a great red ape. She dashed forward and seized it in the crawler's arms. Held aloft, it clawed and kicked, hammering the crawler's arms with a smoldering branch. In revulsion and pity, she crushed it. Its bodice of tight-sewn ibis feathers tore, revealing blood-slicked human flesh.

Using the crawler's grips, she tugged at a heavy tuft of feathers on its head. The tight-fitting mask ripped free, and the dead man's head slumped forward. She rolled it back, revealing a face tattooed with stars.

The ornithopter sculled above the burned-out garden, its long red wings beating with dreamlike fluidity. Mirasol watched the Sorienti's painted face as her corporate ladyship stared into the shining viewscreen.

The ornithopter's powerful cameras cast image after image onto the tabletop screen, lighting the Regal's face. The tabletop was lit-

tered with the Sorienti's elegant knickknacks: an inhaler case, a half-empty jeweled squeezebulb, lorgnette binoculars, a stack of tape cassettes.

"An unprecedented case," her ladyship murmured. "It was not a total dieback after all but merely the extinction of everything with lungs. There must be strong survivorship among the lower orders: fish, insects, annelids. Now that the rain's settled the ash, you can see the vegetation making a strong comeback. Your own section seems almost undamaged."

"Yes," Mirasol said. "The natives were unable to reach it with torches before the fire storm had smothered itself."

The Sorienti leaned back into the tasseled arms of her couch. "I wish you wouldn't mention them so loudly, even between ourselves."

"No one would believe me."

"The others never saw them," the Regal said. "They were too busy fighting the flames." She hesitated briefly. "You were wise to confide in me first."

Mirasol locked eyes with her new patroness, then looked away. "There was no one else to tell. They'd have said I built a pattern out of nothing but my own fears."

"You have your faction to think of," the Sorienti said with an air of sympathy. "With such a bright future ahead of them, they don't need a renewed reputation for paranoid fantasies."

She studied the screen. "The Patternists are winners by default. It certainly makes an interesting case study. If the new garden grows tiresome we can have the whole crater sterilized from orbit. Some other faction can start again with a clean slate."

"Don't let them build too close to the edge," Mirasol said.

Her corporate ladyship watched her attentively, tilting her head.

"I have no proof," Mirasol said, "but I can see the pattern behind it all. The natives had to come from somewhere. The colony that stocked the crater must have been destroyed in that huge landslide. Was that your work? Did your people kill them?"

The Sorienti smiled. "You're very bright, my dear. You will do well, up the Ladder. And you can keep secrets. Your office as my secretary suits you very well."

"They were destroyed from orbit," Mirasol said. "Why else would they hide from us? You tried to annihilate them."

"It was a long time ago," the Regal said. "In the early days, when things were shakier. They were researching the secret of starflight, techniques only the Investors know. Rumor says they reached success at last, in their redemption camp. After that, there was no choice."

"Then they were killed for the Investors' profit," Mirasol said. She stood up quickly and walked around the cabin, her new jeweled skirt clattering around the knees. "So that the aliens could go on toying with us, hiding their secret, selling us trinkets."

The Regal folded her hands with a clicking of rings and bracelets. "Our Lobster King is wise," she said. "If humanity's efforts turned to the stars, what would become of terraforming? Why should we trade the power of creation itself to become like the Investors?"

"But think of the people," Mirasol said. "Think of them losing their technologies, degenerating into human beings. A handful of savages, eating bird meat. Think of the fear they felt for generations, the way they burned their own home and killed themselves when they saw us come to smash and destroy their world. Aren't you filled with horror?"

"For humans?" the Sorienti said. "No!"

"But can't you see? You've given this planet life as an art form, as an enormous game. You force us to play in it, and those people were killed for it! Can't you see how that blights everything?"

"Our game is reality," the Regal said. She gestured at the viewscreen. "You can't deny the savage beauty of destruction."

"You defend this catastrophe?"

The Regal shrugged. "If life worked perfectly, how could things evolve? Aren't we posthuman? Things grow; things die. In time the cosmos kills us all. The cosmos has no meaning, and its emptiness is absolute. That's pure terror, but it's also pure freedom. Only our ambitions and our creations can fill it."

"And that justifies your actions?"

"We act for life," the Regal said. "Our ambitions have become this world's natural laws. We blunder because life blunders. We go on because life must go on. When you've taken the long view, from orbit—when the power we wield is in your own hands—then you can judge us." She smiled. "You will be judging yourself. You'll be Regal."

"But what about your captive factions? Your agents, who do your will? Once we had our own ambitions. We failed, and now you isolate us, indoctrinate us, make us into rumors. We must have something of our own. Now we have nothing."

"That's not so. You have what we've given you. You have the Ladder."

The vision stung Mirasol: power, light, the hint of justice, this world with its sins and sadness shrunk to a bright arena far below. "Yes," she said at last. "Yes, we do."

TWENTY
EVOCATIONS

EXPERT SYSTEMS. When Nikolai Leng was a child, his teacher was a cybernetic system with a holographic interface. The holo took the form of a young Shaper woman. Its "personality" was an interactive composite expert system manufactured by Shaper psychotechs. Nikolai loved it.

2. NEVER BORN. "You mean we all came from Earth?" said Nikolai, unbelieving.

"Yes," the holo said kindly. "The first true settlers in space were born on Earth—produced by sexual means. Of course, hundreds of years have passed since then. You are a Shaper. Shapers are never born."

"Who lives on Earth now?"

"Human beings."

"Ohhhh," said Nikolai, his falling tones betraying a rapid loss of interest.

3. A MALFUNCTIONING LEG. There came a day when Nikolai saw his first Mechanist. The man was a diplomat and commercial agent, stationed by his faction in Nikolai's habitat. Nikolai and some children from his crèche were playing in the corridor when the diplomat stalked by. One of the Mechanist's legs was malfunctioning, and it went click-whirr, click-whirr. Nikolai's friend Alex mimicked the man's limp. Suddenly the man turned on them, his plastic eyes dilating. "Gene-lines," the Mechanist snarled. "I can buy you, grow you, sell you, cut you into bits. Your screams: my music."

4. FUZZ PATINA. Sweat was running into the braided collar of Nikolai's military tunic. The air in the abandoned station was still breathable, but insufferably hot. Nikolai helped his sergeant strip the valuables off a dead miner. The murdered Shaper's antiseptic body was desiccated, but perfect. They walked into another section. The body of a Mechanist pirate sprawled in the feeble gravity. Killed during the attack, his body had rotted for weeks inside his suit. An inch-thick patina of grayish fuzz had devoured his face.

5. NOT MERITORIOUS. Nikolai was on leave in the Ring Council with two men from his unit. They were drinking in a free-fall bar called the ECLECTIC EPILEPTIC. The first man was Simon Afriel, a charming, ambitious young Shaper of the old school. The other man had a Mechanist eye implant. His loyalty was suspect. The three of them were discussing semantics. "The map is not the territory," Afriel said. Suddenly the second man picked an almost invisible listening device from the edge of the table. "And the tap is not meritorious," he quipped. They never saw him again.

. . . A Mechanist pirate, malfunctioning, betraying gene-lines. Invisible listening devices buy, grow, and sell you. The abandoned station's ambitious young Shaper, killed during the attack. Falling psychotechs produced by sexual means the desiccated body of a commercial agent. The holographic interface's loyalty was suspect. The cybernetic system helped him strip the valuables off his plastic eyes. . . .

6. SPECULATIVE PITY. The Mechanist woman looked him over with an air of speculative pity. "I have an established commercial position here," she told Nikolai, "but my cash flow is temporarily constricted. You, on the other hand, have just defected from the Council with a small fortune. I need money; you need stability. I propose marriage."

Nikolai considered this. He was new to Mech society. "Does this imply a sexual relationship?" he said. The woman looked at him blankly. "You mean between the two of us?"

7. FLOW PATTERNS. "You're worried about something," his wife told him. Nikolai shook his head. "Yes, you are," she persisted. "You're upset because of that deal I made in pirate contraband.

You're unhappy because our corporation is profiting from attacks made on your own people."

Nikolai smiled ruefully. "I suppose you're right. I never knew anyone who understood my innermost feelings the way you do." He looked at her affectionately. "How do you do it?"

"I have infrared scanners," she said. "I read the patterns of blood flow in your face."

8. OPTIC TELEVISION. It was astonishing how much room there was in an eye socket, when you stopped to think about it. The actual visual mechanisms had been thoroughly miniaturized by Mechanist prostheticians. Nikolai had some other devices installed: a clock, a biofeedback monitor, a television screen, all wired directly to his optic nerve. They were convenient, but difficult to control at first. His wife had to help him out of the hospital and back to his apartment, because the subtle visual triggers kept flashing broadcast market reports. Nikolai smiled at his wife from behind his plastic eyes. "Spend the night with me tonight," he said. His wife shrugged. "All right," she said. She put her hand to the door of Nikolai's apartment and died almost instantly. An assassin had smeared the door handle with contact venom.

9. SHAPER TARGETS. "Look," the assassin said, his slack face etched with weariness, "don't bother me with any ideologies. . . . Just transfer the funds and tell me who it is you want dead."

"It's a job in the Ring Council," Nikolai said. He was strung out on a regimen of emotional drugs he had been taking to combat grief, and he had to fight down recurrent waves of weirdly tainted cheerfulness. "Captain-Doctor Martin Leng of Ring Council Security. He's one of my own gene-line. My defection made his own loyalty look bad. He killed my wife."

"Shapers make good targets," the assassin said. His legless, armless body floated in a transparent nutrient tank, where tinted plasmas soothed the purplish ends of socketed nerve clumps. A body-servo waded into the tank and began to attach the assassin's arms.

10. CHILD INVESTMENT. "We recognize your investment in this child, shareholder Leng," the psychotech said. "You may have created her—or hired the technicians who had her created—but she is not your property. By our regulations she must be treated like any other child. She is the property of our people's corporate republic."

Nikolai looked at the woman, exasperated. "I didn't create her.

She's my dead wife's posthumous clone. And she's the property of my wife's corporations, or, rather, her trust fund, which I manage as executor. . . . No, what I mean to say is that she owns, or at least has a lienhold on, my dead wife's semiautonomous corporate property, which becomes hers at the age of majority. . . . Do you follow me?"

"No. I'm an educator, not a financier. What exactly is the point of this, shareholder? Are you trying to re-create your dead wife?"

Nikolai looked at her, his face carefully neutral. "I did it for the tax break."

. . . Leave the posthumous clone profiting from attacks. Semiautonomous property has an established commercial position. Recurrent waves of pirate contraband. His slack face bothers you with ideologies. Innermost feelings died almost instantly. Smear the door with contract venom. . . .

11. ALLEGIANCES RESENTED. "I like it out here on the fringes," Nikolai told the assassin. "Have you ever considered a breakaway?"

The assassin laughed. "I used to be a pirate. It took me forty years to attach myself to this cartel. When you're alone, you're meat, Leng. You ought to know that."

"But you must resent those allegiances. They're inconvenient. Wouldn't you rather have your own Kluster and make your own rules?"

"You're talking like an ideologue," the assassin said. Biofeedback displays blinked softly on his prosthetic forearms. "My allegiance is to Kyotid Zaibatsu. They own this whole suburb. They even own my arms and legs."

"I own Kyotid Zaibatsu," Nikolai said.

"Oh," the assassin said. "Well, that puts a different face on matters."

12. MASS DEFECTION. "We want to join your Kluster," the Super-bright said. "We must join your Kluster. No one else will have us."

Nikolai doodled absently with his light pen on a convenient vid-eoscreen. "How many of you are there?"

"There were fifty in our gene-line. We were working on quantum physics before our mass defection. We made a few minor break-throughs. I think they might be of some commercial use."

"Splendid," said Nikolai. He assumed an air of speculative pity. "I take it the Ring Council persecuted you in the usual manner—claimed you were mentally unstable, ideologically unsound, and the like."

"Yes. Their agents have killed thirty-eight of us." The Superbright dabbed uneasily at the sweat beading on his swollen forehead. "We are not mentally unsound, Kluster-Chairman. We will not cause you any trouble. We only want a quiet place to finish working while God eats our brains."

13. DATA HOSTAGE. A high-level call came in from the Ring Council. Nikolai, surprised and intrigued, took the call himself. A young man's face appeared on the screen. "I have your teacher hostage," he said.

Nikolai frowned. "What?"

"The person who taught you when you were a child in the crèche. You love her. You told her so. I have it on tape."

"You must be joking," Nikolai said. "My teacher was just a cybernetic interface. You can't hold a data system hostage."

"Yes, I can," the young man said truculently. "The old expert system's been scrapped in favor of a new one with a sounder ideology. Look." A second face appeared on the screen; it was the superhumanly smooth and faintly glowing image of his cybernetic teacher. "Please save me, Nikolai," the image said woodenly. "He's ruthless."

The young man's face reappeared. Nikolai laughed incredulously. "So you've saved the old tapes?" Nikolai said. "I don't know what your game is, but I suppose the data has a certain value. I'm prepared to be generous." He named a price. The young man shook his head. Nikolai grew impatient. "Look," he said. "What makes you think a mere expert system has any objective worth?"

"I know it does," the young man said. "I'm one myself."

14. CENTRAL QUESTION. Nikolai was aboard the alien ship. He felt uncomfortable in his brocaded ambassador's coat. He adjusted the heavy sunglasses over his plastic eyes. "We appreciate your visit to our Kluster," he told the reptilian ensign. "It's a very great honor."

The Investor ensign lifted the multicolored frill behind his massive head. "We are prepared to do business," he said.

"I'm interested in alien philosophies," Nikolai said. "The answers of other species to the great questions of existence."

"But there is only one central question," the alien said. "We have pursued its answer from star to star. We were hoping that you would help us answer it."

Nikolai was cautious. "What is the question?"

" 'What is it you have that we want?' "

15. INHERITED GIFTS. Nikolai looked at the girl with the old-fashioned eyes. "My chief of security has provided me with a record of your criminal actions," he said. "Copyright infringement, organized extortion, conspiracy in restraint of trade. How old are you?"

"Forty-four," the girl said. "How old are you?"

"A hundred and ten or so. I'd have to check my files." Something about the girl's appearance bothered him. "Where did you get those antique eyes?"

"They were my mother's. I inherited them. But you're a Shaper, of course. You wouldn't know what a mother was."

"On the contrary," Nikolai said. "I believe I knew yours. We were married. After her death, I had you cloned. I suppose that makes me your—I forget the term."

"Father."

"That sounds about right. Clearly you've inherited her gifts for finance." He reexamined her personnel file. "Would you be interested in adding bigamy to your list of crimes?"

. . . The mentally unstable have a certain value. Restraint of trade puts a different face on the convenient videoscreen. A few minor breakthroughs in the questions of existence. Your personnel file persecuted him. His swollen forehead can't hold a data system. . . .

16. PLEASURE ROAR. "You need to avoid getting set in your ways," his wife said. "It's the only way to stay young." She pulled a gilded inhaler from her garter holster. "Try some of this."

"I don't need drugs," Nikolai said, smiling. "I have my power fantasies." He began pulling off his clothes.

His wife watched him impatiently. "Don't be stodgy, Nikolai." She touched the inhaler to her nostril and sniffed. Sweat began to break out on her face, and a slow sexual flush spread over her ears and neck.

Nikolai watched, then shrugged and sniffed lightly at the gilded tube. Immediately a rocketing sense of ecstasy paralyzed his nervous system. His body arched backward, throbbing uncontrollably.

Clumsily, his wife began to caress him. The roar of chemical pleasure made sex irrelevant. "Why . . . why bother?" he gasped.

His wife looked surprised. "It's traditional."

17. FLICKERING WALL. Nikolai addressed the flickering wall of monitor screens. "I'm getting old," he said. "My health is good—I was very lucky in my choice of longevity programs—but I just don't have the daring I once did. I've lost my flexibility, my edge. And the Kluster has outgrown my ability to handle it. I have no choice. I must retire."

Carefully, he watched the faces on the screens for every flicker of reaction. Two hundred years had taught him the art of reading faces. His skills were still with him—it was only the will behind them that had decayed. The faces of the Governing Board, their reserve broken by shock, seemed to blaze with ambition and greed.

18. LEGAL TARGETS. The Mechanists had unleashed their drones in the suburb. Armed with subpoenas, the faceless drones blurred through the hallway crowds, looking for legal targets.

Suddenly Nikolai's former Chief of Security broke from the crowd and began a run for cover. In free-fall, he brachiated from handhold to handhold like an armored gibbon. Suddenly one of his prosthetics gave way and the drones pounced on him, almost at Nikolai's door. Plastic snapped as electromagnetic pincers paralyzed his limbs.

"Kangaroo courts," he gasped. The deeply creased lines in his ancient face shone with rivulets of sweat. "They'll strip me! Help me, Leng!"

Sadly, Nikolai shook his head. The old man shrieked: "You got me into this! You were the ideologue! I'm only a poor assassin!"

Nikolai said nothing. The machines seized and repossessed the old man's arms and legs.

19. ANTIQUE SPLITS. "You've really got it through you, right? All that old gigo stuff!" The young people spoke a slang-crammed jargon that Nikolai could barely comprehend. When they watched him their faces showed a mixture of aggression, pity, and awe. To Nikolai, they always seemed to be shouting. "I feel outnumbered," he murmured.

"You *are* outnumbered, old Nikolai! This bar is your museum, right? Your mausoleum! Give our ears your old frontiers, we're listening! Those idiot video ideologies, those antique spirit splits. Mechs and Shapers, right? The wars of the coin's two halves!"

"I feel tired," Nikolai said. "I've drunk too much. Take me home, one of you."

They exchanged worried glances. "This *is* your home! Isn't it?"

20. EYES CLOSED. "You've been very kind," Nikolai told the two youngsters. They were Kosmosity archaeologists, dressed in their academic finery, their gowns studded with awards and medals from the Terraform-Klusters. Nikolai realized suddenly that he could not remember their names.

"That's all right, sir," they told him soothingly. "It's now our duty to remember you, not vice versa." Nikolai felt embarrassed. He hadn't realized that he had spoken aloud.

"I've taken poison," he explained apologetically.

"We know," they nodded. "You're not in any pain, we hope?"

"No, not at all. I've done the right thing, I know. I'm very old. Older than I can bear." Suddenly he felt an alarming collapse within himself. Pieces of his consciousness began to break off as he slid toward the void. Suddenly he realized that he had forgotten his last words. With an enormous effort, he remembered them and shouted them aloud.

"Futility is freedom!" Filled with triumph, he died, and they closed his eyes.

GREEN DAYS
IN BRUNEI

TWO MEN WERE FISHING from the corroded edge of an offshore oil rig. After years of decrepitude, the rig's concrete pillars were thick with barnacles and waving fronds of seaweed. The air smelled of rust and brine.

"Sorry to disturb your plans," the minister said. "But we can't just chat up the Yankees every time you hit a little contretemps." The minister reeled in and revealed a bare hook. He cursed mildly in his native Malay. "Hand me another bait, there's a good fellow."

Turner Choi reached into the wooden bait bucket and gave the minister a large dead prawn. "But I need that phone link," Turner said. "Just for a few hours. Just long enough to access the net in America and download some better documentation."

"What ghastly jargon," said the minister, who was formally known as the Yang Teramat Pehin Orang Kaya Amar Diraja Dato Seri Paduka Abdul Kahar. He was minister of industrial policy for the Sultanate of Brunei Darussalam, a tiny nation on the northern shore of the island of Borneo. The titles of Brunei's aristocracy were in inverse proportion to the country's size.

"It'd save us a lot of time, Tuan Minister," Turner said. "Those robots are programmed in an obsolete language, forty years old. Strictly Neanderthal."

The minister deftly baited his hook and flicked it out in a long spinning cast. "You knew before you came here how the sultanate feels about the world information order. You shall just have to puzzle out this conundrum on your own."

"But you're making weeks, months maybe, out of a three-hour job!" Turner said.

"My dear fellow, this is Borneo," the minister said benignly. "Stop looking at your watch and pay some attention to catching us dinner."

Turner sighed and reeled in his line. Behind them, the rig's squatter population of Dayak fisherfolk clustered on the old helicopter pad, mending nets and chewing betel nut.

It was another slow Friday in Brunei Darussalam. Across the shallow bay, Brunei Town rose in tropical sunlight, its soaring highrises festooned with makeshift solar roofs, windmills, and bulging greenhouse balconies. The golden-domed mosque on the waterfront was surrounded by the towering legacy of the twentieth-century oil boom: boxlike office blocks, now bizarrely transmuted into urban farms.

Brunei Town, the sultanate's capital, had a hundred thousand citizens: Malays, Chinese, Ibans, Dayaks, and a sprinkling of Europeans. But it was a city under a hush. No cars. No airport. No television. From a distance it reminded Turner of an old Western fairy tale: Sleeping Beauty, the jury-rigged high-rises with their cascading greenery like a hundred castles shrouded in thorns. The Bruneians seemed like sleepwalkers, marooned from the world, wrapped in the enchantment of their ideology.

Turner baited his hook again, restive at being away from the production line. The minister seemed more interested in converting him than in letting him work. To the Bruneians, the robots were just another useless memento of their long-dead romance with the West. The old robot assembly line hadn't been used in twenty years, since the turn of the century.

And yet the royal government had decided to retrofit the robot line for a new project. For technical help, they had applied to Kyocera, a Japanese multinational corporation. Kyocera had sent Turner Choi, one of their new recruits, a twenty-six-year-old Chinese Canadian CAD–CAM engineer from Vancouver.

It wasn't much of a job—a kind of industrial archaeology whose main tools were chicken wire and a ball-peen hammer—but it was Turner's first and he meant to succeed. The Bruneians were relaxed to the point of coma, but Turner Choi had his future ahead of him with Kyocera. In the long run, it was Kyocera who would judge his work here. And Turner was running out of time.

The minister, whooping in triumph, hauled hard on his line. A fat, spotted fish broke the surface, flopping on the hook. Turner decided to break the rules and to hell with it.

The local neighborhood organization, the *kampong,* was showing a free movie in the little park fourteen stories below Turner's window. Bright images crawled against the bleak white Bauhaus wall of a neighboring high-rise.

Turner peered down through the blinds. He had been watching the flick all night as he finished his illegal tinkering.

The Bruneians, like Malays everywhere, adored ghost stories. The film's protagonist, or chief horror (Turner wasn't sure which), was an acrobatic monkey-demon with razor-sharp forearms. It had burst into a depraved speakeasy and was slaughtering drunkards with a tremendous windmilling flurry of punches, kicks, and screeches. Vast meaty sounds of combat, like colliding freight trains packed with beef, drifted faintly upward.

Turner sat before his bootleg keyboard, and sighed. He'd known it would come to this ever since the Bruneians had confiscated his phone at the customs. For five months he'd politely tried to work his way around it. Now he had only three months left. He was out of time and out of patience.

The robots were okay, under caked layers of yellowing grease. They'd been roped down under tarps for years. But the software manuals were a tattered ruin.

Just thinking about it gave Turner a cold sinking feeling. It was a special, private terror that had dogged him since childhood. It was the fear he felt when he had to confront his grandfather.

He thought of his grandfather's icy and pitiless eyes, fixed on him with that "Hong Kong Bad Cop" look. In the 1970s, Turner's grandfather had been one of the infamous "millionaire sergeants" of the Hong Kong police, skimming the cream of the Burmese heroin trade. He'd emigrated in the Triad bribery scandals of 1973.

After forty-seven years of silk suits and first-class flights between his mansions in Taipei and Vancouver, Grandfather Choi still had that cold eye and that grim shakedown look. It was an evil memory for Turner, of being weighed and found wanting.

The documentation was hopeless, crumbling and mildewed, alive with silverfish. The innocent Bruneians hadn't realized that the information it held was the linchpin of the whole enterprise. The sultanate had bought the factory long ago, with the last gush of Brunei's oil money, as a stylish, doomed gesture in Western industrial chic. Somehow, robots had never really caught on in Borneo.

But Turner had to seize this chance. He had to prove that he could make it on his own, without Grandfather Choi and the stifling weight of his money.

For days, Turner had snooped around down on the waterfront, with its cubbyholed rows of Chinese junkshops. It was Turner's favorite part of Brunei Town, a white-elephant's graveyard of dead tech. The wooden and bamboo shops were lined with dead, blackened televisions like decaying teeth.

There, he'd set about assembling a bootleg modern phone. He'd rescued a water-stained keyboard and screen from one of the shops. His modem and recorder came from work. On the waterfront he'd found a Panamanian freighter whose captain would illegally time-share on his satellite navigation dish.

Brunei Town was full of phone booths that no one ever seemed to use, grimy old glass-and-plastic units labeled in Malay, English, and Mandarin. A typical payphone stood on the street outside Turner's high-rise. It was an old twentieth-century job with a coin-feed and a rotary dial, and no videoscreen.

In the dead of night he'd crept down there to install a radio link to his apartment on the fourteenth floor. Someone might trace his illegal call back to the phone booth, but no farther. With the radio link, his own apartment would stay safe.

But when he'd punch-jacked the payphone's console off, he'd found that it already had a bootleg link hooked up. It was in fine working order, too. He'd seen then that he wasn't alone, and that Brunei, despite all its rhetoric about the Neo-Colonial World Information Order, was not entirely free of the global communications net. Brunei was wired too, just like the West, but the net had gone underground.

All those abandoned payphones had taken on a new and mildly sinister significance for him since that discovery, but he wasn't going to kick. All his plans were riding on his chance to get through.

Now he was ready. He rechecked the satellite guide in the back of his ASME handbook. *Arabsat 7* was up, in its leisurely low-orbit ramble over the tropics. Turner dialed from his apartment down through the payphone outside, then patched in through the Panamanian dish. Through *Arabsat* he hooked up to an American geosynchronous sat and down into the American ground net. From there he direct-dialed his brother's house.

Georgie Choi was at breakfast in Vancouver, dressed in a French-cuffed pinstripe shirt and varsity sweater. Behind him, Turner's sleek sister-in-law, Marjorie, presided over a table crowded with crisp linen napkins and silver cutlery. Turner's two young nieces decorously spread jam on triangles of toast.

"Is it you, Turner?" Georgie said. "I'm not getting any video."

"I couldn't get a camera," Turner said. "I'm in Brunei—phone quarantine, remember? I had to bootleg it just to get sound."

A monsoon breeze blew up outside Turner's window. The wind-power generators bolted to the high-rise walls whirred into life, and threw broad bars of raw static across the screen. Georgie's smooth brow wrinkled gracefully. "This reception is terrible! You're not even in stereo." He smiled uncertainly. "No matter, we'll make do. We haven't heard from you in ages. Things all right?"

"They will be," Turner said. "How's Grandfather?"

"He's flown in from Taipei for dialysis and his blood change," Georgie said. "He hates hospitals, but I had good news for him." He hesitated. "We have a new great-grandchild on the way."

Marjorie glanced up and bestowed one of her glittering wifely smiles on the camera. "That's fine," Turner said reflexively. Children were a touchy subject with Turner. He had not yet married, despite his family's endless prodding and nagging.

He thought guiltily that he should have spent more time with Georgie's children. Georgie was already in some upscale never-never land, all leather-bound law and municipal politics, but it wasn't his kids' fault. Kids were innocent. "Hi, kids," he said in Mandarin. "I'll bring you something you'll like."

The younger girl looked up, her elegant child's mouth crusted with strawberry jam. "I want a shrunken head," she said in English.

"You see?" Georgie said with false joviality. "This is what comes of running off to Borneo."

"I need some modem software," Turner said, avoiding the issue. Grandfather hadn't approved of Borneo. "Could you get it off the old Hayes in my room?"

"If you don't have a modem protocol, how can I send you a program?" Georgie said.

"Print it out and hold it up to the screen," Turner explained patiently. "I'll record it and type it in later by hand."

"That's clever," Georgie said. "You engineers."

He left to set it up. Turner talked guardedly to Marjorie. He had never been able to figure the woman out. Turner would have liked to know how Marjorie really felt about cold-eyed Bad Cop Grandfather and his eight million dollars in Triad heroin money.

But Marjorie was so coolly elegant, so brilliantly designed, that Turner had never been able to bring himself to probe her real feelings. It would have been like popping open some factory-sealed peripheral that was still under warranty, just so you could sneak a look at the circuit boards.

Even he and Georgie never talked frankly anymore. Not since Grandfather's health had turned shaky. The prospect of finally inheriting that money had left a white hush over his family like fifteen feet of Canadian snow.

The horrible old man relished the competition for his favor. He insisted on it. Grandfather had a second household in Taipei; Turner's uncle and cousins. If Grandfather chose them over his Canadian brood, Georgie's perfect life would go to pieces.

A childhood memory brushed Turner: Georgie's toys, brightly painted little Hong Kong windups held together with folded tin flaps. As a child, Turner had spent many happy, covert hours dexterously prying Georgie's toys apart.

Marjorie chatted about Turner's mother, a neurotic widow who ran an antique store in Atlanta. Behind her, a Chinese maid began clearing the table, glancing up at the camera with the spooked eyes of an immigrant fresh off the boat.

Turner was used to phone cameras, and though he didn't have one he kept a fixed smile through habit. But he could feel himself souring, his face knotting up in that inherited Bad Cop glare. Turner had his grandfather's face, with hollow cheeks, and sunken eyes under heavy impressive brows.

But Canada, Turner's birthplace, had left its mark on him. Years of steak and Wonder Bread had given him a six-foot frame and the build of a linebacker.

Georgie came back with the printout. Turner said goodbye and cut the link.

He pulled up the blinds for the climax of the movie downstairs. The monkey-demon massacred a small army of Moslem extremists in the corroded remnants of a Shell refinery. Moslem fanatics had been stock villains in Brunei since the failure of their coup of '98.

The last of the reel flickered loose. Turner unpinned a banana-leaf wrapping and dug his chopsticks into a midnight snack of rice

fried with green pineapple. He leaned on the open window, prop-
ping one booted foot on the massive window box with its dense
ranks of onions and pepper plants.

The call to Vancouver had sent a shiver of culture shock through
him. He saw his apartment with new eyes. It was decorated with
housewarming gifts from other members of his *kampong*. A flat
leather shadow-puppet, all perforations and curlicues. A gold-framed
photo of the sultan shaking hands with the king of England. A hand-
painted glass ant farm full of inch-long Borneo ants, torpid on
molasses. And a young banyan bonsai tree from the *kampong* headman.

The headman, an elderly Malay, was a political wardheeler for
Brunei's ruling party, the Greens, or "Partai Ekolojasi." In the West,
the Greens had long ago been co-opted into larger parties. But
Brunei's Partai Ekolojasi had twenty years of deep roots.

The banyan tree came with five pages of meticulous instructions
on care and feeding, but despite Turner's best efforts the midget tree
was yellowing and shedding leaves. The tree was not just a gift; it
was a test, and Turner knew it. The *kampong* smiled, but they had
their ways of testing, and they watched.

Turner glanced reflexively at his deadbolt on the door. The locks
were not exactly forbidden, but they were frowned on. The Greens
had converted Brunei's old office buildings into huge multilayered
village longhouses. Western notions of privacy were unpopular.

But Turner needed the lock for his work. He had to be discreet.
Brunei might seem loose and informal, but it was still a one-party
state under autocratic rule.

Twenty years earlier, when the oil crash had hit, the monarchy
had seemed doomed. The Muslim insurgents had tried to murder
them outright. Even the Greens had had bigger dreams then. Turner
had seen their peeling, forgotten wall posters, their global logo of
the Whole Earth half-buried under layered years of want ads and soc-
cer schedules.

The Royal Family had won through, a symbol of tradition and
stability. They'd weathered the storm of the Muslim insurgence, and
stifled the Greens' first wild ambitions. After five months in Brunei,
Turner, like the Royals, had grasped Brunei's hidden dynamics. It was
adat, Malay custom, that ruled. And the first law of *adat* was that you
didn't embarrass your neighbors.

Turner unpinned his favorite movie poster, a big promotional
four-sheet for a Brunei historical epic. In garish four-color printing, a

boatload of heroic Malay pirates gallantly advanced on a sinister Portuguese galleon. Turner had carved a hideout in the sheetrock wall behind the poster. He stowed his phone gear.

Somebody tried the door, hit the deadbolt, and knocked softly. Turner hastily smoothed the poster and pinned it up.

He opened the door. It was his Australian neighbor, McGinty, a retired newscaster from Melbourne. McGinty loved Brunei for its utter lack of televisions. It was one of the last places on the planet in which one could truly get away from it all.

McGinty glanced up and down the hall, stepped inside, and reached into his loose cotton blouse. He produced a cold quart can of Foster's Lager. "Have a beer, chum?"

"Fantastic!" Turner said. "Where'd you get it?"

McGinty smiled evasively. "The bloody fridge is on the blink, and I thought you'd fancy one while they're still cold."

"Right," Turner said, popping the top. "I'll have a look at your fridge as soon as I destroy this evidence." The *kampong* ran on a web of barter and mutual obligation. Turner's skills were part of it. It was tiresome, but a Foster's Lager was good pay. It was a big improvement over the liquid brain damage from the illegal stills down on Floor 4.

They went to McGinty's place. McGinty lived next door with his aged parents; four of them, for his father and mother had divorced and both remarried. The ancient Australians thrived in Brunei's somnolent atmosphere, pottering about the *kampong* gardens in pith helmets, gurkha shorts, and khaki bush vests. McGinty, like many of his generation, had never had children. Now in retirement he seemed content to shepherd these older folk, plying them with megavitamins and morning Tai Chi exercises.

Turner stripped the refrigerator. "It's your compressor," he said. "I'll track you down one on the waterfront. I can jury-rig something. You know me. Always tinkering."

McGinty looked uncomfortable, since he was now in Turner's debt. Suddenly he brightened. "There's a party at the privy councilor's tomorrow night. Jimmy Brooke. You know him?"

"Heard of him," Turner said. He'd heard rumors about Brooke: hints of corruption, some long-buried scandal. "He was a big man when the Partai got started, right? Minister of something."

"Communications."

Turner laughed. "That's not much of a job around here."

"Well, he still knows a lot of movie people." McGinty lowered his voice. "And he has a private bar. He's chummy with the Royal Family. They make allowances for him."

"Yeah?" Turner didn't relish mingling with McGinty's social circle of wealthy retirees, but it might be smart, politically. A word with the old com minister might solve a lot of his problems. "Okay," he said. "Sounds like fun."

The privy councilor, Yang Amat Mulia Pengiran Indera Negara Pengiran Jimmy Brooke, was one of Brunei's odder relics. He was a British tax exile, a naturalized Bruneian, who had shown up in the late '90s after the oil crash. His wealth had helped cushion the blow and had won him a place in the government.

Larger and better-organized governments might have thought twice about co-opting this deaf, white-haired eccentric, a washed-up pop idol with a parasitic retinue of balding bohemians. But the aging rock star, with his decaying glamour, fit in easily with the comic-opera glitter of Brunei's tiny aristocracy. He owned the old Bank of Singapore office block, a *kampong* of remarkable looseness where peccadillos flourished under Brooke's noblesse oblige.

Monsoon rain pelted the city. Brooke's henchmen, paunchy bodyguards in bulging denim, had shut the glass doors of the pent-house and turned on the air conditioning. The party had close to a hundred people, mostly retired Westerners from Europe and Austra-lia. They had the stifling clubbiness of exiles who have all known each other too long. A handful of refugee Americans, still powdered and rouged with their habitual video makeup, munched imported beer nuts by the long mahogany bar.

The Bruneian actress Dewi Serrudin was holding court on a rattan couch, surrounded by admirers. Cinema was a lost art in the West, finally murdered and buried by video; but Brunei's odd policies had given it a last toehold. Turner, who had a mild long-distance crush on the actress, edged up between two hopeful émigrés: a portly Madrasi producer in dhoti and jubbah, and a Hong Kong chop-socky director in a black frogged cotton jacket.

Miss Serrudin, in a gold lamé blouse and a skirt of antique ultrasuede, was playing the role to the hilt, chattering brightly and chain-burning imported Rothmans in a jade holder. She had the ritual concentration of a Balinese dancer evoking postures handed down through the centuries. And she was older than he'd thought she was.

Turner finished his whiskey sour and handed it to one of Brooke's balding gofers. He felt depressed and lonely. He wandered away from the crowd, and turned down a hall at random. The walls were hung with gold albums and old yellowing pub-shots of Brooke and his band, all rhinestones and platform heels, their flying hair lavishly backlit with klieg lights.

Turner passed a library, and a billiards room where two wrinkled, turbaned Sikhs were racking up a game of snooker. Farther down the hall, he glanced through an archway, into a sunken conversation pit lavishly carpeted with ancient, indestructible synthetic plush.

A bony young Malay woman in black jeans and a satin jacket sat alone in the room, reading a month-old issue of *New Musical Express*. It was headlined "Leningrad Pop Cuts Loose!" Her sandaled feet were propped on a coffee table next to a beaten silver platter with a pitcher and an ice bucket. Her bright red, shoulder-length hair showed two long inches of black roots.

She looked up at him in blank surprise. Turner hesitated at the archway, then stepped into the room. "Hi," he said.

"Hello. What's your *kampong?*"

"Citibank Building," Turner said. He was used to the question by now. "I'm with the industrial ministry, consulting engineer. I'm a Canadian. Turner Choi."

She folded the newspaper and smiled. "Ah, you're the bloke who's working on the robots."

"Word gets around," Turner said, pleased.

She watched him narrowly. "Seria Bolkiah Mu'izzaddin Wad-daulah."

"Sorry, I don't speak Malay."

"That's my name," she said.

Turner laughed. "Oh, Lord. Look, I'm just a no-neck Canuck with hay in my hair. Make allowances, okay?"

"You're a Western technician," she said. "How exotic. How is your work progressing?"

"It's a strange assignment," Turner said. He sat on the couch at a polite distance, marveling at her bizarre accent. "You've spent some time in Britain?"

"I went to school there." She studied his face. "You look rather like a Chinese Keith Richards."

"Sorry, don't know him."

"The guitarist of the Rolling Stones."

"I don't keep up with the new bands," Turner said. "A little Russian pop, maybe." He felt a peculiar tension in the situation. Turner glanced quickly at the woman's hands. No wedding ring, so that wasn't it.

"Would you like a drink?" the woman said. "It's grape juice."

"Sure," Turner said. "Thanks." She poured gracefully: innocent grape juice over ice. She was a Moslem, Turner thought, despite her dyed hair. Maybe that was why she was oddly standoffish.

He would have to bend the rules again. She was not conventionally pretty, but she had the kind of neurotic intensity that Turner had always found fatally attractive. And his love life had suffered in Brunei; the *kampongs* with their prying eyes and village gossip had cramped his style.

He wondered how he could arrange to see her. It wasn't a question of just asking her out to dinner—it all depended on her *kampong*. Some were stricter than others. He might end up with half-a-dozen veiled Muslim chaperones—or maybe a gang of muscular cousins and brothers with a bad attitude about Western lechers.

"When do you plan to start production, Mr. Choi?"

Turner said, "We've built a few fishing skiffs already, just minor stuff. We have bigger plans once the robots are up."

"A real factory," she said. "Like the old days."

Turner smiled, seeing his chance. "Maybe you'd like a tour of the plant?"

"It sounds romantic," she said. "Those robots are free labor. They were supposed to take the place of our free oil when it ran out. Brunei used to be rich, you know. Oil paid for everything. The Shellfare state, they used to call us." She smiled wistfully.

"How about Monday?" Turner said.

She looked at him, surprised, and suddenly blushed. "I'm afraid not."

Turner caught her eye. It's not me, he thought. It was something in the way—*adat* or something. "It's all right," he said gently. "I'd like to see you, is that so bad? Bring your whole *kampong* if you want."

"My *kampong* is the Palace," she said.

"Uh-oh." Suddenly he had that cold feeling again.

"You didn't know," she said triumphantly. "You thought I was just some rock groupie."

"Who are you, then?"

"I'm the Duli Yang Maha Mulia Diranee. . . . Well, I'm the princess. Princess Seria." She smiled.

"Good lord." He had been sitting and flirting with the royal princess of Brunei. It was bizarre. He half expected a troupe of bronzed eunuchs to burst in, armed with scimitars. "You're the sultan's daughter?"

"You mustn't think too much of it," she said. "Our country is only two thousand square miles. It's so small that it's a family business, that's all. The mayor of your Vancouver rules more people than my family does."

Turner sipped his grape juice to cover his confusion. Brunei was a Commonwealth country, after all, with a British-educated aristocracy. The sultan had polo ponies and cricket pitches. But still, a princess . . .

"I never said I was from Vancouver," he told her. "You knew who I was all along."

"Brunei doesn't have many tall Chinese in lumberjack shirts." She smiled wickedly. "And those boots."

Turner glanced down. His legs were armored in knee-high engineering boots, a mass of shiny leather and buckles. His mother had bought them for him, convinced that they would save his life from snakebite in savage Borneo. "I promised I'd wear them," he said. "Family obligation."

She looked sour. "You, too? That sounds all too familiar, Mr. Choi." Now that the spell of anonymity was broken, she seemed flustered. Their quick rapport was grinding to a halt. She lifted the music paper with a rustle of pages. He saw that her nails were gnawed down to the quick.

For some perverse reason this put Turner's libido jarringly back into gear. She had that edgy flyaway look that spelled trouble with a capital *T*. Ironically, she was just his type.

"I know the mayor's daughter in Vancouver," he said deliberately. "I like the local version a lot better."

She met his eyes. "It's really too bad about family obligations. . . ."

The privy councilor appeared suddenly in the archway. The wizened rock star wore a cream-colored seersucker suit with ruby cuff links. He was a cadaverous old buzzard with rheumy eyes and a wattled neck. A frizzed mass of snow-white hair puffed from his head like cotton from an aspirin bottle.

"Highness," he said loudly. "We need a fourth at bridge."

Princess Seria stood up with an air of martyrdom. "I'll be right with you," she shouted.

"And who's the young man?" said Brooke, revealing his dentures in an uneasy smile.

Turner stepped nearer. "Turner Choi, Tuan Privy Councilor," he said loudly. "A privilege to meet you, sir."

"What's your *kampong*, Mr. Chong?"

"Mr. Choi is working on the robot shipyard!" the princess said.

"The what? The shipyard? Oh, splendid!" Brooke seemed re-lieved.

"I'd like a word with you, sir," Turner said. "About communications."

"About what?" Brooke cupped one hand to his ear.

"The phone net, sir! A line out!"

The princess looked startled. But Brooke, still not understanding, nodded blankly. "Ah yes. Very interesting . . . My entourage and I will bop by some day when you have the line up! I love the sound of good machines at work!"

"Sure," Turner said, recognizing defeat. "That would be, uh, groovy."

"Brunei is counting on you, Mr. Chong," Brooke said, his wrinkled eyes gleaming with bogus sincerity. "Good to see you here. Enjoy yourself." He shook Turner's hand, pressing something into his palm. He winked at Turner and escorted the princess out into the hall.

Turner looked at his hand. The old man had given him a mari-juana cigarette. Turner shook himself, laughed, and threw it away.

Another slow Monday in Brunei Town. Turner's work crew mean-dered in around midmorning. They were Bruneian Chinese, toting wicker baskets stuffed with garden-fresh produce, and little lac-quered lunchboxes with *satay* shish kebabs and hot shrimp paste. They started the morning's food barter, chatting languidly in Malay-accented Mandarin.

Turner had very little power over them. They were hired by the Industrial Ministry, and paid little or nothing. Their labor was part of the invisible household economy of the *kampongs*. They worked for *kampong* perks, like chickens or movie tickets.

The shipyard was a cavernous barn with overhead pulley tracks and an oil-stained concrete floor. The front section, with its bare launching rails sloping down to deep water, had once been a Dayak *kampong*. The Dayaks had spraybombed the concrete-block walls with giant neon-bright murals of banshees dead in childbirth, and leaping cricket-spirits with evil Day-Glo eyes.

The back part was two-story, with the robots' machine shop at ground level and a glass-fronted office upstairs that looked down over the yard.

Inside, the office was decorated in crass '80s High-Tech Moderne, with round-cornered computer desks between sleek modular parti-tions, all tubular chrome and grainy beige plastic. The plastic had aged hideously in forty years, absorbing a gray miasma of fingerprints and soot.

Turner worked alone in the neck-high maze of curved partitions, where a conspiracy of imported clerks and programmers had once efficiently sopped up the last of Brunei's oil money. He was typing up the bootlegged modem software on the IBM, determined to call America and get the production line out of the Stone Age.

The yard reeked of hot epoxy as the crew got to work. The robots were one-armed hydraulic jobs, essentially glorified tea-trolleys with single swivel-jointed manipulators. Turner had managed to get them up to a certain crude level of donkeywork: slicing wood, stirring glue, hauling heavy bundles of lumber.

But, so far, the crew handled all the craftwork. They laminated the long strips of shaved lumber into sturdy panels of epoxied plywood. They bent the wet panels into hull and deck shapes, steam-sealing them over curved molds. They lapped and veneered the seams, and painted good-luck eye-symbols on the bows.

So far, the plant had produced nothing larger than a twenty-foot skiff. But on the drawing boards was a series of freighter-sized floating *kampongs*, massive sail-powered trimarans for the deep ocean, with glassed-in greenhouse decks.

The ships would be cheap and slow, like most things in Brunei, but pleasant enough, Turner supposed. Lots of slow golden afternoons on the tropical seas, with plenty of fresh fruit. The whole effort seemed rather pointless, but at least it would break Brunei's isolation from the world, and give them a crude merchant fleet.

The foreman, a spry old Chinese named Leng, shouted for Turner from the yard. Turner saved his program, got up, and looked down through the office glass. The minister of industrial policy had arrived, tying up an ancient fiberglass speedboat retrofitted with ribbed lateen sails.

Turner hurried down, groaning to himself, expecting to be invited off for another avuncular lecture. But the minister's zenlike languor had been broken. He came almost directly to the point, pausing only to genially accept some coconut milk from the foreman.

"It's His Highness the Sultan," the minister said. "Someone's put a bee in his bonnet about these robots. Now he wants to tour the plant."

"When?" Turner said.

"Two weeks," said the minister. "Or maybe three."

Turner thought it over, and smiled. He sensed the princess's hand in this and felt deeply flattered.

"I say," the minister said. "You seem awfully pleased for a fellow who was predicting disaster just last Friday."

"I found another section of the manual," Turner lied glibly. "I hope to have real improvements in short order."

"Splendid," said the minister. "You remember the prototype we were discussing?"

"The quarter-scale model?" Turner said. "Tuan Minister, even in miniature, that's still a fifty-foot trimaran."

"Righto. How about it? Do you think you could scatter the blueprints about, have the robots whir by looking busy, plenty of sawdust and glue?"

Politics, Turner thought. He gave the minister his Bad Cop look. "You mean some kind of Potemkin village. Don't you want the ship built?"

"I fail to see what pumpkins have to do with it," said the minister, wounded. "This is a state occasion. We shall have the newsreel cameras in. Of course build the ship. I simply want it impressive, that's all."

Impressive, Turner thought. Sure. If Seria was watching, why not?

Luckily the Panamanian freighter was still in port, not leaving till Wednesday. Armed with his new software, Turner tried another bootleg raid at ten P.M. He caught a Brazilian comsat and tied into Detroit.

Reception was bad, and Doris had already moved twice. But he found her finally in a seedy condominium in the Renaissance Center historical district.

"Where's your video, man?"

"It's out," Turner lied, not wanting to burden his old girlfriend with two years of past history. He and Doris had lived together in Toronto for two semesters while he studied CAD–CAM. Doris was an automotive designer, a Rustbelt refugee from Detroit's collapse.

For Turner, school was a blissful chance to live in the same pair of jeans for days on end, but times were tough in the Rustbelt and Doris had lived close to the bone. He'd ended up footing the bills, which hadn't bothered him (Bad Cop money), but it had preyed on Doris's mind. Months passed, and she spent more each week. He picked up her bills without a word, and she quietly went over the edge. She ended up puking drunk on her new satin sheets, unable to go downstairs for the mail without a line of coke.

But then word had come of his father's death. His father's antique Maserati had slammed head-on into an automated semitrailer rig.

Turner and his brother had attended the cremation in a drizzling Vancouver rain. They put the ashes on the family altar and knelt before little gray ribbons of incense smoke. Nobody said much. They didn't talk about Dad's drinking. Grandfather wouldn't have liked it.

When he'd gone back to Toronto, he found that Doris had packed up and left.

"I'm with Kyocera now," he told her. "The consulting engineers."

"You got a job, Turner?" she said, brushing back a frizzed tangle of blonde hair. "It figures. Poor people are standing in line for a chance to do dishes." She frowned. "What kind of hours you keeping, man? It's seven A.M. You caught me without my vid makeup."

She turned the camera away and walked out of sight. Turner studied her apartment: concrete blocks and packing crates, vinyl beanbag chairs, peeling walls festooned with printout. She was still on the Net, all right. Real Net-heads resented every penny not spent on information.

"I need some help, Doris. I need you to find me someone who can system-crack an old IBM robotics language called AML."

"Yeah?" she called out. "Ten percent agent's fee?"

"Sure. And this is on the hush, okay? Not Kyocera's business, just mine."

He heard her shouting from the condo's cramped bathroom. "I haven't heard from you in two years! You're not mad that I split, huh?"

"No."

"It wasn't that you were Chinese, okay? I mean, you're about as Chinese as maple syrup, right? It's just, the high life was making my sinuses bleed."

Turner scowled. "Look, it's okay. It was a temporary thing."

"I was crazy then. But I've been hooked up to a good shrink program, it's done wonders for me, really." She came back to the screen; she'd put on rouge and powder. She smiled and touched her cheek. "Good stuff, huh? The kind the President uses."

"You look fine."

"My shrink makes me jog every day. So, how you doin', man? Seeing anybody?"

"Not really." He smiled. "Except a princess of Borneo."

She laughed. "I thought you'd settle down by now, man. With some uptown family girl, right? Like your brother and what's-her-face."

"Didn't work out that way."

"You like crazy women, Turner, that's your problem. Remember the time your mom dropped by? She's a fruitcake, that's why."

"Aw, Jesus Christ, Doris," Turner said. "If I need a shrink, I can download one."

"Okay," she said, hurt. She touched a remote control. A television in the corner of the room flashed into life with a crackle of video music. Doris didn't bother to watch it. She'd turned it on by reflex, settling into the piped flow of cable like a hot bath. "Look, I'll see what I can scare you up on the Net. AML language, right? I think I know a—"

BREAK

The screen went blank. Alphanumerics flared up: **ENTERING (C)HAT MODE**

The line zipped up the screen. Then words spelled out in 80-column glowing bright green. **WHAT ARE YOU DOING ON THIS LINE??**

SORRY, Turner typed.

ENTER YOUR PASSWORD:

Turner thought fast. He had blundered into the Brunei underground net. He'd known it was possible, since he was using the prerigged payphone downstairs. **MAPLE SYRUP,** he typed at random.

CHECKING . . . THAT IS NOT A VALID PASSWORD.

SIGNING OFF, Turner typed.

WAIT, said the screen. **WE DON'T TAKE LURKERS LIGHTLY HERE. WE HAVE BEEN WATCHING YOU. THIS IS THE SECOND TIME YOU HAVE ACCESSED A SATELLITE. WHAT ARE YOU DOING IN OUR NET??**

Turner rested one finger on the off switch.

More words spilled out. **WE KNOW WHO YOU ARE, "MAPLE SYRUP." YOU ARE TURNER CHONG.**

"Turner *Choi,*" Turner said aloud. Then he remembered the man who had made that mistake. He felt a sudden surge of glee. He typed: **OKAY, YOU'VE GOT ME—TUAN COUNCILOR JIMMY BROOKE!**

There was a long blank space. Then: **CLEVER,** Brooke typed. **SERIA TOLD YOU. SERIA, ARE YOU ON THIS LINE??**

I WANT HER NUMBER!! Turner typed at once.

THEN LEAVE A (M)ESSAGE FOR "GAMELAN ROCKER," Brooke typed. **I AM "NET HEADHUNTER."**

THANKS, Turner typed.

I'LL LOG YOU ON, MAPLE SYRUP. SINCE YOU'RE ALREADY IN,

YOU'D BETTER BE IN ON OUR TERMS. BUT JUST REMEMBER: THIS IS
OUR ELECTRIC KAMPONG, SO YOU LIVE BY OUR RULES. OUR
"ADAT," OKAY??
    I'LL REMEMBER, SIR.
    AND NO MORE BOOTLEG SATELLITE LINKS, YOU'RE SCREWING
UP OUR GROUND LINES.
    OKAY, Turner typed.
    YOU CAN RENT TIME ON OUR OWN DISHES. NEXT TIME CALL
85-1515 DIRECTLY. OUR GAMES SECTION COULD USE SOME UP-
LOADS, BY THE WAY.
    The words flashed off, replaced by the neatly ranked commands
of a computer bulletin board. Turner accessed the message section,
but then sat sweating and indecisive. In his mind, his quick message
to Seria was rapidly ramifying into a particularly touchy and tentative
love letter.

    This was good, but it wasn't how he'd planned it. He was getting
in over his head. He'd have to think it through.
    He logged off the board. Doris's face appeared at once. "Where
the hell have you been, man?"
    "Sorry," Turner said.
    "I've found you some old geezer out in Yorktown Heights," she
said. "He says he used to work with Big Blue back in prehistory."
    "It's always some old geezer," Turner said in resignation.
    Doris shrugged. "Whaddya expect, man? Birth control got every-
body else."

Down in the yard, the sultan of Brunei chatted with his minister as
technicians in sarongs and rubber sandals struggled with their huge,
ancient cameras. The sultan wore his full regalia, a high-collared red
military jacket with gold-braided shoulder boards, heavy with medals
and pins. He was an elderly Malay with a neatly clipped white mustache and sad, wise eyes.
    His son, the crown prince, had a silk ascot and an air force pilot's
jacket. Turner had heard that the prince was nuts about helicopters.
Seria's formal wear looked like a jazzed-up Girl Guide's outfit, with a
prim creased skirt and a medal-clustered shoulder sash.
    Turner was alone in the programming room, double-checking
one of the canned routines he'd downloaded from America. They'd
done wonders for the plant already; the robots had completed one
hull of the trimaran. The human crew was handling the delicate
work: the glassed-in greenhouse. Braced sections of glass now hung

from ceiling pulleys, gleaming photogenically in geodesic wooden frames.

Turner studied his screen.

IF QMONITOR (FMONS(2)) EQ O THEN RETURN('TOO SMALL')
TOGO = GRIPPER-OPENING+MIN-OFS-QPOSITION(GRIPPER)
DMOVE(XYZ#(GRIPPER), (-TOGO/2*HANDFRAME) (2,2))#(TOGO),
FMONS(2));

This was more like it! Despite its low-powered crudity, AML was becoming obsessive with him, its rhythms sticking like poetry. He picked up his coffee cup, thinking: **REACH-GRASP-TOGO = (MOUTH) +SIP; RETURN.**

The sluggishness of Brunei had vanished overnight once he'd hooked to the Net. The screen had eaten up his life. A month had passed since his first bootleg run. All day he worked on AML; at night he went home to trade electronic mail with Seria.

Their romance had grown through the Net; not through modern video, but through the ancient bulletin board's anonymous green text. Day by day it became more intense, for it was all kept in a private section of memory, and nothing could be taken back. There were over a hundred messages on their secret disks, starting coolly and teasingly, and working slowly up through real passion to a kind of mutual panic.

They hadn't planned it to happen like this. It was part of the dynamic of the Net. For Seria, it had been a rare chance to escape her role and talk to an interesting stranger. Turner was only looking for the kind of casual feminine solace that had never been hard to find. The Net had tricked them.

Because they couldn't see each other. Turner realized now that no woman had ever known and understood him as Seria did, for the simple reason that he had never had to talk to one so much. If things had gone as they were meant to in the West, he thought, they would have chased their attraction into bed and killed it there. Their two worlds would have collided bruisingly, and they would have smiled over the orange juice next morning and mumbled tactful goodbyes.

But that wasn't how it had happened. Over the weeks, it had all come pouring out between them: his family, her family, their resentment, his loneliness, her petty constraints, all those irritants that ulcerate a single person, but are soothed by two. Bizarrely, they had more in common than he could have ever expected. Real things, things that mattered.

The painfully simple local Net filtered human relations down to a single channel of printed words, leaving only a high-flown Platonic essence. Their relationship had grown into a classic, bloodless, spiritual romance in its most intense and dangerous sense. Human beings weren't meant to live such roles. It was the stuff of high drama because it could very easily drive you crazy.

He had waited on tenterhooks for her visit to the shipyard. It had taken a month instead of two weeks, but he'd expected as much. That was the way of Brunei.

"Hello, Maple Syrup."

Turner started violently and stood up. "Seria!"

She threw herself into his arms with a hard thump. He staggered back, hugging her. "No kissing," she said hastily. "Ugh, it's nasty."

He glanced down at the shipyard and hauled her quickly out of sight of the window. "How'd you get up here?"

"I sneaked up the stairs. They're not looking. I had to see you. The real you, not just words on a screen."

"This is crazy." He lifted her off the ground, squeezing her hard. "God, you feel wonderful."

"So do you. Ouch, my medals, be careful."

He set her back down. "We've got to do better than this. Look, where can I see you?"

She gripped his hands feverishly. "Finish the boat, Turner. Brooke wants it, his new toy. Maybe we can arrange something." She pulled his shirttail out and ran her hands over his midriff. Turner felt a rush of arousal so intense that his ears rang. He reached down and ran his hand up the back of her thigh. "Don't wrinkle my skirt!" she said, trembling. "I have to go on camera!"

Turner said, "This place is nowhere. It isn't right for you, you need fast cars and daiquiris and television and jet trips to the goddamn Bahamas."

"So romantic," she whispered hotly. "Like rock stars, Turner. Huge stacks of amps and mobs at the airport. Turner, if you could see what I'm wearing under this, you'd go crazy."

She turned her face away. "Stop trying to kiss me! You Western-ers are weird. Mouths are for eating."

"You've got to get used to Western things, precious."

"You can't take me away, Turner. My people wouldn't let you."

"We'll think of something. Maybe Brooke can help."

"Even Brooke can't leave," she said. "All his money's here. If he tried, they would freeze his funds. He'd be penniless."

"Then I'll stay here," he said recklessly. "Sooner or later we'll have our chance."

"And give up all your money, Turner?"

He shrugged. "You know I don't want it."

She smiled sadly. "You tell me that now, but wait till you see your real world again."

"No, listen—"

Lights flashed on in the yard.

"I have to go, they'll miss me. Let go, let go." She pulled free of him with vast, tearing reluctance. Then she turned and ran.

In the days that followed, Turner worked obsessively, linking subroutines like data tinkertoys, learning as he went along, adding each day's progress to the master program. Once it was all done, and he had weeded out the redundance, it would be self-sustaining. The robots would take over, transforming information into boats. He would be through. And his slow days in Brunei would be history.

After his job, he'd vaguely planned to go to Tokyo, for a sentimental visit to Kyocera corporate headquarters. He'd been recruited through the Net; he'd never actually seen anyone from Kyocera in the flesh.

That was standard practice. Kyocera's true existence was as data, not as real estate. A modern multinational company was not its buildings or its stock. Its real essence was its ability to pop up on a screen, and to funnel that special information known as money through the global limbo of electronic banking.

He'd never given this a second thought. It was old hat. But filtering both work and love life through the screen had left him feeling Net-burned. He took to long morning walks through Brunei Town after marathon sessions at the screen, stretching cramped muscles and placing his feet with a dazed AML deliberation: **TOGO = DMOVE (KNEE)+QPOSITION(FOOT).**

He felt ghostlike in the abandoned streets; Brunei had no nightlife to speak of, and a similar lack of muggers and predators. Everybody was in everyone else's lap, doing each other's laundry, up at dawn to the shrieks of *kampong* roosters. People gossiped about you if you were a mugger. Pretty soon you'd have nightsoil duty and have to eat bruised mangos.

When the rain caught him, as it often did in the early morning, he would take shelter in the corner bus stations. The bus stops were built of tall glass tubes, aquaculture cylinders, murky green soups full of algae and fat, sluggish carp.

He would think about staying then, sheltered in Brunei forever, like a carp behind warm glass. Like one of those little bonsai trees in

its cramped and cozy little pot, with people always watching over
you, trimming you to fit. That was Brunei for you—the whole East,
really—wonderful community, but people always underfoot and in
your face. . . .

But was the West any better? Old people locked away in bursting
retirement homes. . . . Soaring unemployment, with no one knowing
when some robot or expert system would make him obsolete. . . .
People talking over televisions when they didn't know the face of the
man next door. . . .

Could he really give up the West, he wondered, abandon his
family, ruin his career? It was the craziest sort of romantic gesture, he
thought, because even if he was brave or stupid enough to break all
the rules, she wouldn't. Seria would never escape her *adat*. Being
royalty was worse than Triad.

A maze of plans spun through his head like an error-trapping
loop, always coming up empty. He would sit dazedly and watch the
fish circle in murky water, feeling like a derelict, and wondering if he
was losing his mind.

Privy Councilor Brooke bought the boat. He showed up suddenly at
the shipyard one afternoon, with his claque of followers. They'd
brought a truckload of saplings in tubs of dirt. They began at once to
load them aboard the greenhouse, clumping up and down the
stepladders to the varnished deck.

Brooke oversaw the loading for a while, checking a deck plan
from the pocket of his white silk jacket. Then he jerked his thumb at
the glassed-in front of the data center. "Let's go upstairs for a little
talk, Turner."

Mercifully, Brooke had brought his hearing aid. They sat in two of
the creaking, musty swivel chairs. "It's a good ship," Brooke said.

"Thanks."

"I knew it would be. It was my idea, you know."

Turner poured coffee. "It figures," he said.

Brooke cackled. "You think it's a crazy notion, don't you? Using
robots to build tubs out of cheap glue and scrubwood. But your
head's on backwards, boy. You engineers are all mystics. Always
goosing God with some new Tower of Babel. Masters of nature,
masters of space and time. Aim at the stars, and hit London."

Turner scowled. "Look, Tuan Councilor, I did my job. Nothing in
the contract says I have to share your politics."

"No," Brooke said. "But the sultanate could use a man like you.
You're a *bricoleur*, Chong. You can make do. You can retrofit. That's

what *bricolage* is—it's using the clutter and rubble to make something worth having. Brunei's too poor now to start over with fresh clean plans. We've got nothing but the junk the West conned us into buying, every last bloody Coke can and two-car garage. And now we have to live in the rubble, and make it a community. It's a tough job, *bricolage*. It takes a special kind of man, a special eye, to make the ruins bloom."

"Not me," Turner said. He was in one of his tough-minded moods. Something about Brooke made him leery. Brooke had a peculiar covert sleaziness about him. It probably came from a lifetime of evading drug laws.

And Turner had been expecting this final push; people in his *kampong* had been dropping hints for weeks. They didn't want him to leave; they were always stopping by with pathetic little gifts. "This place is one big hothouse," he said. "Your little *kampongs* are like orchids, they can only grow under glass. Brunei's already riddled with the Net. Someday it'll break open your glass bubble, and let the rest of the world in. Then a hard rain's gonna fall."

Brooke stared. "You like Bob Dylan?"

"Who?" Turner said, puzzled.

Brooke, confused, sipped his coffee, and grimaced. "You've been drinking this stuff? Jesus, no wonder you never sleep."

Turner glowered at him. Nobody in Brunei could mind their own business. Eyes were everywhere, with tongues to match. "You already know my real trouble."

"Sure." Brooke smiled with a yellowed gleam of dentures. "I have this notion that I'll sail upriver, lad. A little shakedown cruise for a couple of days. I could use a technical adviser, if you can mind your manners around royalty."

Turner's heart leapt. He smiled shakily. "Then I'm your man, Councilor."

They bashed a bottle of nonalcoholic grape juice across the center bow and christened the ship the *Mambo Sun*. Turner's work crew launched her down the rails and stepped the masts. She was crewed by a family of Dayaks from one of the offshore rigs, an old woman with four sons. They were the dark, beautiful descendants of headhunting pirates, dressed in hand-dyed sarongs and ancient plastic baseball caps. Their language was utterly incomprehensible.

The *Mambo Sun* rode high in the water, settling down into her new element with weird drumlike creaks from the hollow hulls. They put out to sea in a stiff offshore breeze.

Brooke stood with spry insouciance under the towering jib sail, snorting at the sea air. "She'll do twelve knots," he said with satisfaction. "Lord, Turner, it's great to be out of the penthouse and away from that crowd of flacks."

"Why do you put up with them?"

"It comes with the money, lad. You should know that."

Turner said nothing. Brooke grinned at him knowingly. "Money's power, my boy. Power doesn't go away. If you don't use it yourself, someone else will use you to get it."

"I hear they've trapped you here with that money," Turner said. "They'll freeze your funds if you try to leave."

"I let them trap me," Brooke said. "That's how I won their trust." He took Turner's arm. "But you let me know if you have money troubles here. Don't let the local Islamic bank fast-talk you into anything. Come see me first."

Turner shrugged him off. "What good has it done you? You're surrounded with yes-men."

"I've had my crew for forty years." Brooke sighed nostalgically. "Besides, you should have seen them in '98, when the streets were full of Moslem fanatics screaming for blood. Molotovs burning everywhere, pitched battles with the blessed Chinese, the sultan held hostage. . . . My crew didn't turn a hair. Held the mob off like a crowd of teenyboppers when they tried to rush my building. They had grit, those lads."

An ancient American helicopter buzzed overhead, its orange seafloats almost brushing the mast. Brooke yelled to the crew in their odd language; they furled the sails and set anchor, half a mile offshore. The chopper wheeled expertly and settled down in a shimmering circle of wind-flattened water. One of the Dayaks threw them a weighted line.

They hauled in. "Permission to come aboard, sir!" said the crown prince. He and Seria wore crisp nautical whites. They clambered from the float up a rope ladder and onto the deck. The third passenger, a pilot, took the controls. The crew hauled anchor and set sail again; the chopper lifted off.

The prince shook Turner's hand. "You know my sister, I believe."

"We met at the filming," Turner said.

"Ah yes. Good footage, that."

Brooke, with miraculous tact, lured the prince into the greenhouse. Seria immediately flung herself into Turner's arms. "You haven't written in two days," she hissed.

"I know," Turner said. He looked around quickly to make sure the Dayaks were occupied. "I keep thinking about Vancouver. How I'll feel when I'm back there."

"How you left your Sleeping Beauty behind in the castle of thorns? You're such a romantic, Turner."

"Don't talk like that. It hurts."

She smiled. "I can't help being cheerful. We have two days together, and Omar gets seasick."

The river flowed beneath their hulls like thin gray grease. Jungle leaned in from the banks; thick, clotted green mats of foliage over skinny light-starved trunks, rank with creepers. It was snake country, leech country, a primeval reek stewing in deadly humidity, with air so thick that the raucous shrieks of birds seemed to cut it like ripsaws. Bugs whirled in dense mating swarms over rafts of slime. Suspicious, sodden logs loomed in the gray mud. Some logs had scales and eyes.

The valley was as crooked as an artery, snaking between tall hills smothered in poisonous green. Sluggish wads of mist wreathed their tops. Where the trees failed, sheer cliffs were shrouded in thick ripples of ivy. The sky was gray, the sun a muddy glow behind tons of haze.

The wind died, and Brooke fired up the ship's tiny alcohol engine. Turner stood on the central bow as they sputtered upstream. He felt glazed and dreamy. Culture shock had seized him; none of it seemed real. It felt like television. Reflexively, he kept thinking of Vancouver, sailboat trips out to clean pine islands.

Seria and the prince joined him on the bow. "Lovely, isn't it?" said the prince. "We've made it a game preserve. Someday there will be tigers again."

"Good thinking, Your Highness," Turner said.

"The city feeds itself, you know. A lot of old paddies and terraces have gone back to jungle." The prince smiled with deep satisfaction.

With evening, they tied up at a dock by the ruins of a riverine city. Decades earlier, a flood had devastated the town, leaving shattered walls where vines snaked up trellises of rusting reinforcement rods. A former tourist hotel was now a ranger station.

They all went ashore to review the troops: Royal Malay Rangers in jungle camo, and a visiting crew of Swedish ecologists from the World Wildlife Fund. The two aristocrats were gung-ho for a bracing hike through the jungle. They chatted amiably with the Swedes as they soaked themselves with gnat and leech repellent. Brooke pleaded his age, and Turner managed to excuse himself.

Behind the city rose a soaring radio aerial and the rain-blotched white domes of satellite dishes.

"Jamming equipment," said Brooke with a wink. "The sultanate set it up years ago. Islamic, Malaysian, Japanese—you'd be surprised how violently people insist on being listened to."

"Freedom of speech," Turner said.

"How free is it when only rich nations can afford to talk? The Net's expensive, Turner. To you it's a way of life, but for us it's just a giant megaphone for Coca-Cola. We built this to block the shouting of the outside world. It seemed best to set the equipment here in the ruins, out of harm's way. This is a good place to hide secrets." Brooke sighed. "You know how the corruption spreads. Anyone who touches it is tempted. We use these dishes as the nerve center of our own little Net. You can get a line out here—a real one, with video. Come along, Turner. I'll stand Maple Syrup a free call to civilization, if you like."

They walked through leaf-littered streets, where pigs and lean, lizard-eyed chickens scattered from underfoot. Turner saw a tattooed face, framed in headphones, at a shattered second-story window. "The local Murut tribe," Brooke said, glancing up. "They're a bit shy."

The central control room was a small white concrete blockhouse surrounded by sturdy solar-panel racks. Brooke opened a tarnished padlock with a pocket key, and shot the bolt. Inside, the windowless blockhouse was faintly lit by the tiny green-and-yellow power lights of antique disk drives and personal computers. Brooke flicked on a desk lamp and sat on a chair cushioned with moldy foam rubber. "All automated, you see? The government hasn't had to pay an official visit in years. It keeps everyone out of trouble."

"Except for your insiders," Turner said.

"We are trouble," said Brooke. "Besides, this was my idea in the first place." He opened a musty wicker chest and pulled a video camera from a padded wrapping of cotton batik. He popped it open, sprayed its insides with silicone lubricant, and propped it on a tripod. "All the comforts of home." He left the blockhouse.

Turner hesitated. He'd finally realized what had bothered him about Brooke. Brooke was *hip*. He had that classic hip attitude of being in on things denied to the uncool. It was amazing how sleazy and suspicious it looked on someone who was *really old*.

Turner dialed his brother's house. The screen remained dark. "Who is it?" Georgie said.

"Turner."

"Oh." A long moment passed; the screen flashed on to show Georgie in a maroon silk houserobe, his hair still flattened from the pillow. "That's a relief. We've been having some trouble with phone flashers."

"How are things?"

"He's dying, Turner."

Turner stared. "Good God."

"I'm glad you called." Georgie smoothed his hair shakily. "How soon can you get here?"

"I've got a job here, Georgie."

Georgie frowned. "Look, I don't blame you for running. You wanted to live your own life; okay, that's fine. But this is *family business*, not some two-bit job in the middle of nowhere."

"Goddammit," Turner said, pleading, "I *like* it here, Georgie."

"I know how much you hate the old bastard. But he's just a dying old man now. Look, we hold his hands for a couple of weeks, and it's all ours, understand? The Riviera, man."

"It won't work, Georgie," Turner said, clutching at straws. "He's going to screw us."

"That's why I need you here. We've got to double-team him, understand?" Georgie glared from the screen. "Think of my kids, Turner. We're your family, you owe us."

Turner felt growing despair. "Georgie, there's a woman here. . . ."

"Christ, Turner."

"She's not like the others. Really."

"Great. So you're going to marry this girl, right? Raise kids."

"Well . . ."

"Then what are you wasting my time for?"

"Okay," Turner said, his shoulders slumping. "I gotta make arrangements. I'll call you back."

The Dayaks had gone ashore. The prince blithely invited the Swedish ecologists on board. They spent the evening chastely sipping orange juice and discussing Krakatoa and the swamp rhinoceros.

After the party broke up, Turner waited a painful hour and crept into the deserted greenhouse.

Seria was waiting in the sweaty green heat, sitting cross-legged in watery moonlight crosshatched by geodesics, brushing her hair. Turner joined her on the mat. She wore an erotic red synthetic nightie (some groupie's heirloom from the legion of Brooke's women), crisp with age. She was drenched in perfume.

Turner touched her fingers to the small lump on his forearm, where a contraceptive implant showed beneath his skin. He kicked his jeans off.

They began in caution and silence, and ended, two hours later, in the primeval intimacy of each other's musk and sweat. Turner lay on his back, with her head pillowed on his bare arm, feeling a sizzling effervescence of deep cellular pleasure.

It had been mystical. He felt as if some primal feminine energy had poured off her body and washed through him, to the bone. Everything seemed different now. He had discovered a new world, the kind of world a man could spend a lifetime in. It was worth ten years of a man's life just to lie here and smell her skin.

The thought of having her out of arm's reach, even for a moment, filled him with a primal anxiety close to pain. There must be a million ways to make love, he thought languidly. As many as there are to talk or think. With passion. With devotion. Playfully, tenderly, frantically, soothingly. Because you want to, because you need to.

He felt an instinctive urge to retreat to some snug den—anywhere with a bed and a roof—and spend the next solid week exploring the first twenty or thirty ways in that million.

But then the insistent pressure of reality sent a trickle of reason into him. He drifted out of reverie with a stabbing conviction of the perversity of life. Here was all he wanted—all he asked was to pull her over him like a blanket and shut out life's pointless complications. And it wasn't going to happen.

He listened to her peaceful breathing and sank into black depression. This was the kind of situation that called for wild romantic gestures, the kind that neither of them were going to make. They weren't allowed to make them. They weren't in his program, they weren't in her *adat*, they weren't in the plans.

Once he'd returned to Vancouver, none of this would seem real. Jungle moonlight and erotic sweat didn't mix with cool piny fogs over the mountains and the family mansion in Churchill Street. Culture shock would rip his memories away, snapping the million invisible threads that bind lovers.

As he drifted toward sleep, he had a sudden lucid flash of precognition: himself, sitting in the backseat of his brother's Mercedes, letting the machine drive him randomly around the city. Looking past his reflection in the window at the clotted snow in Queen Elizabeth Park, and thinking: *I'll never see her again.*

It seemed only an instant later that she was shaking him awake. "Shh!"

"What?" he mumbled.

"You were talking in your sleep." She nuzzled his ear, whispering. "What does 'Set-position Q-move' mean?"

"Jesus," he whispered back. "I was dreaming in AML." He felt the last fading trail of nightmare then, some unspeakable horror of cold iron and helpless repetition. "My family," he said. "They were all robots."

She giggled.

"I was trying to repair my grandfather."

"Go back to sleep, darling."

"No." He was wide awake now. "We'd better get back."

"I hate that cabin. I'll come to your tent on deck."

"No, they'll find out. You'll get hurt, Seria." He stepped back into his jeans.

"I don't care. This is the only time we'll have." She struggled fretfully into the red tissue of her nightie.

"I want to be with you," he said. "If you could be mine, I'd say to hell with my job and my family."

She smiled bitterly. "You'll think better of it, later. You can't throw away your life for the sake of some affair. You'll find some other woman in Vancouver. I wish I could kill her."

Every word rang true, but he still felt hurt. She shouldn't have doubted his willingness to totally destroy his life. "You'll marry too, someday. For reasons of state."

"I'll never marry," she said aloofly. "Someday I'll run away from all this. My grand romantic gesture."

She would never do it, he thought with a kind of aching pity. She'll grow old under glass in this place. "One grand gesture was enough," he said. "At least we had this much."

She watched him gloomily. "Don't be sorry you're leaving, darling. It would be wrong of me to let you stay. You don't know all the truth about this place. Or about my family."

"All families have secrets. Yours can't be any worse than mine."

"My family is different." She looked away. "Malay royalty are sacred, Turner. Sacred and unclean. We are aristocrats, shields for the innocent. . . . Dirt and ugliness strikes the shield, not our people. We take corruption on ourselves. Any crimes the State commits are our crimes, understand? They belong to our family."

Turner blinked. "Well, what? Tell me, then. Don't let it come between us."

"You're better off not knowing. We came here for a reason, Turner. It's a plan of Brooke's."

"That old fraud?" Turner said, smiling. "You're too romantic about Westerners, Seria. He looks like hot stuff to you, but he's just a burnt-out crackpot."

She shook her head. "You don't understand. It's different in your West." She hugged her slim legs and rested her chin on her knee. "Someday I will get out."

"No," Turner said, "it's *here* that it's different. In the West families disintegrate, money pries into everything. People don't belong to each other there, they belong to money and their institutions. . . . Here at least people really care and watch over each other. . . ."

She gritted her teeth. "Watching. Yes, always. You're right, I have to go."

He crept back through the mosquito netting of his tent on deck, and sat in the darkness for hours, savoring his misery. Tomorrow the prince's helicopter would arrive to take the prince and his sister back to the city. Soon Turner would return as well, and finish the last details, and leave. He played out a fantasy: cruising back from Vanc with a fat cashier's check. Tea with the sultan. *Er, look, Your Highness, my granddad made it big in the heroin trade, so here's two mill. Just pack the girl up in excelsior, she'll love it as an engineer's wife, believe me. . . .*

He heard the faint shuffle of footsteps against the deck. He peered through the tent flap, saw the shine of a flashlight. It was Brooke. He was carrying a valise.

The old man looked around surreptitiously and crept down over the side, to the dock. Weakened by hours of brooding, Turner was instantly inflamed by Brooke's deviousness. Turner sat still for a moment, while curiosity and misplaced fury rapidly devoured his common sense. Common sense said Brunei's secrets were none of his business, but common sense was making his life hell. Anything was better than staying awake all night wondering. He struggled quickly into his shirt and boots.

He crept over the side, spotted Brooke's white suit in a patch of moonlight, and followed him. Brooke skirted the edge of the ruins and took a trail into the jungle, full of ominous vines and the promise of snakes. Beneath a spongy litter of leaves and moss, the trail was asphalt. It had been a highway, once.

Turner shadowed Brooke closely, realizing gratefully that the deaf old man couldn't hear the crunching of his boots. The trail led uphill, into the interior. Brooke cursed good-naturedly as a group of grunting hogs burst across the trail. Half a mile later he rested for ten long minutes in the rusting hulk of a Land-Rover, while vicious gnats feasted on Turner's exposed neck and hands.

They rounded a hill and came across an encampment. Faint moonlight glittered off twelve-foot barbed wire and four dark watchtowers. The undergrowth had been burned back for yards around. There were barracks inside.

Brooke walked nonchalantly to the gate. The place looked dead. Turner crept nearer, sheltered by darkness.

The gate opened. Turner crawled forward between two bushes, craning his neck.

A watchtower spotlight clacked on and framed him in dazzling light from forty yards away. Someone shouted at him through a bullhorn, in Malay. Turner lurched to his feet, blinded, and put his hands high. "Don't shoot!" he yelled, his voice cracking. "Hold your fire!"

The light flickered out. Turner stood blinking in darkness, then watched four little red fireflies crawling across his chest. He realized what they were and reached higher, his spine icy. Those little red fireflies were laser sights for automatic rifles.

The guards were on him before his eyesight cleared. Dim forms in jungle camo. He saw the wicked angular magazines of their rifles, leveled at his chest. Their heads were bulky: they wore night-sight goggles.

They handcuffed him and hustled him forward toward the camp. "You guys speak English?" Turner said. No answer. "I'm a Canadian, okay?"

Brooke waited, startled, beyond the gate. "Oh," he said. "It's you. What sort of dumbshit idea was this, Turner?"

"A really bad one," Turner said sincerely.

Brooke spoke to the guards in Malay. They lowered their guns; one freed his hands. They stalked off unerringly back into the darkness.

"What *is* this place?" Turner said.

Brooke turned his flashlight on Turner's face. "What does it look like, jerk? It's a political prison." His voice was so cold from behind the glare that Turner saw, in his mind's eye, the sudden flash of a telegram. DEAR MADAM CHOI, REGRET TO INFORM YOU THAT YOUR SON STEPPED ON A VIPER IN THE JUNGLES OF BORNEO AND YOUR BOOTS DIDN'T SAVE HIM. . . .

Brooke spoke quietly. "Did you think Brunei was all sweetness and light? It's a nation, damn it, not your toy train set. All right, stick by me and keep your mouth shut."

Brooke waved his flashlight. A guard emerged from the darkness and led them around the corner of the wooden barracks, which was set above the damp ground on concrete blocks. They walked up a short flight of steps. The guard flicked an exterior switch, and the cell inside flashed into harsh light. The guard peered through close-set bars in the heavy ironbound door, then unlocked it with a creak of hinges.

Brooke murmured thanks and carefully shook the guard's hand. The guard smiled below the ugly goggles and slipped his hand inside his camo jacket.

"Come on," Brooke said. They stepped into the cell. The door clanked shut behind them.

A dark-skinned old man was blinking wearily in the sudden light. He sat up in his iron cot and brushed aside yellowed mosquito netting, reaching for a pair of wire-rimmed spectacles on the floor. He wore gray-striped prison canvas: drawstring trousers and a rough, buttoned blouse. He slipped the spectacles carefully over his ears and looked up. "Ah," he said. "Jimmy."

It was a bare cell: wooden floor, a chamber pot, a battered aluminum pitcher and basin. Two wire shelves above the bed held books in English and a curlicued alphabet Turner didn't recognize.

"This is Dr. Vikram Moratuwa," Brooke said. "The founder of the Partai Ekolojasi. This is Turner Choi, a prying young idiot."

"Ah," said Moratuwa. "Are we to be cell mates, young man?"

"He's not under arrest," Brooke said. "Yet." He opened his valise. "I brought you the books."

"Excellent," said Moratuwa, yawning. He had lost most of his teeth. "Ah, Mumford, Florman, and Lévi-Strauss. Thank you, Jimmy."

"I think it's okay," Brooke said, noticing Turner's stricken look. "The sultan winks at these little charity visits, if I'm discreet. I think I can talk you out of trouble, even though you put your foot in it."

"Jimmy is my oldest friend in Brunei," said Moratuwa. "There is no harm in two old men talking."

"Don't you believe it," Brooke said. "This man is a dangerous radical. He wanted to dissolve the monarchy. And him a privy councilor, too."

"Jimmy, we did not come here to be aristocrats. That is not Right Action."

Turner recognized the term. "You're a Buddhist?"

"Yes. I was with Sarvodaya Shramadana, the Buddhist technological movement. Jimmy and I met in Sri Lanka, where the Sarvodaya was born."

"Sri Lanka's a nice place to do videos," Brooke said. "I was still in the rock biz then, doing production work. Finance. But it was getting stale. Then I dropped in on a Sarvodaya rally, heard him speak. It was damned exciting!" Brooke grinned at the memory. "He was in trouble there, too. Even thirty years ago, his preaching was a little too pure for anyone's comfort."

"We were not put on this earth to make things comfortable for ourselves," Moratuwa chided. He glanced at Turner. "Brunei flourishes now, young man. We have the techniques, the expertise, the experience. It is time to fling open the doors and let Right Action spread to the whole earth! Brunei was our greenhouse, but the fields are the greater world outside."

Brooke smiled. "Choi is building the boats."

"Our Ocean Arks?" said Moratuwa. "Ah, splendid."

"I sailed here today on the first model."

"What joyful news. You have done us a great service, Mr. Choi."

"I don't understand," Turner said. "They're just sailboats."

Brooke smiled. "To you, maybe. But imagine you're a Malaysian dock worker living on fish meal and single-cell protein. What're you gonna think of a ship that costs nothing to build, nothing to run, and gives away free food?"

"Oh," said Turner slowly.

"Your sailboats will carry our Green message around the globe," Moratuwa said. "We teachers have a saying: 'I hear and I forget; I see and I remember; I do and I understand.' Mere preaching is only words. When people see our floating *kampongs* tied up at docks around the world, then they can touch and smell and live our life aboard those ships, then they will truly understand our Way."

"You really think that'll work?" Turner said.

"That is how we started here," Moratuwa said. "We had textbooks on the urban farm, textbooks developed in your own West, simple technologies anyone can use. Jimmy's building was our first Green *kampong*, our demonstration model. We found many to help us. Unemployment was severe, as it still is throughout the world. But idle hands can put in skylights, haul nightsoil, build simple windmills. It is not elegant, but it is food and community and pride."

"It was a close thing between our Partai and the Moslem extremists," Brooke said. "They wanted to burn every trace of the West

—we wanted to retrofit. We won. People could see and touch the future we offered. Food tastes better than preaching."

"Yes, those poor Moslem fellows," said Moratuwa. "Still here after so many years. You must talk to the sultan about an amnesty, Jimmy."

"They shot his brother in front of his family," Brooke said. "Seria saw it happen. She was only a child."

Turner felt a spasm of pain for her. She had never told him.

But Moratuwa shook his head. "The royals went too far in protecting their power. They tried to bottle up our Way, to control it with their royal *adat*. But they cannot lock out the world forever, and lock up those who want fresh air. They only imprison themselves. Ask your Seria." He smiled. "Buddha was a prince also, but he left his palace when the world called out."

Brooke laughed sourly. "Old troublemakers are stubborn." He looked at Turner. "This man's still loyal to our old dream, all that wild-eyed stuff that's buried under twenty years. He could be out of here with a word, if he promised to be cool and follow the *adat*. It's a crime to keep him in here. But the royal family aren't saints, they're politicians. They can't afford the luxury of innocence."

Turner thought it through, sadly. He realized now that he had found the ghost behind those huge old Green Party wall posters, those peeling Whole Earth sermons buried under sports ads and Malay movie stars. This was the man who had saved Seria's family— and this was where they had put him. "The sultan's not very grateful," Turner said.

"That's not the problem. You see, my friend here doesn't really give a damn about Brunei. He wants to break the greenhouse doors off, and never mind the trouble to the locals. He's not satisfied to save one little postage-stamp country. He's got the world on his conscience."

Moratuwa smiled indulgently. "And my friend Jimmy has the world in his computer terminal. He is a wicked Westerner. He has kept the simple natives pure, while he is drenched in whiskey and the Net."

Brooke winced. "Yeah. Neither one of us really belongs here. We're both goddamn outside agitators, is all. We came here together. His words, my money—we thought we could change things everywhere. Brunei was going to be our laboratory. Brunei was just small enough, and desperate enough, to listen to a couple of crackpots." He tugged at his hearing aid and glared at Turner's smile.

"You're no prize either, Choi. Y'know, I was wrong about you. I'm glad you're leaving."

"Why?" Turner said, hurt.

"You're too straight, and you're too much trouble. I checked you out through the Net a long time ago—I know all about your granddad the smack merchant and all that Triad shit. I thought you'd be cool. Instead you had to be the knight in shining armor—bloody robot, that's what you are."

Turner clenched his fists. "Sorry I didn't follow your program, you old bastard."

"She's like a daughter to me," Brooke said. "A quick bump-and-grind, okay, we all need it, but you had to come on like Prince Charming. Well, you're getting on that chopper tomorrow, and it's back to Babylon for you, kid."

"Yeah?" Turner said defiantly. "Or else, huh? You'd put me in this place?"

Brooke shook his head. "I won't have to. Think it over, Mr. Choi. You know damn well where you belong."

It was a grim trip back. Seria caught his mood at once. When she saw his Bad Cop scowl, her morning-after smile died like a moth in a killing bottle. She knew it was over. They didn't say much. The roar of the copter blades would have drowned it anyway.

The shipyard was crammed with the framework of a massive Ocean Ark. It had been simple to scale the process up with the programs he'd downloaded. The work crew was overjoyed, but Turner's long-expected triumph had turned to ashes for him. He printed out a letter of resignation and took it to the minister of industry.

The minister's *kampong* was still expanding. They had webbed off a whole city block under great tentlike sheets of translucent plastic, which hung from the walls of tall buildings like giant dew-soaked spiderwebs. Women and children were casually ripping up the streets with picks and hoes, revealing long-smothered topsoil. The sewers had been grubbed up and diverted into long troughs choked with watercress.

The minister lived in a long flimsy tent of cotton batik. He was catching an afternoon snooze in a woven hammock anchored to a high-rise wall and strung to an old lamppost.

Turner woke him up.

"I see," the minister yawned, slipping on his sandals. "Illness in the family, is it? You have my sympathies. When may we expect you back?"

Turner shook his head. "The job's done. Those 'bots will be pasting up ships from now till doomsday."

"But you still have two months to run. You should oversee the line until we're sure we have the beetles out."

"Bugs," Turner said. "There aren't any." He knew it was true. Building ships that simple was monkey-work. Humans could have done it.

"There's plenty of other work here for a man of your talents."

"Hire someone else."

The minister frowned. "I shall have to complain to Kyocera."

"I'm quitting them, too."

"Quitting your multinational? At this early stage in your career? Is that wise?"

Turner closed his eyes and summoned his last dregs of patience. "Why should I care? Tuan Minister, I've never even *seen* them."

Turner cut a last deal with the bootleg boys down on Floor 4 and sneaked into his room with an old gas can full of rice beer. The little screen on the end of the nozzle was handy for filtering out the thickest dregs. He poured himself a long one and looked around the room. He had to start packing.

He began stripping the walls and tossing souvenirs onto his bed, pausing to knock back long shuddery glugs of warm rice beer. Packing was painfully easy. He hadn't brought much. The room looked pathetic. He had another beer.

His bonsai tree was dying. There was no doubt of it now. The cramping of its tiny pot was murderous. "You poor little bastard," Turner told it, his voice thick with self-pity. On impulse, he broke its pot with his boot. He carried the tree gently across the room, and buried its gnarled roots in the rich black dirt of the window box. "There," he said, wiping his hands on his jeans. "Now *grow*, dammit!"

It was Friday night again. They were showing another free movie down in the park. Turner ignored it and called Vancouver.

"No video again?" Georgie said.

"No."

"I'm glad you called, anyway. It's bad, Turner. The Taipei cousins are here. They're hovering around the old man like a pack of buzzards."

"They're in good company, then."

"Jesus, Turner! Don't say that kind of crap! Look, Honorable Grandfather's been asking about you every day. How soon can you get here?"

Turner looked in his notebook. "I've booked passage on a freighter to Labuan Island. That's Malaysian territory. I can get a plane there, a puddle-jumper to Manila. Then a Japan Air jet to Midway and another to Vanc. That puts me in at, uh, eight P.M. your time Monday."

"Three *days?*"

"There are no *planes* here, Georgie."

"All right, if that's the best you can do. It's too bad about this video. Look, I want you to call him at the hospital, okay? Tell him you're coming."

"Now?" said Turner, horrified.

Georgie exploded. "I'm sick of doing your explaining, man! Face up to your goddamn obligations, for once! The least you can do is call him and play good boy grandson! I'm gonna call-forward you from here."

"Okay, you're right," Turner said. "Sorry, Georgie, I know it's been a strain."

Georgie looked down and hit a key. White static blurred, a phone rang, and Turner was catapulted to his grandfather's bedside.

The old man was necrotic. His cheekbones stuck out like wedges, and his lips were swollen and blue. Stacks of monitors blinked beside his bed. Turner spoke in halting Mandarin. "Hello, Grandfather. It's your grandson, Turner. How are you?"

The old man fixed his horrible eyes on the screen. "Where is your picture, boy?"

"This is Borneo, Grandfather. They don't have modern telephones."

"What kind of place is that? Have they no respect?"

"It's politics, Grandfather."

Grandfather Choi scowled. A chill of terror went through Turner. Good God, he thought, I'm going to look like that when I'm old. His grandfather said, "I don't recall giving my permission for this."

"It was just eight months, Grandfather."

"You prefer these barbarians to your own family, is that it?"

Turner said nothing. The silence stretched painfully. "They're not barbarians," he blurted at last.

"What's that, boy?"

Turner switched to English. "They're British Commonwealth, like Hong Kong was. Half of them are Chinese."

Grandfather sneered and followed him to English. "Why they need you, then?"

"They need me," Turner said tightly, "because I'm a trained engineer."

His grandfather peered at the blank screen. He looked feeble suddenly, confused. He spoke Chinese. "Is this some sort of trick? My son's boy doesn't talk like that. What is that howling I hear?"

The movie was reaching a climax downstairs. Visceral crunches and screaming. It all came boiling up inside Turner then. "What's it sound like, old man? A Triad gang war?"

His grandfather turned pale. "That's it, boy. Is all over for you."

"Great," Turner said, his heart racing. "Maybe we can be honest, just this once."

"My money bought you diapers, boy."

"*Fang-pa,*" Turner said. "Dog's-fart. You made our lives hell with that money. You turned my dad into a drunk and my brother into an ass-kisser. That's blood money from junkies, and I wouldn't take it if you begged me!"

"You talk big, boy, but you don't show the face," the old man said. He raised one shrunken fist, his bandaged forearm trailing tubes. "If you were here I give you a good beating."

Turner laughed giddily. He felt like a hero. "You old fraud! Go on, give the money to Uncle's kids. They're gonna piss on your altar every day, you stupid old bastard."

"They're good children, not like you."

"They hate your guts, old man. Wise up."

"Yes, they hate me," the old man admitted gloomily. The truth seemed to fill him with grim satisfaction. He nestled his head back into his pillow like a turtle into its shell. "They all want more money, more, more, more. You want it, too, boy, don't lie to me."

"Don't need it," Turner said airily. "They don't use money here."

"Barbarians," his grandfather said. "But you need it when you come home."

"I'm staying here," Turner said. "I *like* it here. I'm free here, understand? Free of the money and free of the family and free of you!"

"Wicked boy," his grandfather said. "I was like you once. I did bad things to be free." He sat up in bed, glowering. "But at least I helped my family."

"I could never be like you," Turner said.

"You wait till they come after you with their hands out," his grandfather said, stretching out one wrinkled palm. "The end of the world couldn't hide you from them."

"What do you mean?"

His grandfather chuckled with an awful satisfaction. "I leave you all the money, Mr. Big Freedom. You see what you do then when you're in my shoes."

"I don't want it!" Turner shouted. "I'll give it all to charity!"

"No, you won't," his grandfather said. "You'll think of your duty to your family, like I had to. From now on *you* take care of them, Mr. Runaway, Mr. High and Mighty."

"I won't!" Turner said. "You can't!"

"I'll die happy now," his grandfather said, closing his eyes. He lay back on the pillow and grinned feebly. "It worth it just to see the look on their faces."

"You can't make me!" Turner yelled. "I'll never go back, understand? I'm staying—"

The line went dead.

Turner shut down his phone and stowed it away.

He had to talk to Brooke. Brooke would know what to do. Somehow, Turner would play off one old man against the other.

Turner still felt shocked by the turn of events, but beneath his confusion he felt a soaring confidence. At last he had faced down his grandfather. After that, Brooke would be easy. Brooke would find some loophole in the Bruneian government that would protect him from the old man's legacy. Turner would stay safe in Brunei. It was the best place in the world to frustrate the banks of the Global Net.

But Brooke was still on the river, on his boat.

Turner decided to meet Brooke the moment he docked in town. He couldn't wait to tell Brooke about his decision to stay in Brunei for good. He was feverish with excitement. He had wrenched his life out of the program now; everything was different. He saw everything from a fresh new angle, with a *bricoleur*'s eyes. His whole life was waiting for a retrofit.

He took the creaking elevator to the ground floor. In the park outside, the movie crowd was breaking up. Turner hitched a ride in the pedicab of some teenagers from a waterfront *kampong*. He took the first shift pedaling, and got off a block away from the dock Brooke used.

The cracked concrete quays were sheltered under a long rambling roof of tin and geodesic bamboo. Half-a-dozen fishing smacks floated at the docks, beside an elderly harbor dredge. Brooke's first boat, a decrepit pleasure cruiser, was in permanent dry dock with its diesel engine in pieces.

The headman of the dock *kampong* was a plump, motherly Malay grandmother. She and her friends were having a Friday night quilting bee, repairing canvas sails under the yellow light of an alcohol lamp.

Brooke was not expected back until morning. Turner was determined to wait him out. He had not asked permission to sleep out from his *kampong*, but after a long series of garbled translations he established that the locals would vouch for him later. He wandered away from the chatter of Malay gossip and found a dark corner.

He fell back on a floury pile of rice bags, watching from the darkness, unable to sleep. Whenever his eyes closed, his brain ran a loud interior monologue, rehearsals for his talk with Brooke.

The women worked on, wrapped in the lamp's mild glow. Innocently, they enjoyed themselves, secure in their usefulness. Yet Turner knew machines could have done the sewing faster and easier. Already, through reflex, as he watched, some corner of his mind pulled the task to computerized pieces, thinking: simplify, analyze, reduce.

But to what end? What was it really for, all that tech he'd learned? He'd become an engineer for reasons of his own. Because it offered a way out for him, because the gift for it had always been there in his brain and hands and eyes. . . . Because of the rewards it offered him. Freedom, independence, money, the rewards of the West.

But what control did he have? Rewards could be snatched away without warning. He'd seen others go to the wall when their specialties ran dry. Education and training were no defense. Not today, when a specialist's knowledge could be programmed into a computerized expert system.

Was he really any safer than these Bruneians? A thirty-minute phone call could render these women obsolete—but a society that could do their work with robots would have no use for their sails. Within their little greenhouse, their miniature world of gentle technologies, they had more control than he did.

People in the West talked about the "technical elite"—and Turner knew it was a damned lie. Technology roared on, running full-throttle on the world's last dregs of oil, but no one was at the wheel, not really. Massive institutions, both governments and corporations, fumbled for control, but couldn't understand. They had no hands-on feel for tech and what it meant, for the solid feeling in a good design.

The "technical elite" were errand boys. They didn't decide how to study, what to work on, where they could be most useful, or to what end. Money decided that. Technicians were owned by the abstract ones and zeros in bankers' microchips, paid out by silk-suit hustlers who'd never touched a wrench. Knowledge wasn't power, not really, not for engineers. There were too many abstractions in the way.

But the gift was real—Brooke had told him so, and now Turner realized it was true. That was the reason for engineering. Not for money, because there was more money in shuffling paper. Not for power; that was in management. For the gift itself.

He leaned back in darkness, smelling tar and rice dust. For the first time, he truly felt he understood what he was doing. Now that he had defied his family and his past, he saw his work in a new light. It was something bigger than just his private escape hatch. It was a worthy pursuit on its own merits: a thing of dignity.

It all began to fall into place for him then, bringing with it a warm sense of absolute rightness. He yawned, nestling his head into the burlap.

He would live here and help them. Brunei was a new world, a world built on a human scale, where people mattered. No, it didn't have the flash of a hot CAD–CAM establishment with its tons of goods and reams of printout; it didn't have that technical sweetness and heroic scale.

But it was still good work. A man wasn't a Luddite because he worked for people instead of abstractions. The green technologies demanded *more* intelligence, more reason, more of the engineer's true gift. Because they went against the blind momentum of a dead century, with all its rusting monuments of arrogance and waste. . . .

Turner squirmed drowsily into the scrunchy comfort of the rice bags, in the fading grip of his epiphany. Within him, some unspoken knot of division and tension eased, bringing a new and deep relief. As always, just before sleep, his thoughts turned to Seria. Somehow, he would deal with that too. He wasn't sure just how yet, but it could wait. It was different now that he was staying. Everything was working out. He was on a roll.

Just as he drifted off, he half-heard a thrashing scuffle as a *kampong* cat seized and tore a rat behind the bags.

A stevedore shook him awake next morning. They needed the rice. Turner sat up, his mouth gummy with hangover. His T-shirt and jeans were caked with dust.

Brooke had arrived. They were loading provisions aboard his ship: bags of rice, dried fruit, compost fertilizer. Turner, smiling, hoisted a bag over his shoulder and swaggered up the ramp on board.

Brooke oversaw the loading from a canvas deck chair. He was unshaven, nervously picking at a gaudy acoustic guitar. He started violently when Turner dropped the bag at his feet.

"Thank God you're here!" he said. "Get out of sight!" He grabbed Turner's arm and hustled him across the deck into the greenhouse.

Turner stumbled along reluctantly. "What the hell? How'd you know I was coming here?"

Brooke shut the greenhouse door. He pointed through a dew-streaked pane at the dock. "See that little man with the black song-kak hat?"

"Yeah?"

"He's from the Ministry of Islamic Banking. He just came from your *kampong,* looking for you. Big news from the gnomes of Zurich. You're hot property now, kid."

Turner folded his arms defiantly. "I've made my decision, Tuan Councilor. I threw it over. Everything. My family, the West . . . I don't want that money. I'm turning it down! I'm staying."

Brooke ignored him, wiping a patch of glass with his sleeve. "If they get their hooks into your cash flow, you'll never get out of here." Brooke glanced at him, alarmed. "You didn't sign anything, did you?"

Turner scowled. "You haven't heard a word I've said, have you?"

Brooke tugged at his hearing aid. "What? These damn batteries . . . Look, I got spares in my cabin. We'll check it out, have a talk." He waved Turner back, opened the greenhouse door slightly, and shouted a series of orders to the crew in their Dayak dialect. "Come on," he told Turner.

They left by a second door, and sneaked across a patch of open deck, then down a flight of plywood steps into the center hull.

Brooke lifted the paisley bedspread of his cabin bunk and hauled out an ancient steamer chest. He pulled a jingling set of keys from his pocket and opened it. Beneath a litter of ruffled shirts, a shaving kit, and cans of hair spray, the trunk was packed to the gills with electronic contraband: coax cables, multiplexers, buffers and converters, shiny plug-in cards still in their heat-sealed baggies, multiplugged surge suppressors wrapped in tentacles of black extension cord. "Christ," Turner said. He heard a gentle thump as the ship came loose, followed by a rattle of rigging as the crew hoisted sail.

After a long search, Brooke found batteries in a cloisonné box. He popped them into place.

Turner said, "Admit it. You're surprised to see me, aren't you? Still think you were wrong about me?"

Brooke looked puzzled. "Surprised? Didn't you get Seria's message on the Net?"

"What? No. I slept on the docks last night."

"You missed the message?" Brooke said. He mulled it over. "Why are you here, then?"

"You said you could help me if I ever had money trouble," Turner said. "Well, now's the time. You gotta figure some way to get me out of this bank legacy. I know it doesn't look like it, but I've broken with my family for good. I'm gonna stay here, try to work things out with Seria."

Brooke frowned. "I don't understand. You want to stay with Seria?"

"Yes, here in Brunei, with her!" Turner sat on the bunk and waved his arms passionately. "Look, I know I told you that Brunei was just a glass bubble, sealed off from the world, and all that. But I've changed now! I've thought it through, I understand things. Brunei's important! It's small, but it's the ideas that matter, not the scale. I can get along, I'll fit in—you said so yourself."

"What about Seria?"

"Okay, that's part of it," Turner admitted. "I know she'll never leave this place. I can defy my family and it's no big deal, but she's Royalty. She wouldn't leave here, any more than you'd leave all your money behind. So you're both trapped here. All right. I can accept that." Turner looked up, his face glowing with determination. "I know things won't be easy for Seria and me, but it's up to me to make the sacrifice. Someone has to make the grand gesture. Well, it might as well be me."

Brooke was silent for a moment, then thumped him on the shoulder. "This is a new Turner I'm seeing. So you faced down the old smack merchant, huh? You're quite the hero!"

Turner felt sheepish. "Come on, Brooke."

"And turning down all that nice money, too."

Turner brushed his hands together, dismissing the idea. "I'm sick of being manipulated by old geezers."

Brooke rubbed his unshaven jaw and grinned. "Kid, you've got a lot to learn." He walked to the door. "But that's okay, no harm done. Everything still works out. Let's go up on deck and make sure the coast is clear."

Turner followed Brooke to his deck chair by the bamboo railing. The ship sailed rapidly down a channel between mud flats. Already they'd left the waterfront, paralleling a shoreline densely fringed with mangroves. Brooke sat down and opened a binocular case. He scanned the city behind them.

Turner felt a light-headed sense of euphoria as the triple bows cut the water. He smiled as they passed the first offshore rig. It looked like a good place to get some fishing done.

"About this bank," Turner said. "We have to face them sometime —what good is this doing us?"

Brooke smiled without looking up from his binoculars. "Kid, I've been planning this day a long time. I'm running it on a wing and a prayer. But hey, I'm not proud, I can adapt. You've been a lot of trouble to me, stomping in where angels fear to tread, in those damn boots of yours. But I've finally found a way to fit you in. Turner, I'm going to retrofit your life."

"Think so?" Turner said. He stepped closer, looming over Brooke. "What are you looking for, anyway?"

Brooke sighed. "Choppers. Patrol boats."

Turner had a sudden terrifying flash of insight. "You're leaving Brunei. Defecting!" He stared at Brooke. "You bastard! You kept me on board!" He grabbed the rail, then began tearing at his heavy boots, ready to jump and swim for it.

"Don't be stupid!" Brooke said. "You'll get her in a lot of trouble!" He lowered the binoculars. "Oh, Christ, here comes Omar.".

Turner followed his gaze and spotted a helicopter, rising gnatlike over the distant high-rises. "Where is Seria?"

"Try the bow."

"You mean she's here? She's leaving too?" He ran forward across the thudding deck.

Seria wore bell-bottomed sailor's jeans and a stained nylon windbreaker. With the help of two of the Dayak crew, she was installing a meshwork satellite dish in an anchored iron plate in the deck. She had cut away her long dyed hair; she looked up at him, and for a moment he saw a stranger. Then her face shifted, fell into a familiar focus. "I thought I'd never see you again, Turner. That's why I had to do it."

Turner smiled at her fondly, too overjoyed at first for her words to sink in. "Do what, angel?"

"Tap your phone, of course. I did it because I was jealous, at first. I had to be sure. You know. But then when I knew you were leaving, well, I had to hear your voice one last time. So I heard your talk with your grandfather. Are you mad at me?"

"You tapped my phone? You heard all that?" Turner said.

"Yes, darling. You were wonderful. I never thought you'd do it."

"Well," Turner said, "I never thought you'd pull a stunt like this, either."

"Someone had to make a grand gesture," she said. "It was up to me, wasn't it? But I explained all that in my message."

"So you're defecting? Leaving your family?" Turner knelt beside her, dazed. As he struggled to fit it all together, his eyes focused on a cross-threaded nut at the base of the dish. He absently picked up a socket wrench. "Let me give you a hand with that," he said through reflex.

Seria sucked on a barked knuckle. "You didn't get my last message, did you? You came here on your own!"

"Well, yeah," Turner said. "I decided to stay. You know. With you."

"And now we're abducting you!" She laughed. "How romantic!"

"You and Brooke are leaving together?"

"It's not just me, Turner. Look."

Brooke was walking toward them, and with him Dr. Moratuwa, newly outfitted in saffron-colored baggy shorts and T-shirt. They were the work clothes of a Buddhist technician. "Oh, no," Turner said. He dropped his wrench with a thud.

Seria said, "Now you see why I had to leave, don't you? My family locked him up. I had to break *adat* and help Brooke set him free. It was my obligation, my *dharma!*"

"I guess that makes sense," Turner said. "But it's gonna take me a while, that's all. Couldn't you have warned me?"

"I tried to! I wrote you on the Net!" She saw he was crestfallen, and squeezed his hand. "I guess the plans broke down. Well, we can improvise."

"Good day, Mr. Choi," said Moratuwa. "It was very brave of you to cast in your lot with us. It was a gallant gesture."

"Thanks," Turner said. He took a deep breath. So they were all leaving. It was a shock, but he could deal with it. He'd just have to start over and think it through from a different angle. At least Seria was coming along.

He felt a little better now. He was starting to get it under control. Moratuwa sighed. "And I wish it could have worked."

"Your brother's coming," Brooke told Seria gloomily. "Remember this was all my fault."

They had a good head wind, but the crown prince's helicopter came on faster, its drone growing to a roar. A Gurkha palace guard crouched on the broad orange float outside the canopy, cradling a light machine gun. His gold-braided dress uniform flapped in the chopper's downwash.

The chopper circled the boat once. "We've had it," Brooke said. "Well, at least it's not a patrol boat with those damned Exocet missiles. It's family business with the princess on board. They'll hush it all up. You can always depend on *adat*." He patted Moratuwa's shoulder. "Looks like you get a cell mate after all, old man."

Seria ignored them. She was looking up anxiously. "Poor Omar," she said. She cupped her hands to her mouth. "Brother, be careful!" she shouted.

The prince's copilot handed the guard a loudspeaker. The guard raised it and began to shout a challenge.

The tone of the chopper's engines suddenly changed. Plumes of brown smoke billowed from the chromed exhausts. The prince veered away suddenly, fighting the controls. The guard, caught off balance, tumbled headlong into the ocean. The Dayak crew, who had been waiting for the order to reef sails, began laughing wildly.

"What in hell?" Brooke said.

The chopper pancaked down heavily into the bay, rocking in the ship's wake. Spurting caramel-colored smoke, its engines died with a hideous grinding. The ship sailed on. They watched silently as the drenched guard swam slowly up and clung to the chopper's float.

Brooke raised his eyes to heaven. "Lord Buddha, forgive my doubts. . . ."

"Sugar," Seria said sadly. "I put a bag of sugar in brother's fuel tank. I ruined his beautiful helicopter. Poor Omar, he really loves that machine."

Brooke stared at her, then burst into cackling laughter. Regally, Seria ignored him. She stared at the dwindling shore, her eyes bright. "Goodbye, Brunei. You cannot hold us now."

"Where are we going?" Turner said.

"To the West," said Moratuwa. "The Ocean Arks will spread for many years. I must set the example by carrying the word to the greatest global center of unsustainable industry."

Brooke grinned. "He means America, man."

"We shall start in Hawaii. It is also tropical, and our expertise will find ready application there."

"Wait a minute," Turner said. "I turned my back on all that! Look, I turned down a fortune so I could stay in the East."

Seria took his arm, smiling radiantly. "You're such a dreamer, darling. What a wonderful gesture. I love you, Turner."

"Look," said Brooke, "I left behind my building, my title of nobility, and all my old mates. I'm older than you, so my romantic gestures come first."

"But," Turner said, "it was all decided. I was going to help you in Brunei. I had ideas, plans. Now none of it makes any sense."

Moratuwa smiled. "The world is not built from your blueprints, young man."

"Whose, then?" Turner demanded. "Yours?"

"Nobody's, really," Brooke said. "We all just have to do our best with whatever comes up. *Bricolage,* remember?" Brooke spread his hands. "But it's a geezer's world, kid. We got your number, and we got you outnumbered. Fast cars and future shock and that hot Western trip . . . that's another century. We like slow days in the sun. We like a place to belong and gentle things around us." He smiled. "Okay, you're a little wired now, but you'll calm down by the time we reach Hawaii. There's a lot of retrofit work there. You'll be one of us!" He gestured at the satellite dish. "We'll set this up and call your banks first thing."

"It's a good world for us, Turner," Seria said urgently. "Not quite East, not quite West—like us two. It was made for us, it's what we're best at." She embraced him.

"You escaped," Turner said. No one ever said much about what happened after Sleeping Beauty woke.

"Yes, I broke free," she said, hugging him tighter. "And I'm taking you with me."

Turner stared over her shoulder at Brunei, sinking into hot green mangroves and warm mud. Slowly, he could feel the truth of it, sliding over him like some kind of ambiguous quicksand. He was going to fit right in. He could see his future laid out before him, clean and predestined, like fifty years of happy machine language.

"Maybe I wanted this," he said at last. "But it sure as hell wasn't what I planned."

Brooke laughed. "Look, you're bound for Hawaii with a princess and eight million dollars. Somehow, you'll just have to make do."

SPOOK

FOR RUDY RUCKER

THE SPOOK WAS PEELING off from orbit, headed for Washington, D.C., and it felt just great. The spook twisted convulsively in his seat, grinning out the Plexiglas at the cheery red-hot glow of the shuttle's wind edges.

Far below, the unnatural green of genetically altered forests showed the faint scars of old-time roads and fence lines. The spook ran long, narrow, agile fingers through the roots of his short-cropped blue hair. He hadn't made groundfall in ten months. Already the cooped-up feeling of the orbiting zaibatseries was peeling off cold and crisp like a snake's skin.

The shuttle decelerated through Mach 4 with a faint, delicious shiver. The spook twisted in his seat and turned a long slanted green glance past the sleeping plutocrat in the seat beside him and at a woman across the aisle. She had that cool starved zaibatsery look and those hollow veinwebby eyes. . . . Looked like the gravity was giving her trouble already, she'd spent too much time floating along those low-grav zaibatsery axes of rotation. She'd pay for it when they made groundfall, when she'd have to shuffle all cute from waterbed to waterbed, like helpless prey. . . . The spook looked down; his hands were making unconscious twitchy clawing motions in his lap. He picked them up and shook the tension out of them. Silly little hands . . .

The forests of the Maryland Piedmont skinned by like green video. Washington and the DNA recombo labs of Rockville, Maryland, were 1,080 clean ticking seconds away. He couldn't remember when he'd ever had so much fun. Inside his right ear the computer whispered, whispered. . . .

The shuttle albatrossed down on the reinforced runway, and airport groundcraft foamed it cool. The spook decamped, clutching his valise.

A chopper was waiting for him from the private security apparat of the Replicon corporation. While it flew him to Replicon's Rockville HQ, he had a drink, shuddering a little at the intuitive impact of the unspoken paradigms of the chopper's interior. The techniques he had learned in the zaibatsery espionage camp oozed up his hind-brain like psychotic flashbacks. Under the impact of gravity, fresh air, and plush upholstery, whole sections of his personality were decaying at once.

He was as sweet and fluid as the heart of a rotting melon. This was fluidity, slick as grease, all right. . . . Acting on intuition, he opened his valise, took a mechanical comb from a grooming case, and flicked it on with the iridescent nail of his right thumb. Black dye from the comb's vibrating teeth soothed and darkened his blue zaibatsery coif.

He unplugged the tiny jack that was coupled to the auditory nerve of his right ear and unclipped his computer earring. Humming to himself to cover the gaps in its whispering, he opened a flat case clipped inside the valise and restored the minicomp earring to its own padded socket. Inside the case were seven others, little jeweled globes packed with microminiature circuitry, soaked tight with advanced software. He plugged in a new one and hung it from his pale pierced lobe. It whispered to him about his capabilities, in case he had forgotten. He listened with half an ear.

The chopper landed on the Replicon emblem on the rooftop pad of the four-story apparat headquarters. The spook walked to the elevator. He nibbled a bit of skin from the corner of his nail and flicked it into the recessed slot of a biopsy analyzer, then rocked back and forth on his clean new heels, grinning, as he was weighed and scanned and measured by cameras and sonar.

The elevator door slid open. He stepped inside, staring ahead easily, happy as a shadow. It opened again, and he walked down a richly paneled hall and into the office suite of the head of Replicon security.

He gave his credentials to the secretary and stood rocking on his heels while the young man fed them through his desktop computer. The spook blinked his narrow green eyes; the corporate Muzak was soaking into him like a hot bath.

Inside, the security chief was all iron gray hair and tanned wrinkles and big ceramic teeth. The spook took a seat and went limp as wax as the man's vibrations poured over him. The man bubbled over with ambition and corruption like a rusting barrel full of chemical waste. "Welcome to Rockville, Eugene."

"Thank you, sir," the spook said. He sat up straighter, taking on the man's predatory coloration. "It's a pleasure."

The security chief looked idly into a hooded data screen. "You come highly recommended, Eugene. I have data here on two of your operations for other members of the Synthesis. In the Amsterdam Gill Piracy case you stood up under pressure that would have broken a normal operative."

"I was at the head of my class," said the spook, smiling guilelessly. He didn't remember anything about the Amsterdam case. It had all slicked aside, erased by the Veil. The spook looked placidly at a Japanese kakemono wall hanging.

"We here at Replicon don't often enlist the help of your zaibatsery apparat," the chief said. "But our cartel has been allotted a very special operation by the Synthesis coordinating board. Although you're not a member of the Synthesis, your advanced zaibatsery training is crucial to the mission's success."

The spook smiled blandly, waving the toe of his decorated shoe. Talk of loyalties and ideologies bored him. He cared very little about the Synthesis and its ambitious efforts to unite the planet under one cybernetic-economic web.

Even his feelings about his native zaibatseries were not so much "patriotism" as the sort of warm regard that a worm feels for the core of an apple. He waited for the man to come to the point, knowing that his earring computer could replay the conversation if he missed anything.

The chief toyed with an electronic stylus, leaning back in his chair. "It hasn't been easy for us," he said, "facing the ferment of the postindustrial years, watching a relentless brain drain into the orbital factories, while overpopulation and pollution wrecked the planet. Now we find we can't even put the pieces back together without help from your orbiters. You can appreciate our position, I hope."

"Perfectly," said the spook. Using his zaibatsery training and the advantages of the Veil, it wasn't hard at all to put on the man's skin and see through his eyes. He didn't like it much, but it wasn't difficult.

"Things are settling down now, since most of the craziest groups have killed themselves off or emigrated into space. The Earth cannot afford the cultural variety you have in your orbiting city-states. Earth must unite its remaining resources under the Synthesis aegis. The conventional wars are over for good and all. What we face now is a war of states of mind."

The chief began doodling absently with the light pen on a convenient videoscreen. "It's one thing to deal with criminal groups, like the Gill Pirates, and another entirely to confront those, ah, cults and sects who refuse outright to join the Synthesis. Since the population diebacks of the 2000s, large sections of the undeveloped world have gone to seed. . . . This is especially true of Central America, south of the People's Republic of Mexico. . . . It's there that we face a dissident cult calling itself the Maya Resurgence. We Synthetics are confronting a cultural mind-set, what your apparat, Eugene, would call a paradigm, that is directly opposed to everything that unites the Synthesis. If we can stop this group before it can solidify, all will be well. But if their influence continues to spread, it may provoke militancy among the Synthesis. And if we are forced to resort to arms, our own fragile concordance will come apart at the seams. We can't afford to remilitarize, Eugene. We can't afford those suspicions. We need everything we have left to continue to fight ecological disaster. The seas are still rising."

The spook nodded. "You want me to destabilize them. Make their paradigm untenable. Provoke the kind of cognitive dissonance that will cause them to crumble from within."

"Yes," the chief said. "You are a proven agent. Tear them apart."

The spook said delicately, "If I find it necessary to use interdicted weapons . . . ?"

The chief paled, but set his teeth and said bravely, "Replicon must not be implicated."

It took four days for the small solar-powered zeppelin to float and whir its way from the dikes of Washington, D.C., to the bloated Gulf of Honduras. The spook rode alone, on a sealed flight. He spent most of the trip in a semiparalyzed state, with the constant whisper of his computer taking the place of conscious thought.

At last the zep's programming brought it to a grayish waterlogged section of wave-lapped tropical forest near the dock of New

Belize. The spook had himself lowered by cable to a firm patch by the churned-up earth of the docks. He waved cheerily to the crew of a three-masted schooner, who had been disturbed from their afternoon siesta by his almost silent arrival.

It was good to see people again. Four days with only his fragmentary self for company had left the spook antsy and hungry for companionship.

It was suffocatingly hot. Wooden crates of bananas were ripening odoriferously on the dock.

New Belize was a sad little town. Its progenitor, Old Belize, was underwater somewhere miles out in the Caribbean, and New Belize had been hastily cobbled together from leftovers. The center of the town was one of the prefabricated geodomes the Synthesis used for headquarters in its corporate concessions. The rest of the town, even the church, clung to the dome's rim like the huts of villagers around a medieval fortress. When and if the seas rose farther, the dome would move easily, and the native structures would drown with the rest.

Except for its dogs and flies, the town slept. The spook picked his way through the mud to a bumpy street of corduroyed driftwood. An Amerindian woman in a filthy shawl watched him from her butcher's stall beside one of the dome's airlocks. She brushed flies from a suspended pig's carcass with a palm-leaf fan, and as his eyes locked with hers he felt a paradigmatic flash of her numb misery and ignorance, like stepping on an electric eel. It was weird and intense and new, and her stupefied pain meant absolutely nothing to him except for its novelty; in fact, he could barely stop himself from leaping over her dirty counter and embracing her. He wanted to slide his hands up under her long cotton blouse and slip his tongue into her wrinkled mouth; he wanted to *get right under her skin* and peel it off like a snake's. . . . Wow! He shook himself and went in through the airlock.

Inside, it smelled of the Synthesis, compressed and tangy like the air in a diving bell. It was not a large dome, but not a lot of room was needed for the modern management of information. The dome's lower floor was loosely divided into working offices with the usual keyboards, voice decoders, translators, videoscreens, and com channels for satellites and electric mail. The personnel ate and slept upstairs. In this particular station, most of them were Japanese.

The spook mopped sweat from his forehead and asked a secretary in Japanese where he might find Dr. Emilio Flores.

Flores ran a semi-independent health clinic that had slipped suspiciously from Synthetic control. The spook was forced to take a seat in the doctor's waiting room, where he played antique videogames on a battered old display screen.

Flores had an endless clientele of the lame, halt, diseased, and rotting. These Belizeans seemed bewildered by the dome and moved tentatively, as if afraid that they might break the walls or floor. The spook found them intensely interesting. He studied their infirmities—mostly skin diseases, fevers, and parasitic infestations, with a sprinkling of septic wounds and fractures—with an analytic eye. He had never before seen people so sick. He tried to charm them with his expertise on the videogames, but they preferred to murmur to one another in English patois or sit huddled and shivering in the air conditioning.

At last the spook was allowed to see the doctor. Flores was a short, balding Hispanic, wearing a physician's traditional white business suit. He looked the spook up and down. "Oh," he said. "Now your illness, young man, is one I have seen before. You want to travel. Into the interior."

"Yes," the spook said. "To Tikal."

"Have a seat." They sat down. Behind Flores's chair a nuclear magnetic resonator sat ticking and blinking to itself. "Let me guess," the doctor said, steepling his fingers. "The world seems like a dead end to you, young man. You couldn't make the grade or get the training to migrate to the zaibatseries. And you can't bear wasting your life cleaning up a world your ancestors ruined. You dread a life under the thumb of huge cartels and corporations that starve your soul to fill their pockets. You long for a simpler life. A life of the spirit."

"Yes, sir."

"I have the facilities here to change your hair and skin color. I can even arrange the supplies that will give you a decent chance of making it through the jungle. You have the money?"

"Yes, sir. Bank of Zurich." The spook produced an electronic charge card.

Flores fitted the card into a desktop slot, studied the readout, and nodded. "I won't deceive you, young man. Life among the Maya is harsh, especially at first. They will break you and remold you exactly as they want. This is a bitter land. Last century this area fell into the hands of the Predator Saints. Some of the diseases the Predators unleashed are still active here. The Resurgence is heir to Predator fanaticism. They, too, are killers."

The spook shrugged. "I'm not afraid."

"I hate killing," the doctor said. "Still, at least the Maya are honest about it, while the cost-benefit policies of the Synthetics have made the entire local population into prey. The Synthetics will not grant me funds of any kind to prolong the lives of so-called nonsurvival types. So I compromise my honor by accepting the money of Synthetic defectors, and finance my charities with treason. I am a Mexican national, but I learned my profession at a Replicon university."

The spook was surprised. He hadn't known there was still a Mexican "nation." He wondered who owned its government.

The preparations took eight days. The clinic's machines, under Flores's token direction, tinted the spook's skin and irises and re-worked the folds around his eyes. He was inoculated against the local and the artificially introduced strains of malaria, yellow jack, typhus, and dengue fever. New strains of bacteria were introduced into his gut to avoid dysentery, and he was given vaccines to prevent allergic reactions to the inevitable bites of ticks, fleas, chiggers, and, worst of all, burrowing screwworms.

When the time came for him to bid farewell to the doctor, the spook was reduced to tears. As he mopped his eyes, he pressed hard against his left cheekbone. There was a clicking sound inside his head and his left sinus cavity began to drain. He carefully but unobtrusively caught the draining fluid in his handkerchief. When he shook hands in farewell, he pressed the wet cloth against the bare skin of the doctor's wrist. He left the handkerchief on Flores's desk.

By the time the spook and his mules had passed the cornfields and entered the jungle, the schizophrenic toxins had taken effect and the doctor's mind had shattered like a dropped vase.

The jungle of lowland Guatemala was not a happy place for an orbiter. It was a vast canny morass of weeds run wild that had known man for a long time. In the twelfth century it had been cauterized for the irrigated cornfields of the original Maya. In the twentieth and twenty-first it had been introduced to the sinister logic of bulldozers, flamethrowers, defoliants, and pesticides. Each time, with the death of its oppressors, it had sprung back, nastier and more desperate than before.

The jungle had once been threaded by the trails of loggers and chicleros, seeking mahogany and chicle trees for the international market. Now there were no such trails, because there were no such trees left.

This was not the forest primeval. It was a human artifact, like the genetically altered carbon-dioxide gobblers that stood in industrial ranks across the Synthetic forests of Europe and North America. These trees were the carpetbaggers of an ecological society smashed and in disarray: thorn, mesquite, cabbage palm, winding lianas. They had swallowed whole towns, even, in places, whole oil refineries. Swollen populations of parrots and monkeys, deprived of their natural predators, made nights miserable.

The spook took constant satellite checks of his position and was in no danger of losing his way. He was not having any fun. Disposing of the rogue humanitarian had been too easy to enjoy. His destination was the sinister hacienda of the twentieth-century American millionaire, John Augustus Owens, now the headquarters of the Mayan brain trust.

The stuccoed roof-combs of the Tikal pyramids were visible from treetops thirty miles away. The spook recognized the layout of the Resurgent city from satellite photographs. He traveled till dark and spent the night in the decaying church of an overgrown village. In the morning he killed his two mules and set out on foot.

The jungle outside Tikal was full of hunters' trails. A mile outside the city the spook was captured by two sentries armed with obsidian-studded clubs and late-twentieth-century automatic rifles.

His guards looked too tall to be actual Mayans. They were probably outside recruits rather than the indigenous Guatemalan Indians who made up the core of the city's population. They spoke only Maya, mixed with distorted Spanish. With the help of his computer, the spook began eagerly sucking in the language, meanwhile complaining plaintively in English. The Veil gave a talent for languages. He had already learned and forgotten over a dozen.

His arms were bound behind him and he was searched for weapons, but not otherwise harmed. His captors marched through a suburban complex of thatched houses, cornfields, and small gardens. Turkeys scratched and gobbled underfoot. He was turned over to the theocrats in an elaborate wooden office at the foot of one of the secondary pyramids.

There he was interrogated by a priest, who put aside a headdress and jade lip plug to assume the careful colorlessness of a bureaucrat. The priest's English was excellent, and his manner had that ingrained remoteness and casual assumption of total power that only a long acquaintance with industrial-scale power structures could breed. The spook slipped easily into the expected responses. With immediate success, he posed as a defector from the Synthesis, in search of the so-called "human values" that the Synthesis and the zaibatseries had dismissed as obsolete.

He was escorted up the pyramid's limestone stairs and impri-

soned near the apex in a small but airy stone cell. His integration into
Mayan society, he was told, would come only when he had emptied
himself of old falsehoods and was cleansed and reborn. In the meantime he would be taught the language. He was instructed to watch
the daily life of the city and to expect a vision.

The cell's barred windows provided a splendid view of Tikal.
Ceremonies were carried out every day on the largest temple pyramid; priests climbed like sleepwalkers up its steep stairs, and stone
caldrons sent black threads of smoke rising into the pitiless Guatemalan sky. Tikal held almost fifty thousand people, a tremendous
number for a preindustrial city.

At dawn, water glittered from a hand-dug limestone reservoir
east of the city. At dusk the sun set in the jungle beyond a sacred
cenote, or sacrificial well. About a hundred yards from the cenote
was a small but elaborate stone pyramid, closely guarded by men
with rifles, which had been erected over the bombproof shelter of
the American millionaire, Owens. When the spook craned his neck
and peered through the stone bars, he could see the entrances and
exits there of the city's highest-ranking priests.

The cell went to work on him the first day. The combination of
his spook training, the Veil, and his computer protected him, but he
observed the techniques with interest. During the day he was hit
with occasional blasts of subsonics, which bypassed the ear and dug
right into the nervous system, provoking disorientation and fear. At
night hidden speakers used hypnagogic indoctrination techniques,
peaking around three A.M. when biorhythmic resistance was lowest.
Mornings and evenings, priests chanted aloud at the temple's sum-
mit, using a mantralike repetition as old as humanity itself. Combined
with the mild sensory deprivation of the chamber, its effect was powerful. After two weeks of this treatment, the spook found himself
chanting his language lessons aloud with an ease that seemed
magical.

In the third week they began drugging his food. When things
began to trail and pattern about two hours after lunch, the spook
realized he was not facing the usual vibratory thrill of subsonics but a
powerful dose of psilocybin. Psychedelics were not the spook's
drugs of choice, but he rode out the dose without much difficulty.
The peyote next day was considerably harder—he could taste its
bitter alkaloids in his tortillas and black beans—but he ate it all anyway, suspecting that his intake and output were monitored. The day
crawled by, with spasms of nausea alternating with elation-states that

made him feel his pores were bleeding spines. He peaked sometime after sunset, when the city gathered by torchlight to watch two young women in white robes plummet fearlessly from a stone catafalque into the cold green depths of the sacred well. He could almost taste the chill green limestone water in his own mouth as the drugged girls quietly drowned.

In the fourth and fifth weeks his diet of native psychedelics was cut back. He was acculturated by being escorted around the city by two young priestesses of his own apparent age. They rounded out the subliminal language lessons and began to introduce him to the Resurgence's carefully crafted theology. By now a normal man would have been sufficiently pulverized to cling to them like a child. It had been a severe ordeal even for the spook, and he sometimes had to struggle against the urge to rip both priestesses to pieces like a pair of tangerines.

Halfway through his second month he was put to work on probation in the cornfields, and allowed to sleep in a hammock in a thatched house. Two other recruits shared the hut, where they struggled to reintegrate their shattered psyches along approved cultural lines. The spook didn't like being cooped up with them; they were so broken up that there was nothing left for him to pick up on.

He was tempted to creep out at night, ambush a couple of priests, and break them up, just to get a healthy flow of disintegrative paranoia going, but he bided his time. It was a tough assignment. The power elite's consumption of drugs had accustomed them to psychotomimetic states, and if he used his implanted schizophrenic weaponry prematurely he might actually reinforce the local paradigm. Instead he began to plan an assault on the millionaire's bunker. Presumably, most of the arsenal of the Predator Saint was still intact: cultured plague germs, chemical agents, possibly even a privately owned warhead or two. The more he thought about it, the more tempted he was to simply murder the entire colony. It would save him a lot of grief.

On the night of the next full moon he was allowed to attend a sacrifice. The rainy season was due, and it was necessary to coax the rain gods with the death of four children. The children were drugged with mushrooms and adorned with flint and jade and thickly embroidered robes. Pepper was blown into their eyes to evoke the rain tears of sympathetic magic, and they were escorted to the edge of the catafalque. Drums and flutes and a chanted litany combined with the moonlight and torchlight to throw an intensely hypnotic ambience over the worshipers. The air reeked of copal incense, and to the spook's empathic senses it seemed as thick as cheese. He let himself soak into the crowd, and it felt wonderful. It was the first time he'd had any fun in ages.

A high-ranking priestess weighted down with armlets and a towering feathered headdress paced slowly along the front lines of the crowd, distributing ladles of fermented balche from a jug. The spook shuffled forward for his share.

There was something very odd about the priestess. At first he thought she was just blasted on psychedelics, but her eyes were clear. She held out the ladle for him to sip, and when his fingers touched hers, she looked into his face and screamed.

Suddenly he knew what was wrong. "Eugenia!" he gasped. She was another spook.

She went for him. There was nothing elegant about the hand-to-hand combat techniques of spooks. The martial arts, with their emphasis on calmness and control, didn't work for operatives only partly conscious to begin with. Instead, ingrained conditioning simply stripped them down into screaming, clawing, adrenalin-crazed maniacs, impervious to pain.

The spook felt murderous hysteria rising up within him. To stand and fight was certain death; his only hope was to escape into the crowd. But as he fended off the woman's rush, strong hands were already seizing him. Snarling, he broke free, spinning toward the lip of the broad edge of the sacred well, then turned, looked: torches, ugly fear, a crazed face, the plumes of warriors nearing, the clack of automatic rifles, no time for a rational decision. Pure intuition, then. He turned and threw himself headfirst into the wide, dank, empty gloom of the sacred well.

The water was a hard shock. He floated on his back, rubbing the sting of impact from his face. The water was thready with filaments of algae. A fish nibbled his bare leg beneath his cotton shirt. He knew all too well what it ate. He looked at the cenote walls. No hope there—they were as smooth as glass, as smooth as if they had been fused with lasers, or fireball-blasted.

Time passed. A white form came plummeting downward, belly-flopping into the water with a lethal smack. They were sacrificing the children.

Something grabbed his foot and pulled him under.

Water filled his nose. He was too busy choking to fight his way free. He was pulled down into the blackness. Water seared his lungs and he passed out.

The spook awoke in a straitjacket and looked up at a ceiling of creamy antiseptic white. He was in a hospital bed. He moved his head on the pillow and realized that his scalp had been shaved.

To his left an antique monitor registered his pulse and breathing. He felt awful. He waited for his computer to whisper something, and realized that it was gone. Rather than feeling its loss, however, he felt, somehow, repulsively *whole*. His brain ached like an overstuffed stomach.

From his right he heard faint, harsh breathing. He twisted his head to look. Sprawled on a waterbed was a withered, naked old man, cyborged into a medusa complex of life-support machinery. A few locks of colorless hair clung to the old man's age-spotted scalp, and his sunken sharp-nosed face had the look of long-forgotten cruelty. . . . An EEG registered a few flickers of comatose delta waves from the hindbrain. It was John Augustus Owens.

The sound of sandals on stone. It was the female spook. "Welcome to the Hacienda Maya, Eugene."

He stirred feebly in his straitjacket, trying to pick up her vibrations. It was like trying to swim in air. With growing panic, he realized that his paradigmatic empathy was gone. "What in hell . . ."

"You're whole again, Eugene. It feels strange, doesn't it? After all those years of being a junkyard of other people's feelings? Can you remember your real name yet? That's an important first step. Try."

"You're a traitor." His head weighed ten tons. He sank back into the pillow, feeling too stupid even to regret his indiscretion. Tattered remnants of his spook training said he ought to flatter her. . . .

"My real name," she said precisely, "was Anatolya Zhukova, and I was sentenced to corrective education by the Brezhnevograd People's Zaibatsery. . . . You were a dissident or so-called criminal of some kind also, before the Veil robbed you of your personality. Most of our top people here are from orbit, Eugene. We're not the stupid Terran cultists you were led to believe. Who hired you, anyway? Yamato Corporation? Fleisher S.A.?"

"Don't waste your time."

She smiled. "You'll come around. You're human now, and the Resurgence is humanity's brightest hope. Look."

She held up a glass flask. Inside it, something like a threaded cloudy film floated slowly in a yellowish plasma. It seemed to squirm. "We took this out of your head, Eugene."

He gasped. "The Veil."

"Yes, the Veil. It's been riding on the top of your cortex for God knows how long now, breaking you up, keeping you fluid. Robbing you of your personality. You were nothing better than a psychopath in harness."

He closed his eyes, stunned. She said, "We understand Veil technology here, Eugene. We use it ourselves, sometimes, on sacrificial victims. They can emerge from the well, touched by the Gods. Troublemakers turned divinely into saints. It fits in well with the old Mayan traditions of trepanation; a triumph of social engineering, really. They're very competent here. They managed to capture me without knowing anything about the spook apparat but rumors."

"You tried to take them out?"

"Yes. They caught me alive and won me over. And even without the Veil I have enough perception left to tell a spook when I see one." Again, she smiled. "I was faking mania when I attacked you. I only knew you had to be stopped at any cost."

"I could have ripped you apart."

"Then, yes. But now you've lost your maniac phase, and we've killed your implanted weapons. Cloned bacteria producing schizophrenic toxins in your sinuses. Altered sweat glands oozing emotional hormones. Nasty! But you're safe now. You're nothing more or less than a normal human being."

He consulted his interior state. His brain felt like a dinosaur's. "Do people really feel like this?"

She touched his cheek. "You haven't begun to feel. Wait until you've lived with us awhile, seen the plans we've made, in the finest traditions of the Predator Saints. . . ." She looked reverently at the machine-pumped corpse across the room. "Overpopulation, Eugene —that's what ruined us. The Saints took the moral effort of genocide upon themselves. Now the Resurgents have taken up the challenge of building a stable society—without the dehumanizing technology that has always, inevitably, been turned against us. The Mayans had the right idea—a civilization of social stability, ecstatic communion with the Godhead, and a firm appreciation of the cheapness of human life. They simply didn't go far enough. They didn't kill enough people to keep their population in check. With a few small changes in the Mayan theology we have brought the whole system into balance. It's a balance that will outlast the Synthesis by centuries."

"You think primitives armed with stone knives can triumph over the industrialized world?"

She looked at him pityingly. "Don't be naive. Industry really belongs in space, where there's room and raw materials, not in a biosphere. Already the zaibatseries are years ahead of Earth in every major field. The Earth's industrial cartels are so drained of energy and resources trying to clean up the mess they inherited that they can't even handle their own industrial espionage. And the Resurgent elite is armed to the teeth with the weaponry, and the spiritual inheritance, of the Predator Saints. John Augustus Owens dug the cenote of Tikal with a low-yield neutron bomb. And we own stores of twentieth-century binary nerve gas that we could smuggle, if we wanted, into Washington, or Kyoto, or Kiev. . . . No, as long as the elite exists, the Synthetics can't dare to attack us head-on—and we intend to go on protecting this society until its rivals are driven into space, where they belong. And now you and I, together, can avert the threat of paradigmatic attack."

"There'll be others," he said.

"We've co-opted every attack made upon us. People want to live real lives, Eugene—to feel and breathe and love and be of simple human worth. They want to be something more than flies in a cybernetic web. They want something realer than empty pleasures in the luxury of a zaibatsu can-world. Listen, Eugene. I'm the only person who has ever put on the spook's Veil and then returned to humanity, to a thinking, feeling, genuine life. We can understand each other."

The spook considered this. It was frightening and bizarre to be rationally thinking on his own, without a computer helping to manage his stream of consciousness. He hadn't realized how stiff and painful thinking was. The weight of consciousness had crushed the intuitive powers that the Veil had once set free. He said incredulously, "You think we could *understand* each other? By ourselves?"

"Yes!" she said. "You don't know how much I've needed it!"

The spook twitched in his straitjacket. There was a roaring in his head. Half-smothered segments of his mind were flaming, like blown coals, back into blazing life. "Wait!" he shouted. "Wait!" He had remembered his name and, with it, what he was.

Outside Replicon's Washington headquarters, snow was sifting over the altered evergreens. The head of security leaned back in his chair, fiddling with his light pen. "You've changed, Eugene."

The spook shrugged. "You mean the skin? The zaibatsery apparat can deal with that. I'm dead tired of this bodyform, anyway."

"No, it's something else."

"Of course, I was robbed of the Veil." He smiled flatly. "To continue. Once the traitress and I had become lovers, I was able to discover the location and guard codes of the nerve gas armaments. Immediately thereafter I faked an emergency, and released the chemical agents within the sealed bunker. They had all sought safety there, so their own ventilation system destroyed all but two of them. Those two I hunted down and shot later the same night. Whether the cyborg Owens 'died' or not is a matter of definition."

"You won the woman's trust?"

"No. That would have taken too long. I simply tortured her until she broke." Again, he smiled. "Now the Synthesis can move in and dominate the Mayan population, as you would any other preindustrial culture. A few transistor radios will knock the whole flimsy structure over like a deck of cards."

"You have our thanks," said the chief. "And my personal congratulations."

"Save it," said the spook. "Once I've faded back into the shadows under the Veil, I'll forget all this anyway. I'll forget that my name is Simpson. I'll forget that I am the mass murderer responsible for the explosion of the Leyland Zaibatsery and the death of eight thousand orbiters. By any standards I am a deadly hazard to society who fully deserves to be psychically destroyed." He fixed the man with a cold, controlled, and feral grin. "And I face my own destruction happily. Because now I've seen life from both sides of the Veil. Because now I know for sure what I've always suspected. Being human just isn't enough fun."

THE BEAUTIFUL
AND THE SUBLIME

May 30, 2070

Y DEAR MACLUHAN:

You, my friend, who know so well a lover's troubles, will understand my affair with Leona Hillis.

Since my last letter to you, I have come to know Leona's soul. Slowly, almost despite myself, I opened those reservoirs of sympathy and feeling that turn a simple liaison into something much deeper. Something that partakes of the sublime.

It is love, my dear MacLuhan. Not the appetite of the body, easily counterfeited with pills. No, it is closer to *agape,* the soaring spiritual union of the Greeks.

I know the Greeks are out of favor these days, especially Plato with his computerlike urge toward abstract intellect.

Forgive me if my sentiments take this somewhat over-Westernized expression. I can only express what I feel, simply and directly.

In other words, I am free of that sense of evanescence that poisoned my earlier commitments. I feel as if I had always loved Leona; she has a place within my soul that could never be filled by another woman.

I know it was rash of me to leave Seattle. Aksyonov was eager to have me complete the set design for his new drama. But I felt taxed and restless, and dreaded the days of draining creative effort. Inspiration comes from nature, and I had been too long pent in the city.

So, when I received Leona's invitation to her father's birthday gala in the Grand Canyon, the lure was irresistible. It combined the best of both worlds: the companionship of a charming woman, against the background of a natural wonder unrivaled for sublimity.

I left poor Aksyonov only a hasty note over the mailnet, and fled to Arizona.

And what a landscape! Great sweeping mesas, long blasted vistas in purple and rose, great gaudy sunsets reaching ethereal fingers of pure radiance halfway to the zenith! It is the opposite pole to our green, introspective Seattle; a bright yang to the drizzling yin of the Pacific Coast. The air, sharpened by sagebrush and pinyon pine, seems to scrub the brain like a loofah. At once I felt my appetite return, and a new briskness lent itself to my step.

I spoke with several Arizonans about their Global Park. I found them to be sensitive and even noble people, touched to the core by the staggering beauty of their eerie landscape. They are quite modern in their sentiments, despite the large numbers of retirees—crotchety industrial-age relics. Since the draining of Lake Powell, the former floodplain of the reservoir has been opened to camping, sports, and limited development. This relieves the crowding in the Grand Canyon itself, which, under wise stewardship, is returning to a pristine state of nature.

For Dr. Hillis's celebration, Hillis Industries had hired a modern hogan, perching on the northern canyon rim. It was a broad two-story dome, wrought from native cedar and sandstone, which blended into the landscape with admirable restraint and taste. A wide cedar porch overlooked the river. Behind the dome, white-barked Ponderosa pines bordered a large rock garden.

Freed of its obnoxious twentieth-century dams, the primal Colorado raged gloriously below the cliffsides, leaping and frothing in great silted billows and surges, flinging rocks and driftwood with tigerlike abandon. In the days that followed, its hissing roar would never be far from my thoughts.

The long drowning beneath the man-made lake had added an eerie charm to these upper reaches of the great canyon. Its shale and sandstone walls were stained a viridian green. In gulfs and eddies amid the canyon's sinuous turns, old lake sediments still clung in warping slopes, clotted by the roots of cottonwoods and flowering scrub.

On the hogan porch, overlooking the cliffs, I plugged my wrist-ward into the house system and made my presence known. Also on the porch were a pair of old people. I checked their identities with my newly charged ward. But with the typical callousness of their generation, they had not plugged into the house system, and remained unknown to me.

It was with some relief, then, that I saw our old friend Mari Kuniyoshi emerge from the hogan to greet me. She and I had corresponded faithfully since her return to Osaka; mostly about her fashion business, and the latest gossip in Japanese graphic design.

I confess I never understood the magnetic attraction Mari has for so many men. My interest lies in her talent for design, and in fact I find her romances rather heartless.

My ward identified Mari's companion: her production engineer and chief technician, Claire Berger. Mari was dressed somewhat ahead of the latest taste, in a bright high-throated peach sateen jacket and subtly clinging fluted anklewrap skirt. Claire Berger wore expedition pants, a cotton trek blouse, and hiking boots. It was typical of Mari that she would use this gawky young woman as a foil.

The three of us were soon chastely sipping fruit juice under one of the porch umbrellas and admiring the view. We traded pleasantries while I waited for Mari's obvious aura of trouble to manifest itself.

It emerged that Mari's current companion, a nineteen-year-old model and aspiring actor, had become a source of friction. Also present at the Hillis birthday fete was one of Mari's older flames, the globe-trotting former cosmonaut, Friedrik Solokov. Mari had not expected Fred's appearance, though he had been traveling with Dr. Hillis for some time. Mari's model friend had sensed the rekindled rapport between Mari and Fred Solokov, and he was extravagantly jealous.

"I see," I said. "Well, at some convenient time I can take your young friend aside, for a long talk. He's an actor with ambitions, you say. Our troupe is always looking for new faces."

"My dear Manfred," she sighed, "how well you understand my little problems. You look very dashing today. I admire your ascot. What a charming effect. Did you tie it yourself or have a machine do it?"

"I confess," I said. "This ascot has pre-stressed molecular folds."

"Oh," said Claire Berger distantly. "Really roughing it."

I changed the subject. "How is Leona?"

"Ah. Poor Leona," Mari said. "You know how fond she is of solitude. Well, as the preparations go on, she wanders through these great desolate canyons . . . climbing crags, staring down into the mists of that fierce river. . . . Her father is not at all well." She looked at me meaningfully.

"Yes." It was well-known that old Dr. Hillis's eccentricities, even cruelties, had advanced with the years. He never understood the new society his own great work had created. It was one of those ironic strokes you're so fond of, my dear MacLuhan.

However, my Leona had paid for his reactionary stubbornness, so I failed to smile. Poor Leona, the child of the old man's age, had been raised as his industrial princess, expected to master profits and losses and quarterly reports, the blighting discipline of his grisly drudgery. In today's world, the old man might as well have trained her to be a Spanish conquistador. It's a tribute to her spirit that she's done as much for us as she has.

"Someone should be looking after her," Mari said.

"She's wearing her ward," Claire said bluntly. "She'd have to work to get lost."

"Excuse me," I said, rising. "I think it's time I met our host."

I walked into the dome, where the pleasant resinous tang of last night's pine fire still clung to the cold ashes of the hearth. I admired the interior: buffalo hides and vigorous Hopi blankets with the jagged look of old computer graphics. Hexagonal skylights poured light onto a floor of rough masculine sandstone.

Following the ward's lead, I took my bags to a charming interior room on the second floor, with great braced geodesics of rough cedar, and whitewashed walls, hung with quaint agricultural tools.

In the common room downstairs, the old man had gathered with two of his elderly cronies. I was shocked to see how that famous face had aged: Dr. Hillis had become a cadaverous cheek-sucking invalid. He sat within his wheelchair, a buffalo robe over his withered legs. His friends still looked strong enough to be dangerous: crocodilian remnants from a lost age of violence and meat. The two of them had also not registered with the house system, but I tactfully ignored this bit of old-fashioned rudeness.

I joined them. "Good afternoon, Dr. Hillis. A pleasure to share this occasion with you. Thank you for having me."

"This is one of my daughter's friends," Hillis croaked. "Manfred de Kooning, of Seattle. He's an ar-tist."

"Aren't they all," said Crocodile #1.

"If that's so," I said, "we owe our happy estate to Dr. Hillis. So it's a double honor to celebrate with him."

Crocodile #2 reached into his old-fashioned business suit and produced, of all things, a cigarette. He lit it and blew a lungful of cancerous reek among us. Despite myself, I had to take half a step back. "I'm sure we'll meet again," I said. "In the meantime I should greet our hostess."

"Leona?" said Dr. Hillis, scowling. "She's not here. She's out on a private walk. With her fiancé."

I felt a sudden icy pang at this. But I could not believe that Leona had deceived me in Seattle; if she'd had a formal liaison, she would have told me. "A sudden proposal?" I hedged. "They were carried away by passion?"

Crocodile #1 smirked sourly, and I realized that I'd touched a sore spot. "Damn it," Hillis snapped, "it's not some overblown modern claptrap with ridiculous breast-beating and hair-tearing. Leona's a sensible girl with old-fashioned standards. And Dr. Somps certainly fulfills those in every degree." He glared at me as if daring me to contradict him.

Of course I did no such thing. Dr. Hillis was gravely ill; it would have been cruelty to upset a man with such a leaden look. I murmured a few noncommittal pleasantries and excused myself.

Once outside again, I quickly consulted my ward. It gave me the biographical data that Dr. Somps had placed in the house system, for the use of guests.

My rival was a man of impressive accomplishments. He had been a child prodigy possessed of profound mathematical gifts. He was now twenty-nine, two years younger than myself, and a professor of aeronautical engineering at the Tsiolkovsky Institute in Boulder, Colorado. He had spent two years in space, as a guest in the Russian station. He was the author of a textbook on wing kinematics. He was an unsurpassed expert on wind-tunnel computer simulations, as performed by the Hillis Massively Parallel Processor.

You can imagine my profound agitation at learning this, my dear MacLuhan. I imagined Leona leaning her ringleted head on the shoulder of this suave spaceman. For a moment I succumbed to rage.

Then I checked my ward, and realized that the old man had lied. The ward's locator told me that Dr. Somps was on a plateau to the west, and his companion was not Leona but his fellow cosmonaut, Fred Solokov. Leona was alone, exploring an arroyo two miles upstream, to the east!

My heart told me to rush to her side, and as always in such matters, I obeyed it.

It was a bracing hike, skirting declines and rockslides, with the sullen roar of the mighty Colorado to my right. Occasional boatloads of daredevils, paddling with might and main, appeared amid the river's surges, but the trails were almost deserted.

Leona had climbed a fanglike promontory, overlooking the river. She was hidden from ground level, but my ward helped me find her. Filled with ardor, I ignored the trail and scrambled straight up the slope. At the cost of a few cactus spines, I had the pleasure of appearing suddenly, almost at her side.

I swept my broad-brimmed hat from my head. "My dear Ms. Hillis!"

Leona sat on a paisley groundcloth; she wore a loose bush jacket over a lace blouse, its white intricacy complemented by the simple lines of a calf-length Serengeti skirt. Her blue-green eyes, whose very faint protuberance seems to multiply her other charms, were red-rimmed from weeping. "Manfred!" she said, raising one hand to her lips. "You've found me despite myself."

I was puzzled. "You asked me to come. Did you imagine I'd refuse you anything?"

She smiled briefly at my galanterie, then turned to stare moodily over the savage river. "I meant this to be a simple celebration. Something to get Father out of his black mood. . . . Instead, my troubles have multiplied. Oh, Manfred, if only you knew."

I sat on a corner of the groundcloth and offered her my canteen of Apollinaris water. "You must tell me everything."

"How can I presume on our friendship?" she asked. "A kiss or two stolen backstage, a few kind words—what recompense is that? It would be best if you left me to my fate."

I had to smile at this. The poor girl equated our level of physical intimacy with my sense of obligation; as if mere physical favors could account for my devotion. She was oddly old-fashioned in that sense, with the old industrial mentality of things bought and sold. "Nonsense," I said. "I'm resolved not to leave your side until your mind is eased."

"You know I am affianced?"

"I heard the rumor," I said.

"I hate him," she said, to my vast relief. "I agreed to it in a moment of weakness. My father was so furious, and so set on the idea, that I did it for his sake, to spare him pain. He's very ill, and the chemotherapy has made him worse than ever. He's written a book—

full of terrible, hateful things. It's to be released under specific conditions—upon proof of his suicide. He threatens to kill himself, to shame the family publicly."

"How horrible," I said. "And what about the gentleman?"

"Oh, Marvin Somps has been one of Father's protégés for years. Flight simulations were one of the first uses of Artificial Intelligence. It's a field that's dear to Father's heart, and Dr. Somps is brilliant at it."

"I suppose Somps worries about his funding," I said. I was never a devotee of the physical sciences, especially in their current shrunken state, but I could well imagine the agitation of Somps should his ready pool of capital dry up. Except for eccentrics like Hillis, there were few people willing to pay expensive human beings to think about such things.

"Yes, I suppose he worries," she said morosely. "After all, science is his life. He's at the airfield, up on the mesa, now. Testing some wretched machine."

For a moment I felt sorry for Somps, but I thrust the feeling aside. The man was my rival; this was love and war! I checked my ward. "I think a word with Dr. Somps is in order."

"You mustn't! Father will be furious."

I smiled. "I have every respect for your father's genius. But I'm not afraid of him." I donned my hat and smoothed the brim with a quick snap of my hand. "I'll be as polite as I can, but if he needs his eyes opened, then I am the man to do it."

"Don't!" she cried, seizing my hand. "He'll disinherit me."

"What's mere pelf in the modern age?" I demanded. "Fame, glory —the beautiful and the sublime—now those are goals worth striving for!" I took her shoulders in both my hands. "Leona, your father trained you to manage his abstract riches. But you're too soulful, too much a full human being for such a mummified life."

"I like to think so," she said, her upturned eyes full of pain. "But Manfred, I don't have your talent, or the sophistication of your friends. They tolerate me for my wealth. What else do I have to offer? I haven't the taste or grace or wit of a Mari Kuniyoshi."

I felt the open ache of her exposed insecurities. It was perhaps at that moment, my dear MacLuhan, that I truly fell in love. It is easy to admire someone of grace and elegance, to have one's eye caught by the sleek drape of a skirt or by a sidelong glance across the room. In certain circles it is possible to live through an entire affair which is composed of nothing more than brittle witticisms. But the love of the spirit comes when the dark yin of the soul is exposed in the lover's sight; vanities, insecurities, those tender crevices that hold the potential of real pain.

"Nonsense," I said gently. "Even the best art is only a symptom of an inner greatness of soul. The purest art is silent appreciation of beauty. Later, calculation spoils the inner bloom to give an outer mask of sophisticated taste. But I flatter myself that I can see deeper than that."

After this, things progressed rapidly. The physical intimacies which followed were only a corollary of our inner rapport. Removing only selected articles of clothing, we followed the delightful practice of *carezza*, those embraces that enflame the mind and body, but do not spoil things with a full satisfaction.

But there was a specter at our love feast: Dr. Somps. Leona insisted that our liaison be kept secret; so I tore myself away, before others could track us with their wards and draw unwelcome conclusions.

Having arrived as an admirer, I left as a lover, determined that nothing should spoil Leona's happiness. Once on the trail again, I examined my ward. Dr. Somps was still on the tall mesa, west of the hogan.

I turned my steps in that direction, but before I had gone more than a mile I had a sudden unexpected encounter. From overhead, I heard the loud riffling of fabric wings.

I consulted my ward and looked up. It was Mari Kuniyoshi's current escort, the young model and actor, Percival Darrow. He was riding a hang glider; the machine soared with cybernetic smoothness across the banded cliff-face. He turned, spilling air, and landed on the trail before me, with an athletic bound. He stood waiting.

By the time I reached him the glider had folded itself, its prestressed folds popping and flapping into a neat orange backpack. Darrow leaned against the sun-warmed rock with a teenager's false nonchalance. He wore a sleek cream-colored flyer's jumpsuit, its elastic sleeves pushed up to reveal the brawny arms of a gymnast. His eyes were hidden by rose-colored flyer's goggles.

I was polite. "Good afternoon, Mr. Darrow. Fresh from the airfield?"

"Not that fresh," he said, a sneer wrinkling his too-perfect features. "I was floating over you half an hour ago. The two of you never noticed."

"I see," I said coldly, and walked on. He hurried after me.

"Where do you think you're going?"

"Up to the airfield, if it's any of your business," I said.

"Solokov and Somps are up there." Darrow looked suddenly desperate. "Look, I'm sorry I mentioned seeing you with Ms. Hillis. It was a bad gambit. But we both have rivals, Mr. de Kooning. And they're together. So you and I should also have an understanding. Don't you think so?"

I slowed my pace a bit. My shoes were better than his; Darrow winced as he hopped over rocks in his thin flight slippers. "What exactly do you want from me, Mr. Darrow?"

Darrow said nothing; a slow flush built up under his tanned cheeks. "Nothing from you," he said. "Everything from Mari Kuniyoshi."

I cleared my throat. "Don't say it," Darrow said, raising a hand. "I've heard it all; I've been warned away from her a dozen times. You think I'm a fool. Well, perhaps I am. But I went into this with my eyes open. And I'm not a man to stand aside politely while a rival tramples my happiness."

I knew it was rash to involve myself with Darrow, who lacked discretion. But I admired his spirit. "Percival, you're a man of my own heart," I confessed. "I like the boldness of a man who'll face even longer odds than my own." I offered my hand.

We shook like comrades. "You'll help me, then?" he said.

"Together we'll think of something," I said. "Truth to tell, I was just going to the airfield to scout out our opposition. They're formidable foes, and an ally's welcome. In the meantime it's best that we not be seen together."

"All right," Darrow said, nodding. "I already have a plan. Shall we meet tonight and discuss it?"

We agreed to meet at eight o'clock at the lodge, to plot confusion to cosmonauts. I continued down the trail, while Darrow climbed an escarpment to find a spot to launch himself.

I stopped at the hogan again to refill my canteen and enjoy a light tea. A cold shower and quick pill relieved the stresses of *carezza*. The excitement, the adventure, were doing me good. The cobwebs of sustained creative effort had been swept from my brain. You may smile, my dear MacLuhan; but I assure you that art is predicated on living, and I was now in the very thick of real life.

I was soon on my way, refreshed and groomed. An afternoon's hike and a long climb brought me to the glider grounds, an airfield atop a long-drowned mesa now known as the Throne of Adonis. Reborn from the depths of Lake Powell, it was named in consonance with the various Osirises, Vishnus, and Shivas within Grand Canyon

Global Park. The hard sandstone caprock had been cleaned of sediment and leveled near one edge, with a tastefully unobtrusive light aircraft hangar, a fiberglass control tower, changing rooms, and a modest teahouse. There were perhaps three dozen flyers there, chatting and renting gliders and powered ultralights. Only two of them, Somps and Solokov, were from our party.

Solokov was his usual urbane, stocky self. He had lost some hair since I'd last seen him. Somps was a surprise. Tall, stooped, gangling, with a bladelike nose, he had coarse windblown hair and long flopping hands. They both wore flightsuits; Solokov's was of modish brown corduroy, but Somps's was wrinkled day-wear from the Kosmograd space station, a garish orange with grease-stained cuffs and frayed Cyrillic mission patches.

They were muttering together over a small experimental aircraft. I stepped into sight. Solokov recognized me and nodded; Somps checked his ward and smiled briefly and distractedly.

We studied the aircraft together. It was a bizarre advanced ultralight, with four flat, paired wings, like a dragonfly's. The translucent wings were long and thin, made of gleaming lightweight film over netted struts of tough plastic. A cagelike padded rack beneath the wings would cradle the pilot, who would grip a pair of joysticks to control the flight. Behind the wings, a thick torso and long counterbalancing tail held the craft's engine.

The wings were meant to flap. It was a one-man powered ornithopter. I had never seen its like. Despite myself, I was impressed by the elegance of its design. It needed a paint job, and the wiring had the frazzled look of a prototype, but the basic structure was delightful.

"Where's the pilot?" I said.

Solokov shrugged. "I am he," he said. "My longest flight being twenty seconds."

"Why so brief?" I said, looking around. "I'm sure you'd have no lack of volunteers. I'd like a spin in it myself."

"No avionics," Somps mumbled.

Solokov smiled. "My colleague is saying that the Dragonfly has no computer on board, Mr. de Kooning." He waved one arm at the other ultralights. "These other craft are highly intelligent, which is why anyone can fly them. They are user-friendly, as they used to say. They have sonar, updraft and downdraft detection, aerofoil control, warpage control, and so forth and so forth. They almost fly themselves. The Dragonfly is different. She is seat-of-the-pants."

As you may imagine, my dear MacLuhan, this news amazed and

intrigued me. To attempt to fly without a computer! One might as well eat without a plate. It then occurred to me that the effort was surely very hazardous.

"Why?" I said. "What happened to its controls?"

Somps grinned for the first time, exposing long, narrow teeth. "They haven't been invented yet. I mean, there aren't algorithms for its wing kinematics. Four wings flapping—it generates lift through vortex-dominated flow fields. You've seen dragonflies."

"Yes?" I hedged.

Solokov spread his hands. "It is a breakthrough. Machines fly through calculation of simple, fixed wings. A computer can fly any kind of traditional aircraft. But, you see, the mathematics that determine the interactions of the four moving wings—no machine can deal with such. No such programs exist. The machines cannot write them because they do not know the mathematics." Solokov tapped his head. "Only Marvin Somps knows them."

"Dragonflies use perturbations in the flow field," Somps said. "Steady-state aerodynamic theory simply can't account for dragonfly lift values. I mean, consider its major flight modes: stationary hovering, slow hovering in any direction, high-speed upward and downward flight, as well as gliding. Classic aerodynamic design can't match that." He narrowed his eyes. "The secret is unsteady separated lift flows."

"Oh," I said. I turned to Solokov. "I didn't know you grasped the mathematics, Fred."

Solokov chuckled. "No. But I took cosmonaut's pilot training, years ago. A few times we flew the primitive craft, without avionics. By feel, like riding the bicycle! The brain does not have to know, to fly. The nervous system, it has a feel. Computers fly by thinking, but they feel nothing!"

I felt a growing sense of excitement. Somps and Solokov were playing from the central truism of the modern age. Feeling—perception, emotion, intuition, and taste—these are the indefinable elements that separate humanity from the shallow logic of our modern-day intelligent environment. Intelligence is cheap, but the thrill of innate mastery is precious. Flying the Dragonfly was not a science, but an art!

I turned to Somps. "Have you tried it?"

Somps blinked and resumed his normal hangdog expression. "I don't like heights."

I made a mental note of this, and smiled. "How can you resist? I was thinking of renting a common glider here, but having seen this contraption, I feel cheated!"

Somps nodded. "My thinking exactly. Moderns . . . they like novelty. Glitter and glamour. It ought to do well if we can get it into production. Commercially, I mean." His tone wavered from resignation to defiance. I nodded encouragingly as a number of choice epithets ran through my head: money-grubbing poltroon, miserly vivisectionist, and so forth. . . .

The basic idea seemed sound. Anything with the innate elegance of Somps's aircraft had definite appeal for today's leisure society. However, it would have to be designed and promoted properly, and Somps, who struck me as something of an idiot savant, was certainly not the man for the job. You could tell just from the way he mooned over it that the machine was, in its own odd way, a labor of love. The fresh grease on his cuffs showed that Somps had spent precious hours up on the plateau, fiddling with his knobs and switches, while his bride-to-be despaired.

Such technician's dedication might have passed muster in the days of the steam engine. But in today's more humane age Somps's behavior seemed close to criminal. This head-in-the-clouds deadbeat saw my poor Leona as a convenient way to finance his pointless intellectual curiosity.

My encounter with the two ex-cosmonauts gave me much to ponder. I withdrew with polite compliments and rented one of the local hang gliders. I circled the Throne of Adonis a few times to establish my bona fides, and then flew back to the hogan.

The effect was enchanting. Cradled by the machine's slow and careful swoops and glides, one felt the majesty of an archangel. Yet I found myself wondering what it would be like without the protective shroud of computer piloting. It would be cold sweat and naked risk and a rush of adrenalin, in which the shadowed crevices far beneath one's feet would be, not an awesome panorama, but a sheer drop!

I admit I was glad to send the machine back to the mesa on its own.

Inside the hogan I enjoyed the buffet supper, carefully avoiding the reeking plates of scorched beef served to the elders. ("Barbecue," they called it. I call it murder.) I sat at a long table with Claire Berger, Percival Darrow, and several of Leona's West Coast friends. Mari herself did not make an appearance.

Leona arrived later, when machines had cleared the meal away and the younger guests had gathered round the fire. Leona and I pretended to avoid one another, but traded stolen glances in the firelight. Under the influence of the mellow light and the landscape, the talk drifted to those poles of the modern existence: the beautiful and the sublime. We made lists: the land is beautiful, the sea is sublime; day is beautiful, night is sublime; craft is beautiful, art is sublime, and so forth.

The postulate that the male is beautiful while the female is sublime provoked much heated comment. While the discussion raged, Darrow and I unstrapped our wards and left them in the common room. Anyone checking our location would see our signals there, while we actually conspired among the machines in the kitchen.

Darrow revealed his plan. He meant to accuse Solokov of cowardice, and seize his rival's glory by testing the Dragonfly himself. If necessary, he would steal the machine. Solokov had done nothing more than take a few fluttering efforts around the top of the mesa. Darrow, on the contrary, meant to fling himself into space and break the machine to his will.

"I don't think you realize the danger involved," I said.

"I've been flying since I was a kid," Darrow sneered. "Don't tell me you're spooked too."

"Those were computer-guided," I said. "This is a blind machine. It could kill you."

"Out on Big Sur we used to rig them," Darrow said. "We'd cut out the autopilot on a dare. It's simple if you find the main sensor thingamajig. It's illegal, but I've done it. Anyway, it makes it easy for you, right? If I break my neck, your Somps will look like a criminal, won't he? He'll be discredited."

"This is outrageous!" I said, but was unable to restrain a smile of admiration. There was a day when my blood ran as hot as Darrow's, and, if I no longer wore my heart on my sleeve, I could still admire the grand gesture.

"I'm going to do it anyway," Darrow insisted. "You needn't worry on my account. You're not my keeper, and it's my decision."

I thought it over. Clearly he could not be argued out of it. I could inform against him, but such a squalid betrayal was completely beneath me. "Very well," I said, clapping him on the shoulder. "How can I help?"

Our plans progressed rapidly. We then returned to the gathering and quietly resumed our wrist-wards and our places near the hearth. To my delight, I found that Leona had left a private note on my ward. We had a midnight assignation.

After the party broke up I waited in my room for her arrival. At last the welcome glow of lamplight came down the corridor. I eased the door open silently.

She wore a long nightgown, which she did not remove, but otherwise we spared ourselves nothing, except for the final sating pleasure. When she left an hour later, with a last tender whisper, my nerves were singing like synthesizers. I forced myself to take two pills and waited for the ache to subside. For hours, unable to sleep, I stared at the geodesic cedar beams of the ceiling, thinking of spending days, weeks, years, with this delightful woman.

Darrow and I were up early next morning, our minds grainy and sharp with lack of sleep and a lover's adrenalin. We lurked in ambush for the unwitting Solokov as he returned from his morning jog.

We mousetrapped him badly as he prepared to go in for a much-needed shower. I stopped him, enthusing about my glider flight. Darrow then joined our conversation "accidentally" and made a number of sharp comments. Solokov was genial and evasive at first, shrugging off Darrow's insinuations. But my loud, innocent questions made things worse for poor Fred. He did his best to explain Somps's cautious testing program for the Dragonfly. But when he was forced to admit that he had only been in the air twenty seconds, the gathering crowd tittered audibly.

Things became hectic with the arrival of Crocodile #1. I had since been informed that this obnoxious old man was Craig Deakin, a medical doctor. He had been treating Dr. Hillis! Small wonder that Leona's father was near death.

Frankly, I've always had a morbid fear of doctors. The last time I was touched by an actual human doctor was when I was a small child, and I can still remember his probing fingers and cold eyes. Imagine it, my dear MacLuhan—putting your health, your very life, into the charge of a fallible human being, who may be drunk, or forgetful, or even corrupt! Thank God that medical expert-systems have made the profession almost obsolete.

Deakin entered the fray with a cutting remark toward Darrow. By now my blood was up, and I lost all patience with this sour old relic. To make things short, we created a scene, and Darrow and I got the best of it. Darrow's fiery rhetoric and my icy sarcasm made an ideal combination, and poor Solokov, gravely puzzled and embarrassed, was unwilling to fight back. As for Dr. Deakin, he simply disgraced himself. It took no skill to show him up for what he was—an arrogant, tasteless old fraud, completely out of touch with the modern world.

Solokov finally fled to the showers, and we carried the day.

Deakin, still leaking venom, tottered off shortly thereafter. I smiled at the reaction of our small eavesdropping audience. They hustled out of Deakin's way as if afraid of his touch. And small wonder! Imagine it, MacLuhan—probing diseased flesh, for money! It gives you a chill.

Flushed with success, we now sought out the unsuspecting Marvin Somps.

To our surprise, our wards located Somps with Mari Kuniyoshi and her ever-present foil, Claire Berger. The three of them were watching the preparations for the evening's festivities: projection screens and an address system were being erected in the rock garden behind the hogan.

I met them first while Darrow hung back in the trees. I greeted Somps with civil indifference, then gently detached Mari from the other two. "Have you seen your Mr. Darrow recently?" I murmured.

"Why, no," she said, and smiled. "Your doing, yes?"

I shrugged modestly. "I trust things have gone well with Fred. What's he doing here, anyway?"

"Oh," she said, "old Hillis asked him to help Somps. Somps has invented some dangerous machine that no one can control. Except for Fred, of course."

I was skeptical. "Word inside was that the thing has scarcely left the ground. I had no idea Fred was the pilot. Such timidity certainly doesn't seem his style."

"He was a cosmonaut!" Mari said hotly.

"So was *he,*" I said, lifting an eyebrow at Somps. In the gentle breeze Somps's lank hair was flying all over his head. He and Claire Berger were in some animated technician's shoptalk about nuts and bolts, and Somps's long hands flopped like a puppet's. In his rumpled, tasteless business suit, Somps looked the very opposite of spacefaring heroism. I smiled reassuringly. "It's not that I doubt Fred's bravery for a moment, of course. He probably distrusts Somps's design."

Mari narrowed her eyes and looked sidelong at Somps. "You think so?"

I shrugged. "They say in camp that flights have only lasted ten seconds. People were laughing about it. But it's all right. I don't think anyone knows it was Fred."

Mari's eyes flashed. She advanced on Somps. I lifted my hat and smoothed my hair, a signal to the lurking Darrow.

Somps was only too happy to discuss his obsession. "Ten seconds? Oh, no, it was twenty. I timed it myself."

Mari laughed scornfully. "Twenty? What's wrong with it?"

"We're in preliminary test mode. These are novel methods of lift production. It's a whole new class of fluid dynamic uses," Somps droned. "The testing's slow, but that's our methodical risk avoidance." He yanked an ink-stained composition book from inside his rumpled jacket. "I have some stroke cycle summaries here. . . ."

Mari looked stunned. I broke in casually. "I heard that the go-slow approach was your pilot's decision."

"What? Fred? Oh, no, he's fine. I mean, he follows orders."

Darrow ambled forward, his hands in his pockets. He was looking at almost everything except the four of us. He was so elaborately casual that I feared Mari would surely catch on. But that remark about public laughter had stung Mari's Japanese soul. "Follows orders?" she told Somps tightly. "People are laughing. You are crushing your test pilot's face."

I took her arm. "For heaven's sake, Mari. This is a commercial development. You can't expect Dr. Somps to put his plane into the hands of a daredevil."

Somps smiled gratefully. Suddenly Claire Berger burst out in his defense. "You need training and discipline for the Dragonfly. You can't just jump in and pop off like bread from a toaster! There are no computers on Marvin's flyer."

I signaled Darrow. He closed in. "Flyer?" he ad-libbed. "You're heading for the airfield, too?"

"We were just discussing Dr. Somps's aircraft," I said artlessly.

"Oh, the Ten-Second Wonder?" Darrow said, grinning. He crossed his muscular arms. "I'd certainly like a shot at that. I hear it has no computer and has to be flown by feel! Quite a challenge, eh?"

I frowned. "Don't be a fool, Percival. It's far too risky for an amateur. Besides, it's Fred Solokov's job."

"It's not his *job*," Somps mumbled. "He's doing a favor."

But Darrow overrode him. "Sounds to me like it's a bit beyond the old man. You need someone with split-second reflexes, Dr. Somps. I've flown by feel before; quite often in fact. If you want someone to take it to the limit, I'm your man."

Somps looked wretched. "You'd crash it. I need a technician, not a daredevil."

"Oh," said Darrow with withering scorn. "A *technician*. Sorry. I had the idea you needed a *flyer*."

"It's expensive," Somps said pitifully. "Dr. Hillis owns it. He financed it."

"I see," Darrow said. "A question of money." He rolled up his sleeves. "Well, if anyone needs me, I'll be on the Throne of Adonis. Or better yet, aloft." He left.

We watched him swagger off. "Perhaps you should give him a shot," I advised Somps. "We've flown together, and he really is quite good."

Somps flushed dully. On some level, I believe he suspected that he had been had. "It's not one of your glamour toys," he mumbled bitterly. "Not yet, anyway. It's my experiment and I'm doing aeronautic science. I'm not an entertainer and I'm not doing sideshow stunts for your benefit, Mr. de Kooning."

I stared at him. "No need to snap," I said coolly. "I sympathize completely. I know things would be different if you were your own man." I touched my hat. "Ladies, good day."

I rejoined Darrow, out of sight, down the trail. "You said you could talk him into it," Darrow said.

I shrugged. "It was worth a try. He was weakening for a moment there. I didn't think he'd be such a stick-in-the-mud."

"Well, now we do things my way," Darrow said. "We have to steal it." He stripped off his ward, set it on top of a handy sandstone ledge, and whacked it with a fist-sized rock. The ward whined, and its screen flared into static. "I think my ward broke," Darrow observed. "Take it in for me and plug me out of the house system, won't you? I wouldn't want anyone to try locating me with my broken ward. That would be rude."

"I still advise against stealing it," I said. "We've made both our rivals look like idiots. There's no need for high drama."

"Don't be petty, Manfred," Darrow said. "High drama is the only way to live!"

I ask you, my dear MacLuhan—who could resist a gesture like that?

That afternoon crawled by. As the celebration started in earnest, wine was served. I was nervous, so I had a glass. But after a few sips I regretted it and set it aside. Alcohol is such a sledgehammer drug. And to think that people used to drink it by the barrel and case!

Dusk arrived. There was still no sign of Darrow, though I kept checking the skies. As preparations for the outdoor banquet neared completion, corporate helicopters began arriving, disgorging their cargos of aging bigwigs. This was, after all, a company affair; and whole hordes of retirees and cybernetic pioneers were arriving to pay tribute to Hillis.

Since they lacked the relaxed politesse of us moderns, their idea of a tribute was harried and brief. They would pack down their plates of scorched meat, swill far too much hard liquor, and listen to speeches . . . then they would check their pacemakers and leave.

A ghastly air of stuffiness descended over the hogan and its surroundings. Leona's contingent of beautiful people was soon outnumbered; pressed on all sides, they flocked together like birds surrounded by stegosaurs.

After a brief delay, a retrospective tribute to Dr. Hillis flashed onto the rock-garden's screen. We watched it politely. There were the familiar scenes, part of the folklore of our century. Young Hillis at MIT, poring over the work of Marvin Minsky and the cognitive psychologists. Hillis at Tsukuba Science City, becoming the heart and soul of the Sixth Generation Project. Hillis, the Man with a Mission, incorporating in Singapore and turning silicon to gold with a touch.

And then all that cornucopia of riches that came with making intelligence into a utility. It's so easy to forget, MacLuhan, that there was once a time when the ability to reason was *not* something that comes through wires just like electricity. When "factory" meant a place where the "blue-collar" caste went to work!

Of course Hillis was only one of a mighty host of pioneers. But as the Nobel Prize winner and the author of Structured Intelligent Multiple Processing he has always been a figurehead for the industry. No, more than that; a figurehead for the age itself. There was a time, before he turned his back on the modern world, when people spoke the name Hillis in the same breath with Edison, Watt, and Marconi.

It was not at all a bad film, of its sort. It didn't tell the whole truth, of course; it was conspicuously quiet about Hillis's regrettable involvement in politics during the '40s, the EEC bribery scandal, and that bizarre episode at the Tyuratam Launch Center. But one can read about those things anywhere. Actually, I confess that I felt the loss of those glory days, which we now see, in hindsight, as the last sunset glow of the Western analytic method. Those lost battalions of scientists, technicians, engineers!

Of course, to the modern temperament, this lopsided emphasis on rational thought seems stifling. Admittedly, machine intelligence has its limits; it's not capable of those human bursts of insight that once advanced scientific knowledge by leaps and bounds. The march of science is now the methodical crawling of robots.

But who misses it? We finally have a stable global society that accommodates man's higher feelings. A world of plenty, peace, and leisure, where the beautiful and the sublime reign supreme. If the film caused me a qualm, it was a credit to our modern mastery of propaganda and public relations. Soft intuitive arts, maybe; the dark yin to the bright yang of the scientific method. But powerful arts, and, like it or not, the ones that shape our modern age.

We had advanced from soup to fish when I caught my first glimpse of Darrow. The Dragonfly emerged from the depths of the canyon in a brief frenzied arc, its four wings thrashing in the twilit air. Strangely, my first impression was not of a struggling pilot but of a poisoned bug. The thing vanished almost at once.

I must have turned pale, for I noticed Mari Kuniyoshi watching me strangely. But I held my peace.

Crocodile #2 took the podium. This gentleman was another artifact of the vanished age. He'd been some kind of military bigwig, a "Pentagon chief of staff" I think they called him. Now he was Hillis Industries' "Chief of Security," as if they needed one in this day and age. It was clear that he'd been drinking heavily. He gave a long lachrymose introduction to Hillis, droning on and on about "air force" this and "space launch" that, and Hillis's contribution to the "defense industry." I noticed then that Fred Solokov, resplendent in tie and tails, began to look noticeably offended. And who could blame him?

Hillis at last took the podium, standing erect with the help of a cane. He was applauded loudly; we were overjoyed to see Crocodile #2 go. It isn't often that you see someone with the bad taste to mention atomic weapons in public. As if sensing the scotched nerves of our Soviet friend, Hillis departed from his prepared speech and began rambling about his "latest project."

Imagine, my dear MacLuhan, the exquisite embarrassment of the moment. For as Hillis spoke, his "latest project" appeared on the fringes of camp. Darrow had mastered the machine, caught an up-draft from the depths of the canyon, and was now fluttering slowly around us. Murmurs began spreading among the crowd; people began to point.

Hillis, not a gifted speaker, was painfully slow to catch on. He kept talking about the "heroic pilot" and how his Dragonfly would be airborne "sooner than we knew." The audience thought poor Hillis was making some elaborate joke, and they began laughing. Most people thought it was clever publicity. In the meantime, Darrow swooped nearer. Sensing with a model's intuition that he was the cynosure of all eyes, he began stunting.

Still avoiding the crowd, he threw the aircraft into a hover. The wings hummed audibly, their tips flapping in complex loops and circles. Slowly, he began flying backward, the craft's long tail waggling in barely controlled instability. The crowd was amazed; they cheered aloud. Hillis, frowning, squinted across the table, his drone dying into a mumble. Then he realized the truth and cried out. Crocodile #2 took his arm, and Hillis tottered backward into his near-by chair.

Dr. Somps, his long face livid, scrambled to the podium. He flung out an arm, pointing. "Stop that man!" he screeched. This provoked hysterical laughter, shading close to authentic hysteria when Darrow spun the craft twice tailfirst and caught himself at the last moment, the wings kicking up clouds of dust over the rear of the crowd. Diners, shrieking, leapt from their chairs and fled for cover. Darrow fought for height, throwing full power into the wings and blowing two tables over with a crash and spatter of tureens and cutlery. The Dragonfly shot up like a child's toy rocket.

Darrow regained control almost at once, but it was clear that the sudden lurch upward had strained one of the wings. Three of them beat smoothly at the twilit air, but the fourth, the left rear one, was out of sync. Darrow began to fall, sliding out of the sky, listing backward to his left.

He tried to throw more power into the wings again, but we all heard the painful flopping and rasping as the injured wing refused to function. At the end the craft spun about again a few feet from earth, hit a pine at the edge of our rock garden, and crashed.

That effectively ended the festivities. The crowd was horrified. A number of the more active attendees rushed to the crash site while others babbled in shock. Crocodile #2 took the microphone and began yelling for order, but he was of course ignored. Hillis, his face twisted, was hustled inside in his chair.

Darrow was pale and bloodied, still strapped into the bent ribs of the pilot's cage. He had a few scrapes, and he had managed to break his ankle. We fished him out. The Dragonfly did not look badly damaged. "The wing gave out," Darrow kept muttering stubbornly. "It was equipment failure. I was doing fine!"

Two husky sorts formed an arm-cradle for Darrow and lugged him back to the hogan. Mari Kuniyoshi hurried after him, her face pale, her hands fluttering in shock. She had a dramatic, paralyzed look.

Lights blazed from the hogan, along with the excited babbling of the crowd. The outside floodlights in the rock garden dimmed suddenly. From the clearings around us, corporate helicopters began to lift, whirring almost silently into the fragrant Arizona night.

The crowd dispersed around the damaged craft. Soon I noticed that there were only three of us left; myself, Dr. Somps, and Claire Berger. Claire shook her head. "God, it's so sad," she said.

"I'm sure he'll recover," I said.

"What, that thief?" she said. "I hope not."

"Oh. Right," I said. I examined the Dragonfly critically. "She's just a little bent, that's all. Nothing broken. She only needs a few biffs with a lug-wrench or what-have-you."

Somps glared at me. "Don't you understand? Dr. Hillis has been humiliated. And my work was the cause of it. I'd be ashamed to speak to him now, much less ask for his support."

"You still have his daughter," Claire Berger said bluntly. We both looked at her in surprise. She looked back boldly, her arms stiff at her sides.

"Right," Somps said at last. "I've been neglecting Leona. And she's so devoted to her father. . . . I think I'd better go to her. Talk to her. Do whatever I can to make this up."

"Plenty of time for that later, when things calm down," I said. "You can't just leave the Dragonfly here! The morning dew will soak her. And you don't want gawkers out here tonight—poking at her, maybe laughing. Tell you what—I'll help you carry her up to the airfield."

Somps hesitated. It did not take long, for his devotion to his machine burst all bounds. With her long wings hinged back, the Dragonfly was easy to carry. Somps and I hoisted the heavy torso to our shoulders, and Claire Berger took the tail. All the way to the mesa Somps kept up a steady monologue of self-pity and disaster. Claire did her clumsy best to cheer him up, but the man was crushed. Clearly a lifetime of silent spleen had built up, requiring just such a calamity to uncork it. Even though he sensed that I was a rival and meant him ill, he could not entirely choke back his need for sympathy.

We found some flyers at the base of the Throne of Adonis. They were curious and eager to help, so I returned to camp. Once he had the Dragonfly in her hangar and his tools at hand, I was sure that Somps would be gone for hours.

I found the camp in uproar. With amazing crassness, Crocodile #2, Hillis's security man, wanted to arrest Darrow. A furious argument broke out, for it was brutally unfair to treat Darrow as a common thief when his only crime had been a daring gesture.

To his credit, Darrow rose above this ugly allegation. He rested in a wicker peacock chair, his bandaged ankle propped on a leather hassock and his pale blond hair swept back from a bruised forehead. The craft was brilliantly designed, he said; it was only the shoddy workmanship of Hillis Industries that had put his life into danger. At various dramatic cruxes, he would lean back with a faint shudder of pain and grasp the adoring hand of Mari Kuniyoshi. No jury in the world would have touched him. All the world loves a lover, Mac-Luhan.

Old Dr. Hillis had retired to his rooms, shattered by the day's events. Finally, Leona broke in and settled things. She scolded Darrow and threw him out, and Mari Kuniyoshi, swearing not to leave his side, went with him. Most of the modern contingent left as well, partly as a gesture of solidarity with Darrow, partly to escape the source of embarrassment and transmute it, somewhere else, into endlessly entertaining gossip.

Poor Fred Solokov, made into the butt of jokes through absolutely no fault of his own, also stormed off. I was with the small crowd as he threw his bags into a robot chopper at midnight. "They do not treat me like this," he insisted loudly. "Hillis is mad. I thought so ever since Tyuratam. Why people admire such young vandals as Darrow these days I do not know."

Truly, I felt sorry for him. I went out of my way to shake his hand. "Sorry to see you go, Fred. I'm sure we'll meet again under better circumstances."

"Never trust women," Fred told me darkly. He paused on the running board to belt his trenchcoat, then stepped in and slammed the vacuum-sealed door. Off he went with a whir of wings. A fine man and a pleasure to know, MacLuhan. I shall have to give some thought to making things up to him.

I then hurried back to my room. With so many gone, it would now be easier for Leona and me to carry on our assignation. Unfortunately I had not had time to arrange the final details with her. And I had a lover's anxiety that she might not even arrive. The day had been a trying one, after all, and *carezza* is not a practice for harried nerves.

Still, I waited, knowing it would be a lover's crime should she arrive and find me sleeping.

At half past one I was rewarded by a dim flicker of lamplight under the door. But it passed me.

I eased the door open silently. A figure in a white nightgown was creeping barefoot around the dome's circular hall. She was too short and squat for the willowy Leona, and her trailing, loosened hair was not blonde, but an unremarkable brown. It was Claire Berger.

I tied my pajamas and shuffled after her with the stealth of a medieval assassin.

She stopped, and scratched at a door with one coy forefinger. I did not need my ward to tell me this was the room of Dr. Somps. The door opened at once, and I ducked back just in time to avoid Claire's quick glance up and down the hall.

I gave the poor devils fifteen minutes. I retired to my room, wrote a note, and returned to Somps's door. It was locked, of course, but I scratched lightly and slid my note under it.

The door opened after a hurried conclave of whispers. I slipped inside. Claire was glowering, her face flushed. Somps's fists were clenched. "All right," he grated. "You have us. What is it you want?"

"What does any man want?" I said gently. "A little companionship, some open sympathy, the support of a soul mate. I want Leona."

"I thought that was it," Somps said, trembling. "She's been so different since Seattle. She never liked me, but she didn't hate me, before. I knew there was someone after her. Well, I have a surprise for you, Mr. de Kooning. Leona doesn't know this, but I've talked to Hillis and I know. He's almost bankrupt! His firm is riddled with debts!"

"Oh?" I said, interested. "So?"

"He's thrown it all away, trying to bring back the past," Somps said, the words tumbling out of him. "He's paid huge salaries to his old hangers-on and backed a hundred dud ideas. He was depending on my success to restore his fortunes. So without me, without the Dragonfly, his whole empire falls apart!" He glared at me defiantly.

"Really?" I said. "That's terrific! I always said Leona was enslaved by this nonsense. Empire indeed; why, the whole thing's a paper tiger. Why, the old fraud!" I laughed aloud. "Very well, Marvin. We're going to have it out with him right now!"

"What?" Somps said, paling.

I gave him a bracing whack on the shoulder. "Why carry on the pretense? You don't want Leona; I do. So there's a few shreds of money involved. We're talking about love, man! Our very happiness! You want some old fool to come between you and Claire?"

Somps flushed. "We were only talking."

"I know Claire better than that," I said gallantly. "She's Mari Kuniyoshi's friend. She wouldn't have stayed here just to trade technical notes."

Claire looked up, her eyes reddened. "You think that's funny?

Don't ruin it for us. Please," she begged. "Don't ruin Marvin's hopes. We have enough against us as it is."

I dragged Somps out the door by main force and closed it behind me. He wrenched free and looked ready to hit me. "Listen," I hissed. "That woman is devoted to you. How dare you trample her finer feelings? Have you no sympathy, no intuition? She puts your plans above her own happiness."

Somps looked torn. He stared at the door behind him with the aspect of a man poleaxed by infatuation. "I never had time for this. I . . . I never knew it could be like this."

"Damn it, Somps, be a man!" I said. "We're having it out with the old dragon right now."

We hustled downstairs to Hillis's suite. I tried the double doors; they were open.

Groaning came from the bedroom.

My dear MacLuhan. You are my oldest and closest friend. Often we have been one another's confessors. You remember the ancient pact we swore, as mere schoolchildren, never to tell each other's mischiefs, and to hold each other's secrets silent to the grave. The pact has served us well, and many times it has eased us both. In twenty years of friendship we have never given each other cause to doubt. However, we are now adults, men steeped in life and its complications; and I'm afraid that you must bear the silent burden of my larger mischiefs with me.

I know you will not fail me, for the happiness of many people rests on your discretion. But someone must be told.

The bedroom door was locked. Somps, with an engineer's directness, knocked out its hinge pins. We rushed inside.

Dr. Hillis had fallen off the bed. A deadly litter on the bedside table told the awful truth at once. Hillis, who had been treating himself with the aid of the servile human doctor, had access to the dangerous drugs normally safely stored in machines. Using an old hand-powered hypodermic, he had injected himself with a fatally large dose of painkiller.

We tugged his frail body back into the bed. "Let me die," the old man croaked. "Nothing to live for."

"Where's his doctor?" I said.

Somps was sweating freely in his striped cotton pajamas. "I saw him leave earlier. The old man threw him out, I think."

"All bloodsuckers," Hillis said, his eyes glazed. "You can't help me. I saw to that. Let me die, I deserve to."

"We can keep him moving, maybe," Somps said. "I saw it in an old film once." It seemed a good suggestion, with our limited knowledge of medicine.

"Ignorant," Hillis muttered, as the two of us pulled his limp arms over our shoulders. "Slaves to machines! Those wards—handcuffs! I invented all that . . . I killed the scientific tradition." He began weeping freely. "Twenty-six hundred years since Socrates and then, me." He glared and his head rolled like a flower on a stalk. "Take your hands off me, you decadent weasels!"

"We're trying to help you, Doctor," Somps said, frightened and exasperated.

"Not a cent out of me, Somps," the old man raved weakly. "It's all in the book."

I then remembered what Leona had told me about the old man's book, to be published on his suicide. "Oh, no," I said. "He's going to disgrace us all and disgrace himself."

"Not a penny, Somps. You failed me. You and your stupid toys. Let me go!"

We dropped him back onto the bed. "It's horrible," Somps said, trembling. "We're ruined."

It was typical of Somps that he should think of himself at a moment like that. Anyone of spirit would have considered the greater interests of society. It was unthinkable that this titan of the age should die in such squalid circumstances. It would give no one happiness, and would cause pain and disillusion to uncounted millions.

I pride myself that I rose to the challenge. My brain roared with sudden inspiration. It was the most sublime moment of my life.

Somps and I had a brief, fierce argument. Perhaps logic was not on my side, but I ground him down with the sheer passion of my conviction.

By the time I had returned with our clothes and shoes, Somps had fixed the door and disposed of the evidence of drugs. We dressed with frantic haste.

By now the old man's lips were bluish and his limbs were like wax. We hustled him into his wheelchair, wedging him in with his buffalo robe. I ran ahead, checking that we were not seen, while Somps wheeled the dying man along behind me.

Luckily there was a moon out. It helped us on the trail to the Throne of Adonis. It was a long exhausting climb, but Somps and I were men possessed.

Roseate summer dawn was touching the horizon by the time we had the Dragonfly ready and the old man strapped in. He was still

breathing shallowly, and his eyelids fluttered. We wrapped his gnarled hands around the joysticks.

When the first golden rim of the sunlight touched the horizon, Somps flicked on the engine. I jammed the aircraft's narrow tail beneath my arm, braced like a lance. Then I ran forward and shoved her off into the cold air of dawn!

MacLuhan, I'm almost sure that the rushing chilly air of the descent revived him briefly. As the aircraft fell toward the roiling waters below, she began to pitch and buck like a live thing. I feel in my heart that Hillis, that seminal genius of our age, revived and fought for life in his last instants. I think he went like a hero. Some campers below saw him hit. They, too, swore he was fighting to the last.

The rest you know. They found the wreckage miles downstream, in the Global Park, next day. You may have seen Somps and myself on television. I assure you, my tears were not feigned; they came from the heart.

Our story told it as it should have happened. The insistence of Dr. Hillis that he pilot the craft, that he restore the fair name of his industries. We helped him unwillingly, but we could not refuse the great man's wishes.

I admit the hint of scandal. His grave illness was common knowledge, and the autopsy machines showed the drugs in his body. Luckily, his doctor admitted that Hillis had been using them for months to fight the pain.

I think there is little doubt in most people's minds that he meant to crash. But it is all in the spirit of the age, my dear MacLuhan. People are generous to the sublime gesture. Dr. Hillis went down fighting, struggling with a machine on the cutting edge of science. He went down defending his good name.

As for Somps and myself, the response has been noble. The mailnet has been full of messages. Some condemn me for giving in to the old man. But most thank me for helping to make his last moments beautiful.

I last saw poor Somps as he and Claire Berger were departing for Osaka. I'm afraid he still feels some bitterness. "Maybe it was best," he told me grudgingly as we shook hands. "People keep telling me so. But I'll never forget the horror of those last moments."

"I'm sorry about the aircraft," I said. "When the notoriety wears off, I'm sure it will be a great success."

"I'll have to find another backer," he said. "And then put it into production. It won't be easy. Probably take years."

"It's the yin and yang," I told him. "Once poets labored in garrets while engineers had the run of the land. Things change, that's all. If one goes against the grain, one pays the price."

My words, meant to cheer him, seemed to scald him instead. "You're so damned smug," he almost snarled. "Damn it, Claire and I build things, we shape the world, we try for real understanding! We don't just do each other's nails and hold hands in the moonlight!"

He is a stubborn man. Maybe the pendulum will one day swing his way again, if he lives as long as Dr. Hillis did. In the meantime he has a woman to stand by him and assure him that he is persecuted. So maybe he will find, in the good fight, some narrow kind of sublimity.

So, my dear MacLuhan, love has triumphed. Leona and I will shortly return to my beloved Seattle, where she will rent the suite next to my own. I feel that very soon we will take the great step of abandoning *carezza* and confronting true physical satisfaction. If all goes well then, I will propose marriage! And then, perhaps, even children.

In any case, I promise you, you will be the first to know.

Yours as always,
de K.

FANTASY STORIES

TELLIAMED

ONSIEUR BENOÎT DE MAILLET, formerly
His Majesty's grand consul in Egypt, now retired, tottered down the slope of the beach on the arm of his
manservant, Torquetil. When they reached the usual
spot beside the great striped rock, de Maillet leaned
on his cane, breathing heavily. The walk was a hard one for a man in
his eighties. De Maillet's wig was askew, and his wise old face was
pinched with concealed suffering.

Torquetil unfolded the campstool. De Maillet sat on it with a
brief sigh of relief. Torquetil set up the parasol. It was an immense
and gaudy parting gift from the Sultan of Egypt, and de Maillet was
particularly proud of it. The servant set a wicker basket of provisions
by the old philosopher's swollen knees. "Will there be anything else,
monsieur?"

"When you get back, have the carriage master come and examine those straps," de Maillet said firmly. He opened his wicker box
and pulled out a black-ribboned pair of spectacles. He sat upright
again with an effort and put his hand to the side of his substantial
paunch. "And tell the cook—no more curries!"

"Very well, monsieur." The young Breton bounded back up the
slope toward the carriage.

De Maillet balanced the spectacles on his large and fleshy nose. He reached into the basket for a letter, and broke its wax seal with his thumb.

Pont Gardeau, Suriname
February 12, 1737

To the Sieur Benoît de Maillet,
Grand Consul and Envoy
Plenipotentiary, ret'd.,
in Marseille.

Cher Monsieur:

Please forgive this execrable handwriting, which, I know, is almost as bad as your own. It seems that my secretary has fallen ill with one of the manifold agues of this pestilential region. Without the aid of this invaluable boy my studies of natural theology have fallen into a lamentable state. I myself am not so well as I should be; but it is nothing serious. I imagine that neither of us can claim the vigor we had in those faraway days in Egypt.

I regret that I am unable to send you the samples of rock you requested; during the past several months I have been upriver, in the interior, humbly struggling for the propagation of His Catholic Majesty's most perfect Faith. During such time I collected a number of very curious worms and insects, with which I hope to confound the pedantic System of the infidel Linnaeus.

The natives of the interior are stubbornly set in their heathen errors, yet full of remarkable stories of men with tails, ancestral giants, and the like, which I hope to convey to you when I have more thoroughly mastered their language.

And now I must chide you. A friend of mine in the Royal Society of London, a colleague in natural theology (though very lamentably a Protestant), has told me that he has read a certain manuscript circulated secretly among the savants of France and England, which he called *Telliamed; or, Discourses On the Diminution of the Sea.* He was full of praise for this manuscript, which, he being an infidel, does nothing for the sanctity of your reputation. And you need not protest your innocence; for a child could see that the supposed Indian sage, named *Telliamed,* who narrates this new System of Geology, merely has your own name spelled backward.

Perhaps the sea really has diminished; I should find this hard to deny, since I, too, have seen the desert of petrified ships in the Bahar-Balaama west of Cairo. But this should not be interpreted to go against Revelation. As your spiritual adviser, I must warn you, my old friend: you are no longer so young as to be able to neglect the very pressing matter of the salvation of your soul. In the end the Dogma must triumph, and no amount of sophistical "evidences," "hypotheses," or "deductions" will save you when you argue before the Throne of Judgment.

I should hate to think that the collections of rocks and fossils that I have sent you had been used for an impious purpose. Yet I cannot leave you without a gift of some sort; and knowing your fondness for snuff, I have sent you some of the aboriginals' own nasal aliment, which they derive from a number of curious bushes and vines. It is not tobacco, but upon the use of it, they receive the word of the Faith more readily, with excitement and rejoicing; so I cannot think that it is bad. I include the small birdbone snuffing tool with which they inhale the substance, for your collection.

In return, I ask that you burn a few candles for the repose of the soul of poor Bérard Procureur; and please try to go to confession with regularity. I pray for you,

Your ancient friend,
Fr. Gérard le Bovier de Fuillet, S.J.

De Maillet smiled. "It is not at all a bad thing to have one's spiritual adviser in another country," he mused aloud. He pulled from within the heavy envelope another, smaller envelope, which rustled. He peeled the gummed endpaper loose, and the snuff within the packet released a pleasant, faintly bitter aroma of exotic spices.

The smell unlocked a chain of memories within de Maillet's mind: cones of black incense smoldering in a perforated silver bowl, dark coffee in a china cup, the nude rump of an Egyptian courtesan spread across a brocade pillow. With these unexpected and pleasant memories came a sudden comfortable loosening in de Maillet's bowels. He felt a brief sense of animal well-being, a warm flickering from the ashen coals of youth.

His doctor had forbidden him snuff. It had been several months since he had last felt his nostrils solidly plugged. He peered carefully into the paper packet. The fine-ground leaves looked harmless enough. He fingered the light, hollow birdbone, then plunged it into the packet and snorted recklessly.

"Yoww!" he shouted, leaping to his feet. His spectacles flew off into the sand. Cursing, de Maillet stomped heavily around the pole of the parasol, his old eyes leaking tears. The pagan snuff had stung his tissues like an angry wasp, hurting so much that he could not even sneeze. He clutched his cheekbone and sinus with one age-spotted leathery hand.

Slowly the pain faded to a strange numbness, not entirely unpleasant. De Maillet straightened his back, then bent to pick up his silver-headed cane and his spectacles. It had been a long time since he had bent so easily. He sat on the campstool without puffing for breath.

He noted with interest that his sensibilities seemed heightened. When he felt the smooth ebony of his cane, it was as if he had never felt it before. Even his eyesight seemed improved; the blue summer sky over the crystalline Mediterranean seemed to shimmer as if it had just been created. Even the sand grains on his silver-buckled pumps seemed to have been placed each just so, forming a tiny constellation of their own against the black leather.

He was just contemplating filling his other nostril when he saw a young townsman running toward him from a rockier section of the coast. Here there were a number of secluded dells and hollows where the young gallants of Marseille were wont to take their mistresses, or other young women whom they wished to persuade to assume that estate. The stranger was a handsome fellow of the commercial class with a face slightly marred by smallpox.

"Did you hear a cry for help?" the young man demanded, stopping in the broad shadow of de Maillet's parasol.

"My word," said de Maillet, embarrassed. "I'm afraid that I myself cried out. I, er, am somewhat troubled with the gout. I wasn't aware that there was anyone within earshot."

"It can't have been you, monsieur," the young man said reasonably, tucking in his linen shirttail. "It was followed by a spate of the most horrible cursing, some of it in a foreign language. My companion was so frightened that she fled immediately."

"Oh," de Maillet said. Suddenly he smiled. "Well, perhaps there was a boatload of sailors, then. My eyes are not so good as they were. I might have missed them completely."

The young man grinned. "All is well. Women always want to prolong a rendezvous long after its natural summation." His eyes fell on de Maillet's cane, a presentation item from the city fathers of Marseille. "Forgive me," the young man said. "You are the Sieur de Maillet, the famous savant, are you not?"

De Maillet smiled. "You know I am. You just read my name from the cane."

"Nonsense," said the young tradesman vigorously. "Everyone knows who Monsieur de Maillet is. Marseille owes its prosperity to you. My father is Jean Martine of the Martine Oriental Import-Export Company. I am his eldest son, Jean Martine the Younger." He bowed. "He has spoken of you often. My family owes you a very large debt of gratitude."

"Yes, I believe I know your father," de Maillet said generously. He loved flattery. "He deals in Egyptian trade-stuffs, does he not? Bitumen, antiquities, and the like." De Maillet shrugged with an aristocrat's proper vagueness about such matters.

"The very same," said Martine. "We have sometimes had the honor of supplying Your Excellency with curios for your very famous cabinet of natural wonders." He hesitated. "Without meaning to intrude, Your Excellency, I cannot help but wonder why I find you alone here on this deserted beach."

De Maillet looked at the tradesman's open, guileless face and felt the natural urge of the old, the learned, and the garrulous to instruct the young. "It has to do with my System," he said. "My life's work in natural philosophy, upon which my posthumous fame will rest. For many years, in my travels, I have examined seashores, and studied the history of the world as revealed in its rocks. It is my contention that the level of the sea is dropping, at a rate I calculate at perhaps three feet every thousand years. During my life I have amassed evidence of this diminution, and I believe it to be proved beyond a shadow of a doubt."

"Very remarkable," said Martine slowly. "But surely you are not sitting here in order to watch it drop."

"No," said de Maillet, "but when the weather is fine, I often come here, to think over old times, to examine my notes and journals, and to extend my chain of deductions.

"For instance. If you grant that the sea is diminishing, then it follows quite rigorously that there must have been a time, many thousands of centuries ago, when the entire earth was covered by the sea. And you may prove this quite easily. I have examined the cabinet of Herr Scheuchzer in Zurich, which contains a great many fossilized fish that that worthy man pried from the stones of the Swiss mountains. In the writings of the savant Fulgose we find the story of an entire ship, with its sails, cordage, and anchors, and the bones of forty of its crew, found fossilized a hundred fathoms down an iron mine in the Canton of Bern. Herodotus writes of iron mooring-rings found far up the slopes of the mountains of Mokatan, near Memphis. How else can we account for these vestiges, than to assume that the sea was once deep enough to drown these mountains?"

De Maillet jabbed his cane into the sand. "So. It follows, then, that life must have arisen from the sea, and that such creatures as sea adders, sea apes, sea dogs, and sea lions must have swarmed in the depths when there was no land at all. Similarly, sea grapes, sea lettuce, sea moss, and sea trees must have supplied the land with its greenery."

"This is very troubling," the young man said. "What of men, then? Do you believe that men, too, arose from the sea?"

"To be sure, it is troubling," de Maillet said. "But the *evidence,* young man; one cannot ignore the *evidence.* I admit that I have never seen mermen. But I have seen the bones of giants. Thirty years ago, in the quarry of Cape Coronne, just a few miles from here, I saw the bones of a giant, lying on his back, enclosed in the stone. When you have seen a marvel like that with your own eyes, you may confidently put aside your doubts. . . ." A strange feeling was creeping up and down the length of de Maillet's spine. He closed his eyes and felt a weird tremor below the soles of his feet, as if the bowels of the earth had shifted. When he opened his eyes, with a crawling sense of vertigo, he saw a phenomenon so odd that he rejected it almost at once as a trick of the light.

It was as if the hand of God had dropped a formless pane of tinted glass on the horizon. Then this mighty pane, or this wall of invisible essence, had swept forward from out of the distance and flashed past him. It was as if this formless wall had combed the sea to its depths, and had passed through the very substance of the earth, leaving no ripple of its passage, yet leaving everything somehow subtly changed. He himself felt different, stirred somehow, with an odd tingling sensation, as he sometimes had before a thunderstorm. A strange cool breeze began to blow steadily off the sea. It seemed to de Maillet that the suspicious breeze had a faint marshy reek of roiled mud, from the subaqueous depths of the world.

He looked at the young man sitting in the sand at his feet. Some manner of subtle transformation had affected the young tradesman. He was eyeing de Maillet with a bold and speculative look, as if he were about to buy the world and was ready to offer de Maillet as a down payment. De Maillet said faintly, "You didn't see . . . ?"

"See what, Your Excellency?"

"A certain . . . flash, a certain wind? No? No, of course not." De Maillet shivered. "Where were we?"

"Your Excellency was speaking of mermen."

"Mermen." Although it was one of his favorite topics, the word sounded strange to de Maillet, as if in a single instant the word had aged a thousand years and was now some dusty and totally discredited apparition from the remote past. Had he ever really believed in mermen and merwomen? Surely he must have, for they merited an entire subchapter in his masterwork.

"Ah yes, mermen. Though I have never seen one, I have garnered many references from writers of unquestioned veracity. We must omit the tales of ancients such as Pliny, who speaks of flute-playing tritons and the like; they were entirely too credulous.

"Avoiding old wives' tales, then, and sticking strictly to the facts: I have read the works of al-Qaswini, the celebrated Arabian writer, in the original. In his narrative of the travels of Salim, envoy of the Caliph Vathek of the Abassids, he mentions a fishing party on the Caspian Sea, where a mergirl was rescued whole from the belly of a monstrous fish. She was not half-fish and half-woman, as popular error has it, but a woman entire. On being parted from the water, she sobbed and tore her hair, but could not speak any human words. This was in the year of the Hegira 288, or the year 842 of our era.

"In the year 1430, after a great flood in the Zuider Zee, a mergirl was captured from the mud behind the dikes. The good women of Edam taught her to dress herself, to spin, and to make the sign of the cross, which, one must suppose, was the entirety of the accomplishments of the women of that rather dull country. . . . In later life she attempted to return to the water on a number of occasions, but her lungs had accustomed themselves to the breathing of air, and she was not able to do it. Such was no doubt the case with our remotest ancestors, who, emerging from the sea onto the first uncovered islands, found after a certain time that they could not return. I imagine that this process happens even today. I have read accounts of savage men, the orangoutans of the Dutch East Indies, who are covered with hair and cannot speak human language. Obviously they are not far removed from their merhood.

"From time to time tailed men are found among the European races. A courtesan I knew in Pisa told me of a lover of hers whose body hair was black and thick, whose strength was that of several men, and who had a tail. Doubtless a race of tailed mermen exists somewhere in the sea's unplumbed depths. New species of all kinds must creep from the sea at one time or another; how else are we to account for the flora and fauna of remote islands? No one has ever seen such an emergence. But how many have watched the shoreline patiently, for years on end, knowing for what to look?"

"I suppose that no one but Your Excellency could be so

qualified," Martine said. "Is this, then, the reason for your vigil? You expect some prodigy to emerge from the sea?"

De Maillet smiled sadly. "No, of course not. The chances are infinitesimal that I could actually witness such a thing. But what else am I to do? My legs are too weak and gouty for me to leap about in cliffs and quarries, as I did in my youth. All I have now are my eyes and my brain. Even if a merman were to emerge at this moment, I would not be able to capture or subdue him. But if I saw him, I would be sure of my System—surer even than I am now, after amassing evidence for years. I could die knowing that History is sure to vindicate me."

He looked out wistfully across the waters. "Suppose that, at this moment, one were to see a strange movement among those waves that roll and pitch so oddly in this wind. Suppose one were to see that patch of sea-foam begin to eddy and twist—yes, just as it is doing now, only faster. Faster, becoming unmistakable!" De Maillet heaved himself to his feet and pointed with his cane. "My God, look!"

The young man stared out to sea. "I see nothing. . . ."

"Use your eyes, fool! Do you not see where that whirlpool gyres and spreads? Its rim glitters with foam like diamonds, and its waters are the green of . . . of ancient bronze, or Chinese jade, or the sheen of an insect in amber, or . . . or. . . ." The words ground to a mumble in the sudden torrent of images. De Maillet pointed dumbly with his cane. The young man looked at de Maillet, then back at the sea, then at de Maillet again. Suddenly he turned and ran off headlong down the beach.

De Maillet ignored the fleeing youth and took two tottering steps closer to the apparition. About the whirlpool's foamy edges, half-translucent phantoms were chasing one another in the wind, streaking around and around the whirlpool's center in a riot of films and veils. Some of the phantoms embraced one another; other, darker spirits moved sluggishly, as if poisoned by earthly biles; yet others, with streaming hair and rolling eyes, blew curling gasps of wind from their mouths. Their looks and movements proclaimed them senseless things, mere servants and harbingers of the prodigy that was to come.

More and more of the aerial spirits were cast off from the frantic whirling of the jade-green maelstrom; mere blobs of foam at first, they took on form in their flight and spiraled upward, forming before de Maillet's amazed eyes a slowly whirling tower of unearthly presences. Above them, a surf of clouds boiled out across the empty, crawling sky.

A shaft of muddy green light sprang upward from the maelstrom's depth, and another presence, a greater one by far, began to emerge from the whirlpool's core. She rose with slow majesty from the bottom of the sea, whirling like a dervish entranced: a Dark Girl, whose skin was the color of slate and whose black, slimy hair had the damp, clinging look of kelp or sea moss. She was nude, her secret parts concealed by her hand across her breast and the curling of a mass of hair across her hip. As her knees and ankles rose above the water's rim, the whirlpool slowed and vanished, showing her bare feet perched within the mother-of-pearl bowl of an enormous clamshell.

Awed by the majesty of this dark giantess, de Maillet fell painfully to one knee. The Dark Girl's eyes opened; they were the color of the whirlpool's waters, a dark archaic green.

Two of the wind-spirits offered the Dark Girl a long cloak or veil, made of their own intangible essence. As it touched her dark shoulders, it at once assumed weight and substance, and became a miraculous cloak, arcanely worked with embroidered symbols of manticores, rocs, krakens, one-eyed giants, and other monstrous beasts and prodigies.

The Dark Girl's curving lips opened slightly. "Greetings, philosopher."

Hearing that she knew of him, de Maillet's amazement was quelled, and his old stubborn courage at once filled his ancient heart. He heaved himself to his feet with the help of his cane and bent forward in a stiff and courtly bow. "A very good day to Your Ladyship," he said.

The Dark Girl smiled the strange hieratic smile seen on the oldest statues of Greece and Egypt. "You know my name?"

"I know that you are the Dark Girl from the Sea; surely that should be title enough, since there could never be two such entities."

"Ah," she said, "old philosopher, you have lost none of your cleverness. It is well that you flatter me now, after having done me so many grievous injuries during your long career. We are old enemies, you and I. You have faced me many times, and stolen your knowledge from my dark realm. You built your System to do me hurt. But now you face me incarnate." The Dark Girl's great eyelids closed and opened, and she fixed him with her gaze of serpent green.

"Listen, philosopher!" she cried. "This is a Day of days, when a

Great Tide of Change sweeps across the World, and the Spirit of the Age—which is to say, the minds of men—is transformed forever. During this awe-filled Moment, the iron laws of necessity and fate that govern this world are held in abeyance, and the dark essences and spirits that ruled this plane of being may walk abroad for the last time."

De Maillet said, "I have read that in a man's last days he may glimpse hidden truths and have prophetic visions. Am I dying, then?"

"O mortal, the whole world is dying, and a new world is being born: a world that you yourself, and the others of your kind, have brought into being. It will be a barer, sharper world, where a harsh and pitiless Enlightenment burns from men's minds the old, warm clutter of legends and dogmas and romances."

"But my System," de Maillet cried. "In this new world of clarity and light, will my System be triumphant? Will my name live on? Will the evidence support me?"

The Dark Girl laughed aloud, revealing a gray mouthful of sharp, serrated teeth. "You ask me to prophesy? I am the Mother of Fantasies, the Mother of Faith, Hope, and the Church."

De Maillet stared, clutching his ebony cane to his chest. "You are Ignorance."

"I am," the Dark Girl said. "So ask of me no favors, you who have pursued and harried me throughout this world; you, who through your learned books and the example of your life, shall harry me still, even after your death. Ask questions of my daughters, if ask you must."

The Dark Girl gestured with her slate-gray hand, and three weird Sisters sprang up from the sand at de Maillet's feet.

"I am Faith," said the first of the Sisters. "I am she who enters the mind of man when his power to reason is exhausted, and he clings stubbornly to his own wishes and ambitions, and believes in them, for fear of madness otherwise. You have chased me from your own mind and, with your books, sometimes from the minds of others; but I will persist as long as there is ignorance and fear."

"Why do you cringe, then?" said de Maillet. "And why is your face so pale?"

"O savant, you have wounded me. In the new age that dawns, it will be possible to live without me, as you have lived. You and your brethren, with eyes that see everything and fear nothing, will make me a thing of catalogs and dissertations and claw me with harsh arguments and skeptical logics. That is why I tremble and cannot meet your eyes."

"What of my System, then, Spirit? Will it be revealed as truth?"

"You must believe that it will," said Faith, and seeped away into the sand.

The second Sister stepped before him. "I am Hope," she said accusingly, "and I, too, shall be wounded grievously. I shall no longer be the great, blind Hope of Salvation, but only trivial fragments of hope: for power, or riches, or earthly glory, or simply for an end to pain. This era to come will not be a time of great hopes, but of plans, predictions, theories, and hypotheses, when man will seize the reins of fate in his own hands, and have only himself to blame or credit. I shall not be totally destroyed; but you shall rob me of my glory."

"What of my System, then, Spirit? You whose eyes are fixed always on the future? Will my work persist?"

"You must hope that it will," she said, and vanished into the sand.

De Maillet faced the specter of the Church. "You should have been mine!" said the last of the Sisters, pointing at him with a bony arm lopped off clean at the wrist. Within her hooded veil, the crone's eyes were tightly shut. "If not one of my theologians, then mine to burn!"

"I never opposed you," said de Maillet. "Not openly."

"But your logics have chopped off my hands!" the Spirit wailed. "In the days to come, your successors will cry, 'Crush the infamous thing!' and make of me a mockery, a thing to be shunned by freethinking men.

"Your heart was not mine, philosopher. It belonged to science and to worldly fame. Each time you despised and doubted the flames of hell, those flames guttered a little lower. As you have discovered His worldly machineries, you have withered the God of the Prophets to a watchmaker's God, a phantom mechanic. The demons that lurked in the wastes; the spirits of woods and dells; the legions of ghosts and angels, all, all will shrivel in the pitiless light!

"No more will I gather the souls of believers for rapture and punishment. When the great Change is through, there will be no souls. Men will stand revealed as cunning animals, born from the loins of apes. Their sharpened minds will cut all my fine fictions into pieces." Weeping, the Church turned her back on the philosopher.

De Maillet leaned on his cane. "You should not have concealed the truth," he said.

"The Truth!" cried Ignorance. "O mortal, the truth exists in the minds of men. It is you who have brought this great Change upon the world. The round and cozy firmament was too small for your ambitions. No, you would have stars in Newton's orbits, and whole universes reeling to your laws! Every law and datum wrenched from the great Mystery enfeebles God, to put man in His place! I see my fate is written on your brow. The day will come, in stark futurity, when the mind of man will encompass all, and his omniscience will utterly destroy me. So know my hatred!"

From the depths of the sea, a wall of turgid water roared upon the land and struck de Maillet down. His stick was knocked from his grasp and his nostrils were filled with the smell of muck. As he floundered in the dark water, blinded, he seized a smooth and rounded pebble from the beach. He lurched splashing to his feet.

His spectacles were gone. He looked around wildly for the apparition of the Dark Girl. "This!" he shouted, shaking the pebble in his clenched fist. "This will defeat you, Dark Spirit! This is the *evidence;* I put my Faith and Hope in that, and in myself. . . ."

A dull roaring came from out to sea. Dimly, de Maillet saw the waves receding, and a vast wall surging toward the land, bright with lightnings. The storm burst upon him with appalling speed, crackling, rumbling, and roaring, with a sound like the walls of Heaven itself, crumbling under siege.

Gasping, stumbling, clutching his pebble to his pounding heart, Benoît de Maillet fled into the ultimate darkness.

A pure and searing light beat down on the old man's eyelids. Groaning, de Maillet opened his eyes upon a brilliant summer dawn.

Suddenly the face of his servant Torquetil was thrust before his own. De Maillet seized the shoulder of the young man's livery coat. "Torquetil!"

"Huzza!" cried Torquetil, pulling loose and leaping into the air in joy. "He stirs, he lives! My master speaks to me!"

A hoarse, ragged cheer broke out. De Maillet, dizzily, sat up. A motley collection of house servants, fisherfolk, and townsmen had gathered around him, some of them clutching burned-out torches. "We have searched for you all night," said Torquetil. "I brought the carriage as soon as the weather turned bad, but you had gone!"

"Help me up," de Maillet said. The young Breton put his shoulder under de Maillet's arm and hoisted him to his feet. "Monsieur's clothes are drenched," Torquetil said.

Blinking myopically, de Maillet stared at the pebble he held in his hand.

"It was the young gentleman here who first thought of looking among the Lovers' Rocks," said Torquetil, gesturing politely at the confident well-dressed figure of Jean Martine the Younger.

"It was nothing," the young merchant said, stepping closer. "After we, ah, parted, I felt some concern for Your Excellency. The weather turned foul quite suddenly, and I thought Your Excellency might have sought shelter here." He smiled patronizingly at de Maillet, obviously pleased at his own ingenuity in tracking down an eccentric dotard. "The rocks were very high; in the wind and darkness my servants lost their way. I do hope Your Excellency is not injured."

"I've lost my spectacles," de Maillet said. "Torquetil, do you have my spare ones?"

"Of course, monsieur." He produced them. De Maillet hurriedly pinched them on and studied the wave-smoothed pebble. "Remarkable," he said. "Remarkable! Have I played by the shore of this great ocean so long, to have no more than this? Still, I have this. I do. This, at least, is mine."

Torquetil glanced pleadingly at Jean Martine; the merchant stifled a smile. "We must get Your Excellency into some dry clothes," he said. "My carriage is on the road, not far from here. It is at your service."

"Come along, monsieur," said Torquetil with exaggerated gentleness. He lowered his voice. "It is not well that the common folk should see you like this."

There was a sudden bustle at the back of the small crowd, and three ragged children burst forth. "We found it, we found it!" they cried. One of them carried de Maillet's ebony cane.

"Splendid!" de Maillet said. "Give them a little something, Torquetil." The servant tossed them a few coppers; they scrambled for them wildly. "And what about my parasol?" de Maillet said.

Torquetil looked sad. "Alas, monsieur, your wonderful parasol, so strange and colorful! The winds, the terrible winds, have blown it all to pieces; it is all cast down and wrecked."

"I see," de Maillet said. He was silent for a moment, then heaved a heavy sigh.

Martine cleared his throat. "If Your Excellency should care to visit my father's warehouse in town, perhaps we could find you another."

"Never mind," de Maillet said stoically. He polished the pebble across the front of his soggy waistcoat and dropped it into his pocket. Seeing him do this, the children pointed at him and giggled behind their hands.

"They laugh," de Maillet observed. "Posterity will laugh. Thus am I answered." He leaned heavily on his cane, then turned to go. Torquetil helped him up the slope.

Suddenly de Maillet stopped and squared his shoulders. "And what if they do?" he demanded. "At least, if they laugh at you, then you know you are still alive! Eh, Torquetil?"

Torquetil smiled. "Just as you say, monsieur." He brushed sand from his master's shoulders. "Let us go home. The cook has promised: no more curries."

CFE LITTLE
MAGIC SHOP

HE EARLY LIFE of James Abernathy was rife with ominous portent.

His father, a New England customs inspector, had artistic ambitions; he filled his sketchbooks with mossy old Puritan tombstones and spanking new Nantucket whaling ships. By day, he graded bales of imported tea and calico; during evenings he took James to meetings of his intellectual friends, who would drink port, curse their wives and editors, and give James treacle candy.

James's father vanished while on a sketching expedition to the Great Stone Face of Vermont; nothing was ever found of him but his shoes.

James's mother, widowed with her young son, eventually married a large and hairy man who lived in a crumbling mansion in upstate New York.

At night the family often socialized in the nearby town of Albany. There, James's stepfather would talk politics with his friends in the National Anti-Masonic Party; upstairs, his mother and the other women chatted with prominent dead personalities through spiritualist table rapping.

Eventually, James's stepfather grew more and more anxious over the plotting of the Masons. The family ceased to circulate in society. The curtains were drawn and the family ordered to maintain a close watch for strangers dressed in black. James's mother grew thin and pale, and often wore nothing but her houserobe for days on end.

One day, James's stepfather read them newspaper accounts of the angel Moroni, who had revealed locally buried tablets of gold that detailed the Biblical history of the Mound Builder Indians. By the time he reached the end of the article, the stepfather's voice shook and his eyes had grown quite wild. That night, muffled shrieks and frenzied hammerings were heard.

In the morning, young James found his stepfather downstairs by the hearth, still in his dressing gown, sipping teacup after teacup full of brandy and absently bending and straightening the fireside poker.

James offered morning greetings with his usual cordiality. The stepfather's eyes darted frantically under matted brows. James was informed that his mother was on a mission of mercy to a distant family stricken by scarlet fever. The conversation soon passed to a certain upstairs storeroom whose door was now nailed shut. James's stepfather strictly commanded him to avoid this forbidden portal.

Days passed. His mother's absence stretched to weeks. Despite repeated and increasingly strident warnings from his stepfather, James showed no interest whatsoever in the upstairs room. Eventually, deep within the older man's brain, a ticking artery burst from sheer frustration.

During his stepfather's funeral, the family home was struck by ball lightning and burned to the ground. The insurance money, and James's fate, passed into the hands of a distant relative, a muttering, trembling man who campaigned against liquor and drank several bottles of Dr. Rifkin's Laudanum Elixir each week.

James was sent to a boarding school run by a fanatical Calvinist deacon. James prospered there, thanks to close study of the scriptures and his equable, reasonable temperament. He grew to adulthood, becoming a tall, studious young man with a calm disposition and a solemn face utterly unmarked by doom.

Two days after his graduation, the deacon and his wife were both found hacked to bits, their half-naked bodies crammed into their one-horse shay. James stayed long enough to console the couple's spinster daughter, who sat dry-eyed in her rocking chair, methodically ripping a handkerchief to shreds.

James then took himself to New York City for higher education.

It was there that James Abernathy found the little shop that sold magic.

James stepped into this unmarked shop on impulse, driven inside by muffled screams of agony from the dentist's across the street.

The shop's dim interior smelled of burning whale-oil and hot lantern-brass. Deep wooden shelves, shrouded in cobwebs, lined the walls. Here and there, yellowing political broadsides requested military help for the rebel Texans. James set his divinity texts on an apothecary cabinet, where a band of stuffed, lacquered frogs brandished tiny trumpets and guitars. The proprietor appeared from behind a red curtain. "May I help the young master?" he said, rubbing his hands. He was a small, spry Irishman. His ears rose to points lightly shrouded in hair; he wore bifocal spectacles and brass-buckled shoes.

"I rather fancy that fantod under the bell jar," said James, pointing.

"I'll wager we can do much better for a young man like yourself," said the proprietor with a leer. "So fresh, so full of life."

James puffed the thick dust of long neglect from the fantod jar. "Is business all it might be, these days?"

"We have a rather specialized clientele," said the other, and he introduced himself. His name was Mr. O'Beronne, and he had recently fled his country's devastating potato famine. James shook Mr. O'Beronne's small papery hand.

"You'll be wanting a love-potion," said Mr. O'Beronne with a shrewd look. "Fellows of your age generally do."

James shrugged. "Not really, no."

"Is it budget troubles, then? I might interest you in an ever-filled purse." The old man skipped from behind the counter and hefted a large bearskin cape.

"Money?" said James with only distant interest.

"Fame then. We have magic brushes—or if you prefer newfangled scientific arts, we have a camera that once belonged to Montavarde himself."

"No, no," said James, looking restless. "Can you quote me a price on this fantod?" He studied the fantod critically. It was not in very good condition.

"We can restore youth," said Mr. O'Beronne in sudden desperation.

"Do tell," said James, straightening.

"We have a shipment of Dr. Heidegger's Patent Youthing

Waters," said Mr. O'Beronne. He tugged a quagga hide from a nearby brassbound chest and dug out a square glass bottle. He uncorked it. The waters fizzed lightly, and the smell of May filled the room. "One bottle imbibed," said Mr. O'Beronne, "restores a condition of blushing youth to man or beast."

"Is that a fact," said James, his brows knitting in thought. "How many teaspoons per bottle?"

"I've no idea," Mr. O'Beronne admitted. "Never measured it by the spoon. Mind you, this is an old folks' item. Fellows of your age usually go for the love-potions."

"How much for a bottle?" said James.

"It is a bit steep," said Mr. O'Beronne grudgingly. "The price is everything you possess."

"Seems reasonable," said James. "How much for two bottles?"

Mr. O'Beronne stared. "Don't get ahead of yourself, young man." He recorked the bottle carefully. "You've yet to give me all you possess, mind."

"How do I know you'll still have the waters, when I need more?" James said.

Mr. O'Beronne's eyes shifted uneasily behind his bifocals. "You let me worry about that." He leered, but without the same conviction he had shown earlier. "I won't be shutting up this shop—not when there are people of your sort about."

"Fair enough," said James, and they shook hands on the bargain. James returned two days later, having sold everything he owned. He handed over a small bag of gold specie and a bank draft conveying the slender remaining funds of his patrimony. He departed with the clothes on his back and the bottle.

Twenty years passed.

The United States suffered civil war. Hundreds of thousands of men were shot, blown up with mines or artillery, or perished miserably in septic army camps. In the streets of New York, hundreds of antidraft rioters were mown down with grapeshot, and the cobbled street before the little magic shop was strewn with reeking dead. At last, after stubborn resistance and untold agonies, the Confederacy was defeated. The war became history.

James Abernathy returned.

"I've been in California," he announced to the astonished Mr. O'Beronne. James was healthily tanned and wore a velvet cloak, spurred boots, and a silver sombrero. He sported a large gold turnip-watch, and his fingers gleamed with gems.

"You struck it rich in the goldfields," Mr. O'Beronne surmised.

"Actually, no," said James. "I've been in the grocery business. In Sacramento. One can sell a dozen eggs there for almost their weight in gold dust, you know." He smiled and gestured at his elaborate clothes. "I did pretty well, but I don't usually dress this extravagantly. You see, I'm wearing my entire worldly wealth. I thought it would make our transaction simpler." He produced the empty bottle.

"That's very farsighted of you," said Mr. O'Beronne. He examined James critically, as if looking for hairline psychic cracks or signs of moral corruption. "You don't seem to have aged a day."

"Oh, that's not quite so," said James. "I was twenty when I first came here; now I easily look twenty-one, even twenty-two." He put the bottle on the counter. "You'll be interested to know there were twenty teaspoons exactly."

"You didn't spill any?"

"Oh, no," said James, smiling at the thought. "I've only opened it once a year."

"It didn't occur to you to take two teaspoons, say? Or empty the bottle at a draught?"

"Now what would be the use of that?" said James. He began stripping off his rings and dropping them on the counter with light tinkling sounds. "You did keep the Youthing Waters in stock, I presume."

"A bargain's a bargain," said Mr. O'Beronne grudgingly. He produced another bottle. James left barefoot, wearing only shirt and pants, but carrying his bottle.

The 1870s passed and the nation celebrated its centennial. Railroads stitched the continent. Gaslights were installed in the streets of New York. Buildings taller than any ever seen began to soar, though the magic shop's neighborhood remained obscure.

James Abernathy returned. He now looked at least twenty-four. He passed over the title deeds to several properties in Chicago and departed with another bottle.

Shortly after the turn of the century, James returned again, driving a steam automobile, whistling the theme of the St. Louis Exhibition and stroking his waxed mustache. He signed over the deed to the car, which was a fine one, but Mr. O'Beronne showed little enthusiasm. The old Irishman had shrunken with the years, and his tiny hands trembled as he conveyed his goods.

Within the following period, a great war of global empires took place, but America was mostly spared the devastation. The 1920s arrived, and James came laden with a valise crammed with rapidly appreciating stocks and bonds. "You always seem to do rather well for yourself," Mr. O'Beronne observed in a quavering voice.

"Moderation's the key," said James. "That, and a sunny disposition." He looked about the shop with a critical eye. The quality of the junk had declined. Old engine parts lay in reeking grease next to heaps of moldering popular magazines and spools of blackened telephone wire. The exotic hides, packets of spice and amber, ivory tusks hand-carved by cannibals, and so forth, had now entirely disappeared. "I hope you don't mind these new bottles," croaked Mr. O'Beronne, handing him one. The bottle had curved sides and a machine-fitted cap of cork and tin.

"Any trouble with supply?" said James delicately.

"You let me worry about that!" said Mr. O'Beronne, lifting his lip with a faint snarl of defiance.

James's next visit came after yet another war, this one of untold and almost unimaginable savagery. Mr. O'Beronne's shop was now crammed with military surplus goods. Bare electric bulbs hung over a realm of rotting khaki and rubber.

James now looked almost thirty. He was a little short by modern American standards, but this was scarcely noticeable. He wore high-waisted pants and a white linen suit with jutting shoulders.

"I don't suppose," muttered Mr. O'Beronne through his false teeth, "that it ever occurs to you to share this? What about wives, sweethearts, children?"

James shrugged. "What about them?"

"You're content to see them grow old and die?"

"I never see them grow all *that* old," James observed. "After all, every twenty years I have to return here and lose everything I own. It's simpler just to begin all over again."

"No human feelings," Mr. O'Beronne muttered bitterly.

"Oh, come now," said James. "After all, I don't see *you* distributing elixir to all and sundry, either."

"But I'm in the magic shop *business*," said Mr. O'Beronne, weakly. "There are certain unwritten rules."

"Oh?" said James, leaning on the counter with the easy patience of a youthful centenarian. "You never mentioned this before. Supernatural law—it must be an interesting field of study."

"Never you mind that," Mr. O'Beronne snapped. "You're a *customer,* and a human being. You mind your business and I'll mind mine."

"No need to be so touchy," James said. He hesitated. "You know, I have some hot leads in the new plastics industry. I imagine I could make a great deal more money than usual. That is, if you're interested in selling this place." He smiled. "They say an Irishman never forgets the Old Country. You could go back into your old line—pot o' gold, bowl of milk on the doorstep. . . ."

"Take your bottle and go," O'Beronne shouted, thrusting it into his hands.

Another two decades passed. James drove up in a Mustang convertible and entered the shop. The place reeked of patchouli incense, and Day-Glo posters covered the walls. Racks of demented comic books loomed beside tables littered with hookahs and hand-made clay pipes.

Mr. O'Beronne dragged himself from behind a hanging beaded curtain. "You again," he croaked.

"Right on," said James, looking around. "I like the way you've kept the place up to date, man. Groovy."

O'Beronne gave him a poisonous glare. "You're a hundred and forty years old. Hasn't the burden of unnatural life become insupportable?"

James looked at him, puzzled. "Are you kidding?"

"Haven't you learned a lesson about the blessings of mortality? About how it's better not to outlive your own predestined time?"

"Huh?" James said. He shrugged. "I did learn something about material possessions, though. . . . Material things only tie a cat down. You can't have the car this time, it's rented." He dug a hand-stitched leather wallet from his bell-bottom jeans. "I have some fake ID and credit cards." He shook them out over the counter.

Mr. O'Beronne stared unbelieving at the meager loot. "Is this your idea of a joke?"

"Hey, it's all I possess," James said mildly. "I could have bought Xerox at fifteen, back in the '50s. But last time I talked to you, you didn't seem interested. I figured it was like, you know, not the bread that counts, but the spirit of the thing."

Mr. O'Beronne clutched his heart with a liver-spotted hand. "Is this never going to end? Why did I ever leave Europe? They know how to respect a tradition there. . . ." He paused, gathering bile. "Look at this place! It's an insult! Call this a magic shop?" He snatched up a fat mushroom-shaped candle and flung it to the floor.

"You're overwrought," James said. "Look, you're the one who said a bargain's a bargain. There's no need for us to go on with this any longer. I can see your heart's not in it. Why not put me in touch with your wholesaler?"

"Never!" O'Beronne swore. "I won't be beaten by some cold-blooded . . . bookkeeper."

"I never thought of this as a contest," James said with dignity.

"Sorry to see you take it that way, man." He picked up his bottle and left.

The allotted time elapsed, and James repeated his pilgrimage to the magic shop. The neighborhood had declined. Women in spandex and net hose lurked on the pavement, watched from the corner by men in broad-brimmed hats and slick polished shoes. James carefully locked the doors of his BMW.

The magic shop's once-curtained windows had been painted over in black. A neon sign above the door read ADULT PEEP 25¢.

Inside, the shop's cluttered floor space had been cleared. Shrink-wrapped magazines lined the walls, their fleshy covers glaring under the bluish corpse-light of overhead fluorescents. The old counter had been replaced by a long glass-fronted cabinet displaying knotted whips and flavored lubricants. The bare floor clung stickily to the soles of James's Gucci shoes.

A young man emerged from behind a curtain. He was tall and bony, with a small, neatly trimmed mustache. His smooth skin had a waxy subterranean look. He gestured fluidly. "Peeps in the back," he said in a high voice, not meeting James's eyes. "You gotta buy tokens. Three bucks."

"I beg your pardon?" James said.

"Three bucks, man!"

"Oh." James produced the money. The man handed over a dozen plastic tokens and vanished at once behind the curtains.

"Excuse me?" James said. No answer. "Hello?"

The peep machines waited in the back of the store, in a series of curtained booths. The vinyl cushions inside smelled of sweat and butyl nitrate. James inserted a token and watched.

He then moved to the other machines and examined them as well. He returned to the front of the shop. The shopkeeper sat on a stool, ripping the covers from unsold magazines and watching a small television under the counter.

"Those films," James said. "That was Charlie Chaplin. And Douglas Fairbanks. And Gloria Swanson . . ."

The man looked up, smoothing his hair. "Yeah, so? You don't like silent films?"

James paused. "I can't believe Charlie Chaplin did porn."

"I hate to spoil a magic trick," the shopkeeper said, yawning. "But they're genuine peeps, pal. You ever hear of Hearst Mansion? San Simeon? Old Hearst, he liked filming his Hollywood guests on the sly. All the bedrooms had spy holes."

"Oh," James said. "I see. Ah, is Mr. O'Beronne in?"

The man showed interest for the first time. "You know the old guy? I don't get many nowadays who knew the old guy. His clientele had pretty special tastes, I hear."

James nodded. "He should be holding a bottle for me."

"Well, I'll check in the back. Maybe he's awake." The shopkeeper vanished again. He reappeared minutes later with a brownish vial. "Got some love-potion here."

James shook his head. "Sorry, that's not it."

"It's the real stuff, man! Works like you wouldn't believe!" The shopkeeper was puzzled. "You young guys are usually into love-potions. Well, I guess I'll have to rouse the old guy for you. Though I kind of hate to disturb him."

Long minutes passed, with distant rustling and squeaking. Finally the shopkeeper backed through the curtains, tugging a wheelchair. Mr. O'Beronne sat within it, wrapped in bandages, his wrinkled head shrouded in a dirty nightcap. "Oh," he said at last. "So it's you again."

"Yes, I've returned for my—"

"I know, I know." Mr. O'Beronne stirred fitfully on his cushions. "I see you've met my . . . associate. Mr. Ferry."

"I kind of manage the place, these days," said Mr. Ferry. He winked at James, behind Mr. O'Beronne's back.

"I'm James Abernathy," James said. He offered his hand.

Ferry folded his arms warily. "Sorry, I never do that."

O'Beronne cackled feebly and broke into a fit of coughing. "Well, my boy," he said finally, "I was hoping I'd last long enough to see you one more time . . . Mr. Ferry! There's a crate, in the back, under those filthy movie posters of yours. . . ."

"Sure, sure," Ferry said indulgently. He left.

"Let me look at you," said O'Beronne. His eyes, in their dry, leaden sockets, had grown quite lizardlike. "Well, what do you think of the place? Be frank."

"It's looked better," James said. "So have you."

"But so has the world, eh?" O'Beronne said. "He does bang-up business, young Ferry. You should see him manage the books. . . ." He waved one hand, its tiny knuckles warped with arthritis. "It's such a blessing, not to have to care anymore."

Ferry reappeared, lugging a wooden crate, crammed with dusty six-packs of pop-top aluminum cans. He set it gently on the counter.

Every can held Youthing Water. "Thanks," James said, his eyes widening. He lifted one pack reverently, and tugged at a can.

"Don't," O'Beronne said. "This is for you, all of it. Enjoy it, son. I hope you're satisfied."

James lowered the cans, slowly. "What about our arrangement?"

O'Beronne's eyes fell, in an ecstasy of humiliation. "I humbly apologize. But I simply can't keep up our bargain any longer. I don't have the strength, you see. So this is yours now. It's all I could find."

"Yeah, this must be pretty much the last of it," nodded Ferry, inspecting his nails. "It hasn't moved well for some time—I figure the bottling plant shut up shop."

"So many cans, though . . ." James said thoughtfully. He produced his wallet. "I brought a nice car for you, outside. . . ."

"None of that matters now," said Mr. O'Beronne. "Keep all of it, just consider it my forfeit." His voice fell. "I never thought it would come to this, but you've beaten me, I admit it. I'm done in." His head sagged limply.

Mr. Ferry took the wheelchair's handles. "He's tired now," he said soothingly. "I'll just wheel him back out of our way, here. . . ." He held the curtains back and shoved the chair through with his foot. He turned to James. "You can take that case and let yourself out. Nice doing business—goodbye." He nodded briskly.

"Goodbye, sir!" James called. No answer.

James hauled the case outside to his car, and set it in the backseat. Then he sat in front for a while, drumming his fingers on the steering wheel.

Finally he went back in.

Mr. Ferry had pulled a telephone from beneath his cash register. When he saw James he slammed the headset down. "Forget something, pal?"

"I'm troubled," James said. "I keep wondering . . . what about those unwritten rules?"

The shopkeeper looked at him, surprised. "Aw, the old guy always talked like that. Rules, standards, quality." Mr. Ferry gazed meditatively over his stock, then looked James in the eye. "What *rules,* man?"

There was a moment of silence.

"I was never quite sure," James said. "But I'd like to ask Mr. O'Beronne."

"You've badgered him enough," the shopkeeper said. "Can't you see he's a dying man? You got what you wanted, so scram, hit the road." He folded his arms. James refused to move.

The shopkeeper sighed. "Look, I'm not in this for my health. You want to hang around here, you gotta buy some more tokens."

"I've seen those already," James said. "What else do you sell?"

"Oh, machines not good enough for you, eh?" Mr. Ferry stroked his chin. "Well, it's not strictly in my line, but I might sneak you a gram or two of Señor Buendia's Colombian Real Magic Powder. First taste is free. No? You're a hard man to please, bub."

Ferry sat down, looking bored. "I don't see why I should change my stock, just because you're so picky. A smart operator like you, you ought to have bigger fish to fry than a little magic shop. Maybe you just don't belong here, pal."

"No, I always liked this place," James said. "I used to, anyway. . . . I even wanted to own it myself."

Ferry tittered. "You? Gimme a break." His face hardened. "If you don't like the way I run things, take a hike."

"No, no, I'm sure I can find something here," James said quickly. He pointed at random to a thick hardbound book, at the bottom of a stack, below the counter. "Let me try that."

Mr. Ferry shrugged with bad grace and fetched it out. "You'll like this," he said unconvincingly. "Marilyn Monroe and Jack Kennedy at a private beach house."

James leafed through the glossy pages. "How much?"

"You want it?" said the shopkeeper. He examined the binding and set it back down. "Okay, fifty bucks."

"Just cash?" James said, surprised. "Nothing magical?"

"Cash *is* magical, pal." The shopkeeper shrugged. "Okay, forty bucks and you have to kiss a dog on the lips."

"I'll pay the fifty," James said. He pulled out his wallet. "Whoops!" He fumbled, and it dropped over the far side of the counter.

Mr. Ferry lunged for it. As he rose again, James slammed the heavy book into his head. The shopkeeper fell with a groan.

James vaulted over the counter and shoved the curtains aside. He grabbed the wheelchair and hauled it out. The wheels thumped twice over Ferry's outstretched legs. Jostled, O'Beronne woke with a screech.

James pulled him toward the blacked-out windows. "Old man," he panted. "How long has it been since you had some fresh air?" He kicked open the door.

"No!" O'Beronne yelped. He shielded his eyes with both hands. "I have to stay inside here! That's the rules!" James wheeled him out onto the pavement. As sunlight hit him, O'Beronne howled in fear and squirmed wildly. Gouts of dust puffed from his cushions, and his bandages flapped. James yanked open the car door, lifted O'Beronne bodily, and dropped him into the passenger seat. "You can't do this!" O'Beronne screamed, his nightcap flying off. "I belong behind walls, I can't go into the world. . . ."

James slammed the door. He ran around and slid behind the wheel. "It's dangerous out here," O'Beronne whimpered as the engine roared into life. "I was safe in there. . . ."

James stamped the accelerator. The car laid rubber. He glanced behind him in the rearview mirror and saw an audience of laughing, whooping hookers. "Where are we going?" O'Beronne said meekly.

James floored it through a yellow light. He reached into the backseat one-handed and yanked a can from its six-pack. "Where was this bottling plant?"

O'Beronne blinked doubtfully. "It's been so long . . . Florida, I think."

"Florida sounds good. Sunlight, fresh air . . ." James weaved deftly through traffic, cracking the pop-top with his thumb. He knocked back a hefty swig, then gave O'Beronne the can. "Here, old man. Finish it off."

O'Beronne stared at it, licking dry lips. "But I can't. I'm an owner, not a customer. I'm simply not allowed to do this sort of thing. I own that magic shop, I tell you."

James shook his head and laughed.

O'Beronne trembled. He raised the can in both gnarled hands and began chugging thirstily. He paused once to belch, and kept drinking.

The smell of May filled the car.

O'Beronne wiped his mouth and crushed the empty can in his fist. He tossed it over his shoulder.

"There's room back there for those bandages, too," James told him. "Let's hit the highway."

FLOWERS
OF EDO

UTUMN. A FULL MOON floated over old Edo, behind the thinnest haze of high cloud. It shone like a geisha's night-lamp through an old mosquito net. The sky was antique browned silk.

Two sweating runners hauled an iron-wheeled rickshaw south, toward the Ginza. This was Kabukiza District, its streets bordered by low tile-roofed wooden shops. These were modest places: coopers, tobacconists, cheap fabric shops where the acrid reek of dye wafted through reed blinds and paper windows. Behind the stores lurked a maze of alleys, crammed with townsmen's wooden hovels, the walls festooned with morning glories, the tinder-dry thatched roofs alive with fleas.

It was late. Kabukiza was not a geisha district, and honest workmen were asleep. The muddy streets were unlit, except for moonlight and the rare upstairs lamp. The runners carried their own lantern, which swayed precariously from the rickshaw's drawing-pole. They trotted rapidly, dodging the worst of the potholes and puddles. But with every lurching dip, the rickshaw's strings of brass bells jumped and rang.

Suddenly the iron wheels grated on smooth red pavement. They had reached the New Ginza. Here, the air held the fresh alien smell of mortar and brick.

The amazing New Ginza had buried its old predecessor. For the Flowers of Edo had killed the Old Ginza. To date, this huge disaster had been the worst, and most exciting, fire of the Meiji Era. Edo had always been proud of its fires, and the Old Ginza's fire had been a real marvel. It had raged for three days and carried right down to the river.

Once they had mourned the dead, the Edokko were ready to re-build. They were always ready. Fires, even earthquakes, were noth-ing new to them. It was a rare building in Low City that escaped the Flowers of Edo for as long as twenty years.

But this was Imperial Tokyo now, and not the Shogun's old Edo anymore. The Governor had come down from High City in his horse-drawn coach and looked over the smoldering ruins of Ginza. Low City townsmen still talked about it—how the Governor had folded his arms—like this—with his wrists sticking out of his Western frock coat. And how he had frowned a mighty frown. The Edo townsmen were getting used to those unsettling frowns by now. Hard, no-nonsense, modern frowns, with the brows drawn low over cold eyes that glit-tered with Civilization and Enlightenment.

So the Governor, with a mighty wave of his modern frock-coated arm, sent for his foreign architects. And the Englishmen had besieged the district with their charts and clanking engines and tubs full of brick and mortar. The very heavens had rained bricks upon the black and flattened ruins. Great red hills of brick sprang up—were they houses, people wondered, were they buildings at all? Stories spread about the foreigners and their peculiar homes. The long noses, of course—necessary to suck air through the stifling brick walls. The pale skin—because bricks, it was said, drained the life and color out of a man. . . .

The rickshaw drew up short with a final brass jingle. The older rickshawman spoke, panting, "Far enough, gov?"

"Yeah, this'll do," said one passenger, piling out. His name was Encho Sanyutei. He was the son and successor of a famous vaudeville comedian and, at thirty-five, was now a well-known performer in his own right. He had been telling his companion about the Ginza Brick-town, and his folded arms and jutting underlip had cruelly mimicked Tokyo's Governor.

Encho, who had been drinking, generously handed the older man a pocketful of jingling copper sen. "Here, pal," he said. "Do something about that cough, will ya?" The runners bowed, not bothering to overdo it. They trotted off toward the nearby Ginza crowd, hunting another fare.

Parts of Tokyo never slept. The Yoshiwara District, the famous Nightless City of geishas and rakes, was one of them. The travelers had just come from Asakusa District, another sleepless place: a brawling, vibrant playground of bars, Kabuki theaters, and vaudeville joints.

The Ginza Bricktown never slept either. But the air here was different. It lacked that earthy Low City workingman's glow of sex and entertainment. Something else, something new and strange and powerful, drew the Edokko into the Ginza's iron-hard streets.

Gaslights. They stood hissing on their black foreign pillars, blasting a pitiless moon-drowning glare over the crowd. There were eighty-five of the appalling wonders, stretching arrow-straight across the Ginza, from Shiba all the way to Kyobashi.

The Edokko crowd beneath the lights was curiously silent. Drugged with pitiless enlightenment, they meandered down the hard, gritty street in high wooden clogs, or low leather shoes. Some wore hakama skirts and jinbibaori coats, others modern pipe-legged trousers, with top hats and bowlers.

The comedian Encho and his big companion staggered drunkenly toward the lights, their polished leather shoes squeaking merrily. To the Tokyo modernist, squeaking was half the fun of these foreign-style shoes. Both men wore inserts of "singing leather" to heighten the effect.

"I don't like their attitudes," growled Encho's companion. His name was Onogawa, and until the Emperor's Restoration, he had been a samurai. But Imperial decree had abolished the wearing of swords, and Onogawa now had a post in a trading company. He frowned, and dabbed at his nose, which had recently been bloodied and was now clotting. "It's all too free-and-easy with these modern rickshaws. Did you see those two runners? They looked into our faces, just as bold as tomcats."

"Relax, will you?" said Encho. "They were just a couple of street runners. Who cares what they think? The way you act, you'd think they were Shogun's Overseers." Encho laughed freely and dusted off his hands with a quick, theatrical gesture. Those grim, spying Overseers, with their merciless canons of Confucian law, were just a bad dream now. Like the Shogun, they were out of business.

"But your face is known all over town," Onogawa complained.

"What if they gossip about us? Everyone will know what happened back there."

"It's the least I could do for a devoted fan," Encho said airily.

Onogawa had sobered up a bit since his street fight in Asakusa. A scuffle had broken out in the crowd after Encho's performance—a scuffle centered on Onogawa, who had old acquaintances he would have preferred not to meet. But Encho, appearing suddenly in the crowd, had distracted Onogawa's persecutors and gotten Onogawa away.

It was not a happy situation for Onogawa, who put much stock in his own dignity, and tended to brood. He had been born in Satsuma, a province of radical samurai with stern unbending standards. But ten years in the capital had changed Onogawa, and given him an Edokko's notorious love for spectacle. Somewhat shamefully, Onogawa had become completely addicted to Encho's sidesplitting skits and impersonations.

In fact, Onogawa had been slumming in Asakusa vaudeville joints at least twice each week, for months. He had a wife and small son in a modest place in Nihombashi, a rather straitlaced High City district full of earnest young bankers and civil servants on their way up in life. Thanks to old friends from his radical days, Onogawa was an officer in a prosperous trading company. He would have preferred to be in the army, of course, but the army was quite small these days, and appointments were hard to get.

This was a major disappointment in Onogawa's life, and it had driven him to behave strangely. Onogawa's long-suffering in-laws had always warned him that his slumming would come to no good. But tonight's event wasn't even a geisha scandal, the kind men winked at or even admired. Instead, he had been in a squalid punch-up with low-class commoners.

And he had been rescued by a famous commoner, which was worse. Onogawa couldn't bring himself to compound his loss of face with gratitude. He glared at Encho from under the brim of his bowler hat. "So where's this fellow with the foreign booze you promised?"

"Patience," Encho said absently. "My friend's got a little place here in Bricktown. It's private, away from the street." They wandered down the Ginza, Encho pulling his silk top-hat low over his eyes, so he wouldn't be recognized.

He slowed as they passed a group of four young women, who were gathered before the modern glass window of a Ginza fabric shop. The store was closed, but the women were admiring the tailor's dummies. Like the dummies, the women were dressed with daring modernity, sporting small Western parasols, cutaway riding-coats in brilliant purple, and sweeping foreign skirts over large, jutting bustles. "How about that, eh?" said Encho as they drew nearer. "Those foreigners sure like a rump on a woman, don't they?"

"Women will wear anything," Onogawa said, struggling to loosen one pinched foot inside its squeaking shoe. "Plain kimono and obi are far superior."

"Easier to get into, anyway," Encho mused. He stopped suddenly by the prettiest of the women, a girl who had let her natural eyebrows grow out, and whose teeth, unstained with old-fashioned tooth-blacking, gleamed like ivory in the gaslight.

"Madame, forgive my boldness," Encho said. "But I think I saw a small kitten run under your skirt."

"I beg your pardon?" the girl said in a flat Low City accent.

Encho pursed his lips. Plaintive mewing came from the pavement. The girl looked down, startled, and raised her skirt quickly almost to the knee. "Let me help," said Encho, bending down for a better look. "I see the kitten! It's climbing up inside the skirt!" He turned. "You'd better help me, older brother! Have a look up in there."

Onogawa, abashed, hesitated. More mewing came. Encho stuck his entire head under the woman's skirt. "There it goes! It wants to hide in her false rump!" The kitten squealed wildly. "I've got it!" the comedian cried. He pulled out his doubled hands, holding them before him. "There's the rascal now, on the wall!" In the harsh gaslight, Encho's knotted hands cast the shadowed figure of a kitten's head against the brick.

Onogawa burst into convulsive laughter. He doubled over against the wall, struggling for breath. The women stood shocked for a moment. Then they all ran away, giggling hysterically. Except for the victim of Encho's joke, who burst into tears as she ran.

"Wah," Encho said alertly. "Her husband." He ducked his head, then jammed the side of his hand against his lips and blew. The street rang with a sudden trumpet blast. It sounded so exactly like the trumpet of a Tokyo omnibus that Onogawa himself was taken in for a moment. He glanced wildly up and down the Ginza prospect, expecting to see the omnibus driver, horn to his lips, reining up his team of horses.

Encho grabbed Onogawa's coat-sleeve and hauled him up the street before the rest of the puzzled crowd could recover. "This way!" They pounded drunkenly up an ill-lit street into the depths of Bricktown. Onogawa was breathless with laughter. They covered a block, then Onogawa pulled up, gasping. "No more," he wheezed, wiping tears of hilarity. "Can't take another . . . ha ha ha . . . step!"

"All right," Encho said reasonably, "but not here." He pointed up. "Don't you know better than to stand under those things?" Black telegraph wires swayed gently overhead.

Onogawa, who had not noticed the wires, moved hastily out from under them. "Kuwabara, kuwabara," he muttered—a quick spell to avert lightning. The sinister magic wires were all over the Bricktown, looping past and around the thick, smelly buildings.

Everyone knew why the foreigners put their telegraph wires high up on poles. It was so the demon messengers inside could not escape to wreak havoc amongst decent folk. These ghostly, invisible spirits flew along the wires as fast as swallows, it was said, carrying their secret spells of Christian black magic. Merely standing under such a baleful influence was inviting disaster.

Encho grinned at Onogawa. "There's no danger as long as we keep moving," he said confidently. "A little exposure is harmless. Don't worry about it."

Onogawa drew himself up. "Worried? Not a bit of it." He followed Encho down the street.

The stonelike buildings seemed brutal and featureless. There were no homey reed blinds or awnings in those outsized windows, whose sheets of foreign glass gleamed like an animal's eyeballs. No cozy porches, no bamboo wind chimes or cricket cages. Not even a climbing tendril of Edo morning glory, which adorned even the worst and cheapest city hovels. The buildings just sat there, as mute and threatening as cannonballs. Most were deserted. Despite their fireproof qualities and the great cost of their construction, they were proving hard to rent out. Word on the street said those red bricks would suck the life out of a man—give him beriberi, maybe even consumption.

Bricks paved the street beneath their shoes. Bricks on the right of them, bricks on their left, bricks in front of them, bricks in back. Hundreds of them, thousands of them. Onogawa muttered to the smaller man. "Say. What *are* bricks, exactly? I mean, what are they made of?"

"Foreigners make 'em," Encho said, shrugging. "I think they're a kind of pottery."

"Aren't they unhealthy?"

"People say that," Encho said, "but foreigners live in them and I haven't noticed any shortage of foreigners lately." He drew up short. "Oh, here's my friend's place. We'll go around the front. He lives upstairs."

They circled the two-story building and looked up. Honest old-fashioned light, from an oil lamp, glowed against the curtains of an upstairs window. "Looks like your friend's still awake," Onogawa said, his voice more cheery now.

Encho nodded. "Taiso Yoshitoshi doesn't sleep much. He's a little high-strung. I mean, peculiar." Encho walked up to the heavy, ornate front door, hung foreign-style on large brass hinges. He yanked a bellpull.

"Peculiar," Onogawa said. "No wonder, if he lives in a place like this." They waited.

The door opened inward with a loud squeal of hinges. A man's disheveled head peered around it. Their host raised a candle in a cheap tin holder. "Who is it?"

"Come on, Taiso," Encho said impatiently. He pursed his lips again. Ducks quacked around their feet.

"Oh! It's Encho-san, Encho Sanyutei. My old friend. Come in, do."

They stepped inside into a dark landing. The two visitors stopped and unlaced their leather shoes. In the first-floor workshop, beyond the landing, the guests could dimly see bound bales of paper, a litter of tool chests and shallow trays. An apprentice was snoring behind a shrouded wood-block press. The damp air smelled of ink and cherry-wood shavings.

"This is Mr. Onogawa Azusa," Encho said. "He's a fan of mine, down from High City. Mr. Onogawa, this is Taiso Yoshitoshi. The popular artist, one of Edo's finest."

"Oh, Yoshitoshi the artist!" said Onogawa, recognizing the name for the first time. "Of course! The wood-block print peddler. Why, I bought a whole series of yours, once. *Twenty-eight Infamous Murders with Accompanying Verses.*"

"Oh," said Yoshitoshi. "How kind of you to remember my squalid early efforts." The ukiyo-e print artist was a slight, somewhat pudgy man, with stooped, rounded shoulders. The flesh around his eyes looked puffy and discolored. He had close-cropped hair parted in the middle and wide, fleshy lips. He wore a printed cotton house robe, with faded bluish sunbursts, or maybe daisies, against a white background. "Shall we go upstairs, gentlemen? My apprentice needs his sleep."

They creaked up the wooden stairs to a studio lit by cheap pottery oil lamps. The walls were covered with hanging prints, while dozens more lay rolled, or stacked in corners, or piled on battered bookshelves. The windows were heavily draped and tightly shut. The naked brick walls seemed to sweat, and a vague reek of mildew and stale tobacco hung in the damp, close air.

The window against the far wall had a secondhand set of exterior shutters nailed to its inner sill. The shutters were bolted. "Telegraph wires outside," Yoshitoshi explained, noticing the glances of his guests. The artist gestured vaguely at a couple of bedraggled floor cushions. "Please."

The two visitors sat, struggling politely to squeeze some comfort from the mashed and threadbare cushions. Yoshitoshi knelt on a thicker cushion beside his worktable, a low bench of plain pine with ink stick, grinder, and water cup. A bamboo tool jar on the table's corner bristled with assorted brushes, as well as compass and ruler. Yoshitoshi had been working; a sheet of translucent rice paper was pinned to the table, lightly and precisely streaked with ink.

"So," Encho said, smiling and waving one hand at the artist's penurious den. "I heard you'd been doing pretty well lately. This place has certainly improved since I last saw it. You've got real bookshelves again. I bet you'll have your books back in no time."

Yoshitoshi smiled sweetly. "Oh—I have so many debts . . . the books come last. But yes, things are much better for me now. I have my health again. And a studio. And one apprentice, Toshimitsu, came back to me. He's not the best of the ones I lost, but he's honest at least."

Encho pulled a short foreign briar-pipe from his coat. He opened the ornate tobacco-bag on his belt, an embroidered pouch that was the pride of every Edo man-about-town. He glanced up casually, stuffing his pipe. "Did that Kabuki gig ever come to anything?"

"Oh, yes," said Yoshitoshi, sitting up straighter. "I painted bloodstains on the armor of Onoe Kikugoro the Fifth. For his role in *Kawanakajima Island*. I'm very grateful to you for arranging that."

"Wait, I saw that play," said Onogawa, surprised and pleased. "Say, those were wonderful bloodstains. Even better than the ones in that murder print, *Kasamori Osen Carved Alive by Her Stepfather*. You did that print too, am I right?" Onogawa had been studying the prints on the wall, and the familiar style had jogged his memory. "A young girl yanked backwards by a maniac with a knife, big bloody hand-prints all over her neck and legs. . . ."

Yoshitoshi smiled. "You liked that one, Mr. Onogawa?"

"Well," Onogawa said, "it was certainly a fine effort for what it was." It wasn't easy for a man in Onogawa's position to confess a liking for mere commoner art from Low City. He dropped his voice a little. "Actually, I had quite a few of your pictures, in my younger days. Ten years ago, just before the Restoration." He smiled, remembering. "I had the *Twenty-eight Murders*, of course. And some of the *One Hundred Ghost Stories*. And a few of the special editions, now that I think of it. Like Tamigoro blowing his head off with a rifle. Especially good sprays of blood in that one."

"Oh, I remember that one," Encho volunteered. "That was back in the old days, when they used to sprinkle the bloody scarlet ink with powdered mica. For that deluxe bloody gleaming effect!"

"Too expensive now," Yoshitoshi said sadly.

Encho shrugged. "Remember *Naosuke Gombei Murders His Master*? With the maniac servant standing on his employer's chest, ripping the man's face off with his hands alone?" The comedian cleverly mimed the murderer's pinching and wrenching, along with loud sucking and shredding sounds.

"Oh, yes!" said Onogawa. "I wonder whatever happened to my copy of it?" He shook himself. "Well, it's not the sort of thing you can keep in the house, with my age and position. It might give the children nightmares. Or the servants ideas." He laughed.

Encho had stuffed his short pipe; he lit it from a lamp. Onogawa, preparing to follow suit, dragged his long ironbound pipe from within his coat-sleeve. "How wretched," he cried. "I've cracked my good pipe in the scuffle with those hooligans. Look, it's ruined."

"Oh, is that a smoking-pipe?" said Encho. "From the way you used it on your attackers, I thought it was a simple bludgeon."

"I certainly would not go into the Low City without self-defense of some kind," Onogawa said stiffly. "And since the new government has seen fit to take our swords away, I'm forced to make do. A pipe is an ignoble weapon. But as you saw tonight, not without its uses."

"Oh, no offense meant, sir," said Encho hastily. "There's no need to be formal here among friends! If I'm a bit harsh of tongue I hope you'll forgive me, as it's my livelihood! So! Why don't we all have a drink and relax, eh?"

Yoshitoshi's eye had been snagged by the incomplete picture on his drawing table. He stared at it raptly for a few more seconds, then came to with a start. "A drink! Oh!" He straightened up. "Why, come to think of it, I have something very special, for gentlemen like

yourselves. It came from Yokohama, from the foreign trade zone."
Yoshitoshi crawled rapidly across the floor, his knees skidding inside
the cotton robe, and threw open a dented wooden chest. He un-
wrapped a tall glass bottle from a wad of tissue and brought it back
to his seat, along with three dusty sake cups.

The bottle had the flawless symmetrical ugliness of foreign
manufacture. It was full of amber liquid, and corked. A paper label
showed the grotesquely bearded face of an American man, framed
by blocky foreign letters.

"Who's that?" Onogawa asked, intrigued. "Their king?"

"No, it's the face of the merchant who brewed it," Yoshitoshi said
with assurance. "In America, merchants are famous. And a man of
the merchant class can even become a soldier. Or a farmer, or priest,
or anything he likes."

"Hmmph," said Onogawa, who had gone through a similar transi-
tion himself and was not at all happy about it. "Let me see." He examined the printed label closely. "Look how this foreigner's eyes bug
out. He looks like a raving lunatic!"

Yoshitoshi stiffened at the term. An awkward moment of frozen
silence seeped over the room. Onogawa's gaffe floated in midair
among them, until its nature became clear to everyone. Yoshitoshi
had recovered his health recently, but his illness had not been a
physical one. No one had to say anything, but the truth slowly oozed
its way into everyone's bones and liver. At length, Onogawa cleared
his throat. "I mean, of course, that there's no accounting for the
strange looks of foreigners."

Yoshitoshi licked his fleshy lips and the sudden gleam of desperation slowly faded from his eyes. He spoke quietly.

"Well, my friends in the Liberal Party have told me all about it.
Several of them have been to America and back, and they speak the
language, and can even read it. If you want to know more, you can
read their national newspaper, the *Lamp of Liberty,* for which I am
doing illustrations."

Onogawa glanced quickly at Encho. Onogawa, who was not a
reading man, had only vague notions as to what a "liberal party" or a
"national newspaper" might be. He wondered if Encho knew better.
Apparently the comedian did, for Encho looked suddenly grave.

Yoshitoshi rattled on. "One of my political friends gave me this
bottle, which he bought in Yokohama, from Americans. The Americans have many such bottles there—a whole warehouse. Because the
American Shogun, Generalissimo Guranto, will be arriving next year

to pay homage to our Emperor. And the Guranto, the 'Puresidento,' is especially fond of this kind of drink! Which is called borubona, from the American prefecture of Kentukki."

Yoshitoshi twisted the cork loose and dribbled bourbon into all three cups. "Shouldn't we heat it first?" Encho said.

"This isn't sake, my friend. Sometimes they even put ice in it!"

Onogawa sipped carefully and gasped. "What a bite this has! It burns the tongue like Chinese peppers." He hesitated. "Interesting, though."

"It's good!" said Encho, surprised. "If sake were like an old stone lantern, then this borybona would be gaslight! Hot and fierce!" He tossed back the rest of his cup. "It's a pity there's no pretty girl to serve us our second round."

Yoshitoshi did the honors, filling their cups again. "This serving girl," Onogawa said. "She would have to be hot and fierce too—like a tigress."

Encho lifted his brows. "You surprise me. I thought you were a family man, my friend."

A warm knot of bourbon in Onogawa's stomach was reawakening an evening's worth of sake. "Oh, I suppose I seem settled enough now. But you should have known me ten years ago, before the Restoration. I was quite the tough young radical in those days. You know, we really thought we could change the world. And perhaps we did!"

Encho grinned, amused. "So! You were a shishi?"

Onogawa had another sip. "Oh, yes!" He touched the middle of his back. "I had hair down to here, and I never washed! Touch money? Not a one of us! We'd have died first! No, we lived in rags and ate plain brown rice from wooden bowls. We just went to our kendo schools, practiced swordsmanship, decided what old fool we should try to kill next. . . ." Onogawa shook his head ruefully. The other two were listening with grave attention.

The bourbon and the reminiscing had thawed Onogawa out. The lost ideals of the Restoration rose up within him irresistibly. "I was the despair of my family," he confided. "I abandoned my clan and my daimyo. We shishi radicals, you know, we believed only in our swords and the Emperor. Sonno joi! Remember that slogan?" Onogawa grinned, the tears of mono no aware, the pathos of lost things, coming to his eyes.

"Sonno joi! The very streets used to ring with it. 'Revere the Emperor, destroy the foreigners!' We wanted the Emperor restored to full and unconditional power! We demanded it in the streets! Because the Shogun's men were acting like frightened old women. Frightened of the black ships, the American black warships with their steam and cannon. Admiral Perry's ships."

"It's pronounced 'Peruri,' " Encho corrected gently.

"Peruri, then . . . I admit, we shishi went a bit far. We had some bad habits. Like threatening to commit hara-kiri unless the townsfolk gave us food. That's one of the problems we faced because we refused to touch money. Some of the shopkeepers still resent the way we shishi used to push them around. In fact that was the cause of tonight's incident after your performance, Encho. Some rude fellows with long memories."

"So that was it," Encho said. "I wondered."

"Those were special times," Onogawa said. "They changed me, they changed everything. I suppose everyone of this generation knows where they were, and what they were doing, when the foreigners arrived in Edo Bay."

"I remember," said Yoshitoshi. "I was fourteen and an apprentice at Kuniyoshi's studio. And I'd just done my first print. *The Heike Clan Sink to Their Horrible Doom in the Sea.*"

"I saw them dance once," Encho said. "The American sailors, I mean."

"Really?" said Onogawa.

Encho cast a storyteller's mood with an irresistible gesture. "Yes, my father, Entaro, took me. The performance was restricted to the Shogun's court officials and their friends, but we managed to sneak in. The foreigners painted their faces and hands quite black. They seemed ashamed of their usual pinkish color, for they also painted broad white lines around their lips. Then they all sat on chairs together in a row, and one at a time they would stand up and shout dialogue. A second foreigner would answer, and they would all laugh. Later two of them strummed on strange round-bodied samisens, with long thin necks. And they sang mournful songs, very badly. Then they played faster songs and capered and danced, kicking out their legs in the oddest way, and flinging each other about. Some of the Shogun's counselors danced with them." Encho shrugged. "It was all very odd. To this day I wonder what it meant."

"Well," said Onogawa. "Clearly they were trying to change their appearance and shape, like foxes or badgers. That seems clear enough."

"That's as much as saying they're magicians," Encho said, shaking his head. "Just because they have long noses, doesn't mean they're mountain goblins. They're men—they eat, they sleep, they want a woman. Ask the geishas in Yokohama if that's not so." Encho smirked. "Their real power is in the spirits of copper wires and black iron and burning coal. Like our own Tokyo-Yokohama Railway that the hired English built for us. You've ridden it, of course?"

"Of course!" Onogawa said proudly. "I'm a modern sort of fellow."

"That's the sort of power we need today. Civilization and Enlightenment. When you rode the train, did you see how the backward villagers in Omori come out to pour water on the engine? To cool it off, as if the railway engine were a tired horse!" Encho shook his head in contempt.

Onogawa accepted another small cup of bourbon. "So they pour water," he said judiciously. "Well, I can't see that it does any harm."

"It's rank superstition!" said Encho. "Don't you see, we have to learn to deal with those machine-spirits, just as the foreigners do. Treating them as horses can only insult them. Isn't that so, Taiso?"

Yoshitoshi looked up guiltily from his absentminded study of his latest drawing. "I'm sorry, Encho-san, you were saying?"

"What's that you're working on? May I see?" Encho crept nearer.

Yoshitoshi hastily plucked out pins and rolled up his paper. "Oh, no, no, you wouldn't want to see this one just yet. It's not ready. But I can show you another recent one. . . ." He reached to a nearby stack and dexterously plucked a printed sheet from the unsteady pile. "I'm calling this series *Beauties of the Seven Nights.*"

Encho courteously held up the print so that both he and Onogawa could see it. It showed a woman in her underrobe; she had thrown her scarlet-lined outer kimono over a nearby screen. She had both natural and artificial eyebrows, lending a double seductiveness to her high forehead. Her mane of jet black hair had a killing little wispy fringe at the back of the neck; it seemed to cry out to be bitten. She stood at some lucky man's doorway, bending to blow out the light of a lantern in the hall. And her tiny, but piercingly red mouth was clamped down over a roll of paper towels.

"I get it!" Onogawa said. "That beautiful whore is blowing out the light so she can creep into some fellow's bed in the dark! And she's taking those handy paper towels in her teeth to mop up with, after they're through playing mortar-and-pestle."

Encho examined the print more closely. "Wait a minute," he said. "This caption reads 'Her Ladyship Yanagihara Aiko.' This is an Imperial lady-in-waiting!"

"Some of my newspaper friends gave me the idea," Yoshitoshi said, nodding. "Why should prints always be of tiresome, stale old actors and warriors and geishas? This is the modern age!"

"But this print, Taiso . . . it clearly implies that the Emperor sleeps with his ladies-in-waiting."

"No, just with Lady Yanagihara Aiko," Yoshitoshi said reasonably. "After all, everyone knows she's his special favorite. The rest of the Seven Beauties of the Imperial Court are drawn, oh, putting on their makeup, arranging flowers, and so forth." He smiled. "I expect big sales from this series. It's very topical, don't you think?"

Onogawa was shocked. "But this is rank scandal-mongering! What happened to the good old days, with the nice gouts of blood and so on?"

"No one buys those anymore!" Yoshitoshi protested. "Believe me, I've tried everything! I did *A Yoshitoshi Miscellany of Figures from Literature*. Very edifying, beautifully drawn classical figures, the best. It died on the stands. Then I did *Raving Beauties at Tokyo Restaurants*. Really hot girls, but old-fashioned geishas done in the old style. Another total waste of time. We were dead broke, not a copper piece to our names! I had to pull up the floorboards of my house for fuel! I had to work on fabric designs—two yen for a week's work! My wife left me! My apprentices walked out! And then my health . . . my brain began to . . . I had nothing to eat . . . nothing. . . . But . . . But that's all over now."

Yoshitoshi shook himself, dabbed sweat from his pasty upper lip, and poured another cup of bourbon with a steady hand. "I changed with the times, that's all. It was a hard lesson, but I learned it. I call myself Taiso now, Taiso, meaning 'Great Rebirth.' Newspapers! That's where the excitement is today! *Tokyo Illustrated News* pays plenty for political cartoons and murder illustrations. They do ten thousand impressions at a stroke. My work goes everywhere—not just Edo, the whole nation. The nation, gentlemen!" He raised his cup and drank. "And that's just the beginning. The *Lamp of Liberty* is knocking them dead! The Liberal Party committee has promised me a raise next year, and my own rickshaw."

"But I like the old pictures," Onogawa said.

"Maybe you do, but you don't buy them," Yoshitoshi insisted. "Modern people want to see what's happening now! Take an old theme picture—Yorimitsu chopping an ogre's arm off, for instance. Draw a thing like that today and it gets you nowhere. People's tastes are more refined today. They want to see real cannonballs blowing off real arms. Like my eyewitness illustrations of the Battle of Ueno. A sensation! People don't want print peddlers anymore. 'Journalist il-lustrator'—that's what they call me now."

"Don't laugh," said Encho, nodding in drunken profundity. "You should hear what they say about me. I mean the modern writer fellows, down from the University. They come in with their French novels under their arms, and their spectacles and slicked-down hair, and all sit in the front row together. So I tell them a vaudeville tale or two. Am I 'spinning a good yarn'? Not anymore. They tell me I'm 'creating naturalistic prose in a vigorous popular vernacular.' They want to publish me in a book." He sighed and had another drink. "This stuff's poison, Taiso. My head's spinning."

"Mine, too," Onogawa said. An autumn wind had sprung up out-side. They sat in doped silence for a moment. They were all much drunker than they had realized. The foreign liquor seemed to bubble in their stomachs like tofu fermenting in a tub.

The foreign spirits had crept up on them. The very room itself seemed drunk. Wind sang through the telegraph wires outside Yoshi-toshi's shuttered window. A low eerie moan.

The moan built in intensity. It seemed to creep into the room with them. The walls hummed with it. Hair rose on their arms.

"Stop that!" Yoshitoshi said suddenly. Encho stopped his ventrilo-quial moaning, and giggled. "He's trying to scare us," Yoshitoshi said. "He loves ghost stories."

Onogawa lurched to his feet. "Demon in the wires," he said thickly. "I heard it moaning at us." He blinked, red-faced, and stag-gered to the shuttered window. He fumbled loudly at the lock, ignor-ing Yoshitoshi's protests, and flung it open.

Moonlit wire clustered at the top of a wooden pole, in plain sight a few feet away. It was a junction of cables, and leftover coils of wire dangled from the pole's crossarm like thin black guts. Onogawa flung up the casement with a bang. A chilling gust of fresh air entered the stale room, and the prints danced on the walls. "Hey, you foreign de-mon!" Onogawa shouted. "Leave honest men in peace!"

The artist and entertainer exchanged unhappy glances. "We drank too much," Encho said. He lurched to his knees and onto one unsteady foot. "Leave off, big fellow. What we need now. . . ." He belched. "Women, that's what."

But the air outside the window seemed to have roused Ono-gawa. "We didn't ask for you!" he shouted. "We don't need you! Things were fine before you came, demon! You and your foreign ser-vants . . ." He turned half-round, looking red-eyed into the room. "Where's my pipe? I've a mind to give these wires a good thrashing."

He spotted the pipe again, stumbled into the room and picked it up. He lost his balance for a moment, then brandished the pipe threateningly. "Don't do it," Encho said, getting to his feet. "Be reasonable. I know some girls in Asakusa, they have a piano. . . ." He reached out.

Onogawa shoved him aside. "I've had enough!" he announced. "When my blood's up, I'm a different man! Cut them down before they attack first, that's my motto! Sonno joi!"

He lurched across the room toward the open window. Before he could reach it there was a sudden hiss of steam, like the breath of a locomotive. The demon, its patience exhausted by Onogawa's taunts, gushed from its wire. It puffed through the window, a gray gaseous thing, its lumpy misshapen head glaring furiously. It gave a steam-whistle roar, and its great lantern eyes glowed.

All three men screeched aloud. The armless, legless monster, like a gray cloud on a tether, rolled its glassy eyes at all of them. Its steel teeth gnashed, and sparks showed down its throat. It whistled again and made a sudden gnashing lurch at Onogawa.

But Onogawa's old sword-training had soaked deep into his bones. He leapt aside reflexively, with only a trace of stagger, and gave the thing a smart overhead riposte with his pipe. The demon's head bonged like an iron kettle. It began chattering angrily, and hot steam curled from its nose. Onogawa hit it again. Its head dented. It winced, then glared at the other men.

The townsmen quickly scrambled into line behind their champion. "Get him!" Encho shrieked. Onogawa dodged a halfhearted snap of teeth and bashed the monster across the eye. Glass cracked and the bowl flew from Onogawa's pipe.

But the demon had had enough. With a grumble and crunch like dying gearworks, it retreated back toward its wires, sucking itself back within them, like an octopus into its hole. It vanished, but hissing sparks continued to drip from the wire.

"You humiliated it!" Encho said, his voice filled with awe and admiration. "That was amazing!"

"Had enough, eh!" shouted Onogawa furiously, leaning on the sill. "Easy enough mumbling your dirty spells behind our backs! But try an Imperial warrior face to face, and it's a different story! Hah!"

"What a feat of arms!" said Yoshitoshi, his pudgy face glowing. "I'll do a picture. *Onogawa Humiliates a Ghoul.* Wonderful!"

The sparks began to travel down the wire, away from the window. "It's getting away!" Onogawa shouted. "Follow me!"

He shoved himself from the window and ran headlong from the

studio. He tripped at the top of the stairs, but did an inspired shoulder-roll and landed on his feet at the door. He yanked it open.

Encho followed him headlong. They had no time to lace on their leather shoes, so they kicked on the wooden clogs of Yoshitoshi and his apprentice and dashed out. Soon they stood under the wires, where the little nest of sparks still clung. "Come down here, you rascal," Onogawa demanded. "Show some fighting honor, you skulking wretch!"

The thing moved back and forth, hissing, on the wire. More sparks dripped. It dodged back and forth, like a cornered rat in an alley. Then it made a sudden run for it.

"It's heading south!" said Onogawa. "Follow me!"

They ran in hot pursuit, Encho bringing up the rear, for he had slipped his feet into the apprentice's clogs and the shoes were too big for him.

They pursued the thing across the Ginza. It had settled down to headlong running now, and dropped fewer sparks.

"I wonder what message it carries," panted Encho.

"Nothing good, I'll warrant," said Onogawa grimly. They had to struggle to match the thing's pace. They burst from the southern edge of the Ginza Bricktown and into the darkness of unpaved streets. This was Shiba District, home of the thieves' market and the great Zojoji Temple. They followed the wires. "Aha!" cried Onogawa. "It's heading for Shinbashi Railway Station and its friends the locomotives!"

With a determined burst of speed, Onogawa outdistanced the thing and stood beneath the path of the wire, waving his broken pipe frantically. "Whoa! Go back!"

The thing slowed briefly, well over his head. Stinking flakes of ash and sparks poured from it, raining down harmlessly on the ex-samurai. Onogawa leapt aside in disgust, brushing the filth from his derby and frock coat. "Phew!"

The thing rolled on. Encho caught up with the larger man. "Not the locomotives," the comedian gasped. "We can't face those."

Onogawa drew himself up. He tried to dust more streaks of filthy ash from his soiled coat. "Well, I think we taught the nasty thing a lesson, anyway."

"No doubt," said Encho, breathing hard. He went green suddenly, then leaned against a nearby wooden fence, clustered with tall autumn grass. He was loudly sick.

They looked about themselves. Autumn. Darkness. And the moon. A pair of cats squabbled loudly in an adjacent alley.

Onogawa suddenly realized that he was brandishing, not a sword, but a splintered stick of ironbound bamboo. He began to tremble. Then he flung the thing away with a cry of disgust. "They took our swords away," he said. "Let them give us honest soldiers our swords back. We'd make short work of such foreign foulness. Look what it did to my coat, the filthy creature. It defiled me."

"No, no," Encho said, wiping his mouth. "You were incredible! A regular Shoki the Demon Queller."

"Shoki," Onogawa said. He dusted his hat against his knee. "I've seen drawings of Shoki. He's the warrior demigod, with a red face and a big sword. Always hunting demons, isn't he? But he doesn't know there's a little demon hiding on the top of his own head."

"Well, a regular Yoshitsune, then," said Encho, hastily grasping for a better compliment. Yoshitsune was a legendary master of swordsmanship. A national hero without parallel.

Unfortunately, the valorous Yoshitsune had ended up riddled with arrows by the agents of his treacherous half-brother, who had gone on to rule Japan. While Yoshitsune and his high ideals had to put up with a shadow existence in folklore. Neither Encho nor Onogawa had to mention this aloud, but the melancholy associated with the old tale seeped into their moods. Their world became heroic and fatal. Naturally all the bourbon helped.

"We'd better go back to Bricktown for our shoes," Onogawa said.

"All right," Encho said. Their feet had blistered in the commandeered clogs, and they walked back slowly and carefully.

Yoshitoshi met them in his downstairs landing. "Did you catch it?"

"It made a run for the railroads," Encho said. "We couldn't stop it; it was way above our heads." He hesitated. "Say. You don't suppose it will come back here, do you?"

"Probably," Yoshitoshi said. "It lives in that knot of cables outside the window. That's why I put the shutters there."

"You mean you've seen it before?"

"Sure, I've seen it," Yoshitoshi muttered. "In fact I've seen lots of things. It's my business to see things. No matter what people say about me."

The others looked at him, stricken. Yoshitoshi shrugged irritably. "The place has atmosphere. It's quiet and no one bothers me here. Besides, it's cheap."

"Aren't you afraid of the demon's vengeance?" Onogawa said.

"I get along fine with that demon," Yoshitoshi said. "We have an understanding. Like neighbors anywhere."

"Oh," Encho said. He cleared his throat. "Well, ah, we'll be moving on, Taiso. It was good of you to give us the borubona." He and Onogawa stuffed their feet hastily into their squeaking shoes. "You keep up the good work, pal, and don't let those political fellows put anything over on you. Their ideas are weird, frankly. I don't think the government's going to put up with that kind of talk."

"Someday they'll have to," Yoshitoshi said.

"Let's go," Onogawa said, with a sidelong glance at Yoshitoshi. The two men left.

Onogawa waited until they were well out of earshot. He kept a wary eye on the wires overhead. "Your friend certainly is a weird one," he told the comedian. "What a night!"

Encho frowned. "He's gonna get in trouble with that visionary stuff. The nail that sticks up gets hammered down, you know." They walked into the blaze of artificial gaslight. The Ginza crowd had thinned out considerably.

"Didn't you say you knew some girls with a piano?" Onogawa said.

"Oh, right!" Encho said. He whistled shrilly and waved at a distant two-man rickshaw. "A piano. You won't believe the thing; it makes amazing sounds. And what a great change after those dreary geisha samisen routines. So whiny and thin and wailing and sad! It's always, 'Oh, How Piteous Is A Courtesan's Lot,' and 'Let's Stab Each Other To Prove You Really Love Me.' Who needs that old-fashioned stuff? Wait till you hear these gals pound out some 'opera' and 'waltzes' on their new machine."

The rickshaw pulled up with a rattle and a chime of bells. "Where to, gentlemen?"

"Asakusa," said Encho, climbing in.

"It's getting late," Onogawa said reluctantly. "I really ought to be getting back to the wife."

"Come on," said Encho, rolling his eyes. "Live a little. It's not like you're just cheating on the little woman. These are high-class modern girls. It's a cultural experience."

"Well, all right," said Onogawa. "If it's cultural."

"You'll learn a lot," Encho promised.

But they had barely covered a block when they heard the sudden frantic ringing of alarm bells, far to the south.

"A fire!" Encho yelled in glee. "Hey, runners, stop! Fifty sen if you get us there while it's still spreading!"

The runners wheeled in place and set out with a will. The

rickshaw rocked on its axle and jangled wildly. "This is great!" Onogawa said, clutching his hat. "You're a good fellow to know, Encho. It's nothing but excitement with you!"

"That's the modern life!" Encho shouted. "One wild thing after another."

They bounced and slammed their way through the darkened streets until the sky was lit with fire. A massive crowd had gathered beside the Shinagawa Railroad Line. They were mostly low-class townsmen, many half-dressed. It was a working-class neighborhood in Shiba District, east of Atago Hill. The fire was leaping merrily from one thatched roof to another.

The two men jumped from their rickshaw. Encho shouldered his way immediately through the crowd. Onogawa carefully counted out the fare. "But he said fifty sen," the older rickshawman complained. Onogawa clenched his fist, and the men fell silent.

The firemen had reacted with their usual quick skill. Three companies of them had surrounded the neighborhood. They swarmed like ants over the roofs of the undamaged houses nearest the flames. As usual, they did not attempt to fight the flames directly. That was a hopeless task in any case, for the weathered graying wood, paper shutters, and reed blinds flared up like tinder, in great blossoming gouts.

Instead, they sensibly relied on firebreaks. Their hammers, axes, and crowbars flew as they destroyed every house in the path of the flames. Their skill came naturally to them, for, like all Edo firemen, they were also carpenters. Special bannermen stood on the naked ridgepoles of the disintegrating houses, holding their company's ensigns as close as possible to the flames. This was more than bravado; it was good business. Their reputations, and their rewards from a grateful neighborhood, depended on this show of spirit and nerve.

Some of the crowd, those whose homes were being devoured, were weeping and counting their children. But most of the crowd was in a fine holiday mood, cheering for their favorite fire teams and laying bets.

Onogawa spotted Encho's silk hat and plowed after him. Encho ducked and elbowed through the press, Onogawa close behind. They crept to the crowd's inner edge, where the fierce blaze of heat and the occasional falling wad of flaming straw had established a boundary.

A fireman stood nearby. He wore a knee-length padded fireproof coat with a pattern of printed blocks. A thick protective headdress fell stiffly over his shoulders, and long padded gauntlets shielded his forearms to the knuckles. An apprentice in similar garb was soaking him down with a pencil-thin gush of water from a bamboo hand-pump. "Stand back, stand back," the fireman said automatically, then looked up. "Say, aren't you Encho the comedian? I saw you last week."

"That's me," Encho shouted cheerfully over the roar of flame. "Good to see you fellows performing for once."

The fireman examined Onogawa's ash-streaked frock coat. "You live around here, big fella? Point out your house for me, we'll do what we can."

Onogawa frowned. Encho broke in hastily. "My friend's from uptown! A High City company man!"

"Oh," said the fireman, rolling his eyes.

Onogawa pointed at a merchant's tile-roofed warehouse, a little closer to the tracks. "Why aren't you doing anything about that place? The fire's headed right for it!"

"That's one of merchant Shinichi's," the fireman said, narrowing his eyes. "We saved a place of his out in Kanda District last month! And he gave us only five yen."

"What a shame for him," Encho said, grinning.

"It's full of cotton cloth, too," the fireman said with satisfaction. "It's gonna go up like a rocket."

"How did it start?" Encho said.

"Lightning, I hear," the fireman said. "Some kind of fireball jumped off the telegraph lines."

"Really?" Encho said in a small voice.

"That's what they say," shrugged the fireman. "You know how these things are. Always tall stories. Probably some drunk knocked over his sake kettle, then claimed to see something. No one wants the blame."

"Right," Onogawa said carefully.

The fire teams had made good progress. There was not much left to do now except admire the destruction. "Kind of beautiful, isn't it?" the fireman said. "Look how that smoke obscures the autumn moon." He sighed happily. "Good for business, too. I mean the carpentry business, of course." He waved his gauntleted arm at the leaping flames. "We'll get this worn-out trash out of here and build something worthy of a modern city. Something big and expensive with long-term construction contracts."

"Is that why you have bricks printed on your coat?" Onogawa asked.

The fireman looked down at the block printing on his dripping cotton armor. "They do look like bricks, don't they?" He laughed. "That's a good one. Wait'll I tell the crew."

Dawn rose above old Edo. With red-rimmed eyes, the artist Yoshitoshi stared, sighing, through his open window. Past the telegraph wires, billowing smudge rose beyond the Bricktown rooftops. Another Flower of Edo reaching the end of its evanescent life.

The telegraph wires hummed. The demon had returned to its tangled nest outside the window. "Don't tell, Yoshitoshi," it burbled in its deep humming voice.

"Not me," Yoshitoshi said. "You think I want them to lock me up again?"

"I keep the presses running," the demon whined. "Just you deal with me. I'll make you famous, I'll make you rich. There'll be no more slow dark shadows where townsmen have to creep with their heads down. Everything's brightness and speed with me, Yoshitoshi. I can change things."

"Burn them down, you mean," Yoshitoshi said.

"There's power in burning," the demon hummed. "There's beauty in the flames. When you give up trying to save the old ways, you'll see the beauty. I want you to serve me, you Japanese. You'll do it better than the clumsy foreigners, once you accept me as your own. I'll make you all rich. Edo will be the greatest city in the world. You'll have light and music at a finger's touch. You'll step across oceans. You'll be as gods."

"And if we don't accept you?"

"You will! You must! I'll burn you until you do. I told you that, Yoshitoshi. When I'm stronger, I'll do better than these little flowers of Edo. I'll open seeds of Hell above your cities. Hell-flowers taller than mountains! Red blooms that eat a city in a moment."

Yoshitoshi lifted his latest print and unrolled it before the window. He had worked on it all night; it was done at last. It was a landscape of pure madness. Beams of frantic light pierced a smoldering sky. Winged locomotives, their bellies fattened with the eggs of white-hot death, floated like maddened blowflies above a corpse-white city. "Like this," he said.

The demon gave a gloating whir. "Yes! Just as I told you. Now show it to them. Make them understand that they can't defeat me. Show them all!"

"I'll think about it," Yoshitoshi said. "Leave me now." He closed the heavy shutters.

He rolled the drawing carefully into a tube. He sat at his work-table again, and pulled an oil lamp closer. Dawn was coming. It was time to get some sleep.

He held the end of the paper tube above the lamp's little flame. It browned at first, slowly, the brand-new paper turning the rich antique tinge of an old print, a print from the old days when things were simpler. Then a cigar-ring of smoldering red encircled its rim, and blue flame blossomed. Yoshitoshi held the paper up, and flame ate slowly down its length, throwing smoky shadows.

Yoshitoshi blew and watched his work flare up, cherry-blossom white and red. It hurt to watch it go, and it felt good. He savored the two feelings for as long as he could. Then he dropped the last flaming inch of paper in an ashtray. He watched it flare and smolder until the last of the paper became a ghost-curl of gray.

"It'd never sell," he said. Absently, knowing he would need them tomorrow, he cleaned his brushes. Then he emptied the ink-stained water over the crisp dark ashes.

DINNER IN AUDOGHAST

> Then one arrives at Audoghast, a large and very populous
> city built in a sandy plain. . . . The inhabitants live in ease and
> possess great riches. The market is always crowded; the mob
> is so huge and the chattering so loud that you can scarcely
> hear your own words. . . . The city contains beautiful
> buildings and very elegant homes.
>
> —DESCRIPTION OF NORTHERN AFRICA,
> ABU UBAYD AL-BAKRI (A.D. 1040–94)

DELIGHTFUL AUDOGHAST! Renowned through
the civilized world, from Cordova to Baghdad, the city
spread in splendor beneath a twilit Saharan sky. The setting sun threw pink and amber across adobe domes, ma-
sonry mansions, tall, mud-brick mosques, and open
plazas thick with bristling date-palms. The melodious calls of market
vendors mixed with the remote and amiable chuckling of Saharan
hyenas.

Four gentlemen sat on carpets in a tiled and whitewashed portico, sipping coffee in the evening breeze. The host was the genial
and accomplished slave-dealer, Manimenesh. His three guests were
Ibn Watunan, the caravan-master; Khayali, the poet and musician;
and Bagayoko, a physician and court assassin.

The home of Manimenesh stood upon the hillside in the aristo-
cratic quarter, where it gazed down on an open marketplace and the
mud-brick homes of the lowly. The prevailing breeze swept away the
city reek, and brought from within the mansion the palate-sharpen-
ing aromas of lamb in tarragon and roast partridge in lemons and
eggplant. The four men lounged comfortably around a low inlaid
table, sipping spiced coffee from Chinese cups and watching the ebb
and flow of market life.

The scene below them encouraged a lofty philosophical detach-
ment. Manimenesh, who owned no less than fifteen books, was a
well-known patron of learning. Jewels gleamed on his dark, plump
hands, which lay cozily folded over his paunch. He wore a long tunic
of crushed red velvet, and a gold-threaded skullcap.

Khayali, the young poet, had studied architecture and verse in
the schools of Timbuktu. He lived in the household of Manimenesh
as his poet and praisemaker, and his sonnets, ghazals, and odes were
recited throughout the city. He propped one elbow against the full
belly of his two-string *guimbri* guitar, of inlaid ebony, strung with
leopard gut.

Ibn Watunan had an eagle's hooded gaze and hands callused by
camel-reins. He wore an indigo turban and a long striped djellaba. In
thirty years as a sailor and caravaneer, he had bought and sold Zan-
zibar ivory, Sumatran pepper, Ferghana silk, and Cordovan leather.
Now a taste for refined gold had brought him to Audoghast, for
Audoghast's African bullion was known throughout Islam as the standard of quality.

Doctor Bagayoko's ebony skin was ridged with an initiate's scars,
and his long clay-smeared hair was festooned with knobs of chiseled
bone. He wore a tunic of white Egyptian cotton, hung with gris-gris
necklaces, and his baggy sleeves bulged with herbs and charms. He
was a native Audoghastian of the animist persuasion, the personal
physician of the city's Prince.

Bagayoko's skill with powders, potions, and unguents made him
an intimate of Death. He often undertook diplomatic missions to the
neighboring Empire of Ghana. During his last visit there, the anti-
Audoghast faction had mysteriously suffered a lethal outbreak of
pox.

Between the four men was the air of camaraderie common to
gentlemen and scholars.

They finished the coffee, and a slave took the empty pot away. A
second slave, a girl from the kitchen staff, arrived with a wicker tray
loaded with olives, goat-cheese, and hard-boiled eggs sprinkled with

vermilion. At that moment, a muezzin yodeled the evening call to prayer.

"Ah," said Ibn Watunan, hesitating. "Just as we were getting started."

"Never mind," said Manimenesh, helping himself to a handful of olives. "We'll pray twice next time."

"Why was there no noon prayer today?" said Watunan.

"Our muezzin forgot," the poet said.

Watunan lifted his shaggy brows. "That seems rather lax."

Doctor Bagayoko said, "This is a new muezzin. The last was more punctual, but, well, he fell ill." Bagayoko smiled urbanely and nibbled his cheese.

"We Audoghastians like our new muezzin better," said the poet, Khayali. "He's one of our own, not like that other fellow, who was from Fez. *Our* muezzin is sleeping with a Christian's wife. It's very entertaining."

"You have Christians here?" Watunan said.

"A clan of Ethiopian Copts," said Manimenesh. "And a couple of Nestorians."

"Oh," said Watunan, relaxing. "For a moment I thought you meant real *feringhee* Christians, from Europe."

"From where?" Manimenesh was puzzled.

"Very far away," said Ibn Watunan, smiling. "Ugly little countries, with no profit."

"There were empires in Europe once," said Khayali knowledgeably. "The Empire of Rome was almost as big as the modern civilized world."

Watunan nodded."I have seen the New Rome, called Byzantium. They have armored horsemen, like your neighbors in Ghana. Savage fighters."

Bagayoko nodded, salting an egg. "Christians eat children."

Watunan smiled. "I can assure you that the Byzantines do no such thing."

"Really?" said Bagayoko. "Well, our Christians do."

"That's just the doctor's little joke," said Manimenesh. "Sometimes strange rumors spread about us, because we raid our slaves from the Nyam-Nyam cannibal tribes on the coast. But we watch their diet closely, I assure you."

Watunan smiled uncomfortably. "There is always something new out of Africa. One hears the oddest stories. Hairy men, for instance."

"Ah," said Manimenesh. "You mean gorillas, from the jungles to the south. I'm sorry to spoil the story for you, but they are nothing better than beasts."

"I see," said Watunan. "That's a pity."

"My grandfather owned a gorilla once," Manimenesh said. "Even after ten years, it could barely speak Arabic."

They finished the appetizers. Slaves cleared the table and brought in a platter of fattened partridges, stuffed with lemons and eggplants, on a bed of mint and lettuce. The four diners leaned in closer and dexterously ripped off legs and wings.

Watunan sucked meat from a drumstick and belched politely. "Audoghast is famous for its cooks," he said. "I'm pleased to see that this legend, at least, is confirmed."

"We Audoghastians pride ourselves on the pleasures of table and bed," said Manimenesh, pleased. "I have asked Elfelilet, one of our premiere courtesans, to honor us with a visit tonight. She will bring her troupe of dancers."

Watunan smiled. "That would be splendid. One tires of boys on the trail. Your women are remarkable. I've noticed that they go without the veil."

Khayali lifted his voice in song. "When a woman of Audoghast appears / The girls of Fez bite their lips, / The dames of Tripoli hide in closets, / And Ghana's women hang themselves."

"We take pride in the exalted status of our women," said Manimenesh. "It's not for nothing that they command a premium market price!"

In the marketplace, downhill, vendors lit tiny oil lamps, which cast a flickering glow across the walls of tents and the watering troughs. A troop of the Prince's men, with iron spears, shields, and chain mail, marched across the plaza to take the night watch at the Eastern Gate. Slaves with heavy water-jars gossiped beside the well.

"There's quite a crowd around one of the stalls," said Bagayoko.

"So I see," said Watunan. "What is it? Some news that might affect the market?"

Bagayoko sopped up gravy with a wad of mint and lettuce. "Rumor says there's a new fortune-teller in town. New prophets always go through a vogue."

"Ah yes," said Khayali, sitting up. "They call him 'the Sufferer.' He is said to tell the most outlandish and entertaining fortunes."

"I wouldn't trust any fortune-teller's market tips," said Manimenesh. "If you want to know the market, you have to know the hearts of the people, and for that you need a good poet."

Khayali bowed his head. "Sir," he said, "live forever."

It was growing dark. Household slaves arrived with pottery lamps of sesame oil, which they hung from the rafters of the portico. Others took the bones of the partridges and brought in a haunch and head of lamb with a side dish of cinnamon tripes.

As a gesture of esteem, the host offered Watunan the eyeballs, and after three ritual refusals the caravan-master dug in with relish. "I put great stock in fortune-tellers, myself," he said, munching. "They are often privy to strange secrets. Not the occult kind, but the blabbing of the superstitious. Slave-girls anxious about some household scandal, or minor officials worried over promotions—inside news from those who consult them. It can be useful."

"If that's the case," said Manimenesh, "perhaps we should call him up here."

"They say he is grotesquely ugly," said Khayali. "He is called 'the Sufferer' because he is outlandishly afflicted by disease."

Bagayoko wiped his chin elegantly on his sleeve. "Now you begin to interest me!"

"It's settled, then." Manimenesh clapped his hands. "Bring young Sidi, my errand-runner!"

Sidi arrived at once, dusting flour from his hands. He was the cook's teenage son, a tall young black in a dyed woolen djellaba. His cheeks were stylishly scarred, and he had bits of brass wire interwoven with his dense black locks. Manimenesh gave him his orders; Sidi leapt from the portico, ran downhill through the garden, and vanished through the gates.

The slave-dealer sighed. "This is one of the problems of my business. When I bought my cook she was a slim and lithesome wench, and I enjoyed her freely. Now years of dedication to her craft have increased her market value by twenty times, and also made her as fat as a hippopotamus, though that is beside the point. She has always claimed that Sidi is my child, and since I don't wish to sell her, I must make allowance. I have made him a freeman; I have spoiled him, I'm afraid. On my death, my legitimate sons will deal with him cruelly."

The caravan-master, having caught the implications of this speech, smiled politely. "Can he ride? Can he bargain? Can he do sums?"

"Oh," said Manimenesh with false nonchalance, "he can manage that newfangled stuff with the zeroes well enough."

"You know I am bound for China," said Watunan. "It is a hard road that brings either riches or death."

"He runs the risk in any case," the slave-dealer said philosophically. "The riches are Allah's decision."

"This is truth," said the caravan-master. He made a secret gesture, beneath the table, where the others could not see. His host returned it, and Sidi was proposed, and accepted, for the Brotherhood.

With the night's business over, Manimenesh relaxed, and broke open the lamb's steamed skull with a silver mallet. They spooned out the brains, then attacked the tripes, which were stuffed with onion, cabbage, cinnamon, rue, coriander, cloves, ginger, pepper, and lightly dusted with ambergris. They ran out of mustard dip and called for more, eating a bit more slowly now, for they were approaching the limit of human capacity.

They then sat back, pushing away platters of congealing grease, and enjoying a profound satisfaction with the state of the world. Down in the marketplace, bats from an abandoned mosque chased moths around the vendors' lanterns.

The poet belched suavely and picked up his two-stringed guitar. "Dear God," he said, "this is a splendid place. See, caravan-master, how the stars smile down on our beloved Southwest." He drew a singing note from the leopard-gut strings. "I feel at one with Eternity."

Watunan smiled. "When I find a man like that, I have to bury him."

"There speaks the man of business," the doctor said. He unobtrusively dusted a tiny pinch of venom on the last chunk of tripe, and ate it. He accustomed himself to poison. It was a professional precaution.

From the street beyond the wall, they heard the approaching jingle of brass rings. The guard at the gate called out. "The Lady Elfelilet and her escorts, lord!"

"Make them welcome," said Manimenesh. Slaves took the platters away, and brought a velvet couch onto the spacious portico. The diners extended their hands; slaves scrubbed and toweled them clean.

Elfelilet's party came forward through the fig-clustered garden: two escorts with gold-topped staffs heavy with jingling brass rings; three dancing-girls, apprentice courtesans in blue woolen cloaks over gauzy cotton trousers and embroidered blouses; and four palanquin bearers, beefy male slaves with oiled torsos and callused shoulders. The bearers set the palanquin down with stifled grunts of relief and opened the cloth-of-gold hangings.

Elfelilet emerged, a tawny-skinned woman, her eyes dusted in kohl and collyrium, her hennaed hair threaded with gold wire. Her palms and nails were stained pink; she wore an embroidered blue cloak over an intricate sleeveless vest and ankle-tied silk trousers starched and polished with myrobalan lacquer. A light freckling of smallpox scars along one cheek delightfully accented her broad, moonlike face.

"Elfelilet, my dear," said Manimenesh, "you are just in time for dessert."

Elfelilet stepped gracefully across the tiled floor and reclined face-first along the velvet couch, where the well-known loveliness of her posterior could be displayed to its best advantage. "I thank my friend and patron, the noble Manimenesh. Live forever! Learned Doctor Bagayoko, I am your servant. Hello, poet."

"Hello, darling," said Khayali, smiling with the natural camaraderie of poets and courtesans. "You are the moon, and your troupe of lovelies are comets across our vision."

The host said, "This is our esteemed guest, the caravan-master, Abu Bekr Ahmed Ibn Watunan."

Watunan, who had been gaping in enraptured amazement, came to himself with a start. "I am a simple desert man," he said. "I haven't a poet's gift of words. But I am your ladyship's servant."

Elfelilet smiled and tossed her head; her distended earlobes clattered with heavy chunks of gold filigree. "Welcome to Audoghast."

Dessert arrived. "Well," said Manimenesh. "Our earlier dishes were rough and simple fare, but this is where we shine. Let me tempt you with these *djouzinkat* nutcakes. And do sample our honey macaroons—I believe there's enough for everyone."

Everyone, except of course for the slaves, enjoyed the light and flaky *cataif* macaroons, liberally dusted with Kairwan sugar. The nutcakes were simply beyond compare: painstakingly milled from hand-watered wheat, lovingly buttered and sugared, and artistically studded with raisins, dates, and almonds.

"We eat *djouzinkat* nutcakes during droughts," the poet said, "because the angels weep with envy when we taste them."

Manimenesh belched heroically and readjusted his skullcap. "Now," he said, "we will enjoy a little bit of grape wine. Just a small tot, mind you, so that the sin of drinking is a minor one, and we can do penance with the minimum of alms. After that, our friend the poet will recite an ode he has composed for the occasion."

Khayali began to tune his two-string guitar. "I will also, on demand, extemporize twelve-line *ghazals* in the lyric mode, upon suggested topics."

"And after our digestion has been soothed with epigrams," said their host, "we will enjoy the justly famed dancing of her ladyship's troupe. After that we will retire within the mansion and enjoy their other, equally lauded, skills."

The gate-guard shouted, "Your errand-runner, Lord! He awaits your pleasure, with the fortune-teller!"

"Ah," said Manimenesh. "I had forgotten."

"No matter, sir," said Watunan, whose imagination had been fired by the night's agenda.

Bagayoko spoke up. "Let's have a look at him. His ugliness, by contrast, will heighten the beauty of these women."

"Which would otherwise be impossible," said the poet.

"Very well," said Manimenesh. "Bring him forward."

Sidi, the errand boy, came through the garden, followed with ghastly slowness by the crutch-wielding fortune-teller.

The man inched into the lamplight like a crippled insect. His voluminous dust-gray cloak was stained with sweat, and nameless exudations. He was an albino. His pink eyes were shrouded with cataracts, and he had lost a foot, and several fingers, to leprosy. One shoulder was much lower than the other, suggesting a hunchback, and the stub of his shin was scarred by the gnawing of canal-worms.

"Prophet's beard!" said the poet. "He is truly of surpassing ghastliness."

Elfelilet wrinkled her nose. "He reeks of pestilence!"

Sidi spoke up. "We came as fast as we could, Lord!"

"Go inside, boy," said Manimenesh; "soak ten sticks of cinnamon in a bucket of water, then come back and throw it over him."

Sidi left at once.

Watunan stared at the hideous man, who stood, quivering on one leg, at the edge of the light. "How is it, man, that you still live?"

"I have turned my sight from this world," said the Sufferer. "I turned my sight to God, and He poured knowledge copiously upon me. I have inherited a knowledge which no mortal body can support."

"But God is merciful," said Watunan. "How can you claim this to be His doing?"

"If you do not fear God," said the fortune-teller, "fear Him after seeing me." The hideous albino lowered himself, with arthritic, aching slowness, to the dirt outside the portico. He spoke again. "You are right, caravan-master, to think that death would be a mercy to me. But death comes in its own time, as it will to all of you."

Manimenesh cleared his throat. "Can you see our destinies, then?"

"I see the world," said the Sufferer. "To see the fate of one man is to follow a single ant in a hill."

Sidi reemerged and poured the scented water over the cripple. The fortune-teller cupped his maimed hands and drank. "Thank you, boy," he said. He turned his clouded eyes on the youth. "Your children will be yellow."

Sidi laughed, startled. "Yellow? Why?"

"Your wives will be yellow."

The dancing-girls, who had moved to the far side of the table, giggled in unison. Bagayoko pulled a gold coin from within his sleeve. "I will give you this gold dirham if you will show me your body."

Elfelilet frowned prettily and blinked her kohl-smeared lashes. "Oh, learned Doctor, please spare us."

"You will see my body, sir, if you have patience," said the Sufferer. "As yet, the people of Audoghast laugh at my prophecies. I am doomed to tell the truth, which is harsh and cruel, and therefore absurd. As my fame grows, however, it will reach the ears of your Prince, who will then order you to remove me as a threat to public order. You will then sprinkle your favorite poison, powdered asp venom, into a bowl of chickpea soup I will receive from a customer. I bear you no grudge for this, as it will be your civic duty, and will relieve me of pain."

"What an odd notion," said Bagayoko, frowning. "I see no need for the Prince to call on my services. One of his spearmen could puncture you like a waterskin."

"By then," the prophet said, "my occult powers will have roused so much uneasiness that it will seem best to take extreme measures."

"Well," said Bagayoko, "that's convenient, if exceedingly grotesque."

"Unlike other prophets," said the Sufferer, "I see the future not as one might wish it to be, but in all its cataclysmic and blind futility. That is why I have come here, to your delightful city. My numerous and totally accurate prophecies will vanish when this city does. This will spare the world any troublesome conflicts of predestination and free will."

"He is a theologian!" the poet said. "A leper theologian—it's a shame my professors in Timbuktu aren't here to debate him!"

"You prophesy doom for our city?" said Manimenesh.

"Yes. I will be specific. This is the year 406 of the Prophet's Hejira, and one thousand and fourteen years since the birth of Christ. In forty years, a puritan and fanatical cult of Moslems will arise, known as the Almoravids. At that time, Audoghast will be an ally of the Ghana Empire, who are idol-worshipers. Ibn Yasin, the warrior saint of the Almoravids, will condemn Audoghast as a nest of pagans. He will set his horde of desert marauders against the city; they will be enflamed by righteousness and greed. They will slaughter the men, and rape and enslave the women. Audoghast will be sacked, the wells will be poisoned, and the cropland will wither and blow away. In a hundred years, sand dunes will bury the ruins. In five hundred years, Audoghast will survive only as a few dozen lines of narrative in the travel books of Arab scholars."

Khayali shifted his guitar. "But the libraries of Timbuktu are full of books on Audoghast, including, if I may say so, our immortal tradition of poetry."

"I have not yet mentioned Timbuktu," said the prophet, "which will be sacked by Moorish invaders led by a blond Spanish eunuch. They will feed the books to goats."

The company burst into incredulous laughter. Unperturbed, the prophet said, "The ruin will be so general, so thorough, and so all-encompassing, that in future centuries it will be stated, and believed, that West Africa was always a land of savages."

"Who in the world could make such a slander?" said the poet.

"They will be Europeans, who will emerge from their current squalid decline, and arm themselves with mighty sciences."

"What happens then?" said Bagayoko, smiling.

"I can look at those future ages," said the prophet, "but I prefer not to do so, as it makes my head hurt."

"You prophesy, then," said Manimenesh, "that our far-famed metropolis, with its towering mosques and armed militia, will be reduced to utter desolation."

"Such is the truth, regrettable as it may be. You, and all you love, will leave no trace in this world, except a few lines in the writing of strangers."

"And our city will fall to savage tribesmen?"

The Sufferer said, "No one here will witness the disaster to come. You will live out your lives, year after year, enjoying ease and luxury, not because you deserve it, but simply because of blind fate. In time you will forget this night; you will forget all I have said, just as the world will forget you and your city. When Audoghast falls, this boy

Sidi, this son of a slave, will be the only survivor of this night's gathering. By then he too will have forgotten Audoghast, which he has no cause to love. He will be a rich old merchant in Ch'ang-an, which is a Chinese city of such fantastic wealth that it could buy ten Audoghasts, and which will not be sacked and annihilated until a considerably later date."

"This is madness," said Watunan.

Bagayoko twirled a crusted lock of mud-smeared hair in his supple fingers. "Your gate-guard is a husky lad, friend Manimenesh. What say we have him bash this storm-crow's head in, and haul him out to be hyena food?"

"For that, Doctor," said the Sufferer, "I will tell you the manner of your death. You will be killed by the Ghanaian royal guard, while attempting to kill the crown prince by blowing a subtle poison into his anus with a hollow reed."

Bagayoko started. "You idiot, there is no crown prince."

"He was conceived yesterday."

Bagayoko turned impatiently to the host. "Let us rid ourselves of this prodigy!"

Manimenesh nodded sternly. "Sufferer, you have insulted my guests and my city. You are lucky to leave my home alive."

The Sufferer hauled himself with agonizing slowness to his single foot. "Your boy spoke to me of your generosity."

"What! Not one copper for your driveling."

"Give me one of the gold dirhams from your purse. Otherwise I shall be forced to continue prophesying, and in a more intimate vein."

Manimenesh considered this. "Perhaps it's best." He threw Sidi a coin. "Give this to the madman and escort him back to his raving-booth."

They waited in tormented patience as the fortune-teller creaked and crutched, with painful slowness, into the darkness.

Manimenesh, brusquely, threw out his red velvet sleeves and clapped for wine. "Give us a song, Khayali."

The poet pulled the cowl of his cloak over his head. "My head rings with an awful silence," he said. "I see all waymarks effaced, the joyous pleasances converted into barren wilderness. Jackals resort here, ghosts frolic, and demons sport; the gracious halls, and rich boudoirs, that once shone like the sun, now, overwhelmed by desolation, seem like the gaping mouths of savage beasts!" He looked at the dancing-girls, his eyes brimming with tears. "I picture these maidens, lying beneath the dust, or dispersed to distant parts and far regions, scattered by the hand of exile, torn to pieces by the fingers of expatriation."

Manimenesh smiled on him kindly. "My boy," he said, "if others cannot hear your songs, or embrace these women, or drink this wine, the loss is not ours, but theirs. Let us, then, enjoy all three, and let those unborn do the regretting."

"Your patron is wise," said Ibn Watunan, patting the poet on the shoulder. "You see him here, favored by Allah with every luxury; and you saw that filthy madman, bedeviled by plague. That lunatic, who pretends to great wisdom, only croaks of ruin; while our industrious friend makes the world a better place, by fostering nobility and learning. Could God forsake a city like this, with all its charms, to bring about that fool's disgusting prophesies?" He lifted his cup to Elfelilet, and drank deeply.

"But delightful Audoghast," said the poet, weeping. "All our loveliness, lost to the sands."

"The world is wide," said Bagayoko, "and the years are long. It is not for us to claim immortality, not even if we are poets. But take comfort, my friend. Even if these walls and buildings crumble, there will always be a place like Audoghast, as long as men love profit! The mines are inexhaustible, and elephants are thick as fleas. Mother Africa will always give us gold and ivory."

"Always?" said the poet hopefully, dabbing at his eyes.

"Well, surely there are always slaves," said Manimenesh, and smiled, and winked. The others laughed with him, and there was joy again.